PRAISE FOR A[illegible]
AND THE MATTIE WINSTON MYSTERIES

BOARD STIFF

"Great dialogue and characters enhance this cozy mystery. Starting with the first scene, the book is laugh-out-loud funny and the strong humor continues throughout."

—*RT Book Reviews, Top Pick*

LUCKY STIFF

"Annelise Ryan has done it again! Her heroine Mattie Winston has a way with a crime scene that will keep you reading, laughing and wondering just what can possibly happen next in this entertaining romp. Wisconsin's engaging assistant coroner brings readers another winning mystery!"

—Leann Sweeney, author of the Cats in Trouble Mysteries

"Lucky Stiff is a roller coaster ride of stomach clenching action, sizzling attraction, belly laughs, and a puzzler of a mystery. Annelise Ryan has created a smart and saucy heroine in Mattie Winston, who you just can't help but like especially as she endures what is possibly the worst road trip ever. What a thrill ride!"

—Jenn McKinlay, author of the Cupcake Bakery Mysteries and the Library Lover's Mysteries

FROZEN STIFF

"Ryan mixes science and great storytelling in this cozy series . . . The forensic details ring true and add substance to this fast-paced and funny mystery. Good plotting and relationship drama keep the mystery rolling, while Mattie's humorous take on life provides many comedic moments."

—*RT Book Reviews*

"[Mattie's] competence as a former ER nurse, plus a quirky supporting cast, makes the series intriguing. Ryan has a good eye for forensic and medical detail, and Mattie gets to be the woman of the hour in her third outing."

—*Library Journal*

"Absorbing . . . Ryan smoothly blends humor, distinctive characters, and authentic forensic detail."

—*Publisher's Weekly*

SCARED STIFF

"An appealing series on multiple fronts: the forensic details will interest Patricia Cornwell readers, though the tone here is lighter, while the often slapstick humor and the blossoming romance between Mattie and Hurley will draw Evanovich fans who don't object to the cozier mood."

—*Booklist*

"Ryan's sharp second mystery . . . shows growing skill at mixing humor with CSI-style crime."

—*Publishers Weekly*

WORKING STIFF

"Sassy, sexy, and suspenseful, Annelise Ryan knocks 'em dead in her wry and original Working Stiff."

—Carolyn Hart, author of *Dare to Die*

"Move over, Stephanie Plum. Make way for Mattie Winston, the funniest deputy coroner to cut up a corpse since, well, ever. I loved every minute I spent with her in this sharp and sassy debut mystery."

—Laura Levine, author of *Killer Cruise*

"Mattie Winston, RN, wasn't looking for excitement when she became a morgue assistant—quite the contrary—but she got plenty and so will readers who won't be able to put this book down."

—Leslie Meier, author of *Mother's Day Murder*

"Working Stiff has it all: suspense, laughter, a spicy dash of romance—and a heroine who's guaranteed to walk off with your heart. Mattie Winston is an unforgettable character who has me begging for a sequel. Annelise Ryan, are you listening?"

—Tess Gerritsen, *New York Times* bestselling author of *The Keepsake*

"Mattie is klutzy and endearing, and there are plenty of laugh-out-loud moments . . . her foibles are still fun and entertaining."

—*RT Book Reviews*

"Ryan, the pseudonym of a Wisconsin emergency nurse, brings her professional expertise to her crisp debut . . . Mattie wisecracks her way through an increasingly complex plot."

—*Publishers Weekly*

Books by Annelise Ryan

WORKING STIFF

SCARED STIFF

FROZEN STIFF

LUCKY STIFF

BOARD STIFF

STIFF PENALTY

STIFF COMPETITION

Published by Kensington Publishing Corp.

Stiff Competition

Annelise Ryan

KENSINGTON BOOKS
http://www.kensingtonbooks.com

KENSINGTON BOOKS are published by

Kensington Publishing Corp.
119 West 40th Street
New York, NY 10018

All Kensington titles, imprints and distributed lines are available at special quantity discounts for bulk purchases for sales promotion, premiums, fund-raising, educational or institutional use. Special book excerpts or customized printings can also be created to fit specific needs. For details, write or phone the office of the Kensington Special Sales Manager: Kensington Publishing Corp., 119 West 40th Street, New York, NY, 10018. Attn. Special Sales Department. Phone: 1-800-221-2647.

Kensington and the K logo Reg. U.S. Pat. & TM Off.

ISBN-13: 978-1-61773-410-6
ISBN-10: 1-61773-410-1
First Kensington Mass Market Edition: February 2016

eISBN-13: 978-1-61773-411-3
eISBN-10: 1-61773-411-X
First Kensington Electronic Edition: February 2016

10 9 8 7 6 5 4 3 2

Printed in the United States of America

For Doug

Acknowledgments

So many people are involved in the writing of my books. There are the friends and coworkers who brainstorm with me, and let me steal their witty bon mots, and tell their friends about the books, and provide me with endless observations and traits that I then roll into my characters. Have fun finding bits of yourselves in the text! There is my editor, Peter Senftleben, who is insightful, smart, and a delight to work with. There is my agent, Adam Chromy, who believes in me more than I believe in myself at times. There is Morgan Elwell, whose ongoing efforts to publicize and market my books is appreciated more than she knows. And there are all those folks behind the scenes at Kensington Books whose hard work goes into making my books a success. It is a pleasure and an honor to work with all of you. Thank you.

Of course the most important people are the readers. Without you, none of this would be possible. So thank you from the bottom of my heart. Happy reading!

Chapter 1

Death is sometimes referred to as eternal sleep. It's a nice euphemism, one that brings to mind a far more pleasant picture than the grim realities. At the moment, those grim realities are staring me in the face: waxy, lifeless, bloody, the eyes wide open. It doesn't resemble normal sleep at all, not that I'd recognize normal sleep if it jumped up, slapped me in the face, and yelled at me. Sleep is something I haven't seen much of lately.

My name is Mattie Winston and I work for the medical examiner's office in my hometown of Sorenson, Wisconsin. I'm also a new mother, and for all intents and purposes, a single one. Motherhood is something I'd always planned on, but the path I took to get here has been a circuitous, twisted mess with lots of detours, hazards, and side trips along the way. Still, my son, Matthew Hurley, is my greatest accomplishment in life thus far. I adore his soft, black hair and his big blue eyes, which he gets from his dad, and his round face and chubby thighs, which he gets from me. His smile, which is slightly crooked and has the ability to melt my heart, is uniquely his. I love everything about him, but I wish he would sleep a little more.

It's been eight weeks since he was born, and yesterday was my first official day back on the job. Fortunately it was an easy one because death took a holiday. But that guy with the scythe is a relentless pursuer, and today he came knocking again. I'm standing beside his latest victim: a man dressed in the same blaze orange accoutrements that I and the people who are with me are wearing.

It's deer hunting season, an occasion that is as much of a holiday for many in Wisconsin as is Christmas, or Thanksgiving, which is right around the corner. Even as we stand here in a wooded copse with bright morning sunlight beaming down on us, the sounds of gunshots can be heard echoing through the air. It's a bit unnerving knowing there are hordes of men (and the occasional woman) wandering around out here armed with tons of alcohol, a desire to kill something, and the guns to do it. Given that, it's not hard to imagine that some of the hunters, as well as some of the hunted, end up dead as a result. Most years there is a human victim or two, and the vast majority of them have something to do with stupidity. Hunting season casualties always reinforce my belief in Darwinism.

Despite all the gunshots, the man lying on the ground at our feet wasn't killed by a gun of any sort. His end came with much more stealth judging from the arrow sticking out both sides of his throat.

A crashing sound in the trees behind us makes everyone look that way. A doe bounds into our small clearing and then stops short to stare at us with wide, frightened eyes, steam rising from her flared nostrils. After a few seconds her hindquarters quiver and in a blink she bounds back the way she came, disappearing from view.

"These poor deer don't know which way to run," I say.

"Apparently our victim didn't either," Izzy says, and everyone's focus shifts back to the body on the ground.

Izzy is my neighbor, my boss, and my best friend. I live in a cottage behind his house, a cottage that just happens to be right next door to the house I used to share with my ex-husband, David Winston—though technically I've never lived in the house that currently stands on that property. The first house burned to the ground, nearly taking David's life in the process. He has since rebuilt and is now sharing it with his fiancée, Patty Volker, the insurance rep who at one time sold us the coverage that made the rebuild possible. I received a share of the proceeds as part of my divorce settlement, a chunk of money I considered fair at the time. But David is a surgeon at our local hospital, and he makes a lot of money. His original plan to build a more modest home to replace the mini mansion we once shared apparently fell by the wayside. The new house is as big, if not bigger, than the one we had. It makes me wonder if David was hiding some money when our divorce settlement was being sorted out.

My cottage is tiny in comparison: a one-bedroom, one-bathroom affair that is all of nine hundred square feet. Izzy had it built for his mother, Sylvie, who lived in it for a year when her health was failing, and then moved out when her recovery proved nothing short of amazing. She might have stayed in it even then if not for her son's lifestyle, something she has made clear she doesn't like. Izzy is gay and has been living with his partner, Dom, for nearly a decade now. Sylvie tells everyone it's just a phase her son is going through, and that she's sure he'll come to his senses any day now and settle down with a nice young woman.

Standing in the woods with Izzy and me are two uniformed cops: Brenda Joiner and a new guy named

Karl Young, who has already been saddled with the nickname KY, which inevitably leads to conversational segues laced with sexual innuendo. Being paired up with Brenda doesn't help since her initials lend themselves to similar insinuations. Also present are Jonas Kriedeman, the evidence technician for the Sorenson Police Department, Charlotte "Charlie" Finnegan, the PD's videography specialist, and Steve Hurley, a detective with the Sorenson PD, the love of my life, and the father of my child.

"Anyone know who he is?" Hurley asks, staring down at the dead man.

"Hard to say since we can't see much of his face," I say. Our victim is lying on the ground, face up, his sightless eyes open and staring at the sky. But aside from the fact that his eyes are blue, it's hard to tell anything else about him because his face is covered with partially dried blood.

Izzy reaches into the man's front pants pockets, pulls a cell phone out of one and a set of keys from the other, and hands them to Jonas. Then he goes into the back pockets, finds a wallet, and hands it to Hurley, who opens it and removes a driver's license.

"Assuming this is his license, it seems our dead man is one Lars Sanderson," Hurley says, looking from the license to the man on the ground and back to the license again. He then shows us the picture.

"Looks like it could be a match," KY says.

Izzy frowns. "It does bear a resemblance, but we'll get a better idea once we clean his face off. Let's not jump to any conclusions yet." Izzy is extremely cautious when it comes to identifying our victims, in part because he's very professional and thorough when it comes to his job, but also because of an embarrassing debacle that occurred fifteen years ago, early on during his career here in Sorenson. A wallet found on a man killed in a horrific auto crash was used by the local cops to identify the victim despite caution from Izzy. The name on the driver's license matched that on the car's registration and it seemed pretty clear who the victim was. Hair color, size, and weight matched the driver's license info, but the injuries were severe enough that any facial recognition was impossible. Still, the identity seemed obvious and the cops notified the man's wife of her husband's death.

As it turned out, her husband was alive, though barely, after being beaten by the man who stole his wallet and car. The husband, who had lain unconscious in a field for several hours, finally came to in the middle of the night and was able to stagger his way home. He didn't have his keys, and both the front and back doors were locked, so he entered through a bedroom window that he and his wife typically left open at night. His wife, who had been amply dosed with sedatives after receiving the shocking news of her husband's death, awoke in something of a haze to find a man standing in her bedroom. She screamed, assumed it was an intruder, and in her muddled haze she managed to open the drawer of the bedside table and take out the gun that was kept there. Then she shot her husband. The wound proved fatal, though not immediately. He lived long enough to explain what had happened and to tell his wife he forgave her. She, however, was not so magnanimous and she filed a lawsuit against the police department and the city. It ended up getting settled a year later, but not before both of the cops involved in the presumptuous death notification moved on to other cities and jobs.

"Izzy is right that we need to be careful in jumping to conclusions," I say, mindful of the past incident, "but it does look like Lars. He has a distinctive hook nose and a mole on his left cheek."

"You know this Lars guy?" Hurley asks, then before I can answer he says, "Dumb question. Of course you do. I swear you know everyone in Sorenson."

"Not everyone, but I did grow up here, and Sorenson isn't a very big town. I didn't know Lars personally, but I met him once at a hospital function. And he's pretty recognizable in these parts because his picture has been in the local paper a number of times."

"Why?" Hurley asks.

"He's a real estate developer who came to town a few years ago and made a big splash. Not everybody has been happy about getting wet. Some of his projects have been rather controversial."

"Great," Hurley mutters. "Why can't we ever get victims who are mostly liked by everyone? It would make the investigations a lot easier."

"Maybe because people don't tend to kill people they like?" I suggest with more than a hint of sarcasm.

Hurley smiles at me and then looks over at Izzy. "Any chance this was a hunting accident?"

Izzy does a half wince as he stares down at the dead man. "Can't say for sure until I get him back to the morgue, but I'm leaning toward no. Look at the angle of the arrow. It enters the left side of his neck just above the collar bone and comes out on the right side just below his jaw line, close to a forty-five-degree angle. If the arrow was shot from a distance away, it would have had a downward trajectory, or a level one, but not an upward one. For the arrow to have gone the direction it did, he had to have been shot by someone who was standing below him." Izzy pauses and looks up at the trees around us. "I don't see a tree stand anywhere nearby so I don't think it happened that way. And these woods are dense, so I'm thinking that whoever shot him had to have been close. In fact, I'd wager they were here in this small clearing with our victim. It isn't easy to hit a person with an arrow from any distance."

Hurley, who is squatting beside the body, looks up at Izzy and says, "What if the shooter was kneeling, squatting, or sitting, and Lars was standing?"

Izzy contemplates this a moment. "I suppose it's possible," he says. "But there are problems with that scenario. It would be hard to pull sufficiently and get a decent aim with a regular bow in a squatting, sitting, or kneeling position. . . . Not impossible, but definitely awkward."

Hurley looks up at me and mimes shooting at me with a bow and arrow. Then he looks back down at Lars. "Think the arrow came from a crossbow?"

Izzy shakes his head. "It's the wrong kind of arrow. Crossbows use a bolt. This looks like it came from a compound bow, or perhaps an old-fashioned bow and arrow, though you don't see many of those out here these days. Besides, if the arrow came from a crossbow and it was fired close by, the force behind it would have sent it clear through the victim's neck and out the other side. The fact that it's still embedded suggests that the arrow didn't have that kind of momentum behind it."

"Look at this," I say, pointing to a disturbance in the dirt on my side of the body, not far from the arrow point. "Could Lars have been on the ground when he was shot? There's a depression in the ground and it looks like there's dirt on the arrow tip. Couldn't that suggest that Lars was on the ground, perhaps on his side when he was shot, and then he rolled onto his back?"

Everyone contemplates the question until Izzy responds. "Mattie's scenario is definitely a possibility. In fact, to me it makes the most sense. Even with a regular bow, the arrow could easily go clear through the neck musculature. If he was on the ground, the impact of hitting the dirt would have stopped it."

Hurley says, "What if Lars fell from a standing or kneeling position after he was shot and landed on the side where the arrow point is protruding? Wouldn't that leave the same sort of evidence?"

Izzy looks thoughtful. "It could, yes. I won't be able to determine that until I open him up. If he fell and landed on the side where the arrow head is protruding, I should be able to see reciprocal damage, reverse sheering to the internal musculature of the neck that shows a force counter to the direction of the arrow. If he was shot while lying in the side position and then rolled onto his back, I would anticipate finding only forward motion of the arrow shaft and one directional tissue damage. It's possible to stab someone in the neck with an arrow and have it go all the way through, too, but I don't see that as a possibility because of the upward angle. If someone was stabbing"—Izzy pauses and mimes the motion—"the trajectory would be downward. So I'm leaning more toward Mattie's theory. It fits better with the angles of the arrow, the trajectory, and the final lie."

Hurley asks, "Why would he have been on the ground when he was shot?"

Izzy wraps his gloved hands around the victim's head and begins to palpate. "Ah, yes," he says as he feels the back of the scalp. "We have a significant wound back here that indicates trauma of some sort from a blunt object. It doesn't feel like anything that would have been fatal, but it definitely could have stunned him." He sets the head down gently and looks around. "I'd check out some of these rocks around here."

Everyone looks around the small clearing. There are a handful of stones on the ground and KY, Brenda, Jonas, Hurley, and I each go after one of them. It's KY who strikes gold.

"Here we go," he says, showing us a long, thick, craggy rock a little bit bigger than a hardcover book. There is a dark brown stain on one, sharp edge of it.

"Bag it and tag it," Hurley says as Charlie aims her camera at the rock and zooms in on the stained portion before KY places it in a paper evidence bag.

"Can you give me a time of death?" Hurley asks.

Izzy frowns. "I can give you a window, but there are too many variables here to be specific."

"Give me what you can."

"Mattie, can you get a temp for me?"

"How do you want me to do it?"

Izzy looks at the body for a few seconds, pulling at his chin. "Let's go with a liver temp. It won't disturb his position and it will require less clothing movement than a rectal."

I nod, and carefully lift the bottom of Lars's jacket. Then I pull the tail of his shirt from the waist of his pants, exposing an insulated undershirt. I lift that, too, taking care to look for any trace evidence that might be clinging to the clothing. I don't see anything, and once I have Lars's belly exposed I take a scalpel from my scene kit and make a small incision under the rib cage. Then I take out my thermometer and push it through the incision and into the liver. As I'm doing this, Izzy glances at the thermometer he keeps clipped to the side of his kit, and then he starts tapping on his smart phone. "The temperature out here now is forty-two degrees," he says, "and the low this morning was thirty-eight, which would have been just before sunrise at 6:48." He jots this info down on a notepad.

"The body temp is ninety-five," I announce, removing my thermometer and putting Lars's clothing back the way it was. I had photographed the body and the surrounding area when we first arrived, before anything was disturbed, but Izzy likes to keep things as close to the original state as possible when we're in the field.

Izzy starts to reach for Lars's jaw but he pauses and stares at the man's neck. He points to a spot just above the entry point for the arrow and says, "Look at this. What does it look like?"

Hurley and I both lean in and look closely at the spot Izzy has indicated. There is a plaster of dried blood on Lars's neck and the surface of it in one spot is disturbed, lacking the general smoothness of the other areas.

"Looks like a fingerprint," Hurley says.

I don't see it at first, but when I turn my head at a slight angle, the sun hits the area differently and I notice the faint ridges.

"Sure does," Izzy agrees.

I use my camera to get some close-up shots of the area from several different angles and then Charlie films it with her video camera, panning in and out a few times.

"I'll shoot these pics over to the office and see if Arnie can get a good enough picture to run it through AFIS," I say. Then I proceed to e-mail the pictures directly from my camera to Arnie Toffer, our lab tech, who should be working in the office.

Izzy says, "In the meantime, let's try to preserve this spot as best we can." With his gloved hand he prods parts of Lars's face, and then moves Lars's jaw, taking care to avoid the area of the neck where we found the print. "There's no sign of rigor yet," he says. "Given that and the temperatures, I'd say he's been dead for two to four hours."

Hurley glances at his watch. "It's almost nine now, so that means he was shot between five this morning and seven fifty-four when we got the call."

"Who called it in?" I ask.

KY answers. "An employee at the Quik-E-Mart gas station on the edge of town. According to him, a man in a pickup truck pulled in to fuel up and came inside the store for some soda. He overheard two guys talking in the next aisle over, and one of the guys was telling the other about a body he saw in Cooper's Woods. The guy in the pickup mentioned the conversation to the cashier, and the cashier called us."

"Have you talked to him, or any of the others involved?" Izzy asks Hurley.

"I haven't, but I sent Junior Feller over to talk to the cashier and see if there is any security footage. Hopefully that will help us ID the customers involved." Hurley looks over at me. "Mattie, you said Lars did some projects that were controversial. Can you elaborate on that?"

"Sure. He builds stuff nobody wants, like cookie cutter housing developments, strip malls, and cheap condos. At one point he was working with a big box store that wanted to come into town, and he tried to sneak it past the city council members. They stopped him that time, but he's had other slightly shady deals that he's managed to pull off. He's forced a lot of struggling farmers into selling off land for less than it's worth, promising them he will use it for only certain types of developments. Then he changes the plan once he gets his hands on the property. Based on what I've heard through the gripe vine, he promises one thing verbally and then changes it in the written contract, which he then bamboozles people into signing."

"Has anybody sued him?" Hurley asks.

"I've heard Lucien talk about a couple of cases that were filed, but I don't know if any of them ever went to court. He said Lars always hired expensive lawyers from out of town, so most of the people he screwed over couldn't afford to fight him."

Lucien is my brother-in-law and a defense lawyer, though he occasionally dabbles in some other basic legal services, like writing up wills and powers of attorney, or the occasional civil suit. He has a reputation in town, too, one that probably rivals Lars's. The mere mention of his name makes many people shudder, and the sight of him tends to make people cringe, though this latter part is more about what Lucien looks like than it is about his reputation. He wears cheap suits that are often adorned with remnants from his last meal, he greases his strawberry blond hair back with some oily pomade that makes him look like a fuzzy red dipstick, and he has a leering look he's honed to perfection. Accompanying that lecherous look is a politically incorrect, unfiltered mouth that has caused more gasps than the ALS ice bucket challenge.

Lucien fell on some hard times recently. It's not easy to make a living from defending the kinds of crimes that typically occur in a town the size of Sorenson. The police blotter in the local paper often lists such heinous things as cow tipping, illegal tractor parking, and indecent exposure, the latter typically committed by what my sister, Desi, calls the Free Willy Club—drunks who opt to pee outside for some reason and forget to put the animal back in the barn. Ninety percent of the crimes in town involve some level of intoxication, which isn't all that surprising when you consider that there are more bars in town than there are churches. In an effort to pad his bank account, Lucien tried to back up his regular income with some investment strategies using both his own money and some of his clients'. It went well for a short time, but then it all crashed and burned. Lucien struggled to put out the fires but the situation only worsened. He's no longer investing anything, and he's slowly paying back the people whose money he lost. But the debacle nearly cost him his marriage, his livelihood, and his reputation.

Anyone who has met or gone up against Lucien wouldn't think his reputation could sink any lower. But the attitude, appearance, and crass articulation is all a façade—an effective one. People tend to underestimate Lucien because of his appearance and behavior, and that's a big mistake. He's a wolf in sheep's clothing, though I have to admit that his recent setbacks have mellowed him out some. What I won't admit to anyone is that I kind of miss the older, less refined Lucien. He was always entertaining.

Hurley rises to his feet and lets out a perturbed sigh. "It sounds like we'll have no shortage of suspects for this one. I hate cases like this." He turns to Charlie and says, "Make sure we get a close-up of that arrow in case there's anything about it that might help us determine who or where it came from."

Charlie smiles at him and says, "Of course." Then she steps in front of him and squats beside the body, giving Hurley a bird's-eye view of her lovely backside, a view I notice both Hurley and KY take in.

Desperate to distract Hurley's attention, I move away

from the body off to Hurley's right and stare into the trees. "How did Lars get out here?" I ask no one in particular.

"Good question," Hurley says, peering through the trees toward the moraine we hiked through to get here. "Are there any other roads that provide access to these woods?"

KY, Brenda, and I all shake our heads.

"These woods go back a good mile or two," Brenda says. "There's a drumlin that runs along the back edge, and on the other side of the drumlin are more woods. There are some roads leading to that section of woods, but nothing for this area. Where we parked on the county road is the closest access, across that moraine."

The wooded area we are standing in is privately owned property that belongs to the Coopers, a family descended from a long line of farmers who once owned half the county. The modern-day Coopers ran into some financial troubles back in the seventies and they started selling off parcels of land to help pay the bills. But the bills kept coming and the income kept dwindling and over the years the property has been whittled away in chunks like the legs of a diabetic patient with severe vascular disease. Eventually the bulk of the land was either seized or sold off to pay taxes and debts, and today all the family has left is a rambling old farmhouse that sits on a five-acre parcel of land, and this wooded area, which covers over twelve hundred acres. The wooded parcel isn't good for much other than hunting unless someone wanted to go through the work of clearing out all the trees. Apparently no one did because the Coopers never sold it. The patriarch of the family issues land use permits to hunters during deer season because the deer love the woods. But it isn't easy to get to. The county road we parked on is the closest access and then one has to hike a half mile or so across a boulder-strewn field left behind by some Ice Age glacier.

Brenda adds, "I'm guessing one of those cars out there along the road where we parked belongs to our victim."

Hurley nods, takes out his cell phone—diversion accomplished—and punches in a number. Then we all listen in as he talks to Heidi, the day dispatcher at the police station. He instructs her to send an officer out to check the cars parked alongside the road and compare the plates to Sanderson's DMV info. Assuming one of the dozen or so cars that were parked there when we arrived belongs to Lars, it will be towed into the police garage as evidence. The owners of the others will need to be tracked down and questioned.

My reprieve is short-lived because once Hurley has disconnected his call he turns his attention back to Charlie. "The ground is too frozen to leave any footprints, but there are a few patches of snow left here among the trees. Why don't you and Jonas scout around this area and see if you can find any prints in the snow?"

"Sure," Charlie says with a smile. Then, much to my relief, she and Jonas—who looks like he just won the lottery—take off into the woods.

I have to confess there's a tiny part of me that hopes they'll get lost . . . just for a little while.

Chapter 2

Charlie is a relatively new member of our investigative team, thanks to a grant our police chief got in order to tighten up our evidentiary processes and make them more transparent. So far, the most transparent part of this new system is how gaga all the men are over Charlie. She's in her mid- to late twenties, built like a pinup model, and drop-dead gorgeous. On top of that she's a redhead, and not the weird orange kind, but a deep, fiery red with copper and honey highlights. Red-haired women make many men crazy. I don't know of a single guy who hasn't drooled over Charlie other than the gay ones, and even some of them have eyed her with envy.

While Charlie isn't lacking for male attention, the only man she seems interested in is Hurley. She confided as much to the evening dispatcher, Stephanie, who then told me. I also know it because of the way she hangs on Hurley's every word, bats her eyelashes at him, and uses any excuse she can find to touch him.

Charlie is a mixed blessing for me. Clearly I'm not happy about her interest in Hurley, or her stunning good looks, particularly since she's been working side by side with Hurley for the past two months while I've been in postpartum limbo. I tried not to worry about it too much at first because the original grant had Charlie on loan to us for a six-month period, so her time with Hurley was limited. But then her position was made permanent and now she's with us all the time. On the upside, her presence and the grant that came with her made it okay for Hurley and me to have a personal relationship while continuing to work together.

That sounds ideal, but the truth is, lately I've had a more personal relationship with my breast pump than I've had with Hurley. Our time together comes in stolen bits, minutes we manage to cobble together between the demands of our very hungry son, who I swear puts out more than he takes in, and Hurley's daughter, Emily, a fifteen-year-old mess of crazy hormones and teenaged angst. Emily lost her mother, Kate, earlier this year, and it happened only months after she met Hurley for the first time. Up until then, Kate had told Emily her father was dead. So the poor kid is now forced to live with a man who knows nothing about her or about raising a child, and who is on the brink of starting a new family with me. As a result, she has been acting out and doing everything she can to sabotage my relationship with Hurley, a relationship that has already had more bumps than a roll of bubble wrap.

When you add the demands of a newborn to Emily's shenanigans, you get two frustrated, tired, confused people who are desperate to sneak in a little quality time between crises. So far, that quality time has been limited to some snuggling on my couch, a half-eaten lunch interrupted by Matthew's wails, and one attempt at a dinner out that was done in by one of Emily's tantrums. Sex has been off the table while I recovered from my delivery, and I'm worried that Hurley will grow tired of waiting and start looking elsewhere, namely at Charlie. Though to be honest, the sexiest thing Hurley could do for me right now is take care of Matthew for a few hours so I can take a nap.

I've always considered myself a fairly neat and organized person, but the addition of Matthew into my life has changed that. If it wasn't for Dom coming by to help me clean up the cottage and do some laundry, Matthew and I would both be dressed in filthy rags. My dog Hoover hasn't helped the situation. Not only does he need to be walked on a regular basis, he has developed an affinity for chewing up Matthew's dirty diapers. The little genius figured out how to raise the lid of the garbage can I put them in by stepping on the pedal. He then snatches a diaper and ten minutes later there are shredded bits of poopy plastic and padding strewn all over the place. In an effort to not sound like a Debbie Downer all the time, I will admit that the glass is half full on occasion. Thanks to the ready availability of diapers, Hoover has quit chewing the crotches out of my underwear.

Even something as simple as grocery shopping—the only form of shopping I've ever enjoyed—has now become a major ordeal. I not only have to dress myself, I have to dress Matthew and bundle him up against the cold. Then I have to get him into his car seat, an activity that makes my back scream, and when we get to the store I get to remove him and the car seat. Once inside I get to place him in a shopping cart that then has no room left for groceries, not to mention those gigantic packages of disposable diapers that I swear I've bought a thousand of already, so I have to grab a second cart to pull behind me. I also have to undress Matthew enough to keep him from overheating while I shop, and rebundle him before we leave. The prep time alone is longer than it used to take me to make the whole shopping trip.

After a few trips playing choo-choo train at the grocery store, I discovered a new way to shop. One evening after putting Matthew down to sleep, I went surfing on Amazon because my sister told me I could get diapers cheaper by ordering them there. Not only did I find some that were cheaper, I discovered that if I opened up an Amazon Prime account, I could get them shipped and delivered to my door free within two days of ordering them. I haven't bought diapers in a real store since. Then I accidentally discovered an entire grocery section on Amazon. I could order virtually anything, or virtually order anything: peanut butter, pastas, cheeses, breads, meats, spices, coffee, a million canned foods, brand-name baby foods, cookies, milk . . . The list was endless. My trips to the grocery store became fewer and less cumbersome since I no longer needed to buy so much, and food was delivered right to my door. The UPS guy was at my place so often, he started bringing treats for Hoover and joked about opening up a satellite store in my driveway. Dom asked me if I was having an affair with the guy.

While my discovery of Amazon has helped, my life has remained a series of disaster management situations. It wasn't too bad during the first week because I had tons of visitors drop by. My entire family came: my sister, Desi, her husband, Lucien, their kids, Erika and Ethan, and even my mother managed to venture out into the germ-plagued world long enough to visit along with her live-in boyfriend (an ex-date of mine), William. Mom drew the line at changing diapers however. Even a newborn possessed the potential for catastrophic germ warfare and my mother has been waging a war with germs her entire life.

Hurley came by as often as he could, too, which wasn't as often as he liked since his daughter, Emily, did everything in her power to keep us apart. If she suspected he was spending time with me and Matthew, she would skip out of school, or disappear from the house and then call to say she was running away, or wanting to hurt herself. People from my office and other acquaintances dropped by, too, and during that first week I had no shortage of people who were willing to care for Matthew while I napped or showered or just had a few minutes of peace, quiet, and alone time. But once the newness wore off, they all disappeared back to their own lives.

The one constant has been Izzy's partner, Dom, who came by so often during the first few weeks that Izzy started to complain that I saw more of Dom than he did. Dom took to parenting like he was born to do it, and there was never an awkward moment when it came to feeding, changing diapers, bathing, dressing, or just holding and soothing Matthew. At times I felt as if Matthew was more Dom's child than mine. This doubt wasn't helped by the fact that I kept waiting for my maternal attachment to kick in, that overwhelming feeling of love that turns normal human beings into fierce mother bears. But at first Matthew seemed like little more than an adorable blob of flesh that ate, pooped, and slept—though not nearly enough of the latter. I was exhausted, frustrated, and filled with guilt, convinced I was a horrible mother.

Then, when he was a little over a month old, Matthew smiled at me for the first time and I thought my heart would burst with the swell of love I felt. Life didn't get any less chaotic, but suddenly it all seemed worth it.

My chaotic lifestyle was in full swing this morning, so much so that I brought remnants of it with me to the crime scene. I woke up late for work because, for the first time ever, Matthew slept beyond his usual two hours after his four A.M. feeding. And either my alarm didn't go off, or I turned it off and went back to sleep. I can't be sure since what little sleep time I get these days is more like a coma. The first thing I recall from this morning is Dom shaking me awake.

"Mattie, it's almost seven-thirty. Aren't you supposed to be at work by eight?"

I rolled over in my bleary-eyed state, stared at the clock, then at Dom, then at the clock again. Reality kicked in and I flung back the covers and bolted out of bed. "Oh, no! Matthew!" I was convinced my son must be dead because there was no other way I could have slept this long.

"He's fine," Dom said just above a whisper. Then he put a finger to his lips to warn me to be quiet. "He's sleeping."

I walked over to the crib and stared at my sleeping son, momentarily filled with a love so great, it made my heart feel like it would explode from my chest. Then reality tapped me on the shoulder in the form of Dom.

"You need to get a move on," he said.

I kicked back into frantic mode. I realized that the pressure I'd felt in my chest was real. My breasts were about to explode with milk. And I needed coffee, and a shower. I knew there wasn't much point in the shower until I emptied my breasts. They would just leak all over me as soon as I got out. I grabbed my breast pump, headed for the kitchen, and quickly set up the pump—I'd become quite the expert with the diabolical little machine over the past two months for two reasons. One was because of that lie women have been perpetuating for eons, that breast-feeding is normal, natural, and easy. It may be normal and natural, but easy doesn't apply. Matthew was a lazy eater, often not wanting to latch on hard enough and suck long enough to satiate his growing appetite. We spent many an hour together, both of us crying with frustration as we tried to get the hang of it. I was determined to succeed, if for no other reason than because of the benefits I know newborns get from breast milk. But for the first few weeks it was a constant battle. By the time Matthew seemed to get the hang of it, my nipples decided to rebel. They became chafed and sore, and nursing became a form of torture.

The other reason my breast pump is my new best friend is because my breasts don't seem to know when to stop. I produce lots of milk, more than Matthew needs, and I don't want it to go to waste. So I pump and bottle the excess, using it for those occasions when someone comes by for a visit and I can pawn off the kid and the bottle for a few cherished and desperately needed minutes of sleep.

Given my familiarity with the pump, it took me barely more than a minute to set it up, hook it up, and start it up this morning. I stood at the counter, stripped off my pajama top, and dropped the flaps on my bra. I'd invested in the dual chamber pump despite having no idea why I would need it, but I'm glad now I did. I hooked up both sides at the same time and, as the machine chugged away, I went about setting up the coffeepot, turning it on, and grabbing a mug from the cupboard overhead. Then I stood there waiting . . . waiting for both machines to finish their jobs. The coffeepot won the race, and as I poured and tasted that first wondrous sip of hot caffeine, the pump finished, too.

"I can finish that up for you," Dom said behind me.

I looked over my shoulder and saw him standing behind me. You'd think the sight of an essentially bare-breasted woman standing in the kitchen hooked up to a miniature version of The Machine from *The Princess Bride* would have embarrassed him . . . or me . . . but Dom and I have learned to take things in stride. His help has been a lifesaver for me these past few weeks, and he's seen my boobs plenty of times already. Besides, I gave birth in my bathtub with Izzy, Hurley, and another detective, Bob Richmond, all standing by watching. At this point, I have no secrets left.

After detaching myself from the pump this morning, I grabbed my coffee, and headed for the shower, leaving Dom to bottle up the milk. "Thanks," I said.

I lingered in the shower a little longer than I should have, but the luxury of having a few minutes of peace and quiet to myself knowing Matthew was being well looked after, was too much to resist. By the time I dressed and came out of the bathroom, Matthew was awake. Dom had changed him and was sitting on the couch, feeding him from a bottle. The two of them looked so content and serene sitting there, I began to wonder if I should marry Dom instead of Hurley. Or maybe Hurley should marry Dom.

"You're really good with him," I said, watching the two of them. Dom smiled. He had this beatific expression on his face that said it all.

"I want one," he said.

"Want one what?"

"A baby."

"Oh."

"I mean, Izzy and I have been together for a long time now, and we're happy, but sometimes I feel like there's something missing."

"Have you considered a new hobby? Or a vacation?" I asked. "They'd both be cheaper and easier."

Dom scoffed. "Yeah, like Izzy would take a vacation." Matthew had chugged down half the bottle already, so Dom took it from him, set it aside, and hoisted Matthew over his shoulder to burp him. "It took my father dying to get Izzy to take any time off," Dom went on. "And even then he was constantly worrying about work and how things were going up here."

Dom's father had passed away from a heart attack in the spring, and he and Izzy had traveled to Iowa for a week to help with the funeral preparations. It hadn't been an easy trip, and not just because of the death or Izzy's discomfort at being away. Dom's family—except for his mother—has never approved of his lifestyle, and his relationship with his father had always been a contentious one at best. The fact that he has two testosterone-overdosed brothers who are straight as arrows, judgmental as hell, and homophobic, didn't help.

"Izzy's work issues on that trip were partly my fault," I said. "You know . . . that guy I killed? The one who tried to kill me? Izzy was worried about all that."

Dom shot me a look of incredulity. "Come on, Mattie. You know how Izzy is. He's a die-hard workaholic. He isn't happy unless he's knee-deep in dead bodies and paperwork. I don't think he'll ever retire."

"Well, that's something to consider, isn't it?" I said. "How old is Izzy now, fifty-one?"

Dom nodded.

"And you're pushing forty. That's kind of old to be

starting a family. Then there are the simple logistics of how to get a baby. It's not like the two of you can simply decide to have one and plot it out on an ovulation calendar."

"I know," Dom said, frowning at me. "No need to remind me of our limitations."

"It's not a limitation, Dom. It's a simple fact."

"There are other ways," he insisted. "We could adopt."

"Adopting a baby isn't easy. It takes time and money. And there are plenty of married heterosexual couples out there looking, too."

"We could look overseas."

"You could," I admitted, nodding slowly. "But again, it takes a lot of time and money. And there are no guarantees." He looked sad and dejected, a sharp contrast to the blissful expression he'd had when I first entered the room. To try and cheer him up, I said, "You know you can adopt Matthew anytime you want." I was joking of course, but Dom gave me such a serious, questioning look that I immediately added, "What I mean is that you guys are welcome to be as much a part of Matthew's life as you want."

"Thanks, but it's not the same thing. And besides, Matthew should have other kids around. He should have a sibling, or a cousin, or a close playmate. Are you planning to have more kids?"

At the moment, my exhaustion made me want to tell him that I was going to tie my own tubes using a kitchen knife and shoelaces just to make sure I didn't end up in this position again. But when I looked at Matthew's adorable face, the exhaustion didn't seem to matter all that much. I shrugged. "It's possible, if the right situation presents itself and things with Hurley and me get sorted out. But give us time. I'm still in shock below the waist from spitting that one out, and right now we have all we can handle with this little guy and Emily."

"There's always surrogacy," Dom said in a quiet voice. He was watching me closely and it took me a second to realize what he was suggesting.

I stared at him a moment, waiting for the grin that would tell me he was just kidding. It didn't come. "Dom, are you asking me if I'd consider carrying a baby for you and Izzy?"

He shrugged and for a split second I felt relief, but then he nodded. "Would you?"

I was flabbergasted and didn't know what to say. "Um . . . I . . . have you talked to Izzy about this?"

He shook his head and sighed. "Not yet. I thought I should run it by you first to see if it was even a possibility." He paused as we engaged in a stare down. "Is it?"

Was it? I could hardly wrap my mind around the idea. "Dom, I don't know what to say. I mean, I'm flattered that you would consider me for such a thing, but my life is a hot mess at the moment. I really can't think about it right now."

"But will you think about it sometime? At least consider it?"

I hesitated, and then nodded. "Right now I can barely sort out my underwear drawer, much less something as big as this. It's going to take some time, but I promise you I will give it serious thought and consideration at some point."

That seemed to satisfy him. Matthew sealed the moment with a gigantic belch.

"Very good," Dom said with a satisfied smile, and I wasn't sure who he was talking to, me or Matthew. Maybe it was both of us.

I hurried into the kitchen and packed up the breast

pump, which Dom had graciously cleaned and dried, and some extra bottles. If yesterday was any indication, I would be hiding in the bathroom or Izzy's office at least twice, if not three times, during the day, pumping. I glanced in the fridge to make sure there were plenty of filled bottles there, though I had some formula in a cabinet just in case. The formula, however, was superfluous, at least for now. Half of one shelf in my fridge was filled with bottles that Dom had carefully labeled with a time and date, and arranged accordingly. I shook my head and smiled. The man was truly a natural at this. I felt for him and his urge to have a child, but I also felt certain I wouldn't do the surrogacy thing. I would do what he asked and give it some serious consideration when the time was right, but I already knew what my answer would be. I just didn't have the heart to crush his hopes this soon.

When I had everything packed up and ready to go, I headed over to the couch and said, "Let me give my boy a kiss good-bye."

"What about your hair?" Dom asked, eyeing my head with skepticism.

"I'm going to let it air-dry," I said, smoothing down one side with my free hand.

"You really need to go and see Barbara." The wince on his face as he said this told me how serious the situation was.

Barbara is my hairdresser. She works at a local funeral home and ninety-eight percent of her clients are dead. I happen to be one of the lucky ones, though there have been some days recently when I was so tired I wasn't sure *lucky* was the right word.

"I will," I said, knowing he was right. I hadn't been to see Barbara since before Matthew was born and my hair was badly in need of a cut and color. Not only were my roots hideously dark and long, I'd recently spied a couple of gray hairs sprouting from my scalp. That's what the joys of motherhood do for you.

Looking hopeful, Dom said, "Why don't you see if you can get an appointment this evening? I'll be happy to keep Matthew for you until you get home, no matter how late it is."

I was about to object but stopped myself, realizing it would be an automatic response based on some ridiculous Supermom image I was trying to live up to. But even Supermoms need a little self-time once in a while, not to mention that any superhero needs to look good. I knew I was fortunate to have Dom with his top-notch mothering skills and flexible schedule practically at my beck and call, so I said, "You know what, I might just do that. Thank you." I leaned over and gave Dom a quick kiss on the head, making him blush beet red. "Now let me kiss my boy."

Dom pulled the bottle from Matthew's mouth and held him out at arm's length. I gave Matthew a kiss on the cheek and, just as I did, he let loose with another belch. Unfortunately, this one wasn't a dry burp and the eruption, which could have given Vesuvius some serious competition, landed squarely on my shoulder.

Chapter 3

Adorned with baby barf on my blouse, I glanced at my watch and saw that it was already after eight. I had a dilemma. I was going to be late for work—no getting around that—but I wanted to minimize it as much as possible. I'd promised Izzy that I would be able to handle both motherhood and the job just fine, and I was determined to keep that promise. My Supermom role was on the line, not to mention my livelihood.

I still have a decent savings account from my divorce settlement—it would be a lot more decent if I hadn't spent so much time at the casino at the start of the year—but I know I'm going to need that money for things like unexpected medical expenses, and clothes, and diapers, and baby food, and . . . the list seems endless. And that doesn't take into account school fees and a college fund. I know Hurley will help, but he doesn't make that much money, and now he has Emily to support, too. Bottom line: I can't afford to lose my job.

So this morning, in an effort to mitigate my lateness, I didn't bother changing my blouse. Instead I hurried out to the car and, once I was under way, I grabbed a napkin that was on the passenger seat from my last excursion through a drive-through and tried to wipe away the spit-up. My efforts left something to be desired. Instead of a spit-up epaulet on my shoulder, I ended up with a stain sash that extended from my shoulder down to my left breast. Midcurse, my cell phone rang. I dropped the napkin, grabbed the phone, and saw that it was Izzy.

"I'm sorry I'm late," I said before he had a chance to say anything. "I'm only a couple of minutes away."

"Well, turn around and head out of town on the east side, toward Cooper's Woods. We have a dead body out there. It sounds like a hunting accident."

That's how I managed to show up at my first return-to-duty death scene with frizzy, two-toned hair, hastily applied makeup, a stained blouse that I only later realized was buttoned crooked, and the subtle scent of eau de barf cologne wafting in a corona around my shoulders and head. Normally I wouldn't have been too concerned about how I looked or smelled at the scene of a death. I mean, let's face it, the victims couldn't care less and they generally smelled and looked worse than anyone else present. In the past I've shown up at some of my middle-of-the-night calls with raccoon eyes from makeup that I neglected to remove before falling asleep, a major case of bedhead, and wearing all manner of weird thrown-together getups. But now that Charlie was in the mix, I felt like I needed to step up my game.

Of course, she arrived looking like she'd spent all night getting ready. Her hair was perfectly coiffed, her makeup expertly applied, and her clothing clean and pressed. She also smelled divine, and while one part of me wanted to ask her what perfume she was wearing, another part of me would have rather died first.

Feeling self-conscious, I made an effort to smooth down my hair and realized that Matthew's parting gift hadn't been confined to my blouse. On one side of my head was a thick strand of hair that was hard and crusty. Realizing there was little I could do about it at that point, I shifted my focus to the job at hand.

Not a great way to start the day, but now—more than an hour later—we are ready to load Lars Sanderson up and take him back to the morgue. Izzy calls the Johnson Funeral Home to come and transport the body, and informs them it will be a bit of a hike out to the woods from the closest available parking space. The Johnson Funeral Home is a family-run business, and body pickups are typically done by the oldest twin daughters, Cass and Kit, whose Goth-like tastes make them seem perfect for the job. And while the girls are young and relatively fit, hauling a deadweight like Lars half a mile across a rocky field might be more than just the two of them can handle.

Knowing this, Hurley volunteers Brenda to stay and help. Brenda frowns and rolls her eyes. She confided to me once that the Cass-Kit sisters give her the heebie-jeebies. At least she won't be alone. It will take all six of us to walk the deadweight of Lars Sanderson back to the hearse.

I help Izzy bag up Lars in preparation for the twins' arrival, and when we're done, Hurley motions to me. He is standing at the far edge of the small clearing we're in and no one else is around him at the moment.

I walk over to him with a tired smile and he gives me one back.

"I'd really like to kiss you right now," he says in a low voice.

"I don't think I have the energy to kiss you back."

"Still not getting much sleep?"

"Actually, I got a little more than usual this morning. Matthew slept longer than two hours for the first time. I'm hoping it's a sign of things to come."

"My offer still stands."

The offer he is referring to is twofold. One, he wants to marry me, or so he says, but I can't shake the feeling that he's offering only because he feels it's the right and proper thing to do. Two, he has offered to let Matthew and me move into his house so we can share the parenting duties. I would have bit on this one in a heartbeat if it wasn't for Emily. But with all the issues she has right now—including an apparent resentment of Matthew that makes me leery about letting her around him much—I don't think it's a good idea. Plus I have Dom.

"Thanks," I tell him. "I'm still open to the idea down the road, but I think we need to keep the status quo for now. At least until Emily comes around a little more. How are the counseling sessions going?"

Hurley makes a face. "I don't know. I'm not a big fan of shrinks."

"Tell me about it," I say, rolling my eyes. "I *hate* shrinks. But Maggie is really good and I have to admit, she's helped me a lot over the past year." Maggie Baldwin, or Dr. Naggy as I call her, is Emily's shrink, and I know her well. She knows me even better. I spent some time in her office while I was pregnant, sorting out the issues in my own life. As a result, she was familiar with many of Emily's issues long before Emily started seeing her.

"We'll see," Hurley says, scowling and sounding unconvinced. "So far, we've had two sessions together, and Emily has had three alone. Maggie says she wants to continue with Emily alone for now, but I'm not sure it's going to help. I haven't seen any changes in her behavior yet."

"It takes time," I say. "At least she's going. That's some progress."

When Hurley first suggested the counseling idea to Emily, she threatened to run away. I'm not sure if it was insight, frustration, or exhaustion that made Hurley call her bluff, but he did. He told her to go ahead and do it if that's what she really wanted. But if she wanted to stay with him, she was going to have to see a counselor. We both spent a few nail-biting days waiting to see what would happen once Hurley made the first appointment and informed Emily. Her frown deepened, she slammed a few more doors, and she stomped her feet harder, but in the end she went.

"I don't know," Hurley says, still looking skeptical. "I think the whole counseling thing is a long shot. And speaking of shots, when is Matthew due to go to the doctor's again?"

"Not for another month. But I called the pediatrician yesterday with some questions. I was hoping to hold out until the three-month checkup to ask if I could start mixing a little rice cereal in with his bottles, but Matthew seems hungry all the time and this every-two-hour feeding schedule is really wearing me down, especially now that I'm back at work."

"Did he say it would be okay?"

"He did. I started it last night and I think that's why Matthew slept longer this morning." I sighed and shook my head. "I have to tell you, that extra hour of sleep was heavenly. But when I woke up and realized how much time had gone by, I panicked, thinking something had happened to him." My voice catches on the last few words. The memory of that momentary panic is enough to make my emotions well up. *Stupid hormones.*

"I wish I could be there more," Hurley says, looking sad.

I reach over and take his hand, squeezing it. "It will get better," I say, hoping I'm right. "And I'm surviving, thanks to Dom. Although . . ."

Hurley juts his head forward, looking worried. "What?"

"He hit me up with something this morning that kind of caught me off guard."

"He's not going to stop sitting for you, is he?"

"No, not at all. In fact, he wants to add to the fray. He thinks he and Izzy should get a child."

Hurley considers this for a second and then shrugs. "Is that a problem?"

"Possibly." I roll my eyes and then amend my answer. "Probably. For one thing, Dom hasn't discussed it with Izzy yet." I glance over my shoulder to make sure we're still a safe distance from the others. "Izzy is no spring chicken, you know? I don't know if he's going to want to start a family this late in the game, particularly since it will take a fair amount of time to adopt a child, assuming he's even willing to go that route."

"I've heard overseas adoptions can be a lot quicker," Hurley says.

I nod. "True, but even those can be expensive and time-consuming. And a lot of those foreign orphanage kids have emotional and developmental problems. I think that's why Dom is considering a different option." I'm about to tell him about Dom's surprising request when we hear Cass and Kit holler from the edge of the woods.

Half an hour later, we have carried Lars—securely tucked inside a body bag—across the glacial minefield and loaded him into the girls' hearse. It wasn't an easy trek; we almost dropped Lars twice when first Izzy, and then Hurley caught a foot on a half-buried rock. There is a cop car parked behind the hearse, and an officer named Ben Rittenour has walked up to Hurley with a notebook in hand.

"The Lexus over there belongs to your victim," Ben says, pointing toward a beige SUV parked two cars up. He rips a page out of his notebook and hands it to Hurley. "Here's the DMV info on the others that are parked here. I have a tow truck on the way to take the Lexus back to the garage."

Hurley hands Ben an evidence bag that contains the set of keys we found in Lars's pocket. "Is it locked?" Hurley asks.

"It is," Ben says. "Want me to open it here?"

Hurley considers this a moment and then shakes his head. "Nah, just tow it to the garage and let Jonas look it over."

"Will do."

Hurley sends Brenda back to the woods both to help Charlie and KY, and because she is KY's ride. "See if you can find any other hunters in these woods," he tells her. "I want names and data on anyone out here. Get statements from all of them. Find out if anyone heard or saw anything that might be relevant. And be careful. Not only might our killer still be out here, but there's also a bunch of fools with guns running around, and even this early in the day half of them are probably drunk." Brenda nods dutifully and heads back across the rock field.

As Hurley and I head back to our respective cars so we can follow the hearse and Izzy to the morgue, he gets on his phone and has Heidi arrange for an officer to head to Lars's home to see if anyone is there. If not, he instructs her to tell the officer to sit on the place until we can get there.

By the time Hurley disconnects the call, we are back at our cars and he makes good on his kiss wish, giving me a quick peck on the lips. "See you back at the morgue," he says with a wink.

"Now there's a pickup line you don't hear every day."

It takes us about ten minutes to get back to the office and as soon as we arrive, Izzy instructs me to "check Lars in." This task involves supervising the unloading of his body and switching it from the funeral home stretcher to one of our rolling carts. Once this is done, I let the Morticia twins leave, and wheel Lars to a scale that calculates his weight by automatically deducting the weight of the cart and displaying the remainder. From there, I wheel him to the X-ray room and take head-to-toe films. While these are processing, I wheel Lars into the autopsy suite and park his cart next to one of the tables. Then I measure him from head to toe to get his height, document it on the intake sheet, and then add some other details, such as eye color, hair color, and a description of his clothing, jewelry, and other personal items. I also fingerprint him, a task I always find distasteful. Thanks to my nursing career, the sight, smell, and feel of blood and guts doesn't bother me much, though the smell of decomposing bodies can be a challenge. But there's something about the cold, rubbery feel of the hands and fingers when I fingerprint the dead that gives me the creeps.

With that done, I head for the locker room, switch out of my puke-stained clothes and into some scrubs. My breasts are already beginning to tingle, a sign that my milk is letting down, but I don't have time to pump because Izzy will be ready to start by now. So I stuff a couple of extra pads into my bra and head back to the autopsy suite.

Both Hurley and Izzy are in the autopsy room when I arrive and they have already pulled Lars's body onto the autopsy table. With that done, Hurley settles onto a chair off to one side and checks his phone for messages. Not all of the detectives sit in on our autopsies—they are all welcome to do so, though some don't have the stomach for it—but Hurley always does if he has the time.

Sometimes duty calls, however, and autopsies are a time-consuming task. Merely undressing the patient can take half an hour or more, especially when the weather is cold and there are several layers to remove. It's not easy undressing someone who is flaccid and dead, and it's even harder once rigor has set in. Each item has to be examined for trace evidence before it is bagged and tagged. Before we start undressing, Izzy takes a few more photos of the print in the blood on Lars's neck after treating it with some solutions and powders that then make the print glow under a special light. Once we have Lars naked, we carefully examine the body for any other injuries, evidence, or abnormalities. Izzy gently washes Lars's head and face using a hose that extends down from the ceiling. The wash water falls onto the table and into channels that run along the edge. This way any trace evidence that might be rinsed off is captured in a drain at the foot of the table.

With his head and face cleaned off, it's easy to see that our victim is, indeed, Lars, though Izzy won't make the ID official until he has fingerprint or dental records to verify. It's also easier to see the wound Lars has on the back of his head.

"That rock hit him pretty good, causing a two-centimeter laceration in the scalp and significant bruising," Izzy says. "It looks like whoever hit him came up from behind. And there's a slight upward trajectory of the wound, suggesting that whoever hit him was shorter than Lars."

Hurley is writing as Izzy speaks and without looking up from his notebook he asks, "How tall is Lars?"

"He's five-ten," I tell him.

With the head examination complete, Izzy and I move on to the rest of the body. Lars is in pretty good shape for a guy in his late forties, and the only other thing of significance is the elephant in the room—the arrow through his neck.

Izzy goes there next, carefully dissecting the neck tissues until he has exposed the arrow's track. As I snap pictures of the neck and the wound, Izzy turns on the mic hanging down from the ceiling and describes the wound both for Hurley's benefit and for his dictation. "It appears the arrow went in at the base of the neck on the left just above the clavicle, punctured the left carotid artery, the esophagus, and the trachea, and then exited on the right side just below the mandible. There is no evidence of reverse sheering of the neck tissues as one might see if the arrowhead had hit the ground as the victim fell. Therefore, based on evidence at the scene, and the angle of the arrow's track, it appears the victim was shot with the arrow while lying on his side on the ground."

"He bled to death?" Hurley asks.

"Can't say just yet," Izzy says. "He would have bled out quickly based on the damage to the carotid, but most of the blood escaped inside the body, not outside. So he may have drowned in his own blood before he actually bled to death. I'll be able to tell you more once I get a look at his lungs. I think it's safe to say the arrow was the weapon that caused his death, and given the combination of that and the head wound, I'm willing to call this a homicide."

Izzy then makes note of the angles the arrow took through Lars's neck and compares these results to a second set of measurements he takes using the X-ray films. Then, using a rod that is nearly six feet in length, he has me hold the far end while he matches the angle of the arrow with the other end. "Definitely an upward trajectory," he says, snapping some pictures of the rod. "But it's not a steep angle. It's enough to say that there had to have been a distinct difference in the heights of the two people involved, and given the angles, Mattie's theory fits best. Lars was likely on the ground and the shooter was standing close by, near Lars's legs when the arrow was shot."

After setting the rod aside, Izzy removes the arrow and sets it on a tray that I then carry over to a side table. Using a magnifying light, I carefully examine the arrow. "There's a small hair stuck on the tail of this thing," I say, spying a black hair a little over an inch long clinging to one of the arrow's plastic feathers under some dried blood. Using a pair of forceps, I carefully remove the hair and place it in a small plastic baggie and label it. "It's black," I say, holding it under the light, "and Lars has dark blond hair, so it might be significant."

"Good find," Hurley says.

"There are some numbers on the shaft," I say. "Anyone know what they mean?"

Hurley has walked over to look at the hair and as he stares at the numbers, he shrugs.

Izzy says, "Arnie will, or if he doesn't, he'll be able to find out. Send it and the hair up to him." After Hurley jots down the numbers, I bag and tag the arrow and set both it and the hair aside so I can take them up to Arnie's lab later.

Hurley says, "I'm going to head out and assist with the investigative part of this. Let me know if you find anything else on the internal exam that changes the picture."

I look over at him with a sad expression. I don't want him to leave. It seems like we never get to spend much time together lately, and while this is certainly not an ideal setting, these days I take what I can get.

Hurley looks back at me and winks. Then he looks over at Izzy. "Can you free Mattie up to come and assist me once you're done with the autopsy?"

"I don't see why not. Unless we have another body come in."

Hurley looks back at me. "Give me a call when you're done and I'll let you know where we're at, okay?"

I nod, happy that there is a prospect on the horizon of some *us* time, but still sad to see him go. Having the majority of our time together take place amidst dead bodies and homicide investigations isn't the kind of quality time I'd prefer.

We are already an hour into the process by the time Hurley leaves, and as Izzy prepares to make his Y-incision to start the internal exam, he turns off the microphone hanging overhead and switches the focus of our conversation.

"How are things with you two?" he asks.

I shrug. "Not great," I admit. "I feel like there are so

many obstacles in our way all the time. As soon as we eliminate one, another seems to pop up. It's like the Fates are telling us that it's not meant to be."

"Don't think that way," Izzy says. "You have to stay positive. All relationships have their ups and downs, and there will always be times when things seem insurmountable. But if you truly love one another, you'll find a way to work it all out."

"I suppose."

Izzy has made the top of his Y-incision, but he pauses before completing the rest of it and cocks his head to the side, looking at me. "You're not giving up on the two of you, are you?"

I shake my head. "Of course not, but I don't have it in me to fight that hard, at least not now. All of my energy, time, and attention are devoted to Matthew and my job. If Emily wasn't causing such a ruckus, it might be easier, but as it is, the relationship I have with Hurley at the moment is a little too demanding, you know? Sometimes it's just easier to accept the status quo."

"You sound like you might be suffering from some postpartum depression," Izzy says with a worried frown.

"No, I'm suffering from reality," I snap back. "I haven't had more than three hours of consecutive sleep in the past two months, my daily schedule is nonstop, and my little boy is literally changing from day to day. New milestones pop up all the time and I don't want to miss them. I want to relish every last minute of it. Frankly, Emily is too much of a headache, too much of a time drag and killjoy for me to want to be involved with her right now. And I can't be involved with Hurley without being involved with her. So the easiest answer at this point in time is to focus on me and Matthew, let

Hurley deal with Emily, and sneak tidbits of quality time with Hurley whenever I can."

"That's dangerous thinking," Izzy says. "Relationships require work, compromise, and sacrifice from both sides. That's the only way to keep things alive and interesting. If you neglect your relationship with Hurley and get passé about it, it's going to fall apart."

I'm not sure why, but Izzy's little pep speech ticks me off. Maybe it's because I'm so tired and frustrated over being so tired and frustrated. Maybe it's because I feel guilty over not being a better superwoman and I'm worried that he's right. Or maybe it's the lingering hormonal storm going on inside me. Whatever the reason, there is a shrieking harpy inside me dying to come out, and it's all I can do to contain her. I manage not to shriek but I don't exactly keep her contained, either. "So, do you practice your relationship philosophy with Dom?" I ask Izzy, hoping I don't sound as snide as I'm feeling.

"Of course," he says, finishing his incision.

I dig the hole a little deeper. "So, you would support Dom if he wanted to do something different with your relationship?"

Izzy shoots me a glance as he sets his scalpel to separating the tissue in the chest from the ribs. "Yes, within reason, of course. I mean if he wanted to start having threesomes or something like that, I wouldn't agree to it. But if it was something that simply changed the dynamic of our relationship in a way that was going to make him happy, I'd definitely consider it."

"So you support Dom's desire to bring a child into your relationship?"

Izzy drops his scalpel in Lars's chest. He retrieves it

and then stares across the table at me. "What do you mean?"

"I mean just what I said. He wants a child."

"He's never said that."

"Not to you, perhaps, but he said it to me."

Izzy stands there speechless for several seconds, and then gives me a dismissive smile. "I think you misunderstood him," he says, going back to work.

"I didn't misunderstand him, Izzy. He was pretty clear on the matter, not only about wanting a child, but about his plans for getting one."

Izzy sets his scalpel down and lays aside the chest skin flaps, exposing the rib cage. Then he picks up the rib cutters and starts snapping, separating the ribs from the sternal plate. "He's just . . . *snap* . . . enjoying Matthew so much . . . *snap* . . . that he thinks it would . . . *snap* . . . be fun. But he doesn't . . . *snap* . . . mean it . . . *snap*. I think that . . . *snap* . . . losing his dad has left him . . . *snap* . . . melancholy and overly emotional."

He hands me the cutters so I can do my side. I make quick work of the remaining ribs and then set the cutter aside without saying another word. I look over at Izzy, ready for him to remove the breastplate, but he just stands there staring at me with a concerned look.

"What?" I say after several silent seconds.

"There's something you're not telling me."

I shrug, deciding then and there that Izzy isn't ready for the rest of the news yet. "I just don't think you're taking this seriously enough, Izzy. I don't think this is a phase Dom is going through, and I don't think he's going to let it go anytime soon, if at all. Sure, maybe his father's death has been a reminder of his own mortality—and yours," I add pointedly. "But if anything, I think it has served as a reminder to him about what he wants from his life."

Izzy frowns and shakes his head as if he's trying to shake off the whole idea. "This just seems so sudden and out of left field," he mutters. "We've never talked about bringing a child into our relationship."

"Are you sure?"

He looks at me like I've lost my mind. "Yes, I'm sure. I would have remembered any such conversation."

"How often has Dom talked about or done things with kids, like when he took Erika and Ethan out trick-or-treating last year, or asked the high school drama teacher if he could invite some of the students to his thespian group? What about the time he was talking about being a Big Brother? Why do you think he was so eager to volunteer in helping me out with Matthew?"

Izzy stares at me, and I can see the shock of dawning creeping over his face. So I push my advantage.

"He's always been fond of kids, Izzy. And he's good with them, too. You should see him with Matthew. When I can't get him to stop crying, Dom can take him and do it in a heartbeat. He's always gotten along well with Erika and Ethan whenever he's been around them, and they adore him back. Heck, even Emily likes him, and she hates every other adult on the planet along about now."

Izzy blinks hard and turns his focus back to Lars's corpse, working intently to remove the lungs. It's a distraction method I've seen him use a bazillion times and I'm not about to let him get away with it.

"I mean, think about it, Izzy," I go on. "Dom is the cook, the housecleaner, the shopper . . . He is and always has been a natural nurturer. Look at what a great job he does taking care of you. He's been a phenomenal househusband and he'll make a phenomenal parent."

Izzy removes a lung and sets it on a tray so I can weigh and section it. As he goes back in after the second one, he lets out a perturbed sigh and says, "And what about me? What about what I want? Taking on a child is a full-time job that lasts a lifetime and I'm not exactly young anymore."

"Valid points," I admit. "And maybe it won't be the right thing for the two of you. But I think you should at least open up some dialogue on the subject . . . hear Dom out and consider his thoughts on the matter." He opens his mouth to object, but before he can, I hold up my hand like a traffic cop. "What were you just preaching to me? Something about how relationships require work, compromise, and sacrifice on both sides, right? At least give it some serious thought. Don't shoot Dom down right at the start."

"The whole idea is ludicrous," he grouses, setting the second lung on a tray.

I sigh, lace my hands together in front of me, and stare at him as he works at removing Lars's heart. He keeps working, ignoring my posturing. "Do you love Dom?" I ask.

"Of course I do," he retorts. "But that doesn't mean I should engage every whim he has." He removes the heart, sets it aside, and finally looks at me. "Do you know how many times Dom has decided to make some sort of life-changing decision—ones with a lot less impact than this one would have—and then never followed through on them? Like this acting business he's into," he says, pointing his scalpel at me. "Did you know that at one point he wanted us to pull up roots and move to L.A. so he'd have a chance to make it big?

Before that there was the cooking school he wanted to start, and before that was the gay men's clothing line he wanted to launch."

"And why didn't he do any of those things?"

"Because they cost money, and he doesn't have any."

I grab a lung, place it on the scale, record the result, and then return it to the tray. As I go about repeating this action with the second one, I ask, "Did you ever offer to fund Dom for any of his ideas?"

"No," he says irritably, shifting his focus to the lungs on the dissection tray. "It would be a waste of time and money because Dom doesn't stick to any of his ideas for any length of time. They're all whims."

"Perhaps he doesn't stick to them because he doesn't have the resources to do it on his own, and senses your lack of support. He's always been all about supporting you. It seems that so far Dom has been the one doing all the sacrificing and compromising. So maybe it's his turn now."

Izzy is clearly perturbed by this comment. His brow is furrowed, his eyes are narrowed down, and his lips are pursed. He slices open the right lung, revealing that it is filled with partially congealed blood. He does the same to the left lung, with the same results.

Izzy sets his scalpel aside, sighs, and says, "The severing of that left carotid artery was enough to cause death, though if that had been the only injury and someone had applied pressure to the area it's possible Lars might have survived. But because the arrow also tore through the trachea and the esophagus, the blood had an easy escape. Based on the amount of blood on his face he likely tried to cough it up but the flow was too fast, too much. Lars exsanguinated and drowned in his own blood."

The two of us stand there silently for a while, staring at Lars's ashen, claylike face. Though I can't be sure, I guess that Izzy is thinking the same thoughts I am, imagining the grim and terrifying horror of Lars Sanderson's final moments. One thing about this job that has changed the way I think of my own death is that I'm less focused on the inevitable when, and more focused on the how. I used to think the phrase *a good death* was an oxymoron, but I now know better.

I sense Izzy shifting his attention back to me and when I meet his gaze, the sadness I see in his eyes makes my heart ache. It would be easy to assume this despondence stems from the stark reality of Lars's unfortunate demise, but I know it is more than that. A wave of guilt washes over me because I know my attack on his relationship with Dom was a purely defensive and, in some ways, mean-spirited move on my part, an effort to deflect the conversation off of my own ailing state of coupledom.

"I can manage the rest of this on my own," he says, returning his focus to Lars's body and putting his professional, unemotional face back on. "Why don't you go call Hurley and see what you can do to help with the investigation?"

"Izzy, I—"

"I heard what you said, Mattie," he says gruffly, not looking at me. His lips tighten for a second, but then in a softer tone he adds, "I realize I might be a little close-minded on the topic. So if you don't mind, I'd like some time alone to digest things and figure out where I stand on the matter, okay?"

His brow is deeply furrowed and there is a tight rigidness to his posture that tells me he is angry. What I can't tell is who or what he's angry at. Is it himself? Is he angry at me for bringing up the topic? Or is he upset with Dom for . . . well . . . for being Dom? I'm hesitant to leave, but just as reluctant to say anything. Fortunately, Izzy fills the void before I have to decide.

"You're right, Mattie," he says, severing the connections to Lars's stomach. "I've always been the one who's called the shots in our relationship. I'm the one with the power and the purse strings. It's not balanced, and I have to admit that I kind of like it that way. But I also realize that it's not fair to Dom. So I'm willing to entertain the idea that I need to be more open and flexible about things. I just need some time alone to contemplate this particular thing."

"Are we okay?"

He pauses in his work, looks at me, and smiles. It's fleeting, but it appears genuine. "You and I have always been brutally honest with one another about things and situations," he says. "But in the past it's typically been me who's the brutal one. I suppose it's only fair that you turn the tables on me once in a while. You called me out today and rightly so. Now go fawn over Hurley for a while and let me have some time to recover my pride and dignity."

I don't say anything, nor do I make a move. I'm still weighing his mood, taking his emotional temperature.

"You need to leave, Mattie," he says after a few seconds pass. "You're about to create a whole new nipple incident by dripping on my autopsy." He nods toward my chest, arching his eyebrows. I look down and see two large wet spots on my scrub top, one over each nipple.

"Right," I say, backing away from the table. "Sorry about that." I turn and head toward the door, stripping off my gloves and removing my protective headgear in the process. As I'm about to exit, Izzy calls out to me.

"Mattie?"

"Yeah?"

"Think Dom would settle for a dog?"

I decide now is the time. "Nope," I say definitively, shaking my head. "I'm pretty sure he's serious about this. He asked me if I'd be a surrogate for the two of you."

With that I make a hasty exit, the image of a stunned Izzy stamped in my mind.

Chapter 4

After stripping out of my scrubs, I hook up the breast pump and drain, sticking the bottles in the break room fridge when I'm done. Then I give myself a quick once-over in the mirror. It isn't a pretty sight. My hair is still frizzy and the clump I'd found in it earlier has taken on a life of its own, sticking out perpendicular from my head. I give it a quick finger wash and attempt to comb it into submission. I dig in my purse for some makeup and apply some eyeliner, mascara, and blush, hoping it will help. It's better, but still far from what I want. I decide I need to take Dom up on his offer, so I put in a call to my hairstylist, Barbara, to make an appointment. As usual, she has no problem fitting me in. The dead aren't very demanding customers.

I shove my puke-stained top in a bag and grab a spare sweater from my locker. Then I call Hurley.

"I have an official cause of death for you," I tell him. Then I fill him in on the grim details of Lars's demise.

When I'm done, he says, "I've been digging into Lars's recent business deals and his personal life. Turns out the guy has been sued no less than four times in the past two years, all by people he's worked with on some sort of land deal. Two of those were settled out of court, and the other two are still pending. I'm about to go over and take a tour through his house to see what I can find. After that I plan to have a chat with his personal assistant, to deliver the bad news and see what details we can dig up in his office."

"Does Lars have some family we need to notify first?"

"He has elderly parents who live out in Denver. We've got local guys out there making the notification as we speak. Lars has never been married and has no children, so no family locally."

"Want some help?"

"Sure, if Izzy's willing to kick you loose."

"I think he might be willing to do the kick-me part."

"Uh-oh, what did you do now?" Before I can answer he adds, "Grab a scene kit and meet me out front. I'll be there in two minutes and you can tell me all about it."

"Is Charlotte coming along?" I hold my breath, hoping to hear the answer I want.

"No, she's still on site out in the woods."

I breathe a sigh of relief.

"I don't think we need to film a simple notification, but if we do I can handle that myself. I probably will do some filming at Sanderson's home and office though. Do you mind helping with that if need be?"

Mind? I'd take out a hit on Charlotte if I had to in order to keep her away. "Of course I don't mind."

Minutes later I slide into the front seat of Hurley's car. He leans over and kisses me before we head out. His lips linger on mine a tantalizing smidge longer than is proper, considering we are in public view, and I love every illicit second of it. When he finally pulls away, it's all I can do not to grab him and haul him into the backseat. It seems my body is more than ready to resume that part of my life.

"All right, spill it," he says, pulling out into traffic. "What did you do to upset Izzy?"

"I told him about Dom's request."

"The baby thing?"

I nod.

"You didn't."

"I did."

"And you're surprised that he got upset over that?"

"Not surprised really. And anyway, he upset me first." I can hear the petulance in my voice. "He was lecturing me on how to manage our relationship."

"Whose relationship? Yours and his?"

"No, ours," I say, wagging a finger between the two of us. "He told me I'm too complacent about our situation, and that if I don't make some changes, I'm going to lose you." I let the statement hang for a few seconds in order to gauge Hurley's response.

"What does he think you should be doing?" he asks after several agonizing seconds of silence. I was hoping for a quick denial, an affirmation of our commitment to one another, even if we are living essentially separate lives most of the time.

"He didn't say exactly. But when I told him I didn't have the time or the energy right now to deal with all the extra emotional and psychological baggage that would come from trying to live with you and Emily, he implied that I wasn't holding up my end of the relationship."

"Hmm," Hurley says, staring out the windshield.

"Hmm?" I echo with a questioning tone. "What is that supposed to mean?"

"Well, Izzy is right in a way, though I think we're both equally guilty. Let's face it; our relationship *is* kind of stagnant right now. We hardly spend any time together unless it's work related. I can't spend as much time with my son as I want to. You're already exhausted from being a single mom, and that's only going to get worse now that you've returned to work. I have a daughter who seems to hate us both and who's determined to suck up every spare minute I have in a day. I think it's safe to say that we're both emotionally, physically, and psychologically drained right now, and that our relationship, out of necessity or a basic need for survival, has been put on the back burner."

Hearing Hurley say it aloud like that, so blunt and honest, frightens me. "I don't want our relationship to die of neglect, Hurley. If we're going to crash and burn as a couple, so be it, but we at least have to give it a fighting chance."

"That's hard to do when we have to carve out minutes of time to be together."

"I know. It isn't easy . . . I get that. But this business with Emily will take care of itself eventually. Either she'll finally come around, or she'll get old enough to move out."

Hurley shoots me a horrified look. "Are you suggesting that we wait three years before we can be together on a regular basis?"

"Of course I'm not suggesting it. I was being facetious . . . somewhat, anyway. But let's face it; Emily is a problem right now. She's a huge obstacle. And until we can get past that . . ." I leave the rest for him to fill in.

Hurley looks morose and depressed, and I'm mirroring his feelings. The Fates certainly haven't been working to our advantage lately, and I'm starting to wonder if we're doomed as a couple. "Let's keep up with the counseling," I say in a tone that I hope sounds more hopeful than I feel. "Give it a little more time."

Hurley sighs and grips the steering wheel tightly.

"I don't want to give it more time, Mattie. I want to be with you and Matthew now. I want to be a normal family."

"Well, that option is out," I say with a laugh. "We will never be anyone's definition of normal, even if we are together."

"I've been tossing an idea around in my head," Hurley says. "I was thinking about Emily and how she behaves great when she thinks I'm going about my normal daily work, but has a meltdown whenever she thinks I'm spending time with you and Matthew outside of work. What if I tell her I'm going into work early a couple of days during the week and instead come over to your place and get Matthew up for you? That way I'd get to spend some more time with both him and you, and you can get a little extra rest."

I consider the idea and at first blush it sounds like a reasonable, solid plan . . . heavenly, even. But the more I think about it, the less I like it. "This is a small town, Hurley. Things that are secret rarely stay that way. And Emily isn't stupid. She's bound to be suspicious, and she has that gnarly new boyfriend with the driver's license, so it wouldn't be all that hard for her to cruise by my place to check up on us and see if your car is here. If she finds out we lied to her, or tried to dupe her, it's going to set things back and undermine any progress we may have made."

Hurley scowls. "I told her she's not allowed to ride anywhere with the boyfriend."

"And we both know she does everything you tell her to, right?" I say with skepticism.

Emily's new boyfriend is Johnny Chester, son of Kevin Chester, one of my old high school classmates. Kevin was saddled with the nickname Chester the Molester in my day, and it stemmed from more than the obvious rhyming taunt. He had been—and for all I know still is—a very good-looking but not very bright fellow, with sticky fingers and a talent for misbehaving. Kevin's father, Leo, had been blessed with the same good looks, lack of common sense, and penchant for trouble. When Kevin was born, Leo was in jail. He made it out for Kevin's fifth and fourteenth birthdays, but other than that, Leo's permanent mailing address since the late eighties has been the Columbia Correctional Institution. Kevin didn't fare much better. He got locked up during our junior year in high school for robbing the local ice cream parlor. Had it not been for the trail of molten ice cream drops with multicolored sprinkles that led from the scene straight to Kevin's house, he might have gotten away with it. He did a year in juvie and never did finish high school. I heard he got his GED during his second lockup, this time in his father's alma mater, for stealing a car. A third stint came after he was caught shoplifting, and a fourth when he stole a gun from a friend's house, a gun he later used to shoot out the tires on the car of some guy who'd pissed him off. At this point, I suspect the Chester family probably has a wing named after them at the prison.

Kevin's wife, Lila, managed to kick out a trio of kids in between lockups. My feelings regarding Lila are mixed. She was one of those kids in high school who got picked on a lot because her family was poor. She dressed in old, worn clothes that were woefully out of date, she often smelled funny, and she walked around with a morose expression all the time. While these off-putting traits made her a target with a lot of the girls, she had no lack of suitors because word got around that Lila put out, which just goes to show how non-discriminative high school boys can be when it comes to sex.

That Emily chose one of the progeny of the Lila-Kevin union as her main guy hasn't sat well with Hurley, though I suspect he wouldn't be happy with anyone Emily tried to date. Concerned myself, I did pry a little by quizzing my niece, Erika, about Johnny Chester. Surprisingly, she said he seems like a straight arrow and a nice guy. He tells people he's a practitioner of Wicca, but given the practices his forbearers partook in, a little witch worship seems like a mild transgression. And Erika said that even though Johnny likes to act and talk tough around other guys, when he's away from certain people he's a sweet, friendly kid. Even more surprising is the fact that he's an honor roll student. Either Lila had some smarts that she hid well, or Johnny won the gene pool lottery.

In response to my skeptical question, Hurley's scowl deepens and he shakes his head slowly. He says nothing. He doesn't need to. We both know that Emily, like most teenagers, is rebellious enough to do something simply because she was told not to.

"What does Dr. Naggy have to say about your idea of pretending to go to work and sneaking over to my place instead?" I ask Hurley.

"I haven't run that specific idea by her," Hurley admits. "But we discussed the general topic of Matthew and Emily, and trying to find a way to make her more comfortable with this new family dynamic. She keeps telling me to give it more time." Hurley sighs in frustration. "How much more time can I give it?"

"As much as we need to. And I do mean *we.* This is a joint effort, Hurley. I'm in this with you." I reach over and touch his arm. "Right now you have the brunt of the issues with Emily to deal with, but that doesn't mean I'm not with you in thought, even if I can't be with you in deed."

Hurley refuses to be placated. His face tightens and his eyes narrow. "I want to spend more time with my son," he says, his jaw tight. "I want to spend more time with you."

There is a melancholy tone in his voice that makes my heart clutch. I love this man so much it makes me want to cry. I want the same things he does, but the raw facts of our situation are that Emily is a member of his family as much as Matthew and I are. And until we can resolve the issues that are keeping us apart, this is the way it will have to be.

"Put yourself in Emily's shoes," I say. "She has lost all the family she knew and finds herself the outsider in this new family unit she's been forced to live in. She's no doubt scared . . . scared of being abandoned and alone. And because of that, she's testing you. She's testing us. If she gives us a hard enough time and we take it all without giving up on her, maybe she'll start to believe we really are her family and she'll come to trust us. It would be painfully easy to hand her over to the foster system and say we can't deal with her, and she knows that. So she's keeping her emotions locked down, trying to minimize the hurt she fears is coming. Whatever we do, we can't give up on her."

Hurley looks over at me and smiles. "That's one of the things I love about you, Winston. You have a kind heart."

"Mitigated by some really evil thoughts," I say, remembering my actions earlier with Izzy.

Hurley arches his brows at me. "Such as?"

"It doesn't matter, as long as my good side wins out over my evil side most of the time."

"You don't have an evil side," he says.

I wink at him and give him a sly smile. "Oh, but I do. There are things about me you don't know, Hurley. Things that might give you pause the next time you suggest we should live together."

His smile morphs into a worried frown, but it doesn't last long. He dismisses my claim with a *harrumph.* "I don't care how evil you think you can be, Winston. I just want to be with you and my son more than I am now. Somehow we have to find a way to get past this hide-and-seek game we're playing and establish some semblance of normalcy. I feel like things are getting worse instead of better."

He has a point. We've been creative in finding ways to be together over the past two months, stealing minutes whenever and wherever we could—during his lunch breaks, on his way back from an investigation, on his way to the grocery store, on my way back from a doctor's appointment—brief interludes where we pretend that we're a normal couple, a normal family. It was easy at first because Matthew and I were more or less at his beck and call. Now that I'm back to work, finding those niches in time is bound to get more challenging.

"Try to be patient," I say. "I know it isn't easy, and I understand how frustrated you are. But we owe it to ourselves, to Emily, and to Matthew to work this thing out, no matter how long it takes."

Hurley makes no comment because we have arrived at our destination, forcing us to table the topic for now. I make a mental note to drop by Maggie's office and have a chat with her sometime soon. Maybe she can give me some insight to help my relationship with Emily move forward a little faster. Or maybe she'll tell me it's time to give it up and move on. The idea of the latter outcome makes my heart ache.

Chapter 5

Lars Sanderson's home is a town house in a relatively new area of development on the west end. Like many of the newly developed sections bordering the outskirts of Sorenson, the land where the town houses now stand was once farm property. Hurley parks in the lot in front of the unit that belongs to Lars, next to a squad car. Inside the car is Patrick Devonshire, one of the uniformed cops for Sorenson.

Hurley rolls down his window and Patrick does the same. "Anything to tell me?" Hurley asks.

Patrick shakes his head. "I went up and knocked on the door when I got here a little over an hour ago and no one answered. A neighbor was out and she said as far as she knows, Lars lives alone. There is another entrance in back and I checked it to make sure it was locked. I've been sitting here ever since and no one has so much as approached the place."

"Thanks, Patrick. You can go and I'll take it from here. Thanks for sitting on it for me."

"No problem." Patrick starts up his squad car, backs out of his space, and leaves.

Hurley and I sit for a moment, looking around at

the surrounding buildings. The development is one of those hastily constructed things with little thought given to appearances. The structures are covered with vinyl siding, four units to a building, two stories—or perhaps three if there's a basement—to a unit. Lars owns one of the end units, which are typically a bit pricier than the middle ones because they have a private wall and more windows to allow for light. I see that the middle units at least have skylights in the roof to try to make up for the lack of natural light, but I wouldn't be surprised to learn they are more trouble than they're worth. Even I can tell that the construction on the place is subpar and I'm betting that if those skylights don't leak yet, they soon will. The whole development is only four years old, yet I can see windows with fog between the double panes, shingles missing from the roof, and cracks in the siding. The railings on the porches are vinyl, too, and half of them are bent, torn, or otherwise broken. The concrete stairs are filled with chips and cracks. It's the sort of place Lars is known for developing, and I wouldn't be surprised to learn that it's one of his projects. Even if it is, I wonder why Lars would live here. Was his financial situation a tight one? Or was he perhaps hoping to imply that the project is better built than it is? Living in one of the units would certainly send that message.

Hurley finally grabs his camera and gets out of the car. I grab my scene kit, which also contains a camera, though mine is only for stills and short videos, and we head for Lars's end unit. "How are you going to get in?" I ask.

From his coat pocket, Hurley removes an evidence bag that contains the key ring we removed from Lars's pocket earlier, though I notice that the car key that was on it before is now gone. "I had Jonas dust these for prints right away and the only ones that came up were the victim's. I'm hoping one of these keys is to the front door, but if not, I'll call the manager."

"Speaking of keys, have you looked at Lars's car yet?"

"I gave it a cursory inspection but I'm leaving it for Jonas to go over with a fine-tooth comb."

"I take it you didn't find anything of interest in it?"

Hurley shakes his head. "What was interesting is what wasn't in it. There was no hunting gear of any kind. So whatever he was doing out there in the woods, it wasn't hunting."

We climb the stairs to the front door, and Hurley strikes gold with the second key on the ring. We set down the items we are carrying just inside the door and don gloves. Then we take a moment to survey what we can see of the place.

The small foyer we enter opens onto the living room, which is a sight to behold. It is furnished with large, velveteen, mismatched pieces in shades of blood-red, royal purple, and coal black. There is a huge, stuffed, round settee in red, a black chaise lounge, a couple of purple overstuffed chairs, and a black, faux leather couch in case someone doesn't want to sit on something fuzzy. The walls are painted a pale blue with gilded trim and moldings, and the carpet is gold-colored shag. Over in one corner is a metal stand on wheels, the top of it covered with liquor bottles and drinking glasses. The room is garish to the extreme; I feel like I just stepped inside an Austin Powers movie.

The shades are all closed—probably a good thing in this case since it darkens the interior—so Hurley reaches over and flips a switch on the wall. There is a gas fireplace on the front wall of the room and mounted above it is a huge TV. Flanking the bottom of the TV on the mantel are two lava lamps, one in red and the other in purple. On either side of the fireplace are built-in shelves. The ones on the right are filled with DVDs, and a quick scan of the titles reveals a few with ratings near the end of the alphabet. The shelves on the left contain a music system and an assortment of CDs that suggest Lars had eclectic musical tastes.

There is a coffee table in front of the couch—wood with a glass insert on the top and two drawers built into the bottom beneath a shelf. An assortment of magazines on the under shelf suggest Lars had quite the varied reading interests, too. I can see issues of *Playboy* and *Hustler* as well as *Reader's Digest* and *National Geographic*.

Hurley does a quick pan of the room with his video camera while I shoot a bunch of still pictures, hoping my camera doesn't die of embarrassment and humiliation.

There is a small attached dining room, and while it's not as bad as the living room, it will never make it into the pages of *House Beautiful*. The table and chairs look like something out of a knight's castle—dark heavy wood with thick legs and feet on the table, high wood backs on the chairs, and fake rivets in all of it. The wallpaper on one wall is red with gold veins running through it; the other three walls have some kind of textured gold-colored paper. In contrast to the heavy furnishings, a china cabinet in one corner displays a set of delicate bone china in a floral pattern. The contrast is puzzling.

We move on to the kitchen, which is refreshingly ordinary with plain oak cabinets, a double-sided stainless steel sink, and basic white appliances. After snapping a few shots, I sneak a peek inside the fridge where I'm not surprised to find three partially empty wine bottles, an assortment of microbrews, and some cheap, knock-off brands of soda. Foodwise, there isn't much: some cheeses, basic condiments, an outdated half gallon of milk that is still half-full, and an assortment of takeout containers. One of the containers holds a pasta dish of some sort and the others are all Chinese food from the Peking Palace. I hold the containers open while Hurley films the contents, then I grab all the wine and food items that are open and bag and tag them for later scrutiny. I doubt they will have much evidentiary value, but I've learned that even the smallest, seemingly most insignificant thing can sometimes prove to be a case solver.

I close the fridge when I'm done and survey the rest of the room. Next to the sink are two wineglasses, one empty, one with a little bit of red wine still in the bottom. The partially filled glass has the faint remnants of smeared, berry-colored lip prints around its edge, and after pointing this out to Hurley and both of us filming it, I pour the dredges of wine into a container, cap it, and label it. Then I place both glasses into paper evidence bags, and label and seal those.

Next to the kitchen is a laundry room—also refreshingly ordinary—and from there we move on to a washroom that is as garish as the living room. The walls are painted bloodred and the sink and toilet are gleaming black. White shag carpet finishes it off. Aside from being one of the ugliest bathrooms I've ever seen, it offers up little in the way of interest.

The last room on the main floor is an office area, which could also double as a bedroom if one so chose. Entering it is like walking into another dimension. Behind the closed door we find gleaming hardwood floors, tasteful beige walls, a polished oak desk and oak bookcase. We also find someone standing behind the desk: an attractive woman, nicely dressed, blond hair, blue eyes, mid- to late forties.

I recognize her right away—it's not hard to do since her picture can be seen around town—as Kirsten Donaldson, a local real estate broker who worked for one of the chain realty companies up until five years ago. Then, after divorcing her wealthy husband, she started her own realty business. Though her face is familiar, finding her standing here in Sanderson's home office is a shock that unnerves both me and Hurley. Judging from the hand the woman claps over her chest, she is as startled as we are.

"Who the hell are you?" Hurley snaps.

"I'm Kirsten Donaldson. Who the hell are you?" she fires back.

"I'm Detective Steve Hurley with the Sorenson Police Department. And this is Mattie Winston. What are you doing in here? We understood that this was the residence of Lars Sanderson."

"It is."

"And that he lived alone," Hurley adds.

"He does."

"Then I ask again," Hurley says, his patience clearly growing thin. "What are you doing in here? And how did you get in?"

"I have a key to the office door," Kirsten says, ignoring the first question. She gestures toward a windowed door at the rear of the room that opens onto a small yard enclosed with privacy fencing. At the back of the fence is a gate.

"I thought Mr. Sanderson had an office over on Holly Street," Hurley says.

"He does," Kirsten says. "But he also has this one. . . . Different offices for different clients. Whenever he conducts business here in his home, he has people come in through this rear entrance."

It's easy to guess why Lars used the rear entrance after seeing the sheik's harem décor in the rest of the house.

"Lars and I have a . . . well . . . I guess you could say we have an arrangement," Kirsten says with a sheepish smile.

"What sort of arrangement?" Hurley asks.

"I suppose you could call it a sexual arrangement, although it's not just that."

"You and Mr. Sanderson are dating?" Hurley says.

Kirsten makes an equivocal face. "I guess you could call it that. We provide one another with a plus-one from time to time for various social or business occasions, and sometimes we extend those get-togethers into the evening or nighttime. It's not an exclusive relationship; Lars sees other women, too."

"And you are here now because . . . ?" Hurley arches his brows in question.

"Because I left something here last night." She smiles coyly as she says this, but then her expression turns serious. "Why are you here? And where is Lars?"

"Is Mr. Sanderson expecting you?" Hurley says, using his classic answer-a-question-with-another-question maneuver.

"I'm not sure," she says. "I called and left a message earlier to let him know I was coming by, but he didn't return the call."

"So you just show up, not knowing if he's aware you're coming?" Hurley says in a voice rife with skepticism. "And why the back door?"

Kirsten gives him a patient sigh. "I used the back door precisely because I didn't know if Lars knew I was coming. Nor did I know if he was home. If he had a business meeting taking place, I would have been able to see it through this door and could have waited. If he had a more personal type of meeting taking place in the rest of the house, I can be in and out of here with no one being the wiser."

"And Mr. Sanderson is okay with you doing that?"

Kirsten shrugs. "It's not like I do it every day."

"And what is it you left here last night?"

My mind immediately jumps to the wineglasses we found in the kitchen and I suspect I know who the lip prints belong to. The shade of lipstick Kirsten is wearing now doesn't match what was on the glass, but since she's already admitted to being here last night, it seems logical that the wineglasses were hers and Sanderson's.

"I left behind a proposal I was discussing with Lars," she says. "That's another reason why I came in through this door." She points over her shoulder with her thumb. "I figured it would be here in the office somewhere."

"What sort of proposal was it?" Hurley asks.

"A potential development thing," she says, dismissively. "Where is Lars?"

"Development," Hurley says, squinting in thought.

I decide to jump in and help him out. "Kirsten is a real estate broker," I tell him. "Donaldson Realty? You've probably seen her signs around town."

Kirsten nods and smiles, but after a few seconds the smile fades. "Is Lars in some sort of trouble? Is that why you're here?"

I noticed that when Hurley introduced me, he failed to mention my title or office, something I expect was intentional. Now he blurts out the truth. "We're here because Mr. Sanderson was found dead this morning."

If he's hoping to elicit a reaction from Kirsten, he's successful. "Lars is dead?" she gasps. She claps one hand over her chest again while the other one grabs the back of the chair that is tucked in behind the desk. Her eyes are wide with shock. "What happened?"

"It appears he was killed while out hunting," Hurley says.

"Hunting?" Kirsten says, frowning and shaking her head. "Lars doesn't hunt."

"He was out in the woods where a lot of other hunters are," I tell her. "And he was wearing blaze orange." The fact that he apparently wasn't armed in any way and didn't have any hunting equipment in his car is something Kirsten doesn't need to know yet.

"Was he shot?" she asks.

I leave this one for Hurley to answer. I've learned that he prefers to withhold certain facts, or intentionally mislead people at times to see if they will say something incriminating, or provide a previously unknown clue. But Hurley doesn't answer the question at all. He fires back with one of his own.

"Can you tell me where you were this morning between the hours of five and eight?"

Kirsten looks puzzled. "Why would you need to know that?" she asks. "I don't hunt. I don't even own a gun. You can't think I shot him."

"Can you please just answer the question," Hurley says, sounding tired and impatient.

Kirsten scowls at him. "I got up at six this morning, had a cup of coffee, and read the newspaper."

"Where?" I ask her.

She looks over at me and her scowl deepens. "Where what?" she asks in an irritated tone.

"Where were you when you got out of bed this morning? Your house or here?"

"My house."

"What time was it when you left here last night?" I ask her.

"I don't know. Around eleven I suppose?"

"Did you drink any wine while you were here?"

"Sure. Lars and I are both wine connoisseurs."

"And was your evening one of your romantic get-togethers?" I ask.

She cocks her head and gives me a wry smile. "If you're asking whether or not we had sex, then yes, we did. We both had early starts today so I headed home before it got too late."

Hurley says, "Back to this morning and your early start . . . after your coffee and paper what did you do?"

"I showered and got dressed and went to my office," she says. "I got in just before eight."

"Can anyone vouch for that?" Hurley asks.

"My office manager got in a little after eight. Prior to that, I was alone."

"So no," Hurley says.

Kirsten laughs and shakes her head. "Seriously, Detective, what possible reason could I have for wanting Lars dead?"

"I don't know," he says. "You tell me."

"There isn't one," she says. "Lars and I were business associates and good friends."

"Friends with benefits," I say.

"Yes," she says unapologetically. "I'm divorced, and he's single, so where is the harm in that?"

"There isn't any," I say.

"Do you know of anyone who had a grudge against Lars?" Hurley asks.

Kirsten chuckles and rolls her eyes. "Oh my, yes. That's a bit of a list, I'm afraid. There are a lot of people in town who didn't like Lars. You only have to read the Op-Ed page in the paper to see that. He was all about making a buck no matter how it affected other people or the city in general."

Hurley asks, "Did Lars ever talk with you about any of the other women he was seeing?"

"No, and if he had, I would have kicked him out of my bed straightaway. That would have been too rude, even for Lars."

"What sort of business did the two of you do together?"

"I've brokered a number of deals for him," Kirsten says, "including this development. He purchased the land and built these town houses right after he moved here. I handled the sale of all the units for him. That was how we met."

"Why did Lars come to Sorenson?" I ask. "It's not like this area is a hotbed of development opportunities, and he doesn't have any family nearby."

"Ah, but you're wrong about this area," Kirsten says. "It's filled with opportunity. Rural areas located within a reasonable commuting distance to the bigger cities have huge potential for suburban development. You've got all this land that many of the farmers can no longer turn profitably, and you've got these cozy little bedroom communities like Sorenson that give people a small-town atmosphere *and* proximity to cities like Madison and Milwaukee. Lars saw the potential and acted on it."

"Where was he before?" Hurley asks.

"He told me he spent some time working deals down in rural Indiana and Illinois before coming here."

"Why did he leave?" I ask. "Why give up all the connections and professional relationships he built there to move here and start over from scratch?"

"That's a good question," Kirsten says, wagging a

finger at me. "And I asked it of Lars, but he never gave me a good answer. So I did a little digging around based on some of the few details he provided and discovered that the man has always had a knack for pissing people off. He's a bit ruthless when it comes to business and he doesn't care about the people behind the deal. He was all about burning his bridges. So my guess is he moved here to get a fresh start with people who didn't know him or his reputation."

"Do you hunt, Ms. Donaldson?" Hurley asks.

"Heavens, no," she says, with an odd little smile. "I love animals and I'm a vegetarian. In fact, hunting was one of the things that came between me and my ex. He's an avid bow hunter."

With the mention of bow hunting, Hurley and I exchange a look.

"Is your husband the jealous type?" I ask Kirsten.

"I'm afraid so," she says, her eyes wide. "He was very insecure in that way." She looks sheepish for a moment, and then adds, "Brad Donaldson isn't a particularly handsome man. I didn't marry him for his looks, and despite the rumors, I didn't marry him for his money, either, though I'll admit it didn't hurt. I married him because he was one of the kindest, sweetest, most thoughtful men I've ever met."

"So what went wrong?" I ask. I have a morbid fascination of late with the demise of other people's marriages, most likely because I still reel occasionally at how fast my own went to hell.

Kirsten thinks about this for a moment. "He became too possessive. That jealous streak was something I found endearing in the beginning, but over time it became confining, and controlling. His love was stifling me and I had to get out."

"Was he agreeable to the divorce?"

She smiled, and shook her head. "Let's just say it took him a while to see the light."

"Do the two of you stay in touch at all?"

"We do, for the sake of the kids."

"How many do you have?"

"Two girls," she says with a beatific smile. "Avery is a med student at the U of Dub in Madison, and Brittany is a freshman at Harvard studying pre-law."

"Wow, that's impressive," I say. It seems Kirsten has rolled a seven in the crapshoot game of raising children. I'm amazed by how many kids who come from good families with loving parents who try to do everything right still manage to turn out wrong. It's one of my biggest fears with Matthew . . . that and the genetic tendencies he might have inherited. This last thing bothers me the most given that my mother has some serious mental health issues and my father is not only a deadbeat but a wanted felon.

Hurley says, "I need a number where I can reach you, Ms. Donaldson. I might need to talk with you again at some point, but for now I need you to leave these premises. Whatever it is you came here for will have to wait."

"That's fine," she says, reaching into her coat pocket and pulling out a business card. "My office and cell numbers are on there."

Hurley takes the card and sticks it between the pages of the small notebook he always carries in his pocket. "I would also like your key to this place, please."

"Is that really necessary?" she says. "There are files here on some of our joint ventures that I might need to access."

"Once our investigation is concluded and we release the place you can have it back. If there's something you need before then, call me." He concludes the information swap by handing her one of his business cards.

"Very well," Kirsten says with a sigh. She takes a set of keys out of her pocket, removes one from the ring, and goes to hand it to Hurley. But instead of letting it go right away, she takes a step closer to him and looks him right in the eye. "Please don't hesitate to call me if I can be of any further assistance with anything," she says. Her gaze lingers a second or two longer before she finally lets go of the key and leaves.

Chapter 6

"Sheesh," I say, glowering at the door. "So much for being upset over Lars's death. The guy isn't even cold yet and already she's flirting with someone new."

"It sounds like their relationship was more of a business associates with benefits thing rather than friends with benefits," Hurley says. "That sort of arrangement appeals to a lot of successful women, particularly the older ones. And I imagine a lot of men would love that sort of arrangement, too, particularly if they're commitment-phobes."

"Yeah, well, don't get any ideas about establishing a business relationship with Kirsten," I say, making air quotes when I say the word *business.*

Hurley walks over to me, grabs my shoulders, and gives me a nice kiss on the mouth. It's brief, but sweet. "You're all the woman I want or need," he says. Then he winks and hands me his camera. "So start filming while I take a look around."

I man the video camera as Hurley starts routing around through the stuff on top and inside of Lars's desk. There's a lot of it. Both file drawers are crammed full of papers and there are several stacked files in a third drawer. Hurley fingers through some tabbed hanging files and sighs. Then he looks over at the bookcase, the shelves of which are jam-packed with cardboard organizers filled with notebooks and binders.

"It's going to take too much time to go through all of this stuff here," Hurley says. "Let's box it up, take it back to the station, and let Jonas wade through it."

"Sounds good to me," I say, turning off the camera.

Hurley places a call to the station and asks if there is anyone available who can come with Jonas to Lars's residence to assist us. After some juggling of personnel, arrangements are made to send Patrick back our way. With that done, Hurley and I head upstairs.

Given what the rest of the place looks like, I shudder as I think about what horrors await us in Lars's bedroom, and it turns out to be worse than I imagined. The entire ceiling over the bed is covered with mirrored tiles. A faux leopard-skin bedspread covers the king-size bed and the sheets and pillowcases are black satin. The shag carpet has made it into here as well, this time in black. The walls are bloodred like the bathroom. I feel like I'm in a cave, which seems fitting since I'm starting to think Lars was quite the animal.

"Holy crap," Hurley says, staring at the room. "What the hell was this guy thinking? Do women actually like this stuff?"

"This woman doesn't, but it sounds like Lars was something of a ladies' man, so enough of them must. I'm betting that bedspread will light up like a Christmas tree under a UV light."

Hurley curls his lip in disgust. "And I suppose we should take it all in as evidence."

"Do we have to?" I whine. "I don't think I want to touch it."

"Yeah, we need to collect it," Hurley says with a sigh

of resignation. "If Lars was sleeping around, we need to know who's been in this bed. Our killer's DNA could be there." He thinks for a second and then his face brightens. "However, I don't see why we can't let Jonas and Patrick collect it all."

I head into the master bath off the bedroom and open up the medicine cabinet. "It looks like Lars needed a little help keeping up with all his women," I holler out to Hurley, taking a bottle of pills out and bagging them. "He was using Viagra." I look in the trash can bedside the toilet and at first blush it looks like detritus from a kid's birthday party. Then I realize what I'm looking at.

"Sheesh, I think we should call in a biohazard team," I say. "There must be ten used condoms in this trash. And apparently Lars liked to experiment with colors and styles."

"I suppose we should be glad he was practicing safe sex," Hurley says.

There are several other prescription bottles in the cabinet along with an assortment of over-the-counter drugs. I scan the labels on the other medications. "It looks like Lars had himself a little habit. There are several narcotic prescriptions in here—hydrocodone, oxycodone, OxyContin—all prescribed by different doctors and all filled at different pharmacies."

Hurley walks into the bathroom holding up a baggie full of dried leafy stuff. "That's not the only habit he had, apparently," he says. "And to counter all of this mellowing, there's another baggie in the bedside stand with some white powder in it. I'm betting it's coke."

"I wonder where he gets it from. And how he pays for it," I say. An expensive drug habit might explain why Lars was living in his own, cheaply built housing.

"I'll have a look at his banking records," Hurley says.

"Maybe his drug use has something to do with his death."

"Great," I mutter with sarcasm. "Just what we need. More motive and more suspects."

"Speaking of money," Hurley says, "I've been thinking about Emily and her education. She's going to be graduating in a few years and what if she wants to go to college? I don't have money saved up for that sort of thing."

"I'm guessing Kate didn't either?"

He shakes his head. "She didn't have any savings, or any life insurance. What little she did have was used to pay off medical bills."

I suspect Kirsten's kid bragging has triggered this line of thinking, so I say, "You don't have to foot the bill for a fancy, expensive college education, Hurley. There are other options. Depending on what she wants to do, there are lots of affordable community colleges in the area, or she can attend the U of Dub and live at home." I consider offering to help with the tuition, but decide to hold off. Hurley and money is touchy territory. So instead I ask, "Has she talked about any career interests?"

"She hardly talks to me at all," Hurley scoffs. "It's like pulling teeth trying to get her to tell me what she wants to eat for dinner, much less what she wants to be when she grows up."

"She's quite talented in the arts department," I tell him, recalling how Emily once drew a portrait of someone using nothing more than a skeleton that hangs in our office library. The fact that the face she drew looked exactly like the woman whose skeleton it was impressed me. "She might have a career in forensics with her drawing abilities."

"First I have to get her through high school," Hurley grumbles.

We work through the rest of the bedroom and bathroom in silence. Patrick Devonshire shows up along with Jonas, and Hurley heads downstairs to direct them while I venture into the spare bedroom. As I work, I keep thinking about Emily and all the problems she is causing us. In an ideal world, the four of us could be living happily under one roof, but I learned long ago that this world is far from ideal. I understand why Emily's acting out; life hasn't been kind to her this past year, and I know she has to be experiencing a slew of complex emotions. She didn't deserve what fate doled out to her, but then, I couldn't help but feel that Hurley and I didn't deserve our lot in life, either.

I think about how much simpler life would be if Emily wasn't in the picture, but as soon as the thought crosses my mind, I know it's unfair and unkind of me to think this way. Maybe I do deserve the hand I've been dealt.

The spare bedroom doesn't offer up much in the way of useful evidence, so I shoot a bunch of pictures and head downstairs. I can tell right away that something is up with Hurley. His face is a thundercloud. He's still directing Patrick and Jonas on what he wants done and collected, and judging from his tone of voice and what he's saying, I don't think they are the cause of his mood. Turns out I'm right.

As soon as he's done with the two men, he motions me out to the living room and says, "Here we go again. The school just called to inform me that Emily didn't return to class after lunch."

"Has she done that before?"

He nods. "She's gone joyriding a few times with that

boyfriend of hers. The last time she did it, I tried to ground her but she snuck out of the house through her bedroom window, climbed down the tree, and went out anyway."

"Should we go looking for her?"

Hurley shakes his head. "Not yet. Dr. Baldwin told me she thinks Emily does this to get a rise out of me, so if I ignore her, she won't get the kind of feedback she's seeking and she'll stop doing it."

"I guess that makes sense," I say with a shrug. "So where do we go from here?"

Hurley shoots me a wry look. "Are you referring to Emily, us, or the case?"

I consider this a moment. "All three, I suppose."

"You and I are going to figure out a way to spend more time together with one another and with our son, with or without Emily. But we're not going to do it this afternoon, so we might as well focus on the case. Let's go visit Lars's other office and see if his bad taste carries over into his professional life there."

I look around the living room and suppress a shudder. Lars was a very good-looking man, but even so it's hard to imagine him as a lothario, given the décor of this place. "I feel like I'm trapped inside an Austin Powers movie," I say.

"Who is Austin Powers?"

I gape at Hurley, thinking he must be spoofing me. "You really don't know who Austin Powers is?"

Hurley shakes his head.

"You and I need to have a movie date soon," I say, heading for the door. "And if you're lucky, you'll even get some time with your Mini-you."

"My mini what?" Hurley says, opening the door. He has a wicked gleam in his eye that suggests a meaning far from the one I had in mind. "Speaking of which, when are you clear for . . . you know . . . extracurricular activities?"

"Two weeks ago."

Hurley frowns. "Why didn't you tell me?"

"Because being physically ready and mentally ready are two entirely different things. And until both are met, that's off the table. Right now if I lie down even for a minute, I fall asleep. I'm afraid to nurse Matthew unless I'm sitting up for fear I'll fall asleep and roll over on him."

Hurley's frown deepens. "I need to be able to help you more with this stuff."

"It will get better, Hurley. We just need to be patient."

We step outside and head for the car. Surprisingly, Hurley walks around and opens my door for me. It's a sweet and unexpected gesture—Hurley's never been one for the demonstrative, chauvinistic behaviors—and it makes me smile.

That makes him smile, too, and the wicked gleam returns. "You know," he says, "we don't have to do it lying down."

Chapter 7

The office of Lars Sanderson is located in the corner of a relatively new building that covers half a city block and houses several businesses. It borders the downtown area, which is populated with specialty shops housed in older buildings that date back to the late 1800s and early 1900s. This clash of old and new is evident all over Sorenson, in part because the town is spreading each year—kind of like my butt—and in part because some of the older buildings around town were so neglected and run-down that it was determined easier and cheaper to tear them down and rebuild rather than rehab them.

Hurley tells me as we enter the building that Lars's assistant's name is Judy Bennett. This turns out to be unnecessary info since Judy has a large metal plate with her full name engraved on it in gold sitting on the front of her desk. She is a frizzy-haired, bleached blonde with black roots. It appears Judy tried to tame that hair in a taut French twist this morning, but strands of it have sprung out all over her head. Most of the escapees are corkscrew shaped, suggesting that Judy has a good amount of natural curl in her hair. It makes her head look like a skinned-alive, coil spring mattress. Her foundation is so thick that the skin of her face has an odd plaster look to it, one that makes me fear it will crack if she laughs too hard or yawns too wide. Her hazel eyes are outlined with heavy black eyeliner à la Cleopatra topped off with green and brown eye shadow. Apparently she is wearing fake eyelashes because the upper lash on her left eye is sticking out from her eyelid at a thirty-degree angle. Her lipstick and blush appear to be the same vibrant shade, and neither one is subtle.

In sharp contrast to her makeup, Judy's clothing choices are downright sedate. She is wearing a simple tan-colored blouse over a pair of black dress slacks and plain black pumps, and the only jewelry I can see is a small pendant around her neck with a tiny blue gemstone in it.

"Good morning," she greets us in a cheery tone with a smile that looks a tad forced. That stereotypical Midwest politeness is pervasive . . . and oddly annoying at times. "How may I be of help to you nice folks today?"

Hurley takes out his badge and shows it to her. "I'm Steve Hurley with the Sorenson Police Department and this is Mattie Winston with the medical examiner's office. I'm afraid we have some bad news for you."

Judy's smile fades and her eyes look cautiously concerned as her gaze bounces back and forth between me and Hurley.

"Is it true that Lars Sanderson is your boss?" Hurley asks.

Judy shrewdly replies, "Depends on why you're here."

"I'm here because Mr. Sanderson is dead," Hurley says in a soft tone that counters the bluntness of his words.

Judy Bennett's expression doesn't change much.

I'm not sure if it's because she isn't reacting, or if it's because her makeup has her face frozen in place. She stares back at Hurley for several seconds and then finally cracks a smile—and thankfully, doesn't crack the rest of her face. "Good one!" she says with a laugh. "Who put you up to this? Was it Nash? Sandra?"

"This is no joke, Ms. Bennett," Hurley says, wearing his most serious expression. "Mr. Sanderson was found dead earlier this morning out by Cooper's Woods."

Judy finally gets that this isn't a joke and her expression turns serious. "He's really dead?" she says, her eyes disbelieving. Hurley nods solemnly, as do I. Judy looks back and forth between the two of us a couple of times and then says, "Damn. What happened? Did he have a heart attack or something?"

"It appears Mr. Sanderson may have been killed by a hunter," Hurley says.

"He was shot?" Judy says, clapping a hand against her chest. It seems Judy and Kirsten went to the same school of dramatic reactions.

"Did Mr. Sanderson go hunting often?" Hurley counters, ignoring her question and firing off one of his own.

"No," she says, looking befuddled. "Well, not exactly. He's been known to go out on hunting trips with potential clients and customers, but he doesn't actually hunt. He told me he doesn't have the stomach for the killing." She gazes off into space for a few seconds and then says, "Ironic, I guess, isn't it?"

"Do you have any idea why he would have been out by Cooper's Woods?" Hurley asks.

Judy shakes her head, but it evolves into a half-assed shrug as her expression grows uncertain. "Sometimes he meets clients out in the boonies if there's a parcel of land they want to look over."

"Did he have something he was working on in that part of the county?" Hurley asks.

Judy thinks for a minute and then shakes her head. "He didn't tell me about it if he did."

"And would he normally tell you about something like that?" Hurley asks.

"Heck, yeah," Judy says. "I'm his personal assistant." She says this with great pride, announcing it like it's a formidable, accomplished title. Knowing what I do about Lars from the local gossip and the news articles, I imagine the job has its challenges. "I handle his schedule, all of his correspondence, his books, his personal shopping . . . I'm pretty much his go-to person for anything that isn't romantic." She wiggles her eyebrows with this last comment.

"And you don't know of anyone he planned to meet this morning?" Hurley asks again.

Judy shakes her head, looking bewildered. After a moment she looks down and opens a black, spiral-bound datebook. A clip allows her to open it directly to today's date and her finger runs down both the left and right sides of the pages. "Nope, nothing at all this morning," she says. "He has a three o'clock with Harry Olsen to discuss a development proposal, and he's supposed to meet with a contractor for dinner tonight. I had to cancel his date with Ms. Rutherford because of it."

"Who is Harry Olsen? And where was Lars supposed to meet him?"

"Mr. Olsen is the curator of the Sorenson History Museum. He and Lars haven't always seen eye to eye on some of the projects Lars has done because Harry is all about preserving the history. I believe they were going to discuss Lars's ideas for some project the mayor is pushing. And they were supposed to meet at Harry's office at the museum."

Hurley looks at me. "Do you know where that is?"

I nod.

Hurley turns back to Judy. "And who is the contractor he is supposed to meet for dinner?"

"Chuck Obermeyer. They were going to meet at Pesto Change-o at six."

"Do you have contact info for Mr. Obermeyer?" Hurley asks.

Judy nods and scribbles the info down on a piece of paper after looking it up on her computer.

"And finally," Hurley says, taking the slip of paper, "Ms. Rutherford. What is her first name?"

"Bridget."

Hurley writes it down. "Is that someone he saw regularly?" he asks.

Judy smiles coyly. Then she seems to remember the reason behind our visit and her expression sobers with stunning speed. "Lars is . . . was seeing several women," she says. "There are three that he dates with regularity."

"Really?" I say, feigning surprise. "Can you give us the names of these women, and any others he might have been seeing on a less than regular basis?"

Judy nods, takes out a small notepad, and starts scribbling names on it. "It's just the three as far as I know," she says.

"Contact info, too, if you would please," Hurley adds, and without missing a beat, Judy keeps writing, putting down the name, address, and phone number of each woman, apparently from memory. Kirsten Donaldson is on the list.

When she's done writing down all the information we asked for, she hands the list to Hurley. He looks at it a moment and then asks, "Do these women all know about one another?"

Judy shakes her head and gives him a sly grin. "Kirsten and Lars have an open, casual relationship. She knows, but I don't think the others do. Lars has always been careful to keep them separate."

"Has Lars had any arguments or received any threats from anyone recently?"

"No, not that I . . . oh, wait." Judy squints and stares off into space for several seconds. "There was a guy whose mother owned some land that Lars bought last year. He was very unhappy with Lars for talking his mother out of what he referred to as his legacy, his family farm. The place was about to go into foreclosure when Lars bought it from the old woman, so it's not like the guy would have had anything to inherit anyway. But the lady passed away last month and when her son discovered that everything except the house was gone, he got pretty pissed."

"What is this guy's name?" Hurley asks, pen poised over his pocket notebook.

Judy screws her face up and frowns. "It was an odd first name. I can't pull it out right this second. And his last name was different from hers, I'm guessing because she remarried. Her name was Freda Herman and I know Herman was the name of her husband who passed five years ago." She reaches up and scratches her head, freeing a few more of the wild corkscrews. "Dang, what was his name?"

"Don't you have it written down somewhere?" Hurley asks, looking and sounding impatient.

"I don't," she says with a frown. "But maybe Lars wrote it down somewhere. He was handling that one by himself, and apart from answering the phone a few times when the guy called, I had nothing to do with it." She pushes her chair back from the desk and stands.

"Let me look around in Lars's office and see if I can find something with the guy's name on it. I'll know it when I see it."

She doesn't invite us along, but she doesn't say we can't follow, either, so after a quick exchange of looks, Hurley turns on the camera he's been carrying and hands it to me. Then we fall into step behind Judy as she enters Lars's office.

It's surprisingly barren and plain. The desk is an old wooden thing that looks like it weighs a ton and has been through a major war. It is nicked, scratched, and dinged over most of its surface. The wheeled chair behind it is also old, wooden, and battered. On the other side of the desk is a second wooden chair that looks like a castoff from an old dining room set. Along the side wall is a crooked, pressed-wood bookcase with a mishmash of books and papers stacked on the shelves all willy-nilly. There is institutional beige carpeting on the floor, and it's covered with dozens of stains in every color imaginable: red, brown, black, green, blue, yellow, and even a hot pink one that leaves me scratching my head, wondering what made it.

Judy must sense my bemusement over the appearance of the office and she provides some insight. "That pink stain over there is my fault." She shows me the back of one hand and waggles her fingers at me. "Nail polish incident. The rest of the stains belong to Lars. He's not much on neatness and, as you can see, his sense of style is seriously lacking, at least here in the office. His home office is much nicer."

It certainly is.

"Why does he have two offices?" Hurley asks. "Isn't that unusual?"

"He says it's part of his method."

"His method?"

"Yeah, he uses his home office to meet with contractors, politicians, and business leaders."

"And this office?" I ask.

"Mostly for meeting with folks he's buying land from. I suggested he spruce the place up once and he told me it was perfect just the way it is. He thinks the décor makes the clients feel less intimidated, less taken advantage of. Most of his land deals are with farm folk and they tend to be simple, non-fancy people. So he tries to make it look like he's just one of them, that the deal is between two entities who are both struggling to maintain and run a business."

Judy rummages through the papers on top of Lars's desk and Hurley watches over her shoulder, eyeing each piece of paper. I aim the video camera at the desk and capture as much as I can. Finally Judy holds up a sticky note and says, "Here it is. Hartwig Beckenbauer. I told you it was a weird name." She hands the paper to Hurley, who then copies the name and phone number into his notebook.

Judy frowns at the camera and I wonder if she is worried about us invading Lars's privacy or violating some search and seizure law. But then she cups a hand along the twisted mass of hostage curls at the back of her head, making a futile attempt to pat some of the escapees into place, and I realize she's only worried about how she will appear.

"If you're looking for suspects," she says, adjusting a hairpin, "you should probably consider Reece Morton."

"Who is Reece Morton and why would he be a suspect?" Hurley asks.

I manage to beat Judy to the answer. "Reece is a developer who's been around for years here in Sorenson.

He's been behind a number of projects over the years, including The Square downtown. What is now a charming pedestrian area full of shops and cafés was once an ugly old factory that was abandoned back in the sixties. It stayed abandoned until the nineties, when Reece Morton came along and transformed the area."

"And this Mr. Morton would be a suspect because ?"

"Mainly because he's old-fashioned," Judy says. "He's against modernization and growth, and those are the things Lars strives for. So they butt heads a lot."

"It's not that straightforward," I say. "Reece isn't old-fashioned per se; he's interested in preserving Sorenson's small-town atmosphere, culture, and history. He isn't just a developer, he's been *the* developer in Sorenson for the past two decades. Then along comes Lars, who starts stealing some of Reece's business and constructing the sort of stuff Reece is opposed to, like that row of cheap town houses that went up over by Bailey Park, the new condo units on the north edge of town, and the big box store Lars tried to slip in two years ago."

Judy shrugs off my correction and says, "Point is, Lars and Reece didn't get along. In fact, the two of them had a very heated exchange at the Nowhere Bar last week about this latest chunk of land out on the east end that the new mayor wants to turn into a combination residential area and shopping mecca. When Reece found out the mayor was talking to Lars about it instead of him, he got pretty bent. Though I don't know why he was surprised. I mean, it's exactly the kind of development that Reece is against. Plus, Lars was the one putting in the time with the connections lately, you know?"

Hurley and I both shake our heads.

Judy sighs the way she might over a child who doesn't

quite get it. "Lars goes down to the Sorenson Grill every Saturday morning for breakfast and he sits in with a group of older men who have been gathering there for breakfast on Saturdays for years. Some of those guys are aldermen, and all of them have the mayor's ear. Lars managed to worm his way right into the middle of their inner circle, and that resulted in him hearing about development plans and future farm sales that were coming down the line before they became public knowledge. Lars beat Reece out on several land sales and other deals recently, and Reece has made it known that he's none too happy about it."

"Did Reece ever threaten Lars that you know of?"

Judy screws her face up in thought for a few seconds. "He never came right out and said he was going to kill him or anything like that," she says eventually. "Least not as far as I know. But he did tell Lars that he was going to find a way to stop him when they had that to-do down at the Nowhere."

"Do you happen to have Mr. Morton's contact information?" Hurley asks her.

"Sure do," she says with a smile that borders on smug. She writes down the information on a slip of paper and hands it over to Hurley. "Anything else I can help you with, Detective?"

"Yes, there is. I'm going to have some officers and an evidence tech come down here to go through Mr. Sanderson's office. I'll need you to stay out of his office from here on, but if you can be nearby to answer any questions they may have, it would be helpful."

Judy's expression is mixed. "I'm happy to help out however I can," she says, "but Lars has confidential information in his papers and files, and I can't let that stuff leave. We take our clients' privacy concerns very seriously."

Hurley reaches over and puts a hand on Judy's shoulder. Then he turns on what I refer to as his Casanova smile. The combination of that smile and those cornflower blue eyes staring down at you is like being under a deep hypnosis. You're willing to do anything he asks of you, and you're imagining—at least in my case—all kinds of naughty things you'd like to do for him, to him, and with him. I know it works on other women besides me. I've seen it in action.

"I hope Lars knew what a great catch he had in you," Hurley says to Judy. "Your dedication and devotion are truly admirable. I'm sure Lars couldn't have been as successful as he was without you at his side."

Judging from Judy's rapt expression I suspect she is blushing, though it's hard to tell because of the thick plaster of makeup on her face. Clearly she is not immune to Hurley's charms, and I can tell Hurley knows it.

He continues his seductive persuasion. "I promise you I will do everything in my power to keep your reputation safe, Ms. Bennett. Anything we take from this office will be kept securely under lock and key, and we'll only take what is relevant to our investigation. That's where you can help us out. Any background information you can provide about specific people or business dealings will help us figure out which ones might be important. Judy, you could be the key to solving this case and finding Lars's murderer."

The switch from the more formal Ms. Bennett to Judy is a calculated move on Hurley's part, along with the accompanying softening of his voice. When I asked him about it once, he told me he'd learned years ago that he could use his charms to manipulate suspects and witnesses in order to get whatever information or cooperation he wants from them. When I asked him if he'd used it on me when we first met—and at that time I was very much a suspect since the murder he was investigating was that of the woman David cheated on me with—he admitted that he had. "But with you it backfired," he told me. "No matter how much I tried to charm you, you remained stubborn and bullheaded, and determined to do things your way. And oddly enough, I found that incredibly alluring."

Go figure.

Judy is highly susceptible to Hurley's magic and she nods her understanding of everything he has said while staring at him with a doe-eyed, gaga look. Hurley removes his hand from her shoulder and looks over at me. He winks, and then takes out his phone to make some calls. I take Judy back out to her desk, and steer her to her seat.

Hurley has battened down any defenses Judy might have had up, and I want to take advantage of that while I can. I settle in across from her, aim the camera at her, and hit the record button. "Tell me about Lars," I say. "What sort of man was he? Was he easy to work for? Did he have a temper? Did he have any vices or secrets you knew about?"

Judy looks at me with a torn expression. "The man is dead," she says. "I don't want to sully his name."

"So there *is* something?" I say, my radar beeping.

Judy doesn't answer right away. I can tell the magic of Hurley is wearing off.

"It will just be between us," I assure her. "It might help us catch who did this to him. And if it turns out it's not relevant, there's no need for us to make it known to anyone else."

Judy bites her lip, contemplating.

"Is it something to do with his business dealings?"

I prompt. Then, recalling the drugs we found in Lars's house I add, "Or a personal problem, perhaps?"

Judy brightens at this last question and jumps on it . . . a little too eagerly for my tastes, and not in the direction I had hoped. "I did hear that some of the women in his life were getting tired of being strung along and were demanding more exclusivity."

"Anything else?" I ask, pushing a little harder.

Before she can answer, Hurley announces Bob Richmond and an officer will be arriving momentarily to start working on securing Lars's office and going through its contents. This news seems to make Judy nervous, but I can't tell if it's the news or Hurley's renewed attention on her.

"For the record, Ms. Bennett," Hurley says, "can you tell me where you were this morning between the hours of five and eight?"

Judy's expression of adoration shifts to one of disbelief. "You don't seriously think I had anything to do with Lars's death, do you?"

"Of course not," he says quickly, smiling and trying to reestablish his rapport with her. "But in order to have a thorough investigation, we have to ask everyone who knew Lars. It helps us rule out the people who are innocent so we can focus our attention on the more likely suspects. I promise you, it's just routine."

Judy looks mildly placated but still slightly offended, and I sense that any chance I might have had of getting her to divulge any of Lars's deep dark secrets is gone. And her answer to Hurley's question doesn't further our cause much. "I was home in bed until I got up at seven. Then I got ready for work and came here. I stopped at that little drive-through coffee shop to get a latte and a muffin." She gestures toward the trash can beside her desk and I see the cup and an empty muffin wrapper on top of the other garbage. "Other than my stop at the coffee shop, I can't prove any of the rest of it. I live alone, unless you want to count my cats."

So far, I can't see any motive Judy would have for wanting Lars dead, but I do think she might be worth another look or chat in the near future. She may not be a killer but she is the type of nearly invisible yet ever-present person who sees and overhears a lot of things, and I suspect she knows more about our victim than she's letting on.

Chapter 8

A uniformed officer named Grant Culpeper, who's new to the force, arrives along with Bob Richmond, another detective in town who recently returned to full-time work after being semi-retired. Bob has been on a new diet and exercise plan that turned his four-hundred-plus-pounds body into a fit and shapely two-sixty that he carries well thanks to his height. He looks fantastic, and he's been after me to meet him at the gym as often as I can ever since Matthew was born. The two of us were somewhat regular gym partners at one time—my effort to support him in his weight loss efforts—but I was forced to stop working out during the last half of my pregnancy. The neglect shows.

I've lost a decent amount of weight since the birth thanks to breast-feeding, a lack of sleep, and my constant activity, but I still have more to go and I could definitely use some toning, particularly in my tummy. Once I discovered I could order baby clothes from Amazon, I looked to see if I could buy clothes for myself. And of course I can. But because I have to order them without trying them on, I typically order several different sizes in any item I like. Then I return the ones that don't fit. You'd think that finding a size that works in one item would help me order another item, but the sizes are so inconsistent as to be nearly useless. Plus, being pregnant really messed with my body, and things that used to fit don't anymore. My bust is bigger—and it was hard enough to fit before the pregnancy. My thighs are, surprisingly, thinner, but my waist has thickened and my butt is wider than it used to be. Pregnancy even messed with my shoe size. Whereas before I was a solid size twelve—which is a hard enough size to find—I now need a twelve and a half. There isn't a store within fifty miles of here that carries that size, but fortunately, Amazon does.

I haven't spent a ton on new clothes because my body is still changing and I'm determined to lose more weight. I need to start thinking seriously about getting back to the gym, but I've been so exhausted that I've turned Richmond down every time he's invited me to go along. Now that the doctor has released me from my state of celibacy, I need to rethink it all.

"Hey, Mattie," Richmond says when he sees me. "Good to see you back on the job."

"Good to be back, I think."

"Want to hit up the gym with me later tonight?" One thing I can say about Richmond, he's persistent.

"Thanks, but I've got a hair appointment after work that I desperately need to keep."

Richmond and Culpeper both nod and eye my head with understanding, confirming how overdue I am.

"Maybe tomorrow," I say noncommittally. Just thinking about going to the gym makes me feel tired.

After some brief instructions from Hurley, Richmond and Culpeper commandeer Lars's office until more help can arrive. Richmond, like the other detectives, has his own camera since Charlotte can't be in two places at once. She has trained all of the detectives on the equipment and techniques, and in addition to filming stuff herself, she is going to be in charge of downloading, storing, managing, and reviewing all the video we have, including any necessary court displays. That part of her job is going to grow considerably soon because now the uniformed officers are being equipped with body cams. All the recent publicity about police brutality has loosened up purse strings, and since the cost of the cameras is considerably less than that of the typical lawsuit, the people who control the money are starting to see the light. Video evidence is definitely the wave of the future.

Hurley brings Richmond up to speed on the case so far. After filling him in on our visit to Lars's house and our run-in with Kirsten Donaldson, he tells Richmond that the plan for now is for Hurley and me to interview the rest of Sanderson's girlfriends as well as his business associates, guys like Harry Olsen and Reece Morton. "And there's someone named"—Hurley pauses and consults his notebook—"Hartwig Beckenbauer we need to talk to, as well. Apparently he has an ax to grind with Lars regarding some land his mother sold off to Sanderson. But first we have to find the guy. As for this place, we need to take a look at every piece of paper in here. I've got Jonas and Patrick Devonshire doing the same thing over at Sanderson's house where he has a second office. You might want to see if there are any extra hands available, because both they and you could use the help. I'm sure the chief will approve calling in some extra hands if necessary."

Richmond nods and takes out his cell phone. "I'll get right on it," he says. "If need be, we can call in the sheriff's department."

A small town like Sorenson doesn't have a very big

police department, and in situations like this, off-duty officers typically get called in for all kinds of extra stuff, everything from evidence collection and review, to stakeouts. While working extra is always voluntary, there is rarely any shortage of volunteers. Economic times are tough for a lot of folks right now so most of them grab at any overtime they can get. And both the state cops and the county sheriffs are used to chipping in to help when needed, too. While we prefer to keep the investigation as much within our own ranks as possible, sometimes bringing in outsiders can't be helped.

Once Hurley is assured that help is on the way, we head out to his car. As he starts the engine I say, "Who do you think we should tackle first?"

"Let's start with this other developer guy, Reece. And in the meantime, I'd like to get some background info on all these people: Reece, Harry Olsen, this Hartwig Beckenbauer guy, and the various girlfriends. Plus I want to look into the lawsuits Lars has had filed against him. I'm thinking we should put our new gal on it. What do you think?"

The "new gal" he is referring to is Laura Kingston, who used to be an assistant to Gary Henderson, an ME in Madison who came to Sorenson back in May to cover while Izzy was in Iowa with Dom. As it turned out, the first case Laura and Henderson had to investigate was mine. I killed a man, but in my defense, he tried to kill me first.

One good thing we got out of this temporary leadership was some extra staffing. Henderson reported that we were woefully understaffed, and as a result we had some additional positions approved. Laura took on a lab assistant/evidence processing job that is shared between our office and the police department. I think she took the position mainly because she became romantically involved with our resident lab tech and conspiracy theorist, Arnie Toffer, but also because she was tired of being Henderson's lackey. Laura's areas of expertise are varied thanks to her indecisiveness when it came to career choices. Not only is she well versed in several areas of forensic science, she has a business degree. She's also a whiz at tracking down information.

"I'm sure Laura would be happy to help," I tell Hurley, taking out my cell phone to call her.

Laura answers with, "Hey, Mattie, I was just about to call you. You must have ESP."

"Don't tell Arnie that. He'll turn it into some kind of mind control thing. Why were you going to call me?"

"To let you know that we found a partial print on the arrow Izzy took out of Sanderson's neck. That's the good news. The bad news is it looks like it belongs to Sanderson himself."

"What about the print that was in the blood on Sanderson's neck?"

"We're still working on that one, but there's something else we found. There was that small hair you found stuck to the fletching on the arrow."

"Fletching?"

"Fletching is the vanes or feathers, or at least what would be feathers on an old-fashioned arrow, though these days they're typically made out of plastic. The arrow that killed Sanderson has three vanes, which is quite common, though there are some that have four."

"Laura, I—"

"With three vanes there is usually one that's a different color from the other two and that one is called the cock. It's located on the shaft at a right angle from the nock, or notch at the end of the arrow where the bow string goes when you're ready to shoot."

"Laura, you—"

"And the other two vanes are called the hens. They should be situated evenly around the shaft of the arrow, about an inch from the nock. The fact that the hair was beneath some dried blood means that it might have come from whoever fired the arrow because when you—"

"Laura, stop!" I yell into my phone. Hurley jumps and then gives me an annoyed look.

Laura is a talker, and the yell is a tactic we've all grown used to using since she joined our staff. She is self-aware with regard to her verbosity and makes a valiant effort to contain it, but occasionally things get out of control and she needs reminding. Fortunately, she reacts to these abrupt stops with grace and good humor.

"Sorry," she says, and in my mind's eye I can see the sheepish grin I know she's wearing. "Verbal diarrhea."

"You can educate me on arrows later. For now, tell me about the hair."

"It's a cat hair, a black one, but Arnie said there's no root bulb on it so we can't get DNA."

"Okay, good to know. Hurley and I have something we want you to work on if you can."

I tell her what we want her to do and give her the list of names Hurley has written in his notebook.

"I'll get right on it," she says, sounding eager. "Should I call you or do you want to call me to find out what I dig up?"

"We're on our way to talk to Reece Morton, so send me any info you can find on him asap. Texting me is fine," I add, hoping to avoid another bout of her verbal diarrhea. "When you're done with Reece Morton, work your way down the rest of the list, starting with Harry

Olsen and then the girlfriends. Also, look into any lawsuits you can find that involved Lars and see if there's anything there that might provide motive. We'll touch base with you when we're ready to talk to any of these folks to see what you've dug up."

"Will do."

Before she has a chance to expound any more, I say, "Thanks. You're a doll." And then I disconnect the call.

"She's a chatty one," Hurley says with a smile.

"That she is. But she's been a great addition to the staff. She's smart, she's a hard worker, and she and Arnie seem to be hitting it off quite well. Now that he's got a romantic interest in his life, he's backed off on some of his conspiracy mania. Either that or he's venting it all on Laura."

"We might have a new problem," Hurley says, "I've heard Jonas has taken a liking to Laura, too."

"Really? That could get sticky. And speaking of sticky, Arnie said that black hair I found on the feather end of the arrow that killed Lars is a cat hair. He said there isn't enough to get nuclear DNA but at least it's something."

"I don't know," Hurley says, sounding glum. "It could have come from anywhere. It might have been on Lars when he got to the woods."

"But he doesn't have any cats."

"He doesn't need to. All he has to do is know someone who has a cat, or visit a place that has a cat, or sleep with a woman who has a cat," he says with an arch of his brows. "Cat hair adheres very easily. Heck, you could have brought it to the crime scene. Your cat, Tux, has black fur."

"Yes, he does, but this hair was under some dried

blood so it didn't come from me. Though Judy Bennett did mention having some cats."

"Point is, it's of minimal evidentiary value."

"Okay, but if we come across a potential suspect who has a cat with black fur, it might give us a reason to probe a little deeper."

"Fair enough."

We arrive at the address Judy gave us for Reece's place of business. It's also his home. Apparently he doesn't feel the need to have an "official" office the way Lars did. The house is in a ritzier section of town, one with pricey residences that serve as homes to doctors, lawyers, dentists, and the like. David and I almost bought a house in the neighborhood back when we first got married, but we opted instead for a more spacious and secluded property on the edge of town. The homes here are palatial, but they are also crammed surprisingly close together because they are situated on long, narrow lots that back onto a wetland area.

Hurley pulls into the circular driveway and parks in front of the house. It's a two-story brick building, with big arched windows in front and a wide, stone staircase leading up to the front door. Apparently Reece isn't afraid to impress his clients. Understandable, since he no doubt considered himself part of the Good Old Boy network prior to Lars coming to town.

The sun is out and the sky is a brilliant blue that mirrors Hurley's eyes, but it's a deceptive setting because the temperature has dropped since this morning. Our breath as we climb the front steps creates clouds of mist. Hurley makes use of a heavy iron door knocker in the shape of a lion's head. There's a doorbell, too, and for good measure I push it. Hurley shoots me an annoyed look, as if he is taking my use of the doorbell as a personal affront.

A minute or so passes, and I'm beginning to think no one is going to answer when the door is yanked open. The man on the other side is short—barely five-five if that—and balding, though he has stubbornly hung on to a friar's ring of hair. He looks to be in his mid- to late-fifties.

"I don't want whatever crap you're selling," he says with obvious irritation. Before we can say a word he adds, "And a bit of advice. Knock or ring the doorbell, but don't do both. All it does is piss people off." He starts to shut the door in our faces but Hurley throws a hand out and stops him, pushing the door back open while he fishes out his badge.

"Reece Morton, I'm Detective Hurley with the Sorenson PD and this is Mattie Winston with the ME's office. We need to speak with you."

"About what?" Morton is clearly not intimidated by our credentials. Both his frown and the irritation in his voice have deepened, and he takes a harried glance at his watch, letting us know that we are impinging on his time.

Hurley gets straight to the point. "About the murder of Lars Sanderson."

"Somebody killed Lars?" Morton doesn't look surprised.

"Yes, this morning," Hurley says.

"Well, boo-hoo and all that, but what the hell do you think I would know about it?"

"Clearly there is no love lost between the two of you," I say.

"Brilliant deduction," Morton says with obvious arrogance. The man's rude behavior is grating and it's all I can do to keep myself from biting his head off. I mean that metaphorically, but a vision pops into my mind of me snapping forth like some human-snake mutation freak and literally biting his head off. It's a vivid image that makes me shudder.

I realize then that Morton is ogling my chest, which is right at eye level for him. Hurley sees it too, and snaps his fingers in front of the guy's face and says, "Hey, eyes over here."

Morton slowly shifts his gaze with a lecherous little grin. "You got a stake in this one?" he says, nodding his head toward me.

Hurley's face is turning beet red and I sense he is about to explode. Reece Morton knows how to push buttons and obviously isn't afraid to do so. Short man syndrome, I figure. Why else would a man his size intentionally try to tick off two people who could sit on him and squash him like the little bug he is?

"Perhaps you'd prefer to come down to the station to chat," Hurley says, his ire barely contained. He glares at Morton who glares back for several seconds. Then Morton's common sense—or perhaps some survival instinct—kicks in. He steps aside and waves a hand by his side. "Come on in," he says. "Though I have to tell you it's a big waste of time."

We follow him inside and into a great room that makes me feel like I've entered a big city's men's club from the fifties. The walls are paneled in a faux mahogany color and the furnishings are leather and walnut, which would give the room a gloomy feel if not for the many colorful, bright, stained-glass lamps. There is wall-to-wall carpeting in a standard beige tone, and it looks well trampled as if it's been there for years. A heavy scent of stale cigar smoke hangs in the air.

"Sit," Morton says, like he's commanding a dog. He doesn't indicate where, or look to see if we follow his directions, which we don't. Hurley stops in the middle of the room and just stands there. I, the ever dutiful woman, stand by his side. Morton heads for a wet bar in the corner and after scooping some ice into a glass, he proceeds to pour himself a hefty three or four fingers of scotch. When he finally turns around, he shows no surprise at our stance. With a polite smile—the first sign of civility he's displayed—he asks if we would like a drink.

Hurley doesn't answer. He is glaring, shooting death rays at the man. I shake my head.

"I understand that you and Lars were business competitors," Hurley says.

Morton snorts a laugh. "I suppose you could say that, though Lars isn't much competition. He's a fly-by-night, hit-and-run type of developer. Those types never last long. The man was on the way down. He just didn't know it yet."

Morton's obvious disdain for Lars seems like a stupid thing to display, even if he's telling us the truth when he says he knows nothing about the man's murder.

"Are you a hunter?" Hurley asks.

"Of course," Morton says. "It's a rite of passage here in Wisconsin."

"Have you been out this season?"

"Sure. I was out yesterday, in fact."

"How about today?" Hurley asks.

"Nope."

"Do you ever hunt with a bow and arrow?"

"You mean like Cupid?" Morton says with a greasy smile. He looks over at me and winks before turning back to Hurley. "Are you two an item?" he asks, nodding in my direction. "Because if your partner here is available I'd love to show her a good time."

I can't hold back my laugh. It rolls out of me before

I realize what's happening. Apparently, it's a reaction Reece has received one too many times. His expression shifts with the suddenness of a thrown light switch. The smile is gone and he's no longer eyeing me with desire. Now it's something more akin to hate, and at the moment it's not hard to imagine Reece Morton as a killer. The ice in his glass tinkles and I see that his hand is shaking slightly. Anger, nerves, or something else?

"Mr. Morton," Hurley says in a stern voice, "can you please answer my question? Do you ever hunt with a bow and arrow?"

"I've tried it a time or two," he says with a shrug. "These days I prefer a rifle."

"Can you account for your whereabouts this morning between the hours of five and eight?"

"I was here."

"Can anyone verify that?" I ask. "Like a girlfriend perhaps?" I add in a slightly taunting tone.

The glare returns and after several seconds of silence, he says, "No. I was alone." Then with a slight sneer he adds, "By choice." He takes a big gulp of his drink and then sets the glass aside with a trembling hand.

"Rumor has it that you and Mr. Sanderson didn't get along," Hurley says.

Morton's glare lingers on me for a few more seconds before he slowly shifts his gaze back to Hurley. "We have a healthy competition between us."

"I've heard it hasn't been so healthy for you," Hurley says. "I've heard that Lars has been moving in on your old connections and schmoozing with a lot of the power people. Rumor has it he's managed to take away a lot of your business."

"That's ridiculous," Morton grumbles. "Yes, Sanderson managed to secure a couple of projects that I bid on as well, but his utter disregard for the culture and atmosphere of our city, as well as his lack of empathy for our ailing farm community has garnered him a bunch of unhappy patrons and opinions. Like I said before, his days are numbered." A pregnant pause follows and Morton seems to realize what he's just said, and the context in which he said it. "I meant business-wise, of course," he adds by way of explanation.

"It sounds like you had something more serious in mind," Hurley says. "We heard you and Sanderson had a bit of a tiff at the Nowhere Bar recently and you made some comments to him about how you were going to stop him, whatever it took."

Morton frowns, and then he stalls by picking up his scotch again and taking a long slow drink. His hand is shaking and it makes me wonder why he's so nervous. "It's true," he says finally, again setting the glass down. "We did exchange a few heated words at the bar, but it was nothing more than verbal sparring. I admit I was annoyed that he and the mayor seemed to be dealing with one another on a new project that's in the plans, but I've since learned that Lars has been blacklisted by the farmer who sold the land. Apparently when he sold it, he did so with the caveat that he would have a say in what sort of development would go in there and who would design it and do the work. And Lars hasn't earned himself any friends in the farming community around here."

My phone vibrates while Morton is talking and I take it out of my purse and glance at it. It's a text message from Laura, giving me a link to a recent lawsuit between Morton and Lars. "Mr. Morton, what is the basis of the lawsuit you filed against Lars Sanderson earlier this year?" I ask.

Morton's smug expression falters for a second or two, but he recovers quickly. "It was a countersuit for a nuisance suit he brought against me claiming unfair business practices. He's burned too many bridges in these parts and now he's desperate and grasping at any straw he can to try to steal some work. There was no basis to the suit and the court dismissed it."

Based on Laura's message, what Reece just said is true; the case was dismissed. I make a mental note to read the details of the case later as my phone buzzes again with another text message from Laura. The link she includes this time takes me to a Web site that makes Reece Morton look a whole lot more interesting as a suspect.

Chapter 9

I nudge Hurley and show him the Web page. He arches one eyebrow as Morton watches us, his hands trembling. He grabs his glass and takes another gulp, then sets it aside and clasps his hands in his lap, I assume in an effort to make them quit shaking.

Hurley's next comments come with a steely edge in his voice. "Mr. Morton, you own a bow. I need to see it and any arrows you have please."

"Why?"

"Can you please get the bow?" Hurley says, ignoring Morton's counter-question.

Morton puffs himself up to his max height, which is still only about shoulder height on Hurley. He takes a step back, too, distancing himself and lowering the incline of his neck as he looks Hurley in the eye. "It's not here. I told you, I prefer to use a rifle these days."

"Where is it?"

"I keep my archery equipment in a storage unit over on Palmer."

"Then it looks like we're going for a ride."

Morton is clearly not happy about this development.

"Why are you interested in my bow? I haven't used it in months."

"You participate in competitions with it, don't you?" Hurley asks. "We found some online articles about tournaments you've been in, several of which you won."

"I used to compete but I haven't for at least a year now. And I still don't see what it has to do with anything."

"Humor me," Hurley says with a decided lack of humor.

Morton stands there a moment, weighing his options.

"I don't have all day," Hurley says.

"Yeah, okay," Morton says finally, punctuating it with a resigned sigh. "Let me get my coat."

We allow Morton to drive his own car—a Beemer—to the storage site. Once there, we follow him down a row of units, stopping near the far end. He doesn't get out right away, and I can see him sitting in his car talking. Either he's on the phone with someone, or he's having a lively discussion with himself.

We get out, and Hurley grabs the video camera and turns it on. He was Charlie's first student when she came here last spring to train everyone on the filming techniques. I haven't had the chance to be subject to Charlie's tutoring yet, though the plan is for me to be trained as well. But I've been practicing with a video camera that Hurley bought me for my birthday, using Matthew as my main subject. Hurley hands me the camera and says, "Get this, will you?"

Morton finally gets out of his car without a word or a glance in our direction and I follow him with the camera. He looks perturbed and impatient, and I wonder if his annoyance is with us or whoever he was talking to in his car, assuming he was on the phone. His hands are trembling as he grabs the combination lock and starts turning the dials. It takes him several tries—enough so that I start to wonder if he's purposely stalling—before he is able to open the lock. His demeanor does a one-eighty once he rolls up the garage-type door.

Aside from a few stray pieces of hay the unit is empty.

Morton stands at the entrance staring into the concrete room with a puzzled expression. "What the hell. . . ." he mutters.

Hurley and I exchange a look, and I know that Morton's day is about to get a whole lot worse. He looks genuinely shocked by the empty unit, but it could be an act. If he'd known all along that the thing was empty, he had the ride over here to prepare his reaction.

"I don't get it," he says. "I had a bunch of stuff in here . . . my bow, quiver, arrows, targets, some hay bales, my gloves . . . all of my archery equipment."

"So where is it?" Hurley asks. It's obvious his patience is wearing thin.

"Wish the hell I knew," Morton says. He turns and stares into the unit again, as if hoping to discover this is a dream, or a magic trick of some sort. Then he shakes his head. When he turns back to us, he looks angry.

"Who would know the combination on that lock you had on the door?" Hurley asks. I'm not sure if he's giving Morton the benefit of the doubt, or if he's merely trying to keep him talking a little longer to see if he will eventually say something leading, or even better, incriminating.

Morton runs a shaky hand over his head and stares at the ground. "I have no idea."

"Did you set the combination yourself, or did it come preset?"

"I set it," he says. He gives us a sheepish look. "I was born on April ninth, 1962, so I set if for four, nine, six, two."

"You used your birthday?" Hurley says in a tone of disbelief. He sighs and shakes his head. "That seems like an amateur move for a savvy business guy like you."

Morton scowls and for a second he looks like he's about to make a snappy comeback, but then his expression morphs into one of embarrassment instead, and he clamps his mouth shut.

"Mr. Morton, we need to find your archery equipment. Can we go back to your house and look?"

"It's not there," he insists.

"I'd like to make that determination for myself."

Morton frowns and I can tell he doesn't want us going back to his house.

"If you don't want to cooperate I can get a search warrant," Hurley adds. Morton's face lights up at this suggestion, I suspect because he thinks it will delay things, but then Hurley adds, "And in the meantime, you can come down to the station so we can talk some more."

Morton hesitates, but his indecision is short-lived. He glances at his watch and says, "I have an important meeting at three this afternoon. If I let you go look through my house now, will you leave me be so I can keep my appointment?"

"Depends on what we find," Hurley says. "If you're certain your archery equipment isn't in the house, then it shouldn't be a problem."

Something about this whole setup is bothering me, and I decide now is the time to bring it up. Still running the camera, I say, "Mr. Morton, I'm curious about something. Your house is quite large and I saw that you have a shed in your backyard. With all that room, why would you rent a storage facility for your archery equipment? Why not just keep it on the premises somewhere? Surely you must have plenty of storage space there."

"I have room at the house, but I don't use my archery equipment anymore so there isn't much need to have it close by."

"What made you give it up?" I ask. "Based on what we found on the Internet, at one time you were quite the master with your bow and arrows."

He looks away, staring off down the row of storage units, and shrugs. "I just lost interest in it."

He's lying; I'm certain of it. "I'm thinking the reason you gave it up is because of whatever neuromuscular disease you have. You can't do it anymore, can you?"

Morton looks back at me with a shocked expression.

"What is it, Parkinson's?"

"How the hell . . ." Morton mutters. He is staring at me like I'm either the devil incarnate or the second coming of Christ. I can't tell if it's fear or awe on his face. Maybe it's both. I realize Hurley is staring at me with much the same expression.

"He has a tremor," I explain to Hurley. "I saw it back at the house, and I saw it here when he was trying to undo the lock on the unit. Plus there's the way he walks. I'm guessing it's Parkinson's disease." I turn and give Morton a questioning look.

He nods slowly, a sad expression on his face.

"How long have you known?" I ask him.

"Two years. It has progressed quite rapidly since then and I've had to up my medication doses pretty regularly. The doctors tell me that's not a good sign and they want to do some kind of experimental surgery, implant something in my brain that they think will help control the tremors. But my insurance won't cover it. Being self-employed all these years, my insurance costs have been huge so I've always had the minimal coverage. Besides, the procedure is considered experimental. I'm trying to save up enough money to pay for it. That's one of the reasons I've been so angry at Lars for stealing my business."

I lower the camera and turn it off. "So you gave up the archery because you lost your ability to do it well."

Morton scoffs. "I've lost my ability to do it at all. I don't have the strength anymore, and my aim is . . . well . . . it's precarious at best." His face screws up like he's about to cry and he turns away for a few seconds, gathering his emotions. "You don't understand how much that meant to me," he says over his shoulder. "All my life I've been made fun of because of my size, and I was never very good at anything. I got average grades in school, I sucked at sports, I sucked at dating. But archery . . . that was something I got good at. That was something I could do better than anyone else. And now I've lost that, too."

I look over at Hurley and nod toward our car, indicating that I want to talk to him in private. "Hang tight, Morton," I say, and then I head for the car with Hurley on my heels. When we reach the car I turn to Hurley and speak in a low voice. "I realize he seems to have motive and disliked Lars quite a bit, and I can't say for sure that he didn't do this. But I think the likelihood is so slim as to be almost nonexistent. That tremor he has is so severe he wouldn't be able to hit much of anything he aims at. That's not to say that he couldn't have accidentally fired an arrow that just happened to hit

Sanderson, but that's a long shot at best and would make it an accidental death."

Hurley nods. "I see your point, but I'm still concerned about the missing archery equipment. If Morton didn't fire that arrow, it doesn't mean his equipment wasn't used. The fact that it's missing seems auspicious. It could be our murder weapon. We need to find it."

I nod and we return to where Morton is standing. His eyes are a bit red, but he appears to have his emotions in check, at least for now.

Hurley clears his throat and says, "Mr. Morton, Lars Sanderson was murdered this morning with an arrow, so you can see why we are interested in your equipment. And given your competitive, litigious, and antagonistic relationship with Mr. Sanderson, I'm sure you can see why we are interested in you and your whereabouts. However, in light of this latest revelation about your . . . um . . . disorder, I'm less interested in you as a suspect for now. Your equipment, however, remains high on my list, for reasons I'm sure you can understand."

Morton nods but says nothing.

"We need to find your missing equipment. And I want to start by ruling out your home as one of the places it might be. So can we please go back to your house and take a look through it to make sure it isn't there?"

Again Morton nods. Without another word, he heads for his car and settles in behind the wheel. Hurley and I get back into our car and follow Morton home.

"I kind of feel sorry for the guy," I say as Hurley drives. "I loathed him in the beginning, but after that sad little speech back there, I feel like a heel. Clearly he was bullied as a kid and it's damaged his psyche. That kind of stuff scares me when I think about raising a kid."

"Lots of people get bullied as kids," Hurley says. "It's a sad fact of life."

"What if it happens to Matthew?"

Hurley looks over at me and smiles. "You're getting a little ahead of yourself, aren't you?"

"Maybe, but I don't think it's ever too early to start thinking about this stuff."

"The important thing is to prepare your kids and make them feel loved and worthwhile, so that they don't take it too seriously when other kids say hurtful things."

"Has Emily had to deal with any of that stuff at school? It's got to be hard for her as the new kid on the block, especially in a small town like this one where so many of the kids know one another."

"She hasn't said anything to me about it," Hurley says with a frown. "But then, I'm not sure she would."

"Have you talked to her teachers at all?"

Hurley shakes his head and shoots me a guilty look. "I haven't had a reason to. She's been doing okay as far as her grades and her schoolwork are concerned. She won't be making the honor roll, but she's passing."

"It still might be helpful to talk to them to get their take on her behavior and mental status."

"I suppose it couldn't hurt. I'll try to set something up soon."

"We should do it together. I think I'm a big part of her problem, or at least what she perceives as her problem, and maybe her teachers can shed some light on how we can best deal with things."

We arrive back at Morton's house, so we table the discussion for now. Hurley places a call to the station to see who's available to help us search Morton's house. As luck would have it—my bad luck, that is—Charlie is currently free and she offers to come out and handle the filming duties. We also get Junior Feller, who will not only assist with this search but give us an update on his visit to the Quik-E-Mart convenience store.

We follow Morton inside his house and station him in the living room. Charlie arrives a minute or two later, and while we're waiting for Junior to show up, Hurley, Charlie, and I search the main floor, including the kitchen, a dining room, the coat closet, and a family room. We also check out the shed in back of the house, but all we find there is a snowmobile, an all-terrain vehicle, a riding lawnmower, and a bunch of bags of fertilizer. With Charlie present, Hurley and I are free to search and take notes since she can handle the filming, so the process moves along quickly since there aren't that many places in the house where one could hide a bow and a bunch of arrows, not to mention the targets and hay bales Morton claims are also missing.

By the time we're done with the first floor, Junior and his entourage arrive. After Hurley gives the newcomers a quick briefing, the officers and Charlie head upstairs to continue the search. "Don't forget to check the attic area," Junior hollers after them. He then turns to us and says, "I'll check out the basement and then we'll head outside and do the garage. But first, let me tell you what I found out at the convenience store. The cashier's name is Brandon Sveum, and he works every weekday morning at the Quik-E-Mart. He told me this guy named Mike—that's all he knows of the name—came up to him to check out and mentioned a conversation he overheard in the next aisle between the two guys who had just left the store. Mike said the two guys were talking in low voices, and one was telling the other about a body he saw in Cooper's Woods earlier this morning. The guy who saw the body told the other guy that he didn't want to get tied up with some tedious investigation and lose some prime hunting time, so he didn't report it to anyone, figuring someone else would stumble over the body eventually and report it. So it sounds like this first guy was pretty close to the body, close enough to know that Sanderson was dead and how he was killed. Apparently he mentioned the arrow in the neck. So either he's a key witness, or he's our killer."

"I don't suppose you got a name," Hurley asks.

Junior smiles. "Of course I did. The cameras at the store showed both guys and I recognized our body whisperer. It's George Haas."

I know George Haas because I went to school with him. His middle name is Samuel and if you say his name real fast, using just his middle initial, it sounds like *George's ass.* Back in our school days, this was quickly converted to *horse's ass,* which is what George was known as through graduation, a ceremony he barely qualified to attend. George was never the sharpest tool in the shed, but he was a hell of a football player. His teachers tutored him and kept him after school, spending hours trying to get him barely passing grades so he could stay on the football team. It was a group effort that got George through school and graduation. Unfortunately, three days after graduation, George blew out his knee, blew off part of one foot, and lost three of the fingers on one hand trying to get rid of some pesky gophers in his garden. At least that's the official story he gave the cops, though there are many in town who suspect it's a cover story. There's a longstanding rumor that the Haas family operated a still on their farm years ago that produced some of the best moonshine in the county. There has been some speculation that they're still cooking the stuff—or maybe something worse—though there's never been any direct evidence of it that I know of. Still, I'm not too surprised that George doesn't want to attract the attention of the local police over something like a dead body.

"It looks like we need to have a chat with Mr. Haas," Hurley says. "Maybe we should do that before we chat with any of Lars's girlfriends to see if he can shed any new light on the situation."

In response, my stomach churns loudly.

"Maybe we should grab some lunch first," Hurley adds with a wink.

"Good idea. This breast-feeding stuff does give me a big appetite."

No one says anything to this, but I realize that both Junior's and Hurley's eyes have shifted to my chest. I clear my throat and arch my brows at them, and it seems to work. Suddenly they're both looking at something else. Then Junior excuses himself to go help with the search effort.

Hurley says, "Let's eat at my place, if that's okay. I want to check to see if Emily is there. I'm a little concerned that she isn't answering my calls or texts. In the past when she's pulled these disappearing acts, she's always responded to my calls or messages. But today she isn't doing either."

"I thought you were going to ignore her."

He gives me a sheepish smile. "I haven't mastered that ploy just yet."

"Okay," I say with a nod, though I have to admit I'm not keen on having to deal with the surly teenager. I'd much rather go to my place and get in a little cuddle time with my son. Then again, lunch at Hurley's might lead to a little cuddle time with Hurley, which is a perk in and of itself. "Let me call Dom and check on Matthew first."

I step aside to place the call and Dom answers on the first ring. "Hey, Mattie."

"How's my boy doing?"

"He's napping at the moment, but so far he's having a great day. He's a bundle of smiles and I've discovered he's a huge fan of both patty-cake and peekaboo."

There is a childlike quality to Dom's voice as he says this that makes me smile. I miss Matthew like crazy, but it's nice to know he's in good hands. I update Dom on my day, and tell him I'm going to take him up on his offer of some extra time later so I can visit Barbara and get my hair done. "Assuming the offer still stands," I say, not wanting to be too presumptive.

"It does, and I think it's a great idea!" Dom says with an unexpected level of excitement. I wonder if it's because he's excited at the prospect of spending more time with Matthew, or because he's relieved I'm finally going to try and make myself look halfway human again. I thank him, tell him to call me if anything comes up, and then head back to Hurley, who has been corralled by Charlie.

"Ready?" I say to Hurley, eager to break up the two of them.

He nods, says, "Thanks, Charlie," and gives her a squeeze on her shoulder. Then he turns and heads for the door. I follow behind, dying to know why he thanked Charlie, but reluctant to ask. I don't want to come across as a jealous, insecure, needy partner with Hurley.

Even if I am one.

Stupid hormones.

Chapter 10

I needn't have worried about dealing with Emily because she isn't home when we arrive at Hurley's house. And after checking out all the rooms, including Emily's bedroom, which looks like a cyclone has blown through it, it doesn't appear that she stopped here on her way to somewhere else.

"Her book bag isn't here," Hurley says, looking a tad worried. "If she had stopped by the house, she would have dumped the book bag off before going anywhere else. It's the first thing she does when she comes in the door. She always drops it right there in the foyer."

"Maybe she's back at the school by now."

Hurley frowns and shakes his head. "She typically sends me a text once she returns."

"Maybe she's only telling you she returned when she's actually still skipping out."

"No, I've always called the school to verify."

"Do you think she might be at Johnny's house?"

Hurley shakes his head. "Doubt it. That's the first place I used to look when this first started happening, but they were never there. The boyfriend's mom operates a day care out of the house so I don't think they'd find much privacy there."

"Then where do they go?"

Hurley looks frustrated, exasperated, and annoyed. "I don't know," he says irritably. "A few times she told me they went to McDonald's or some other fast food place to eat because the school food sucks. So I offered to pack a lunch for her, but then she said only losers bring a bag lunch to school. Other times she told me they just drove around, or went to a store to buy a few things. When I remind her that she's supposed to be in school during those times, she tells me that she only skips certain classes, the ones she knows she can do well in even if she isn't there all the time." He pauses and sighs. "And her grades bear that out so far. Like I said before, she may not be on the honor roll, but her grades are okay, mostly Bs and Cs."

"I suppose it's possible they're shopping or driving around, but I'm willing to bet they're doing something else entirely." I'm hesitant to voice what I'm thinking—Hurley looks upset enough as it is—but he gives me a questioning look so I go ahead and say it. "I bet she and Johnny are parking somewhere and making out, maybe even having sex."

Hurley's eyebrows draw down into a disapproving V. "Why would you think that?"

"Well, duh. She's a teenage girl with hormones, and he's a teenage guy with hormones and a car. Surely your memory of those years can't be that bad, Hurley."

He frowns and his eyes take on a faraway look that tells me he's tripping down memory lane. "I don't think she'd do that," he says after a moment, shaking his head. But the look on his face tells me he isn't convinced.

"Have you asked her if she's sexually active?"

"No," Hurley answers quickly. His cheeks take on a

rosy hue. "She's too young. And we don't . . . I don't . . . our relationship isn't like that yet."

I give him an exasperated look. "Your relationship with her *has* to be like that, Hurley. You can't just look the other way and pretend these things don't happen. If she has a boyfriend, odds are she's either thinking about having sex or she's already done it. Have you talked to her about safe sex and birth control?"

Hurley shakes his head. "That was her mother's job."

"It's your job now. You need to at least find out what she's been told, if anything. Did Kate talk to her about it?"

"I don't know," Hurley says, mowing his hands through his hair. "The subject never came up when Kate was living here. And later on she was so drugged up most of the time that we never really talked much. Plus I never spent time with her unless Emily was there, so we didn't have any opportunities to talk about Emily in private. I doubt that sort of thing was on her mind much there at the end anyway."

"Then you need to talk to Emily."

"I don't know how," he grumbles, throwing his hands up. "I figured I had another year or two before it became an issue."

"Well, if her hormones are anything like mine were at her age, that ship has sailed. And I think you know what a boy Johnny Chester's age is all about."

Hurley lets out an exasperated sigh. He heads for the kitchen and starts assembling the ingredients for the grilled cheese sandwiches we decided to have for lunch on the drive over. I follow him and settle in at the kitchen table, knowing that there will be no hanky-panky or even cuddle time between us this afternoon, not after the discussion we just had.

"You know, I grew up without a father the same way

Emily did," I say as Hurley preps our sandwiches. "Though I tried to hide it, my father's lack of presence in my life was something that made me feel like an outsider, like I was lacking somehow or wasn't good enough. I can't help but wonder how I would have reacted if he'd suddenly popped into my life the way you popped into Emily's, with another family in the making. When I was in high school I felt really envious of the girls who had fathers, and even though most of them bitched about how their parents would restrict their activities and ground them for stuff all the time, I could tell they felt secure in the love they got from their fathers. I wanted that feeling more than I wanted anything else. I think that's why I made some of the dumb choices I did when it came to boyfriends."

Hurley plops the sandwiches into a frying pan and then puts a lid on it. He turns to me with a crooked grin and says, "Is this that moment in our relationship when we start talking about the exes and comparing numbers?"

"Comparing numbers?" I say with a gulp of dread.

"Yeah, how many other men have you been with before me?"

"I don't know," I say. This is an out and out lie. I know exactly how many there have been. "Well, there was David, of course."

"My number is sixteen," Hurley says.

"Sixteen? Seriously? You've slept with sixteen other women besides me?"

"Fifteen besides you. You're number sixteen. Eleven of them were during my high school and college years and they were either one-night stands or short-lived affairs. I was a bit randy back then," he says with a wink and a sheepish smile.

"I once dated a guy named Randy."

"Did you sleep with him?"

I smile and shake my head. "No, but he made it to second base several times."

"Well, at least he lived up to his name then," Hurley says with a wink. "I got tamer once I finished college. There have only been four women since then, and you already know about two of them: Kate and Callie. In between those two were Jessica and Melanie."

"Jessica came after Kate?"

Hurley picks up a spatula in preparation for flipping our sandwiches and wags it at me. "Oh, no, you don't," he says with a sly smile. "No more details from me until I get your number."

I don't want to tell him my number. It's considerably lower than his and I'm not sure how he's going to interpret that. Will he see it as a good thing that I wasn't a bed-hopper in my younger days? Or will he see it as a sign of how undesirable I am?

"Let's go back to talking about Emily," I say, eager to change the subject.

Hurley narrows his eyes at me for a few seconds and then opens them wide. "What is it? Why don't you want to share your number? Is it huge?"

"No it's not huge," I snap back.

"Then why won't you tell me what it is?"

"Fine. It's five. You are number six. Are you happy?"

He smiles smugly. "David was number five?" he asks.

"Are you asking me if I've slept with anyone else since David and I split up? Because we already covered this subject when we had the whole pregnancy discussion, remember?"

"Just checking. Tell me about numbers one through four." He slides a sandwich onto a plate and brings it to me. Then he goes back for the second one, putting it on a plate for himself and settling in across the table. "Actually, tell me about number one. Who was the first?"

"Mitch Dalrymple." I take a bite of my sandwich to stall for time. Hurley makes killer grilled cheese sandwiches, cooking them nice and slow so that the butter infuses into the bread and all the cheese melts into a gooey, delicious mass. He also sprinkles a little cheese on the outside of the bread, creating a crunchy, cheesy crust.

"How old were you?" Hurley asks.

"Sixteen. We met over the summer between my sophomore and junior years in high school when I was working at the old Dairy Queen that used to be in town. Mitch had just moved here and he told me he was from Los Angeles and had to move because his parents split up. He worked at the DQ, too, and we bonded over the single parent thing because he said his father had stayed in L.A. He told me he was working because his mother had gotten screwed over by his father when it came to money and he had to do what he could to try to help her make ends meet. He seemed so worldly and experienced to me, and he was a big name-dropper, mentioning famous people he'd seen or met when he lived in L.A. Plus he was really handsome, funny, and easy to talk to. He talked me right into his bed by the end of the summer."

"How long did it last?"

"A little over two weeks. Once school started, Mitch realized there were plenty of other cute girls in town and he moved on pretty quickly. He stole the virginity of several of my classmates by the time the school year was out. Then he moved away. We learned later that the whole L.A. story was made up. They were actually from Texas, where his mother was wanted for check forgery."

"Ouch," Hurley says with a grimace.

"Yeah, I suppose," I say with a smile, taking another bite of my sandwich. "But I have to tell you that those two weeks when I was Mitch's girl, I felt like the queen of the ball."

"Were you heartbroken when he moved on?"

"Of course, but I put up a good front. I was good at it by then because I'd been rejected by any number of boys for the same reason Mitch gave me."

"Which was?"

"That I was too tall. He wanted someone smaller, daintier. You have to understand that back then there weren't very many boys who were taller than me. Toward the end of my junior year they started catching up and some even surpassed me, but until then I was the tallest person in my school. It made me very popular during the slow songs at school dances but very unpopular for dating. Which sort of segues into guy number two, Teddy Lawrence."

I pause long enough to finish off my sandwich and lick the butter off my fingers. Hurley's eyes watch me with a steamy interest that makes me rethink the possibilities for some cuddle time. But then he seems to snap to attention. He shoves the rest of his sandwich in his mouth, gets up from the table, and puts both of our plates in the sink. "The tale of Teddy will have to wait for another time," he says. "I'm rethinking the Emily situation. I want to make a quick run by the school to see if she might be out in the parking lot with Johnny. I've smelled cigarette smoke on her a few times so maybe she's just hanging out with him in his car smoking."

We head out to the car and as soon as we are under

way I say, "Turnabout is fair play. I want to hear about your first. How old were you?"

"Sixteen, the same as you. It was with Becky Cooper, a cute little redhead who was in my geometry and biology classes."

I'm not happy to hear that his first was a redhead. Images of Charlie pop into my head. Then images of my color-challenged hair pop into my head.

"Becky had freckles that she hated, but to me they were the cutest things ever. I used to sit in class and daydream about tracking those freckles up her arms, up her legs, down her neck . . . to all the places I couldn't see. But for the longest time, all I had the courage to do was daydream because she was dating the high school quarterback, a senior named Rick McKay. Like the boys you went to school with, I was a little slow in reaching my full potential and at that age I was only about five-six. I didn't hit a major growth spurt until my senior year in high school and then I kept growing during my first two years in college. As a sophomore, Rick McKay scared the crap out of me because he was close to six feet tall and very muscular. I figured I didn't stand a chance with Becky, but then one day we got paired together in biology lab. At first I was so tongue-tied I could barely talk to her, but like your Mitch, she was funny and easygoing, and before I knew it we were getting on like we'd been friends all our lives.

"I'm not sure when I began to suspect that she liked me and was getting tired of Rick, but I noticed she was touching me a lot more all of a sudden. You know . . . a hand on my hand, a brush of her breast against my shoulder as she reached for something, a bit of foot play under the table that may or may not have been intentional. And she started talking smack about Rick, how he ignored her and talked down to her. I saw my chance and made my move. I asked her out to a movie on a Friday night when there was an away football game and I knew Rick wouldn't be in town. She accepted and I was in heaven. I don't even remember what movie we saw because I was busy the entire time trying to plot out the rest of the evening. Little did I know that Becky was plotting, too. She invited me back to her place and I discovered that we had the house to ourselves because her parents and her little brother were out of town for the weekend. Then Becky seduced me. To me it was a turning point in my life, the start of what I knew was going to be a lifelong relationship."

He pauses, shakes his head, and laughs. "How naïve we can be at that age, right?" He doesn't wait for an answer. "Anyway, it turns out that Becky's only interest in bedding me was to make Rick jealous so he'd pay her the attention she felt she was due. As soon as I went home that night, she was on the phone telling her friends what had happened, knowing that eventually it would get back to Rick. I couldn't figure out why she wouldn't take my calls or call me back all weekend, but come Monday at school I came to the truth all too fast. Rick met me in the parking lot before classes started and beat the crap out of me."

"Oh, no," I say, feeling bad for the younger, naïve Hurley.

"Yep, he told me that if I ever so much as spoke to Becky again he'd have me killed. He was a mean kid, too. He might have actually done it. But it didn't matter because Becky was back on his arm, smiling and happy, and I knew I'd been played. Not speaking to her after that was easy except for that damned biology lab. Fortunately we only had two more classes together as a team and I skipped them both. Got a D in the class as a result because we didn't finish our experiment, but I didn't care."

"That's horrible," I tell him. "Whatever happened to the two of them? Did they stay together?"

"No, once Rick graduated, he moved on to college and Becky was left behind. She tried to make another play for me later on, but I'd learned my lesson by then. Though I have to confess, red hair and freckles haunted me throughout the rest of high school."

Red hair again. *Damn.*

We arrive at the high school and Hurley pulls into the student lot and cruises the aisles. After driving the full circuit, he stops and frowns.

"What?" I ask.

"I don't see Johnny Chester's car."

Hurley pulls out of the lot and goes around to the front of the school. It's almost two-thirty, which means the school day will be ending in another hour or so. He parks and turns off the engine.

"What are you doing?" I ask.

"I'm going inside to talk to the principal. Something about this doesn't feel right."

I follow Hurley inside, where he makes straight for the main office. He and I met the high school principal, Jeanette Knowles, last spring while we were investigating the death of one of the school's teachers. Knowles is a grandmotherly-looking woman with a warm smile, gray hair, and a matronly build. But beneath that sweet façade is a stern woman with a disposition made of fire and a spine made of steel. Our last encounter wasn't what I would call friendly, so it's no surprise that she greets us today with scorn and suspicion. She is out in the main area when we enter the office, chatting with the receptionist.

"Detective," she says with obvious disdain. "What on

earth brings you back here to my office? I'm pretty sure all of our teachers are here and alive today, and as far as I know none of our students have killed anyone."

"I'm here on personal business," Hurley says with amazing calm. "It's about my daughter, Emily."

"Ah, yes, our newest truant. I hope you realize that if she keeps skipping out on her classes, she may not pass for the year."

"I'm aware of the issues," he says with a hint of impatience. "And if I'm not mistaken, she's keeping her grades up despite her skips."

"That may be, but if she continues this pattern of behavior, those grades are likely going to plummet. And we do have attendance policies. If she misses much more time without a legitimate excuse, she'll end up with an automatic suspension."

"We can discuss that if and when it happens," Hurley says dismissively. "I'm here because I received a text earlier informing me that Emily hadn't returned to class after lunch. Is she still absent?"

"She is," Knowles says.

"She's not at home and normally when she does this, she's off somewhere with her boyfriend, Johnny Chester. Is he absent also?"

Knowles lets out a humorless chuckle. "In a manner of speaking," she says. "He was suspended for two weeks last Friday."

"What for?"

"He was found with contraband in his locker."

"What sort of contraband?" Hurley asks impatiently.

"I'm not at liberty to share that information with you." Knowles looks smugly pleased as she says this. "Confidentiality, you know."

Hurley narrows his eyes down to a laser glare. I have

to give Knowles credit; she doesn't so much as blink. But Hurley isn't done with her yet.

"Ms. Knowles," he says, tight-lipped, "my daughter is missing and may well be in the company of this Chester boy. If I find out that his suspension was because of some dangerous or illegal behavior that has put my daughter in jeopardy or in any sort of compromising situation, and you didn't inform me of that, I'm going to be all in your business for the foreseeable future. I'm sure you realize that there are any number of ways I can make life difficult for you and the school. So if you're sure you want to play hardball, I'm ready."

Knowles stares back at him for several seconds before firing off her own volley. "*Mr.* Hurley," she says, emphasizing the title in what I suspect is an attempt to belittle his position. "As Emily's parent, it is your responsibility to see to it that your daughter is aware of the dangers inherent in certain things, and to not only teach her the rules, but see to it that she follows them. We here at the school are not the parents of these kids, nor are we their babysitters. So if you want to start laying blame at someone's feet for your daughter's behavior, I suggest you start with your own."

Another round of staring commences, and at first I'm not sure which side to lean toward because I agree with the arguments put forth by both parties. My inherent bias eventually kicks in, making me want to defend, or at least support, Hurley. The receptionist is sitting at her desk looking relaxed and amused. I imagine she finds exchanges like this entertaining.

Sensing that both Knowles and Hurley are equally stubborn and hardheaded, I decide to jump into the fray and appeal to Knowles's softer, more feminine side. "Ms. Knowles, I'm sure you know that Emily has had a very rough time of things this past year. First she was forced to leave her friends behind and move to a town where she doesn't know anyone. Then her mother died, leaving her in the care of a father she doesn't know because up until this year she thought he was dead. On top of that, her newfound father is also the new father of a baby boy, which no doubt makes Emily feel like she doesn't matter. Add to that her age, and all the hormonal ups and downs that go with that, and you've got a very troubled young girl in need of understanding and sympathy."

Knowles turns her steely glare my way, hands on her ample hips, and proceeds to show me just how foolish I am to think she actually has a softer, feminine side. "*Ms.* Winston, given that I know you are a new mother and therefore likely exhausted and hormonal, I'm going to cut you some slack. But before you go lecturing us or pointing your finger at anyone here, let me say again that we are not babysitters. We are eager to help and be a part of the team, but our students' problems are the primary responsibility of their parents, or in this case, parent. And based on our records, that doesn't include you."

I hear Hurley suck air through his teeth and he takes a slight step backward. I, on the other hand, take a step forward until I'm nearly in Knowles's face. I may have soggy boobs and spit-up inspired hair at the moment, but I also have some *cojones* and I'm about to show them to Knowles.

"Your attitude is both appalling and unprincipled," I tell her. "Pun intended," I add with a snippy smile. "Let *me* remind *you* that my brother-in-law is Lucien Colter, a damn fine attorney and first cousin to Gerhardt Townsend, who I believe is the superintendent of schools for our county and therefore your boss. I'm sure they would both be very interested in hearing your position on this matter."

A standoff ensues as Knowles and I stare one another down, but I'm feeling pretty confident. I saw the way her color paled when I mentioned Lucien's name. And once again Lucien's reputation holds sway as Knowles blinks first. "What do you want from me?" she asks through narrowed, tightened lips.

I look over at Hurley with a half smile and step back.

Hurley clears his throat. "Um, for starters, you can tell me why the Chester boy was suspended."

Knowles sighs before she answers. "We found marijuana in his locker after someone made an anonymous tip."

"Thank you," Hurley says. "I want to call the Chester house to see if Emily is there. Can you give me a phone number please?"

Knowles does so grudgingly, nodding toward the receptionist who has been sitting behind her desk looking like she wished she had a big tub of buttered popcorn. The receptionist lets out a mournful little sigh—no doubt disappointed that the brush fire before her didn't turn into a major conflagration—looks up the number on her computer, and writes it on a slip of paper that she then hands to Hurley.

Hurley looks at Knowles and says, "When I'm done I'd like you to have a list for me with the names and contact numbers for all of Emily's teachers."

"Why?" Knowles asks.

"Because I want to speak to them," Hurley retorts. "I want to make them aware of the issues Emily is facing and get their take on her emotional and mental status. And then I want to get them involved in a plan to help her."

"You'll have to do that during the teachers' regular work hours," Knowles says. "I won't have you pestering my staff during their time off, and you'll need to make appointments. I'm not going to have you interfering with our classes over one student's truancy. Your daughter is no more deserving of our staff time and attention than any of the other troubled kids we have here."

Hurley manages to swallow down the incense I know he feels and he steps aside to make his call. We listen in as he gets Lila Chester on the phone. He explains who he is and why he's calling. Then after listening for a few seconds, he looks at me and shakes his head. He puts a hand over the phone and whispers, "She isn't there, but Johnny is." He listens some more, asks if Emily has attempted to reach Johnny, and after listening to what I assume is the answer, he thanks Lila and disconnects the call.

As he summarizes the gist of the call for us, his expression grows more and more concerned. "Lila grounded Johnny and took his car keys, phone, and laptop away from him as part of his punishment, so he hasn't been out of the house since his suspension. She said Emily has never been to their house, and she doesn't even know what she looks like."

"Do you believe her?" I ask him.

He shrugged. "She seemed sincere. I had her check Johnny's phone to see if Emily tried to contact him, and she said there was nothing there since a phone call two days ago."

I turn to Knowles and say, "Are you absolutely sure Emily isn't here at the school? Has anyone checked the bathrooms, or outside on the grounds?"

If looks could kill I'd be lying dead at Knowles's feet right now. I wonder how old she is. Will I have to send

Matthew to a private school in fourteen years, or will Knowles be retired by then?

"We didn't initiate a manhunt, if that's what you're asking," Knowles says with barely contained civility. "The students are responsible for their own attendance. If they choose to skip a class, our job is to notify the parents . . . or parent," she adds, tossing in another jab. "It is not our job to hunt the students down and drag them to class."

"Mind if I have a look around the school while you get the teacher information together?" I ask.

"Yes, I do," Knowles says. "I'll not have you traipsing about the school willy-nilly, interrupting classes and bothering students."

I give her a big smile and say, "No worries, I haven't been able to do the willy-nilly for years. And I'm going to go look in your bathrooms and outside on the grounds, not in your classrooms. If you don't like it, I suppose you can call the cops on me. Oh, wait . . ." I clasp a hand over my mouth and give her a look of mock surprise. "They're here already. Oh well." With that I turn to Hurley, who is barely suppressing his smile, and say, "I'll meet you out front in a bit." Then I leave the office, not giving that witch of a woman a chance to say or do one more thing.

I know the school building well since it's the same one I spent my four years of high school in. It's had some minor upgrades here and there, but it's essentially the same building it was when I attended. There are two girls' and two boys' bathrooms on each floor placed at the ends of the hallways, and I hit up the first floor girls' bathrooms first. It's mid-period, so the hallway and the bathrooms are quiet and empty. Next I climb the stairs to the second floor and do the same with the bathrooms there. It doesn't take long and, when I reach the last one, I finally run into someone: a girl with long, shiny brown hair, big brown eyes, and a heart-shaped face. She is dressed in a cheerleading outfit, primping in front of the mirror as she applies a fresh coat of mascara.

"Hi," I say. "Any chance you know Emily Houston?"

She shoots me a wary look but must not find me too threatening because she says, "I don't know her well but I know who she is. Why?" She turns her attention back to the mirror, chewing on her lower lip as she brushes away a clump of mascara.

Something about her is familiar and after a second it comes to me. "You're Debbie Randall's daughter, Carly, aren't you?"

She turns and gives me a surprised look as she holsters her mascara wand. Then she nods. "Are you a friend of my mom's?"

"I went to school with her. You look just like her and she always chewed on her lip the same way you do."

She stops chewing and swipes at her mouth self-consciously.

"I'm Mattie Winston, used to be Mattie Fjell. Tell your mom I said hi. She and I used to sit next to one another in Mr. Pearson's English class."

"Oh yeah," she says, squinting in thought. "You're the one who works with dead people now, right?"

"Yep, that's me."

"Cool," she says, nodding her approval. Then her expression turns horrified. "Wait, Emily isn't dead, is she?"

"No," I say, but a tiny trill of fear stirs in my chest. "But she's missing and we're trying to figure out where she might be."

"I wouldn't know," she says, dropping the mascara in her purse and rummaging around in there until she comes up with a stick of gum. She makes quick work of the wrapper and pops the gum in her mouth. Then she spares an anxious glance toward the bathroom door and heads that way. "I need to get back to class before I get a detention for being gone too long. Nice to meet you." In a flash, she is out the door.

I walk over to the window at the far end of the bathroom and take a look outside. This particular window looks out over part of the football field, including the home side bleachers, and I flash back on how I and some other girls used to hang here and watch the football players during their practices, mooning and dreaming over how cute and sexy they were. It's a fun, silly memory that makes me smile, but then reality kicks back in. I leave the bathroom and head downstairs and outside, making my way toward the bleachers because I also remember how kids used to hang out on the bleachers—and sometimes beneath and behind them. A lot of tears were shed behind those bleachers, a lot of cigarettes and joints were illicitly smoked back there, and a number of couples solidified their relationships by running the bases back there, too. On the off chance that Emily might be hiding there, I feel compelled to check it out.

She isn't, and after meandering through the parking lot—on foot this time—to the other end of the property where the baseball field and tennis courts are, I feel certain she isn't on the property. I return to the front of the building where Hurley is waiting for me by the car.

"No sign of her on the grounds anywhere," I tell him. "Where do you think she is?"

Hurley runs a hand through his hair, looking perplexed. "I have no idea. Maybe she's finally making good on her threat to run away and join the circus."

"Join the circus? She actually said that?"

"She did, once. It was her response when I asked her what she was going to do for food and shelter after she threatened to run away."

"Fortunately for us, the traveling carnies don't come to town until summertime, so I think we can safely rule that one out. What now?"

Hurley pulls at his chin, looking thoughtful. "I'm going to have some guys at the station try to track her cell. In the meantime, let's get back to our investigation and go talk to this Olsen guy Lars was supposed to meet. You drive."

He tosses me the keys and I slip behind the wheel as he gets on his phone. Despite his attempts to seem unruffled by the whole Emily situation, I can tell he's worried. He's distracted, and that makes it hard to focus on our investigation. So as I pull out, I send a mental message to Emily, knowing it's silly and pointless, but feeling like I need to do something.

Emily, please come home.

Chapter 11

The Sorenson Historical Society and Museum is housed, fittingly, in an old 1800s Victorian home a block off Main Street. Aside from the small, tasteful sign in the front yard, no one would guess that the place was anything other than one of the many ornate Victorian homes in the city. There is an OPEN sign hanging in the window of the front door, and before Hurley and I head inside, we briefly discuss our strategy.

"Let's keep this as a fact-finding mission for now," Hurley says. "Let's see what this guy knows and see if he had any motive or opportunity to do the deed. Bring the camera in case we hit on something and need to conduct a more intense interrogation or search, but for now we can leave it off."

"Got it," I say, hanging the camera around my neck.

We climb onto the porch and enter through the front door. There is no bell to announce our arrival, but sneaking in is out of the question. The old hardwood floors creak, squeak, and groan with every step we take.

In the corner to our right is a desk, but there is no one there at the moment so Hurley and I walk around the room and scan the displays. There are pictures and memorabilia from the founding father of Sorenson, including house and family photos, and some antique toys, dolls, and furnishings. There's also a display of dishes, boxes, and wall hangings featuring the Norwegian art form known as rosemaling, and beside this is a collection of vintage Norwegian clothing, both adult and children's.

In the rooms beyond we can see a vignette of an old-fashioned general store in one and a log cabin in the other. We are about to head into the store vignette when we hear a toilet flush and the creak of a door opening from that direction. A slightly stooped, gray-haired gentleman who looks to be in his seventies comes shuffling through the general store, still working at his fly. He's wearing black slacks, a white shirt, and a red and blue plaid vest, all of which make him look rather dapper. Sorenson has a strong Norwegian heritage and I wonder if his red, white, and blue combo is an attempt at patriotism for America or Norway, since both countries' flags boast the same colors. When the gentleman realizes he isn't alone, he stops short, gapes at us for a few seconds, and then breaks into a smile. He extends his hand to Hurley. Given that we heard a toilet flush seconds ago, but no sound of any other water running, Hurley doesn't offer his hand in exchange. The man seems to realize his gaffe and withdraws his arm.

"Sorry," he says. "A rude oversight. Please forgive me." He wanders over to the desk in the front room and gives himself a couple of squirts of hand sanitizer. As he's rubbing it in, he turns back to us with a big smile and says, "I'm Harry Olsen, the curator here and president of the Sorenson Historical Society. Welcome to our museum. Is there anything in particular you're interested in?"

Olsen looks vaguely familiar to me, though I can't place why yet. The name doesn't ring any bells—not surprising, given that the name Olsen in these parts is more common than Smith or Jones.

Hurley takes out his badge and flashes it. "I'm Detective Steve Hurley with the Sorenson Police Department and this is Mattie Winston with the medical examiner's office. We're interested in the meeting you had scheduled this afternoon with Lars Sanderson."

Olsen spares me a glance during the introduction, but if he knows me, it doesn't show. His smile falters a smidge and he cocks his head to the side. "I wondered why he didn't show. What sort of trouble has Lars stirred up now?"

"What were you supposed to be meeting with him about?" Hurley asks.

Olsen doesn't answer right away. He looks over at me again for a second, before turning back to Hurley. "Why would the police and the medical examiner's office be interested in a meeting I'm having with Lars?"

Hurley loves to answer questions with questions, but at the moment it appears he may have met his match with Olsen.

"Please just answer my question," Hurley says. "What was the topic of your meeting?"

"We were going to discuss some development projects for the city," Olsen says vaguely. I can tell from the look on his face that he's trying to suss out why we're asking him these questions. He gets warmer when he says, "Is someone dead?"

"Yes," Hurley says. "Lars Sanderson."

Olsen doesn't look surprised or particularly upset by this announcement. "What happened?" he asks.

"Did that blowhard finally have a stroke, or a heart attack? I told him a million times that he needed to slow down and learn to take life a little less seriously, but he's one of those guys that only knows how to go full steam ahead."

"Mr. Sanderson was murdered," Hurley says.

All the color drains from Olsen's face. For a moment I fear I'm going to have to resurrect my nursing skills because he has the slightly gray, pasty look of someone who's about to crump. He's breathing fast, and he splays a hand over his chest. With his other hand he reaches behind him and finds the edge of the desk. Then he half staggers, half falls onto it.

"Are you okay, Mr. Olsen?" I ask, hoping he is. A small part of my brain is already running through the steps of CPR, making sure I remember them. While regular CPR training was required by my hospital job and something I used with some regularity when I worked in the ER, I never had to use it during the years I worked in the OR and it's hardly a requirement for my current job.

Olsen doesn't answer right away but I'm reassured by the fact that he's still breathing and moving. Still, I take my phone out, ready to dial 9-1-1 just in case. Movement off to my left distracts me momentarily, and when I glance in that direction I see a black and white cat stroll into the room. Olsen sees the cat, too, and it seems to ground him. He clears his throat—twice—and his color starts to return. "I'm okay," he says, holding the hand that was on his chest out in front of him like a traffic cop trying to stop us. "You just caught me by surprise."

I slip my phone back into my pocket and breathe a little sigh of relief as the cat meanders its way over to Olsen's feet and weaves a path around them.

Hurley takes a step back—he doesn't like cats—and hits Olsen with his next question: "Why were you surprised?" It strikes me as an odd question, but apparently Olsen doesn't think so.

"Well, the murdered part, of course," he says. "When you get to be my age, the news that someone has died is something you get used to. But murder . . . now that's a horse of a different color, isn't it?" He swallows hard and bends down to pet the cat.

"What's the cat's name?" I ask.

"Thor," Olsen says. Then with a wink he adds, "He's the museum caretaker and guard cat."

The idea of a guard cat is absurd enough to make me smile until I look over at Hurley, who is watching Thor with a slightly fearful and wary eye.

Olsen straightens up and looks back at Hurley. "How did it happen, if I may ask?"

Thor heads my way, making Hurley sidestep a few feet. With one eye on Thor, Hurley ignores Olsen's question and fires back with one of his own. "You were supposed to meet with Lars Sanderson at three today, correct?"

"Yes, I was," Olsen says with a sigh.

"Can you be more specific about what you planned to discuss?"

Olsen shakes his head, his lips tight. "Same thing we always talk about: Sanderson's utter lack of respect for the history of this place. Heaven forbid that man would actually try to preserve some of our glorious past. Instead he tromps all over our fine city the way Godzilla did on Tokyo. It's a downright shame some of the things that man has done."

Thor is rubbing against my legs, so I lean down and pick him up. Hurley looks at me like I'm crazy, but I'm not just giving the cat some attention. I want to snag some of his hair. A comparison to the one we found on the arrow may or may not be helpful, but it seems foolish not to get a sample.

"So you were planning on meeting with Lars to discuss these issues in general, or were you going to talk about a particular project?" Hurley asks.

Olsen's eyes dart away from Hurley and he pushes off the desk, momentarily turning his back to us as he heads behind the desk and points to a section of the city map he has hanging on the wall. "There is a piece of land here on the north edge of town that a farmer has offered to sell to the city." He turns back to us, his expression enthused and excited. "I want to develop it into an arts mall that would include shops for making, teaching, and selling artwork . . . anything from painting, wood carving, pottery, stained glass, and metal work to the performing arts like acting and singing. At the core of it all I want to build both an indoor theater for year-round performances and an amphitheater for outdoor concerts and shows. I have an architectural design in mind that would blend in with what the city already has, and I think the level of culture it would bring to Sorenson would be beneficial to our residents, enhance our reputation, and appeal to outsiders. It would bring in more tourist dollars."

"That sounds interesting," I say.

"Of course it is," Olsen says in a tone just shy of condescending. Then his expression turns dour. "But Lars has . . . had a different idea about how to use that land."

Having managed to secure a number of hairs from Thor, I set him back on the floor and he wanders off into one of the rooms. Not knowing what to do with the hairs until I can get to an evidence bag, I keep them in my hand.

"And what was Lars's plan?" Hurley asks.

Olsen shakes his head and looks disgusted. "To create a gated community development with large, cheaply built houses. He thinks that if he can provide big but affordable housing in a setting that appears exclusive, secure, and expensive, that folks will snap them up lickety-split. He says it will attract people who work in Madison but can't afford to live there, and that it will establish Sorenson as a place where people can be part of some ritzy-appearing enclave while still enjoying the perks of small-town living." He pauses and shakes his head woefully. "It's a ridiculous idea, of course, like all of his other projects. It would completely undermine the historic nature of our town and offer nothing to improve our culture. Not to mention that his building practices are often downright shoddy."

Olsen's face has grown redder by the minute, and he's incensed enough that by the end of his little speech he is spraying spittle, though the fact that he has loose dentures might be contributing to this. He seems to realize he's being a bit overzealous and has the good sense to look abashed.

Hurley walks over to the doorway of the log cabin vignette, giving Olsen a few seconds to recover. "I've heard it's going to be a banner year for the deer hunt," he says in an easy, friendly tone. "Do you hunt, Mr. Olsen?"

"Of course I do. It's a tradition in these parts, and I'm always in favor of preserving tradition," he says with a smile.

"What do you typically hunt?"

"Well, I participate in the deer hunt every year, and I used to do duck season, too, though in recent years I've been less religious about that one. I'm also an avid fisherman, though only in the warmer months.

I've given up on the ice fishing. These old bones don't take to the cold very well anymore."

"Is that your trophy?" Hurley asks, nodding toward a deer head on the wall in the vignette room.

"It is," Olsen says with a smile. "Caught that eight-point buck about ten years ago and had it stuffed. It's been hanging on that wall ever since. It fits in well with the cabin theme, so I figured I'd donate it to the museum." He pauses and winces. "And to be honest, I didn't care to have those eyes staring down at me in my home. Don't get me wrong. I love the sport of the hunt, but I try to have respect for the creatures I'm killing."

"That's a bit of an oxymoron, isn't it?" I say, feeling irritated. "You respect the animals so much that you kill them?"

Hurley shoots me a look that tells me to hush up and back off. Then he looks over at Olsen and shakes his head. "Women . . . they don't get it, do they?"

"Most don't," Olsen agrees. "My wife was the same way."

I try shooting eye death rays at both men but they are ignoring me.

"What do you hunt with?" Hurley asks in a sociable tone.

Olsen looks momentarily puzzled. "*What* or *who?*"

"Actually both," Hurley answers with a smile. "Tell me what first."

"Well, in recent years I've tried out some of these newfangled, high-power rifles some of the guys use, but to be honest, I prefer to hunt old school. I have an older rifle, a Winchester that I've used off and on for years. But during the deer hunt, I prefer to use my bow. I believe it gives the animals more of a fighting chance and levels the field a little. I don't want to stack the odds too much in my favor. Some of these fancy guns they use nowadays take all the sport out of the hunt."

"Do you use a crossbow?" Hurley asks.

Olsen makes a face and shakes his head. "Don't like them. I have a compound bow and a regular old-fashioned bow. Frankly, I prefer the old-fashioned one most of the time."

"A bow and arrow," Hurley says with a grudging look of admiration that I know is faked. "That takes some talent and practice."

"My father taught me when I was a boy," Olsen says with obvious pride. "And his father taught him. A family tradition handed down through the generations."

"It sounds like fun," Hurley says with a friendly smile. "Does anyone else around here hunt with a bow and arrow?"

"Sure," Olsen says. "Several guys I know here in town use bows."

"Anyone you can recommend?" Hurley asks. "I'd like to hook up with someone who's good with the arrows. That's the way I prefer to go, too. Like you said, it seems fairer and more sporting that way."

"Bo Jurgenson is quite good. Better than me, though I'd never admit it to his face. I've been out with him a time or two in years past. You can probably find him over at Swenson's hardware store on Third Street. His brother-in-law owns the place and Bo works the afternoon and evening shift there. Bo actually makes arrows for some of the locals and he teaches archery. Dan Hooper is good, too, and he's a diehard bow and arrow man. He's a car salesman over at Kohler's Used Cars but I don't think he's there now. He typically takes a week off during deer season and goes north."

"Thanks," Hurley says, writing down the names. "Have you been out yet this season?"

Olsen nods and smiles. "Sure enough. I went out yesterday with a couple of friends, old farts like myself. Didn't bag anything, though."

"How about today?"

Olsen shakes his head. "Nah, my bones were aching too much, and it's damned cold out there." He shoots me an apologetic look. "Sorry for the language, miss. That one slipped out."

"No problem," I say with a forced smile.

"Anyway, like I said before, these old bones don't take to the cold much anymore and frankly all that walking around tends to inflame my bad hip. Broke it a few years back, and while it works good enough since they fixed it, it gets right cranky when the weather turns. Besides, I had to open up the museum here."

Now I know why Olsen looks familiar. I was on his case when he had his hip repaired.

Thor meanders his way back into the room, making Hurley sidestep again. I realize that anyone entering the museum might end up with cat hair on them and wonder if Olsen keeps a log of visitors.

"Do you have a guest book, Mr. Olsen?"

"Sure do," he says. He points to a book on his desk and I walk over and open it up, scrolling through to the first empty page with my free hand. The most recent people who signed in came two weeks ago, and they listed their home town as Lancaster, Pennsylvania. "Does everyone who comes in here sign in?" I ask.

"I try to get them to, but I can't force them. Most of the out-of-towners do. None of the locals do."

So much for the guest book being of any help.

Hurley says, "Mr. Olsen, can you tell me where you were this morning between the hours of five and eight?"

Olsen stares at Hurley, and after a few seconds he huffs out a little breath of shock and annoyance. "Are you suggesting that I have something to do with Lars being killed?"

"I'm not suggesting anything," Hurley says with amazing patience. "I'm simply asking you a question."

Olsen glares at him, clearly affronted by the implication. "If you must know," he says, tugging at his vest, "I was at home. I came here to open up shop at ten."

"Is there someone who can verify that?" Hurley asks, further incensing Olsen.

"No, there is not," Olsen says, tight-lipped. "I'm a widower and I live alone."

"I'd like to take a look at your archery equipment," Hurley says, smiling in an effort to win back Olsen's trust. But it's too late.

Olsen narrows his eyes and stares at Hurley. "You're not asking about bow hunting because you're interested in doing it, are you?" he says. "Is that how Lars was killed? With an arrow?"

Hurley doesn't answer. He simply looks back at Olsen and lets the silence tick by.

Olsen shakes his head in irritation. "I'm not giving anybody my archery equipment. And if you have any other questions for me, I suggest you call my lawyer. I'll be happy to write down his name for you." He grabs a pen and notepad from the desktop.

"That won't be necessary," Hurley says, and for a few seconds, Olsen looks smug. But his expression rapidly falters when Hurley adds, "You can just bring him with you to the police station the next time we talk. I'll be in touch."

As Hurley and I leave, I can feel the heat of Olsen's glare burning through my back, and my mind conjures up an image of an arrow following the same track.

Chapter 12

I toss the keys at Hurley a little harder than is necessary and, as we settle into the car, I slam my door and give him a dirty look. "What was that comment about women and hunting all about?"

"Sorry. I didn't mean anything by it. I just didn't want you to get Olsen off topic."

"Well, it was kind of insulting."

Hurley looks over at me and sighs. "Is this an example of those hormones you keep talking about?"

My glare turns icier. "Seriously?" I say, scowling at him. "Just because I stick up for some poor defenseless animal and take a stance on a subject, I'm being hormonal?"

"Not then, but maybe now?" Hurley bites his lip and leans back against the driver side door. He looks like he's ready to bolt from the car at any moment, just in case my hormonal blast goes nuclear.

Now it's my turn to sigh. "I'm sorry," I say, "but I can't justify hunting down and killing an animal for sport. If people were dependent upon hunting for food, it would be different."

"You'll get no argument from me. Unless we're talking about cats."

Hurley's comment is clearly an attempt to make me smile. It works. "Speaking of cats, I got a sample of Thor's fur," I tell him, pulling my hand from my pocket. I reach into the glove box where I know Hurley keeps extra evidence bags and place the fur in one. As I'm sealing and labeling it, Hurley checks his phone again and frowns. "Have you ever hunted?" I ask him, hoping to divert him from the Emily problem.

"Nothing four-legged," he answers with a wink and a wicked grin.

"Okay, fair enough. What did you make of Mr. Olsen?"

"He's a bit of a zealot with the history stuff," Hurley says, looking relieved to have the status quo restored. He starts the car and cranks up the heater. "But I don't think he's enough of one to kill someone over it. What did you think?"

"I'm not sure. He does have a cat with some black fur on it."

Hurley nods slowly. "Unfortunately the cat hair just complicates things. Anyone who visited that museum could have picked up a cat hair. So as far as I'm concerned, we're back at square one." His phone rings then and I pray it's Emily. But when he sighs and answers with "What's up?" I know it's not.

I wait as he takes the call, my curiosity burning, wishing I could hear whoever is on the other end because Hurley isn't saying much. It's a thankfully brief call, and after saying, "Thanks," and disconnecting, he fills me in.

"That was Jonas," he says. "We got a hit on that print we found on Lars's neck."

"Really? Whose is it?"

"It belongs to your friend George Haas. Sounds like there might be a little more to his story than what he told his buddy at the convenience store." He glances at his watch. "Haas was out hunting pretty early this morning. Think he might be back home by now?"

"Maybe, but that's assuming he comes home at all. A lot of these guys have cabins they sleep in overnight, like that one you and I stayed in last year. And George is not my friend; he's just an acquaintance. Someone I grew up with."

"O-kay," Hurley says slowly, shooting me a dubious look.

"You'll understand my distinction once you meet him."

"Ah, one of those," Hurley says with a knowing smile. "I can't wait."

The Haas farm is located about two miles outside of town on the west side. It's a livestock farm that used to raise dairy and beef cows, but now houses pigs and chickens. Like many of the other farmers in the area, the Haas family was forced to sell off some of their property in years past in order to keep food on the table and a roof over their heads. Their best grazing fields were the most valuable and salable plats and they, along with the cows, were whittled away over time. Now all the Haas family has left is a ten-acre field that's too rocky to grow anything, fifty acres of wooded land, and an unpleasant aroma that hangs in the air year-round and occasionally drifts into town if the winds are right.

The family home is a typical Wisconsin farmhouse: two stories, once-white clapboard siding in need of paint, and a yard littered with ancient rusted trucks and farm implements. I think there was a law at one time that required farmhouses to be painted white because you hardly ever see any other color, the same way the barns are all red.

The Haas barn is the requisite red color—at least most of it is, because it, like the house, is badly in need of a paint job. We hear the grunts, snuffles, and occasional squeals of the pigs coming from within. There are several other ramshackle buildings around the house, and a fenced-in mud pit that I assume is the pigs' play area.

Hurley grabs his camera and takes a moment to film the house, the barn, the other outbuildings, and the surrounding area. When he's done he turns the camera off and we climb creaky wooden steps onto a large, covered front porch that is furnished with a ragged, torn old couch, the requisite rocking chair, and a small, rusted, wrought-iron table. Several lawn chairs are folded up and leaning against a wall. The front door has a window in the top half of it that's covered with a lace curtain that was probably white at one time but is now a shade of dingy gray. There is no doorbell, so Hurley knocks on the glass.

We can hear the approach of someone inside—a series of heavy footfalls accompanied by the squeak of old floorboards. A vague shape appears behind the curtain, pauses for a moment, and then the door opens, allowing the figure to materialize into a rotund woman of about sixty with steel-gray hair pulled into a bun. She is wearing overalls with a plaid flannel shirt beneath, and mud-rucking boots.

"What can I do ya for?" she asks. Her face is a road map of farm history, etched and carved from time, the elements, and hard work. But her icy blue eyes look lively and alert. I'm betting she doesn't miss much.

"Mrs. Haas?" Hurley says.

"Yeah, what of it?"

"I'm Detective Steve Hurley with the Sorenson Police Department and this is Mattie Winston with the medical examiner's office. We're here to talk to George."

"What you want with my son?" she asks, those eyes narrowing to a steely glint.

"It's regarding an investigation we're conducting."

Mrs. Haas, whose first name is Irma, shifts her gaze to me. "Who's dead?" she asks.

"What makes you ask that?" Hurley says.

She gives him an impatient look. "Do I look stupid, Detective? I know Mattie here works with Doc Izzy and they cut open dead people. So it doesn't take a rocket scientist to figure out that you're here because someone is dead."

"Is George here?" Hurley asks, ignoring her comeback.

"He might be," she says cagily. "Or not. Depends."

Irma has a reputation for being tough as nails and meaner than a badger. And everyone in Wisconsin—and a few colleges around the country—know that badgers can be downright nasty. I know she isn't going to cave easily. So I decide to take a gamble.

"Irma, we can go back and get a search warrant for your place, one that would include the coop. Or you can go and fetch George for us so we can talk to him. It's up to you."

I have no idea if we could actually get a search warrant, but I learned long ago that lying is not only allowed in police investigations, it's frequently encouraged. And I know that Irma thinks the hidden basement beneath her barn is a big secret. George once brought a girl named Angela to that space back when he was in high school, hoping for a little base running. And a week later, during a small slumber party, Angela told me and two other friends all about it. She told us how the entrance to the basement was kept hidden beneath some hay bales, and that the family referred to the space as the coop. She knew this not only because that's what George called it, but because that's what she heard Irma call it, too. That's because Irma had found the two of them down there and had a major meltdown right around the time George was rounding on third base. Irma wasn't upset that George and some girl were half-naked and planning to do the naughty, however, she was upset because George had brought an outsider into the coop.

Angela had been sworn to secrecy, something she readily agreed to because she was embarrassed and eager to escape, and because Irma was an even more frightening force back then than she is now. The only reason Angela told us about it at the slumber party was because she was scared to death of Irma and what she might do to ensure her secret didn't get out. Angela wanted someone else to know—kind of like an insurance policy—and with typical teenaged überdrama, we all agreed to keep it a secret unless Irma had Angela rubbed out. So in the end, there were four of us who knew: me, Angela, and two other friends named Linda and Marta. Sadly, Linda and Marta were killed in a car accident the following year, and Angela moved out to California during our senior year, leaving me as the sole local keeper of the secret as far as I know.

In recent years I've heard rumors that the Haas family is growing and selling pot to augment the income they earn from their pigs, chickens, and eggs. I don't know if it's true, but it's not hard to imagine that barn basement outfitted with some growing lights and garden beds. And given the annoyed and calculating look on Irma's face, I think I might be right. Her lips thin down to a narrow hard line and her eyes fire icicles at me.

"George is sleeping upstairs. He was up early this morning for the hunt. Wait here and I'll fetch him." She slams the door in our faces, leaving us standing on the porch in the cold. That polite Midwest hospitality that so many hear about tends to disappear when you threaten people's families and livelihoods.

"I'm not sure she's going to come back," Hurley says, checking his cell phone.

"I think she will. Give it a minute."

A chorus of squeals emanates from the barn and oddly I feel my milk let down. My boobs begin to ache and as I shiver from the cold, my mind conjures up an image of milksicles hanging off my chest.

I try to shake it off, a little spooked by it. Ever since giving birth, my brain has conjured up all kinds of weird—and sometimes scary—thoughts and images, like that arrow coming at my back when we left the museum. It's as if my newly acquired state of motherhood has opened the door to some dark recess in my brain that was previously sealed and confined. I've imagined all kinds of horrible things that might happen to Matthew, to me, or to Hurley, everything from diseases, pestilence, kidnappings, and worse. It got bad enough that I mentioned it to my doctor, who decided I was experiencing normal mommy angst coupled with a touch of postpartum depression. She prescribed something for me to elevate my mood, but I haven't taken it yet. I'm worried about the effects of the medication on Matthew if it gets into my breast milk. The doctor assured me it was considered safe, but I know what a snow job some of the drug companies can do and I'd rather not risk it. Then again, maybe this concern is just one more dark manifestation, another unrealistic fear conjured up by my mommy-addled brain.

Speaking of addled brains, George appears at the door looking sleepy-eyed and dull. His hair is sticking up in the back, and there are at least three parts I can see in the front. His left cheek is creased from lying on something, and he's putting the finishing touches on a huge yawn as he stops in front of us. The exhalation of his breath hits me square in the face and it's almost enough to make me gag. Trips to the dentist don't appear to be high on George's list of priorities.

"Momma said you guys want to talk to me?" he says, scratching at a roll of belly that's poking out from beneath his yellowed, wife-beater tee.

"Mr. Haas, you went out hunting this morning, correct?" Hurley asks.

"Yeah. So? I got a license. I can show it to ya if ya want."

"Where were you between five and eight this morning?"

George ignores Hurley's question and shifts his gaze to me. "Hey, you're Mattie Fjell, aren't ya?"

"More or less," I say. I've been considering changing my name back to my maiden name now that I'm divorced, but the task has been on a back burner for a while. The paperwork is a headache, and if Hurley and I ever do get married, I'd just have to change it again. Besides, I've never been fond of my maiden name.

"Oh, right," George says, dragging out the last word. "You married some fancy doctor up at the hospital, didn't ya? Heard it didn't turn out so well for ya."

George may not be the sharpest tool in the shed, but he is a master of understatement. "George, can you please answer the detective's question?" I say in an irritated tone.

George's brow furrows, magnifying the Neanderthal ridge he has in his forehead. I can tell he's figuring something out, and for a second I swear I can smell burning rubber from those wheels spinning in his head. "Wait," he says slowly. "You work for that death doctor now, don't ya?" He nods vigorously in answer to his own question and with his flat, splayed nose, prominent brow ridge, and sloping forehead, he looks like a prehistoric bobblehead doll. "This is about that guy I found out in Cooper's Woods, isn't it? Did that damned idiot Axel squeal?"

With that question, I know who George was talking to at the convenience store. Axel Nilsson is another of my ex-classmates, a Sorenson lifer, and George's lifelong friend. They are of a similar caliber mentally, although Axel hasn't been as lucky when it comes to skirting the long arm of the law. He's been busted several times for possession with intent to sell.

"Tell me about it," Hurley says.

"Ain't nothing to tell," George says with a shrug. "Saw the guy all stretched out on the ground with an arrow in his neck. Figured someone would report it, and I was on the trail of a ten-pointer. I checked to make sure he was dead and didn't need the meat wagon."

"You checked?" Hurley says with a questioning arch of one eyebrow.

"Yeah, I felt on his neck for a pulse even though I was pretty sure he was a goner, given all the blood and the way his eyes were staring up at the sky."

Hurley clenches his jaw and sighs heavily.

"What?" George says, looking back and forth between me and Hurley. "I didn't break no law, did I?"

Hurley ignores the question and comes back with one of his own. "Do you hunt with a bow and arrow?"

George grins, revealing his dentition challenges, and holds up a hand. "Kind of hard to do that with this," he says, revealing the one remaining finger and thumb he has on his right hand. "Heck, I have a hard time just pulling a trigger."

"Right," Hurley says with another sigh. "Did you see anyone else out there this morning?"

"Saw that ten-pointer. Almost bagged him, too. But if you mean other people, nope. I didn't see anyone. Heard something though."

"What?" Hurley asks, clearly impatient.

"Sounded like one of them four-wheeler recreational vehicles," George says. "You know, an ATM."

"ATV," I correct.

"Whatever," George replies with an impatient wave of his hand.

"Did you see the ATV?" I ask.

George shakes his head. "Nope, just heard it."

"Where was it?" I ask with a friendly smile. I can tell Hurley's level of patience has worn painfully thin. He is shifting back and forth from one foot to the other and he's glanced at his watch at least three times in the last minute. George has sensed it, too, and I can tell he's about to clam up.

"Sounded like it was over in the field off to the east, by that stream."

I know where he means. There are several small tributaries of the river that runs through town that meander through surrounding fields. One of them divides what used to be the Cooper farmland and runs through Cooper's Woods.

"We should check that area for ATV tracks," I say to Hurley, hoping to get him refocused.

He nods absentmindedly, takes out his cell phone, and looks at it.

Sensing that Hurley is hopelessly lost for the moment, I tell George, "When you find someone dead, you need to report it."

"I will from now on," George says with a vigorous nod and a big smile. "I swear. It's just that I really wanted that buck."

"Did you get him?"

"Not yet, but tomorrow is another day," he says with high optimism. He gives me a quick head-to-toe perusal and pushes his optimistic outlook a little further. "Say, did you get married again after ditching that doctor, or are you available?"

"Not married, and not looking to be," I say. I half expect Hurley to react to this, but he doesn't.

"Well, how about a date? No harm in that, is there? I'll even spring for dinner."

I give his invitation a split second of serious consideration, only because going out for anything right now sounds like a dream, even if I had George for a dinner companion. Then I shake it off, realizing how sad my social life has become. The only thing going out in my house these days is my garbage.

"Thanks, George, but I'm kind of seeing someone." I glance at Hurley, hoping he'll support my claim, but he's still distracted by his phone. Besides, if I'm looking for confirmation of seeing anyone, I'd have better luck with my UPS guy. "Got any trophies from past hunts?" I ask to change the subject and hopefully get Hurley refocused. The Haas farm strikes me as just the sort of creepy place for a bunch of stuffed animals. I wouldn't be surprised to discover that George does his own taxidermy. And I'm trying to find an excuse to get invited inside to see if the Haas house serves as home to any black cats.

"Yeah, we got a twelve-pointer hanging in the living room that my daddy killed years ago when I was a boy. Haven't seen another one like him since. That's why I was hoping to bag that ten-pointer. Not as good, but it would be close and I know my daddy would be smiling down at me from heaven."

"Can I see it?"

George shrugs. "Don't see why not." He steps aside and waves me inside. I look back at Hurley, expecting him to follow, but he's gazing off in the distance.

"Hurley, you coming?"

He waves me off. "You go ahead. I'll wait out here."

To say I'm stymied is an understatement. George isn't *Deliverance* material, but he's not far from it. I can't believe Hurley is letting me go inside this house alone. With a little shake of my head, I square my shoulders, and venture into the unknown.

The Haas family home smells like a mixture of hay and stale cooking oil, though there is a subtle hint of manure underlying the main aroma. From the entry foyer I can see a dining room off to the right, and beyond it a kitchen that looks like it hasn't been remodeled since the fifties. To the left is the living room, which is furnished with two couches—both of which are covered with handmade afghans, and one of which is at a tilt and missing its right legs—and two stuffed chairs covered in some sort of worn, rose-colored brocade. The flooring is wide pine boards, nicked, stained, and scarred along the perimeter I can see, the middle section covered by an oval, rag rug. A huge stone fireplace on one wall has a big soot smear up the front of it, and there are several burn marks on the floor in front of the hearth. Someone has laid a fire ready to light. On the far wall, perpendicular to the fireplace is a wooden flatbed wagon, the hitch end propped up on an old, metal milk can. The boards of the wagon look ancient and brittle, ready to ignite should a spark from the fireplace make it that far, and barely strong enough to support the TV sitting on it. The TV looks like it's from the 1980s—big, boxy body with a small screen. There's no cable service out here in the country so there isn't much reason to have a modern TV. Hanging on the wall above the TV is the promised deer head.

I half expect to find Irma lurking somewhere, but she's nowhere in sight. So I brace myself and settle my gaze on the deer head. I hate seeing trophies like this but I have to admit that whoever preserved it did a great job. The glass eyes look warm and friendly, the fur begs to have a hand run through it, and the stately antlers loom proud and powerful above it all. He was a handsome, majestic beast in his time, and seeing his head mounted like this makes me want to cry.

"Pretty impressive, isn't it?" George says.

I nod, afraid to speak, and turn away. "Got any pets, George?"

"Naw, not really. There's a bunch of cats out in the barn to help keep the mice in check, and we used to have a mutt named Brutus here in the house, but he got some kind of cancer last year and dropped right there in front of the fireplace." George looks sad and shakes his head. "He was a good hunting dog, too."

I make my way back to the front door and George follows on my heels. When I reach the porch, I see Hurley pacing at the foot of the stairs. I look over at the barn thinking that we should probably check it out, too. Then, as if on cue, three cats come scampering out of the barn: one yellow tabby, one calico, and one black and white cat. I'm starting to think that black cats really are a jinx.

I thank George and tell him good-bye as I descend the steps. "We'll be in touch if we have any more questions."

I grab Hurley's arm and steer him back toward the car. "Give me your keys," I tell him. He does so without question. "Still no word from Emily?" I ask rhetorically.

He shakes his head, his face a mask of worry.

"Hurley, I think you need to pass this investigation off to someone else for now, and go look for her. You're obviously distracted and concerned, and I'm sure Richmond can take over for you."

"Yeah, maybe I should."

Hurley's quick capitulation worries me. His investigations are always a priority. The fact that he's willing to hand it off so easily tells me how concerned he is.

"Is there something you're not telling me?" I ask. "Has Emily been talking suicide or anything like that?"

Hurley shakes his head. "No, it's just my gut. I have a bad feeling."

In the time that I've known Hurley I've learned that his gut is pretty darned trustworthy.

"Do you want to have Richmond call George in for more questioning?" I ask him. "We do have his fingerprint on the dead man's neck. And I don't know if you noticed it or not, but there are at least two cats on the property that have black fur—a calico and a black and white one."

Hurley squints up at the sky and shakes his head. "Not yet. Haas's explanation is plausible, and without any other evidence, we don't have anything on him. Besides, with his fingers the way they are, he couldn't have shot a bow and arrow. If something else comes up, we can always come back. Let him think he's off the hook for now so he doesn't try to disappear."

I start the car and head back to the main road. "Call Richmond and ask him to take over this case for you for now."

Hurley nods and punches in Richmond's number. I listen to Hurley's half of the call, a bit spooked by the underlying current of dread I can hear in his voice when he explains to Richmond what's going on with Emily. When he's done with the call, he says, "Drive back to the station and we'll hook up with Richmond there. They've just brought all of Sanderson's home files in for Jonas to start digging through, and Richmond says you and he can start interviewing the girlfriends."

"What are you going to do?"

"I'm going to drive around and look for Emily. I'll check back at the house again. Maybe she just went off somewhere to be by herself for a while before she headed home."

"We should probably check the hospital," I suggest. "Just to make sure nothing has happened to her."

Hurley looks panicked by the idea, and he takes out his phone and calls the hospital ER. I listen in as he asks if Emily is there. After listening for a moment, he then says, "But I'm her father and I'm concerned about her because she's missing. Can't you just tell me if she's there or not?"

I can tell from his rapidly reddening face that he isn't making any progress and I think I know why. He confirms my suspicion once he disconnects the call. "Stupid privacy laws," he mutters. "Whoever that was on the phone told me that they can't reveal the presence of anyone in the ER over the phone."

"That's because they've been tricked before by people who say they're someone other than who they are so they can get info. So they won't say one way or another. They either let the patient make the calls, or if the patient can't, they'll get the cops involved. But I think I know a way to get around it." I take out my phone, dial the ER number, and ask if my ex-coworker and good friend Phyllis—aka Syph—is working in the ER. I breathe a sigh of relief when I find out she is, and when she comes on the phone, I tell her what I need.

"Emily isn't here and hasn't been here," Phyllis says. "If she does show up, I'll call you. Good luck. These darned teenagers can be a handful." I thank her, and as I'm about to disconnect the call, she asks how Matthew is doing and when I'm going to come by and show him off to her and the rest of the staff.

"Soon," I promise. "I'm just getting my feet wet with being back to work. Once I get a little more organized, I'll come by." She finally lets me go and after I've disconnected the call, I pass the information along to Hurley that Emily isn't and hasn't been there.

"Okay, that's good," he says. "At least I think it is."

I shoot him a curious look.

"It's not that I'd want anything to happen to her," he clarifies. "But at least if she was there we'd know where she is."

We arrive at the police station and, as we head inside, Hurley checks his phone for the umpteenth time. I can tell he's growing more concerned by the minute and his worry is contagious. I'm starting to feel a real sense of dread and urgency, as much toward Hurley as Emily.

"Hurley, hold on," I say before we enter the building. "Richmond can handle this investigation without me and I'm worried about you. Why don't I come with you?"

"Thanks, but I don't think it's a good idea. I'd love

to have you along, but I think it's best if you're not with me when I find her . . . assuming I do."

He's probably right, given that I'm an unwelcome complication in Emily's life right now, but I still feel a bit slighted at being left out. "I understand," I say, "but I want you to promise that you'll call me as soon as you know something. And call me later anyway even if you don't. Okay?"

He nods and I lean over to give him a kiss on the cheek. He doesn't kiss me back, but I'm not bothered by the fact. What does bother me is the war going on inside my head. Part of me is fuming at Emily for all the stunts she has pulled and the crap she has put us through. Another part of me empathizes with what she's gone through. And yet another part of me is worried sick that this isn't one of her usual stunts, and that something really bad has happened to her this time.

Chapter 13

We find Richmond sitting at his desk and happy to help—he and Hurley typically work as a team these days anyway—and half an hour later we are all up to speed on the various aspects of the investigation.

Richmond informs us that Jonas and Laura are going through the contents of Lars's office and that, unfortunately, the crew we left behind in the woods this morning didn't find any useful trace evidence, nor did they find anyone in the wooded area who might have been a witness.

"There were people out there, though," he says. "There are still patches of snow on the ground in some places, and they were able to see footprints. They did some photos and casts of them, but Junior said they weren't very clear and he doesn't think they'll be much help."

Hurley tells Richmond about our conversation with George Haas and suggests that Richmond compare the footprints to Haas's shoes. "It's unlikely the guy could have shot the arrow given his hand limitations, but we know he was out there and he might have had an accomplice. While you're at it, we should also have them look for ATV tracks," Hurley adds. "Haas said he heard one off in the distance. Don't know if it's at all significant, but we should probably check it out."

Richmond looks out the window of his office and frowns. "It's almost dark so we might have to let that one wait until morning. And in case you didn't already guess this from my silence on the matter, our search of Morton's house didn't turn up anything either. No bows, no arrows, not so much as a piece of hay. So far we're scoring a big fat zero on this one."

"Maybe something will pan out with the girlfriends," Hurley says, offering up his notebook so Richmond can copy down the names, addresses, and phone numbers. "We had a chat with Kirsten Donaldson already because she made a surprise visit to Lars's house while we were there." He then fills Richmond in on what we learned from and about Kirsten, finishing with "We should check around with her neighbors to see if anyone can verify that she was home this morning. And her ex-husband, Brad, is a potential suspect, too. Sounds like he has a jealous streak, and if he's still carrying a torch for Kirsten, he might have wanted Sanderson dead."

"Kirsten herself might be worth another chat at some point," I add, "if for no other reason than just to see if she has a cat." We then fill Richmond in on the cat hair evidence and spend a few minutes discussing the evidentiary worth—or lack thereof—of the find.

We then place a call to Jonas and ask him if he has anything more for us. As we listen on speakerphone, he tells us that he ran the plates of the other vehicles that were parked out along the road by Cooper's Woods, and he gives us the names of the registered owners. "I also ran the calls on the cell phone we found in Sanderson's pocket," Jonas says. "He had several calls yesterday, the last one around nine o'clock last night from a Harry Olsen. But no calls in or out today. The other calls were all initiated by Sanderson and appear to be work related. One was to the mayor yesterday morning, another was to a guy named Chuck Obermeyer. He's a local contractor. The other two calls were to lumber supply companies. I'll send you up a report on the calls in a bit. I'm getting ready to take a closer look at Sanderson's car and I've got some guys going through those files we retrieved from Sanderson's offices. If anything else comes up I'll let you know."

Hurley tells Jonas to call Richmond with the updates for now, thanks him, and disconnects the call. Then he points to one of the names he has written in his notebook. "Lars was supposed to meet this Chuck Obermeyer for dinner at six tonight at Pesto Change-o," he tells Richmond. "Here's his contact info. You should probably talk to him if for no other reason than to rule him out." Richmond nods and dutifully copies down the info. "I appreciate you helping out with this," Hurley says when Richmond is done and hands him back his notebook. "I have to go, but keep me posted."

"Will do. And good luck."

After Hurley assures me he'll call me later to let me know what's going on, he heads out.

Richmond looks at me and says, "He seems pretty worked up about Emily this time. What's different?"

Richmond is a shrewd judge of character and he's got a real talent for reading people. He doesn't miss much. "It's his gut. He says Emily always contacts him in some way shortly after one of her disappearing acts, but this time she hasn't. He has a feeling something is wrong."

"If Hurley has a gut feeling, he's usually right. Hope the kid is okay."

"Yeah, me, too."

"So it looks like we need to track down Lars's girlfriends and talk to them." He glances at his watch. "It's going on five already. How late can you work today?"

"I have an appointment to get my hair done at seven tonight. Dom is staying with Matthew for the evening, so I'm good to go until six forty-five or so."

"Okay, then, let's start with . . ." Richmond consults the names he copied out of Hurley's notebook. "Why don't we call them first and see where they are?" he says. "It's that time of day when some people might be getting off work, especially with Thanksgiving right around the corner. Plus, with Christmas coming, people are going to be sneaking out of work early so they can go shopping. Let me see who's available for us to talk to."

Christmas. Normally it's a holiday I dread. I hate shopping. I hate trying to come up with gift ideas for people who don't want or need anything. I'm not into all that decorating stuff, either, though I usually cave enough to buy a tree and string a few lights on it, typically getting one of those ugly Charlie Brown trees that no one else will want.

But this year is different. Now I have Matthew. Granted, he's too young to understand or comprehend much, but his presence has imbued me with a new interest in the holiday. Unfortunately, his presence has also left me with much less free time for things like shopping, tree hunting, and decorating. But once again Amazon has come to the rescue. Not only have I been able to whittle down my gift list already, I also bought a Christmas tree and all the trimmings to go with it. My sister, Desi, is hosting Thanksgiving dinner this year and all I'm supposed to bring is dessert. I've arranged to have a cheesecake and a pumpkin pie made for me by one of our local restaurants, Dairy Airs. But I wouldn't be surprised to find that I can order an entire Thanksgiving meal from Amazon and have it delivered right to my door. Online shopping has definitely lessened my holiday pressures.

Speaking of pressure, I need to go and pump, so I leave Richmond to make the calls and head over to my office to do the deed. I poke my head into Izzy's office before I head back out and update him on what we've done and learned so far, and what we're doing next. Then I tell him about Emily.

"Hurley is really worried about her, much more so than I've ever seen before."

"Let's hope he's wrong," Izzy says. He frowns and shakes his head. "It's situations like this one that make me think the idea of having kids isn't a good one."

"No one ever said raising kids is kicks and giggles all the time, though I do think the pluses outweigh the minuses. And keep in mind, this situation with Emily is a unique one. That poor kid has been through a lot lately. Hell, I'd be more surprised if she *wasn't* acting out."

"I'm guessing it isn't helping your situation with Hurley much."

"That's an understatement."

"Anything I can do to help?"

"Not that I can think of, but thanks for asking." I start to leave, but then turn back. "By the way, did Dom tell you he's keeping Matthew for me until around nine o'clock tonight so I can go and get my hair done?"

"He did."

"Is that okay?"

Izzy smiles. "It is, and may I also say it's for a very worthy cause."

"Yeah, I'm really overdue," I say, grimacing and running a hand over the still-stiff strands of hair. "Thanks, and I'll see you later."

By the time I return to the police station, Richmond has our agenda laid out. We're going now to chat with one of Lars's girlfriends, a woman named Cynthia Parker. The other one, Bridget Rutherford, is going to come into the station in the morning.

"By the time we're done talking to Cynthia Parker we can head to Pesto Change-o," Richmond says. "You want to ride with me?"

"Normally I'd say yes, but given what's going on with Emily, would you mind if I took my own car? I'd like to be able to leave if I need to."

"I don't mind, but you might want to park it out of sight for our first stop. Cynthia Parker works at that new Serenity Spa that just opened up over on the east side of town. I'm thinking they might frown on the idea of having a hearse parked in their lot."

I nod my understanding. My midnight blue, slightly used hearse was the only vehicle I could afford when I bought it and I was desperate for some wheels. I thought it would be temporary, but I've grown to love the thing. It's roomy, it drives like a dream, my dog, Hoover, loves all the smells in it, and when I was being stalked by a crazed killer a few months back, Hurley had the thing pimped out like the Popemobile with bulletproof glass and reinforced body panels. It's my safe house. But I understand Richmond's reservations. A hearse might imply a bit more serenity than most spa clients are looking for.

Richmond says, "I left a message for this Chuck Obermeyer. If he doesn't call back by five forty-five, we can head to Pesto Change-o and catch him there."

"I wouldn't mind going to Pesto either way," I say, rubbing my tummy. "I'm getting hungry and Italian is my favorite food group."

"Mine, too," Richmond says with a dreamy smile. He and I are both foodies at heart. "Though I'll probably have to do two extra circuits at the gym to make up for whatever I eat there."

"I have to say, Richmond, I really respect how dedicated you are to your new healthy lifestyle. All your hard work is really paying off. You look fantastic."

"I feel fantastic," he says. "Frankly, that's more motivation for me than how I look."

"Are you sure?" I ask, giving him a sly smile. "The rumor mill has it that you're getting hot and heavy with a certain divorcee we both know."

Richmond blushes. The divorcee in question is one Rose Carpenter, someone we met during an investigation we conducted last September. "We're taking it slow," he says. "Or at least I am. She keeps pushing and I keep putting on the brakes."

"Why? What are you afraid of?"

"It's not fear, it's more . . . I don't know . . . reluctance I suppose. I've never really had a serious, long-term relationship with a woman, and while there are certain perks to being half of a couple, I've been on my own for so long that I don't know if I want to change that."

"And Rose is pushing for the change?"

He nods and rolls his eyes.

"Have you slept with her yet?"

Richmond's blush deepens and he looks away. "Not yet," he says. "Though it's not due to a lack of effort on her part."

"What's holding you back?"

He looks at his feet and shoves his hands in his pockets. "I'm not . . . I haven't . . . I don't have a lot of experience." Richmond is so red now, his face could work as a police light on his car. "It's been twenty years," he says.

"Oh."

"Yeah, oh," he says with a snort of derision. "And I wasn't exactly a lothario prior to that, if you get my drift."

"I do. And let me tell you, these days that's a very attractive trait in a man." Richmond looks at me like he thinks I'm crazy. "I'm serious, Bob. Rose is an experienced woman who knows what she wants. And I'm betting she, like most women out there, would jump at the chance to train a man the way she wants it done. If you confide in her what you just told me, and ask her to help you learn how to make her happy, you will make her very, *very* happy."

Richmond doesn't look convinced.

"Trust me on this one," I say. "And in the meantime, let's get a move on. I want to get these interviews done and hit up Pesto Change-o. My stomach is growling, and time is a wasting." I can practically taste the garlic already.

Richmond gives me the address for the Serenity Spa, and after telling me he'll meet me there, I walk back to my office to fetch my car and head out. It's not a long drive—nothing in Sorenson is much more than ten minutes away—and during the trip I think about Emily, Hurley, Matthew, and me, and my stupid shattered dream of living happily ever after. I plotted out all sorts of imaginary courses for my life when I was younger, but none of them came close to the harsh reality that is my life at the moment. While I couldn't be happier about having Matthew, or the fact that Hurley is his father, our current living situation is beyond frustrating.

I wonder if Amazon sells happily ever afters.

Chapter 14

Cynthia Parker is a receptionist at the Serenity Spa. She's what some might call a handsome woman. She has jet black hair cut very short with curls that snake around her ears and the nape of her neck. Her eyes are huge, pale green in color with flecks of brown, and trimmed with thick, dark lashes. She is built tall and lean, her shoulders broad and straight, her legs and hips narrow and slender. The reason the word handsome comes to mind is because of her features, which are strongly masculine. Her nose is patrician and a bit too large for her face, her forehead is broad, her jaw square, and her lips are narrow and straight, lacking much of a Cupid's bow. Still, the overall package is an attractive one, just not what anyone would call beautiful.

Richmond makes quick work of the introductions since Cynthia is expecting us, and then asks if there is somewhere more private where we can talk.

"Of course," she says in a mellow, cultured voice. "Just let me get someone to relieve me." She makes a phone call and asks someone on the other end to watch the front desk for her. Seconds after she hangs up, a young girl of about twenty comes out of a room down the hallway off to our left. "Thanks, Darla," Cynthia says. Then with a gentle arch of her otherwise straight eyebrows, she says, "Follow me, please," and heads down the same hallway Darla came from. We pass several closed doors along the way, and from beyond those doors I can hear the sounds of soft music playing. It's a mixture of types, ranging from Native American wind flutes in one room to New Age synthesizer in another, with some Oriental-sounding music in between. The hallway is filled with an exotic mix of smells, too, each one suggestive of a different environment. Flowery . . . herbal . . . spicy. Cynthia leads us to the last door on the right, opens it, and gestures us inside. It's a small kitchenette that I guess serves as a break room for the spa staff. The primary aromatherapy in here is coffee.

"Can I get you a water?" Cynthia asks, heading for a glass-door refrigerator filled with every brand of bottled water one can imagine. "Water and hydration are so essential to your health and well-being."

Richmond passes while I accept the offer, and after fetching me a bottle, we settle down at one of two small bistro tables in the room.

"What can I help you with, Detective?" Cynthia asks. "Is this about those burglaries in my neighborhood last week?"

Apparently the gossip mill has been slow to turn today.

Richmond says, "I understand you're dating Mr. Lars Sanderson."

Cynthia again arches her brows ever so slightly. "Yes, I do see Lars from time to time. What does that have to do with anything?"

"When is the last time you saw him?"

Cynthia looks away for a few seconds, narrowing her eyes in thought. "Let's see. It would have been last Friday night. We went out for dinner and then back to my place for aperitifs. Lars left around midnight. Normally he would have stayed the night, but I had to get up early Saturday morning to head for Milwaukee to visit my mother." She gives Richmond a quizzical look. "You don't think Lars has anything to do with those burglaries, do you?"

"I'm not here about the burglaries," Richmond says. "I'm sorry to have to tell you this, but Mr. Sanderson was found dead this morning."

This time there is no subtlety in her reaction. Her eyebrows shoot up as her eyes open wide. "Lars is dead?" she says, clasping a hand to her chest. She looks off to the side and swallows hard. Tears loom in her eyes. "Oh, God," she whispers, squeezing her eyes shut. After a few seconds she opens them and looks back at Richmond. "What happened? Did he have a heart attack? Or was he in an accident of some sort?"

"Mr. Sanderson was murdered," Richmond says softly.

"Murdered?" Cynthia whispers, looking frightened. "How? Where?" She closes her eyes, moans, and lets her head fall back. "Who did he piss off now?" she says to the ceiling.

"Did Mr. Sanderson piss off a lot of people?" Richmond asks.

When Cynthia brings her head forward again, tears roll down her cheeks. She gets up and walks over to a roll of paper towels, rips off a square, and pats it against her face. "He was always making people mad," she says from behind the towel. She resumes her seat and scrunches the towel in her hand. "Couth, subtlety, and manners were traits Lars didn't have, at least when it came to business. He was sweet as could be with me, but when it came to working a deal, he was like Dr. Jekyll and Mr. Hyde."

I'm beginning to wonder if Lars and Lucien might have been separated at birth.

Richmond asks, "Is there anyone in particular you can recall who had a heated disagreement with Lars recently?"

"Well, there's that Olsen fellow who runs the Historic Society. The two of them got to yelling at one another over the phone on Friday night when Lars was at my house. And I know Reece Morton isn't a fan." She squeezes out a few more tears and dabs at her face again. "Can you tell me how it happened?"

I look over at Richmond, wanting to let him handle this one. "Mr. Sanderson was found dead in Cooper's Woods," he says. "At first we thought it might have been a hunting accident, but upon closer inspection it appears someone deliberately killed him."

"He was shot?" Cynthia says. The tears start flowing again. "Please tell me it was quick and merciful."

Richmond doesn't. Instead he hits her with, "Did you know that Lars was dating other women?"

Cynthia scowls at him and she blinks several times. "I knew he went out on social occasions with other women at times, but he always told me I was the only one he was serious about. He said the others were just for business, or for show. He wasn't sleeping with them."

Despite the conviction of this last statement, her expression is doubtful, and a little challenging, as if she's daring us to say she's wrong. It makes me suspect she knew Lars wasn't being faithful. Motive perhaps?

This time it's Richmond who arches his eyebrows. He doesn't say a word. He doesn't need to.

"Oh, dear," Cynthia says. "I guess that's why he always skirted around the question of marriage whenever I brought it up." She falls back against her chair and shakes her head. "I guess I look quite the fool, don't I?"

The woman's pain is obvious, and very uncomfortable. I give Richmond a pleading look and he nods. "I'm sorry to have to deliver such bad news," he says to Cynthia. He takes out a business card and slides it across the table to her. "Call me if you think of anything else that might be helpful to our investigation."

We get up from the table to leave, but before we do, I look back at Cynthia. "Just one more question, Ms. Parker. Do you own a cat?"

"Heavens, no," she says. "I'm allergic to them."

With that we exit the room, leaving a destroyed Cynthia Parker in our wake. When we reach the front door, Darla bestows us with a huge smile and says, "Have a blissful, serene day."

Too late for that.

Chapter 15

Outside the Serenity Spa, Richmond glances at his watch. "Let's head over to Pesto Change-o."

I nod and head for my hearse, which I discreetly parked down the street from the spa. Five minutes later we are pulling into the lot of Pesto Change-o. The heavenly smells of oregano, basil, and garlic fill the air, and as I head inside, it's all I can do not to drool. Richmond is waiting for me just inside the door.

"This is Chuck Obermeyer," he says, showing me a DMV picture on his cell phone. "Should we get a table, or wait here for him?"

"Let's get a table," I say. "I'm ravenous."

A hostess shows us to one of several empty tables. It's Tuesday night, not a busy time for any city night life, much less a city the size of Sorenson.

As soon as we are seated, Giorgio, who is both the proprietor and a magician, comes over to our table to greet us.

"Mattie Winston!" he says, with a dramatic bow. "How good to see you again." He pauses and looks over at Richmond. "And who is this you brought with you tonight? A new boyfriend, perhaps?" Giorgio whips a paper flower bouquet from his sleeve and hands them to Richmond. "You might want to butter her up with these, good sir."

I smile at Richmond, who is blushing as red as the fake poppies in the bouquet. "This is Detective Bob Richmond," I tell Giorgio. "He's a coworker of mine. We've been working on a case together."

"Oh, I see," Giorgio says, looking puzzled. "Please, pardon my gaffe." He stares at Richmond for several seconds and then says, "Are you the same Bob Richmond who used to order takeout from me all the time?"

"Yes, I am," Richmond says with a guilty smile.

"What happened? You no like my food anymore?"

"I love your food," Richmond says. "I loved it a little too much for a lot of years."

Giorgio looks puzzled so I jump in to explain. "Bob has been on a journey of health and fitness for the past year. He's lost well over a hundred pounds."

"Almost one-fifty," Richmond says proudly.

Giorgio nods and looks relieved. "I see," he says. "Well, I will try not to tempt you too much this evening, then." He shifts his attention back to me. "And you have some good news, too, I hear. A bambino?"

"Yes, a little boy named Matthew."

"Wonderful, wonderful!" he says with a big smile. "Do you have a picture?"

I realize I don't, and instantly feel a twinge of guilt. What kind of mother am I if I don't have a picture or two to show off? "I don't have one with me," I say apologetically. "I have lots of videos of him at home, but I haven't taken any regular pictures."

"Well, you best get on that then and bring me one when you can."

"Yes, I best."

With the awkwardness now out of the way, Giorgio excuses himself to greet some new arrivals. I hope it might be Chuck Obermeyer, but it's not.

A waitress comes by with two glasses of water and our menus.

"I don't need the menu," I tell Richmond. "I have it memorized."

He chuckles. "I don't need it either. I don't have it memorized, but I remember my favorite dish." We place our orders—fettuccine alfredo for me and cheese raviolis with a side of sausage for Richmond. We both order salads as well, mine with Italian dressing, Richmond's with bleu cheese.

"So what was your take on Cynthia Parker?" I ask Richmond once the waitress departs.

"I don't see her for it," he says. "She seemed genuinely crushed by the news of Lars's death, so she's either a stellar actress, or she's innocent."

"I agree. She's the first person so far to actually shed a tear over Lars's death, and her pain seemed very real to me."

"It's nice to know someone will mourn the man," Richmond says.

"Presumably his family will."

"Apparently not," Richmond says. "The guys out in Colorado called and told us that Lars has been estranged from his parents for years. They didn't seem too broken up about his death, and they didn't offer to handle the funeral arrangements, either."

"That's sad," I say. Families are complicated, messy, and at times, lifesavers. "Do you have any family nearby, Richmond?"

"I have a brother who lives in Arizona, but we don't talk much. We were never close."

"What about your parents?"

"They're both dead. At least the ones I called Mom and Dad are dead. But since I was adopted, I might have some natural parents alive somewhere."

"You were adopted? I didn't know that. Did you ever try to find your birth parents?"

"Nah, I figured if they didn't want me back when I was a cute little baby, they weren't going to want me when I was overweight and all grown up." He glances over my shoulder and says, "There's Obermeyer." Richmond gets up and heads for the door. I turn and watch as he shows Obermeyer his badge and has a brief discussion with him. Then Richmond gestures toward our table and the two of them come my way.

Chuck Obermeyer looks like the quintessential general contractor. He's tall with a weathered face, clear blue eyes, and blond hair gone to white at the temples. He's dressed in blue jeans, a long-sleeved, corduroy shirt, and a lined denim jacket. Richmond introduces us and then motions for Obermeyer to have a seat.

"We've ordered," Richmond says. "Feel free to do the same."

Obermeyer waves the offer away. "I'm really not that hungry. What's this all about anyway? Where's Sanderson?"

"I'm sorry to tell you he's dead," Richmond says. "Under suspicious circumstances. Can I ask what the two of you were meeting about?"

Obermeyer stares at Richmond, his mouth hanging open. Finally he says, "Sanderson is dead? Seriously?"

"Seriously," Richmond says.

"Well, ain't that a kick in the ass." Obermeyer lets out a perturbed sigh and runs a hand through his hair. "I suppose that means I'm not going to get the job."

"Get the job?" I echo.

"Yeah, Lars was planning to use me as his primary contractor on that new gated development deal. Damn, I really needed that job. Do you know who's going to get it now?"

Richmond and I exchange a look. Clearly Obermeyer has motive, but it's to want Lars alive rather than dead, assuming he's telling the truth and not putting on an act. Judging from the way Richmond is scrutinizing Obermeyer, he's wondering the same thing.

"So the two of you were planning to discuss this job over dinner tonight?" Richmond asks.

"We weren't going to discuss it; we were going to finalize it." Obermeyer reaches inside his jacket and pulls out a sheaf of papers. "I brought the contract for him to sign." He hands the papers to Richmond, who opens and reads them.

Our waitress arrives with our salads and asks Obermeyer if he wants to see a menu.

"No, thanks. I'm not staying."

Richmond looks through the papers and then hands them back to Obermeyer. "Sorry for your loss," he says.

For once that line seems both adequate and appropriate.

"Thanks," Obermeyer says. Though it seems unnecessary, Richmond asks Obermeyer if he's a hunter.

"Hell, no," Obermeyer says, making a face. "I wouldn't have the stomach for it. I love animals too much."

With that, Obermeyer has hit on one of my own annoying dichotomies—trying to come to terms with my love of animals and my love of meat. I realize how hypocritical it is to get upset with hunters who kill deer and other animals for sport when I'm perfectly content to settle down to a nice juicy steak, or gnaw on some barbecued ribs, both of which, I discovered, can be ordered from Amazon.

Obermeyer says, "If you don't need anything else from me, I'm going to go. I've got a crew working overtime on a project out on the lake. I need to go check on them."

"That's fine," Richmond says. "Thanks for talking to us."

With that Obermeyer gets up and leaves.

"I think we can cross him off the list," Richmond says, digging into his salad. "I'll have Jonas see if he can find anything in Lars's office files that verifies his intent to sign up this Obermeyer guy, but even if he doesn't, I don't think Obermeyer had anything to do with the death."

"I agree."

Richmond chews on a bite of salad as I check my cell phone. "Still no word from Hurley?"

I shake my head. "I hate this waiting. I'd rather be doing something about it."

"Not much you can do that Hurley can't."

"I know, but that doesn't make it any easier."

Our entrees arrive, and by some unspoken agreement, Richmond and I spend the next half hour eating and chatting about unimportant stuff that has no bearing on our immediate lives or the case. It's a welcome respite from the intensity of the day, but when we're done, reality noses its way back in.

As I check my phone yet again, Richmond says, "Why don't you send him a message?"

"I did. Back when Obermeyer was leaving. He hasn't answered me."

"Oh. Sorry."

"I want to run home and get in a little time with the kid before I go to my hair appointment. Are you planning to talk to anyone else tonight?"

Richmond shakes his head and consults his notebook. "First thing tomorrow we'll get a crew out to those woods to look for some ATV tracks, and Bridget Rutherford is coming in to the station for a chat at nine. Then I need to try to find this Hartwig Beckenbauer guy. I've got Laura working on it. He's not a local so we're going to have to start with the dead woman, Freda Herman, and see if we can track down any offspring. I suppose we should contact Kirsten Donaldson's ex, too, and invite him in for a chat. Any chance George Haas would let us into his house to take a look at his shoes and those of anyone else in the house so we can compare them to the footprints we found in the woods?"

"George might, but I'm betting his mother, Irma, won't."

"Then I'll have to see if I can get a search warrant."

"You might want to add Harry Olsen to your warrant list. He admitted to owning archery equipment, but by the time Hurley asked him to volunteer it for us to examine, he was incensed and he refused. And Olsen has a black and white cat that lives in the museum."

Richmond nods and writes something in his notebook.

"Also, Hurley asked Laura to look into the lawsuits that have been filed against Lars. That might give us some new leads."

Richmond stops writing and looks at me. "Of the people you saw today, does anyone leap out at you?"

"Reece Morton had motive and we thought he had the means, but his archery equipment is all mysteriously missing. Normally that would keep me focused on him, but he has a bad case of Parkinson's disease with a severe tremor. I can't see him being able to shoot an arrow with any degree of accuracy. He and Lars did have a fight of some sort at the Nowhere Bar last week, and we should probably follow up on that, but at this point I don't think Reece could have done it. However, I am intrigued by the fact that his archery equipment is missing."

"I'll stop by the Nowhere Bar tonight before I head home and see what I can dig up," Richmond says.

"We know George Haas was out there in the woods either at the time of the murder or shortly thereafter, maybe both. I don't see him for shooting the arrow that killed Lars, but Hurley's idea that it might have been more than one person keeps him on my list. Though I don't know what motive George would have. Cynthia Parker and Obermeyer are at the bottom of my list. I don't see either of them for it."

"Let me take a run at Harry Olsen tomorrow to see if I can talk him into letting us look at his archery equipment. Just to be sure, I'll submit the requests for the search warrants first thing in the morning. Want to join me for the interview with Bridget Rutherford?"

"I'd be happy to if there isn't anything going on in my office."

"Why don't we plan to meet at the station around eight forty-five then? If something comes up with Izzy, or with Hurley and Emily, and you can't make it, just let me know."

With that, we split the check and head out, each of us going our separate ways. I skedaddle home hoping to spend the fifteen minutes I have before my hair appointment with Matthew.

I pull up in front of my cottage and, as I head for the front door, I peek inside the window. Dom is sitting on the floor with Matthew on a blanket in front of him.

He's playing peek-a-boo, hiding his face behind his hands and then opening them wide as he lunges toward Matthew's face. Matthew smiles and squirms with delight with each lunge, windmilling his little arms and legs. Sitting on the couch watching is Izzy, but his eyes aren't on Matthew. He's focused on Dom, whose own smile rivals that of my son. Dom's utter enjoyment of this silly little game is obvious, and I can't help but wonder what Izzy is thinking.

I head inside, feeling a little guilty that I'm about to interrupt this fun playtime. As soon as Dom realizes I'm home, he gets up from the floor, scoops Matthew into his arms, and squeals, "Mommy's home!"

The smile on my son's face makes all the day's ugliness and frustration vanish. Dom holds him out to me and I snuggle him against my chest, relishing his warmth, his baby smell, his precious smile. For a few wonderful seconds, the rest of the world retreats and I am happier and more content than I've been in years . . . maybe forever.

"I don't have long," I say to Dom and Izzy. "My hair appointment with Barbara is at seven. But I wanted to come by and see my little guy. I really missed him." I kiss the dark fuzz of hair on top of his head, and he coos. With the sound of his voice, my milk lets down. "My boobs really missed him, too," I say. "I've got enough time to give him five minutes or so on either side. After that, you might need to supplement him."

"No problem," Dom says. "We'll probably take him over to our place after you leave. We were about to head there anyway to make dinner."

"That's fine. I'll pick him up there when I get back. My appointments typically last about an hour and a half, and I have to stop by the office afterward to get the bottles I have in the fridge from today, so it will probably be around nine or so before I return. Is that okay?"

"That's fine," Dom says. "Should I save you some dinner?"

"Thanks, but I already ate. Bob Richmond and I had to meet a person of interest in our current case at Pesto Change-o so I grabbed something there."

"How about dessert?" Dom says. "I'm making apple crisp."

"You could twist my arm on that one," I say. "Count me in."

I take Matthew into my bedroom and settle into the rocking chair I have there. Seconds later he is latched on and feeding.

The next ten minutes of my life are quiet, peaceful, and relaxing. For those few moments, everything seems right with the world. But as I finish nursing my son and make myself ready to head out for my appointment, my cell phone rings. And with that ring, everything gets turned upside down.

Chapter 16

It's Hurley calling. I answer with hope in my voice, wanting him to tell me that Emily has finally returned home and everything is fine. But it's not to be.

"Any good news to report?" I say.

"No. None. She hasn't come home and she still isn't answering her phone or any of the text messages I've sent her. I'm really worried, Mattie."

"Have you talked to Johnny Chester again? Maybe she's been in touch with him."

"I did. I went out to his house and talked to his mom and him, just in case he was lying. According to him, the marijuana that was found in his jacket pocket wasn't his. He said he'd given the jacket to Emily to wear earlier in the day because she was cold, and then later just hung it in his locker when she no longer needed it. He says the marijuana had to have come from her."

"Do you believe him?"

Hurley sighs. "I don't know. He swears he hasn't heard from her recently and his mom showed me his phone to prove it. I'm not sure if I believe him about the marijuana, but he looks and sounds as worried as

I am about the fact that Emily is missing. Of course, maybe it's because he's afraid we'll find out he had something to do with it. Maybe he got mad at her for the marijuana and did something about it. But his mother swears he's been grounded at the house since his suspension, and if that's true, I don't know how he could have anything to do with her disappearance."

"What about her friends? Could she be holed up at someone else's house?"

"According to the teachers and a handful of students I spoke to, she doesn't have that many friends. They say she's a loner who spends most of her time with Johnny. That's not her usual. She was much more involved in activities and school events in Chicago. She even had plans to try out for cheerleading right before they moved up here." He pauses and sighs, and in my mind's eye I can see him raking a hand through his hair the way he does whenever he's upset. "I haven't paid close enough attention," he says. "I knew Emily was upset by all the changes in her life, but I guess I didn't realize how much she herself had changed."

"Don't beat yourself up over this," I tell him. "You've been through a lot lately, too. We all have. And we're all doing the best we know how. Let's stay focused on the task at hand. Let's find her and get her home, and then you can start berating yourself."

"Right," Hurley says with no conviction.

"I assume you've tried tracing her cell phone?"

"I did. It's either turned off or she took the battery out. I've been driving around town, hitting up the spots where the kids tend to hang out, but no has seen her, at least not that they'll admit to."

I rack my brain, trying to think of any other suggestions. "What about your phone records? You pay for the phone, right? Look and see what numbers she has called or texted recently. Maybe that will offer up a new clue."

"I already did that. The only numbers that came up were mine and Johnny's, and those were from last Friday. There haven't been any since then."

"What about e-mails?"

"Her laptop is password protected and I haven't been able to figure it out yet."

"Do you want me to come over there and help you?"

"I would love to have you and Matthew here, but I think it might be best if I'm here alone for now. If she decides to come home and sees you here, it might be enough to push her away again. I've got the guys who are on patrol this evening keeping an eye out for her and I even gave the county and state guys a heads-up. So I think I'll sit tight for now and wait, maybe take another run at that laptop."

"If you change your mind, Matthew and I will be there in a flash, okay?"

"Thanks." He sighs heavily and I can picture him running his hand through his hair again. "I have to say, this parenting stuff is a lot harder than I ever thought it would be."

"Yes, it is," I agree. "And it's been sprung on you without any warning. Twice."

"At least with you I had time to get used to the idea, and I'll have a chance to influence the kid as he grows. With Emily, she's pretty much a done deal already. Changing her isn't going to be easy."

"Maybe she's not the one who needs changing."

There's a long silence on the other end. Then he says, "R-i-g-h-t," drawing the word out with a sarcastic tone. "Don't start preaching and philosophizing to me,

Mattie. There's already one shrink doing that. I don't need another."

"I'm just saying it's worth thinking about, Hurley. You've been on your own for a long time and you're pretty set in your ways. But there are new people in your life now, people who are going to challenge those ways."

"I've made plenty of sacrifices for Emily already," he grumbles. "I've given her a home to live in, a room of her own, food on her table, clothes on her back."

"Those are all great, but they're material things. And I can tell you from my own experiences at that age that while material things matter, they aren't the most important things in life. Emotional things are. How much of *you* have you given her?"

"This psychological mumbo-jumbo is giving me a headache."

"Then I'll stop. I have to go anyway. I have an appointment with Barbara to get my hair done. But I'll keep my cell with me. Call me with any news, okay?"

"Yeah, okay."

I'm about to tell him to hang in there when I realize he has already hung up.

Feeling unsettled, I head back out to the living room and reluctantly turn Matthew over to Dom. Two minutes later I'm on my way to the Keller Funeral Home. Over the past year I've grown accustomed to having a hairdresser who works in the basement of a funeral home, a fact that also requires me to lie down while getting my hair done, sometimes next to another customer who isn't breathing and smells strongly of formaldehyde. It's a little creepy, I suppose, but for the magical ministrations of Barbara, the dead's answer to John Frieda and Vidal Sassoon, it's worth it.

While I've adapted to coming to a funeral home to

get my hair done, today is the first time I've entered the place when it's dark outside other than to attend visitations or funerals that were well lit inside and well attended. Tonight there are no events—or gatherings, as Irene Keller, the owner, calls them—and the funeral home is darkened and seemingly empty. The front door is unlocked—I'm not sure if it would normally be or if it was left open for me—and I step into a large main room with a variety of plush seating lining the walls and situated in two small conversation circles. Various doorways off this area open onto Irene's office, the casket room, three different viewing rooms, and at the far end, the basement. The only interior light at the moment is coming from some wall sconces in the main room—all of which seem to be dimmed—and from inside Irene's office.

I head for the office, my footsteps cushioned by thick carpeting. The acoustics in this place drive me crazy. It's as if the walls eat the sound, and overpowering silence is not all that comfortable when you're tiptoeing through a house of the dead. For some reason I always feel like I need to tread lightly, as if stomping my feet, or making a floorboard creak might somehow upset the dead or the grieving. I also get an overwhelming urge every time I come in here to sing loudly, preferably something fun and slightly irreverent, like Queen's "Another One Bites the Dust" or The Cure's "Hello Goodbye" or "I Dig You."

And the people who work here don't do much to lighten things any. They all have serious, somber faces, wear black suits and shoes, and talk in hushed, monotonic voices. Their demeanor and appearance only serves to up the creep factor in my opinion. And then we get to Irene, who is the ultimate in creepy when it comes to her appearance, though she does display a refreshing attitude of in-your-face honesty and a dark sense of humor that she'll share with those she trusts. But at eighty-something—no one really knows her actual age—Irene looks worse than many of the customers who come in through the basement door. She has skin so thin you can see through it in the places that aren't covered with liver spots or as wrinkled as a shar-pei. Her teeth—what few she has left—are stained and yellowed with age, and she has all the muscular definition of a slug, which is fitting in a way, since she moves at a snail's pace. Her hair grows in white tufts that she tries vainly to tame into something resembling an actual hairdo, and her hands are gnarled and bent from arthritis. For some reason she always wears bright red lipstick and nail polish. I suspect she wears the color in an effort to make herself look younger or at least draw one's eye away from her older bits, but the end result is a garish clash of colors, sights, and textures that draw attention to all the things that make Irene look like the Crypt Keeper.

I'm anticipating the sight of Irene behind the desk in her office, so it's a pleasant surprise when I find a young woman seated there instead. Ever mindful of the nerve-rattling silence of the place, I clear my throat loudly as I enter the office so as not to scare the poor girl.

"Hello," she says, looking up at me with a smile. She is quite pretty, with huge blue eyes, a cascade of curly auburn hair, and pale, translucent skin. She rises from her chair and greets me just inside the door by extending her hand. "I'm Renny. How can I help you?"

I take her hand expecting her to shake it, but instead she clasps mine between both of hers, holding it.

"I'm here to see Barbara," I say, grabbing a length of my hair and holding it out. The girl eyes my head for a second and then nods. "Ah, yes. Sorry, I should have guessed. You must be Mattie Winston."

"Yes, I am." I should probably be offended by the fact that one look told her I was in need of Barbara's services, but I find her honest appraisal rather refreshing, especially in this place. Maybe that means she won't embrace that fine art of cautious, euphemistic lingo that forces funeral home people to say things like *departed,* or *moved on,* or *deceased,* as opposed to the more succinct term *dead.* Those euphemisms created an awkward moment for me in nursing school when I was involved in the care of a southern Baptist family whose patriarch had suffered a heart attack while they were traveling to Minnesota to visit relatives. The heart attack was a bad one and the patient was touch and go during the two days of clinical time I did that week. The following week, when we returned for more clinical time, I saw the wife of the patient standing in the hallway outside his room, leaning against the wall. When I asked how her husband was doing, she said, "He's going home." I whooped with happiness, told her how great that was and how glad it made me. A few minutes later I learned that "going home" was another one of those euphemisms for dying.

"Are you a new employee here?" I ask Renny.

"Sort of. I'm Irene's great-granddaughter. My birth name is Irene also, but everyone has always called me Renny. Anyway, I'm graduating in January with a degree in mortuary science and Grams is grooming me to take over the business since no one else in the family has ever shown an interest. So you and I will likely cross paths from time to time."

Ah yes, that camaraderie that comes from sharing something that many perceive to be a darker side of society that is better neither seen nor heard. "Wow.

Congratulations. Though I have to say, that seems like a . . . lot of responsibility for someone so young." I was about to say it seemed like a dark choice, but then I realized that many of today's younger generation are drawn to such things.

"I suppose it is, but there are so many things I'm looking forward to changing in this business, things that Grams would never consider. She's a bit stuck in her ways."

That's putting it mildly. Irene hasn't changed a thing, including her wardrobe choices or her hairdo, in the decades that I've known her. "That sounds positive," I say. "What sorts of changes do you have in mind?"

"Well, for one thing, this place is going to get a huge makeover, hopefully sooner rather than later. It's too dark, too old, too quiet, too formal. It's like a mausoleum. I want to see some brighter colors, and more sunlight, and furnishings that aren't so heavy and dark."

"I like that idea," I tell her. "In fact I was thinking along those lines when I walked in here."

"See? People these days are much more open to that kind of stuff. Grams thinks everyone expects somber and formal but I disagree. All the baby boomers that are aging now are into a whole different scene. We're talking about former hippies who were into freedom of expression, and fun music, and bright colors. And then there's the whole green movement. Did you know that there's an option now to have your body cremated and your ashes placed into a biodegradable urn along with a plant seed? Once you plant the urn, your ashes become part of the tree, or whatever other plant you may choose. To me that's way cooler than a big, cold gravestone, don't you think?"

It is an interesting idea, enough so that for a moment I consider letting go of my resistance to cremation. For some reason, even though I know that cremation is the only way I'll ever have a smoking hot body, the idea of burning my body into a small pile of gravelly ashes bothers me. I much prefer the idea of being returned to the earth, of being food for the worms and fertilizer for the plants. And besides, Barbara has already shown me how kick-ass good she can make me look for my funeral and I want to preserve that perfect hair for as long as I can.

"That's a cool idea," I say, "but I'm kind of committed to being buried. I know it tends to cost more but I'm fine with not having my body preserved, and I don't want a fancy, expensive coffin. In fact, I have my eye on the one I want already."

"Really?" Renny says, smiling skeptically.

"Really," I tell her. "I found it on Amazon one night when I was looking for a book by an author named Coffin to give as a gift to a friend. I'm not sure what struck me as weirder, the fact that you can buy a coffin from Amazon, or the fact that some of the models come with customer ratings, including one bearing the headline, '*Easy to get into, hard to get out of.*'"

Renny busts out a laugh, a healthy, happy laugh that sounds wonderful and a tad bit rebellious within the confines of this building. "Good one," she says. "That's the kind of thing I want to see more of. There's a movement toward holding wakes rather than memorials, bright, happy gatherings where people can come together and remember the deceased with good humor, and laughter, and a shared story or two. There will always be tears, but rather than focusing on death, I want people to focus on life. I want them to embrace life . . . not only their own, but that of the person who is gone."

"I like your style, Renny," I say with a smile. "Just promise me you won't change anything with Barbara. She's the best hairdresser I've ever had and I hope to keep her right up through to eternity."

"She is good," Renny acknowledges with a nod and a smile. "I've let her do my makeup a time or two. My date for my senior prom would have died if he'd known he stole the virginity of someone who had been lying on an embalming table just hours before."

"Was that a joke?" I say. "He would have *died* knowing?"

Renny claps a hand over her mouth and her eyes grow big. "Oh, that was a good one, wasn't it? And completely accidental. Poor Grams would have a stroke if she heard me say something like that. She's been trying for years to weed words like *dead* and *body* out of my vocabulary."

"Your secret is safe with me," I promise. Then with a glance at my watch, I add, "I'm late so I best get downstairs."

"It was a real pleasure to meet you, Mattie," she says with a genuine smile. "I look forward to working with you."

"Likewise. Is the basement door unlocked or do I need to buzz in?"

"It's locked. That rule is one I have to keep. Regulations and all, you know," she says with a roll of her eyes. "Barbara is expecting you, so go ahead down there. I'm going to close up at eight, so you'll have to leave through the basement door when you're done."

"Okay, thanks. You have a good night." I leave the office and make my way to the door that goes to the basement. Beyond it is a set of stairs that leads down to a locked door. I hit the buzzer on the wall and Barbara opens the door a moment later.

"Mattie, good to see you!" She eyes my head with an expression of horror and disbelief. "And quite overdue, might I add. Where the heck have you been? It's been months since I last saw you."

"I know. Believe me I know." I follow her into an ante room outside the official embalming room. "During the last part of my pregnancy I was being stalked by a crazy man and I was pretty limited in my ability to get out and about. And since the birth I've barely had the time to eat and sleep, much less get my hair done."

"Yes, I heard about your new addition. Congratulations!"

"Thanks."

She pats the top of a metal gurney, which she has topped with a cushy pad, and I hop up and lie down. Barbara is good at what she does, but she comes with a quirk. She does her best work on people who are supine since that's the position the majority of her customers are in by default.

"You had a boy, right?" she says, running her fingers through my hair.

"Yes, his name is Matthew."

"Got a picture?"

Yet another reminder that I need to get some sort of snapshot that I can carry with me. "No, not with me. I have some videos at home, but no pictures yet."

Her fingers get caught in the chunk of dried barf hair on one side of my head. "What is this?" she asks, making a face.

"You don't want to know."

She takes a brush and starts teasing the individual strands in the chunk loose. "You'd be hard put to have anything in your hair grosser than some of the stuff I see on a daily basis in there," she says, gesturing toward the embalming room. "But I'll take your word for it. I'm assuming you want all-over color today and a trim, yes? How much do you want me to take off? Your hair has gotten long."

"I'm thinking of making a change," I tell her. "A big change."

"Ooh, I like that. Want me to make you look like me?" she says with a wink.

When it comes to physical attributes, Barbara and I have almost nothing in common. We both have blue eyes and big bosoms, though mine grew so much during my pregnancy that Hurley named them K-2 and Mt. McKinley, fitting nicknames given that my real first name is Matterhorn. But that's where the similarities end. I'm in my late thirties, tall—five-foot-twelve—and have my father's thick body build. Barbara, on the other hand, is a short, thin woman in her mid-twenties with pale skin and jet black hair that she wears short and spiky. It's a good look on her, but it wouldn't work well on me, especially since the hairdo would only add more height.

"I want to go red," I tell her.

Barbara steps back and scrutinizes me for a few seconds. "I don't think that's a good idea," she says. "If you want change, we could do a darker blond, or even a light brown with gold highlights. But with your skin tone, I'm afraid the red tones will make you look sallow."

"I really want to try the red," I insist. "Where's your book?"

She grabs a binder from a shelf and hands it to me. Inside it are a variety of color samples and when I find one that looks like Charlie's color, I point to it. "I want this one."

"Are you sure?" she says with a frown.

"Absolutely." I snap the binder closed to seal my decision.

"You'll have to change most of your makeup tones," Barbara says.

"That's fine. I barely have time to put on makeup these days anyway. Motherhood doesn't allow me much time for self-indulgence."

"Looking good isn't self-indulgent," she says. "It's a necessity."

"Easy for you to say. You're not buried in mounds of dirty laundry, tied to feedings every two hours, and facing a stack of dirty dishes taller than you are. And on top of that I have a kid and all the stuff he adds to the mix."

It takes Barbara a second or two to get my joke, but once she does, laughter echoes through the funeral home for the second time tonight and I find I like the sound of it.

Chapter 17

You wouldn't think lying on what amounts to a metal slab in the basement of a funeral home would be very relaxing, and yet every time I visit Barbara I come away feeling rested and rejuvenated. It's after nine by the time we're done, and while I'm feeling pretty good at the moment, the fact that Hurley hasn't called or texted me while I've been here doesn't bode well for a restful night.

I'm undecided about my new hair. The color is quite lovely, but it's such a shock when I look in the mirror that I can't decide if I like it on me or not. Barbara tells me to give it a few days to get used to it and see what other people think.

I can always tell when people give me false compliments on a change like this. I learned it in high school when I tried combining teal-colored eye shadow with plum-colored lipstick, and again when I decided to cut my hair supershort, à la Demi Moore in the movie *Ghost.* I have a big, round head, and big round heads don't look good with short, scalp-hugging, pixieish hairdos. When I look back at the pictures of me during that phase, I can't believe my friends and family let me out in public looking like that. Over time I came to realize that when people are on the fence about a new look you're trying, or even firmly off the fence on the grass-is-brown side, they always start out with some innocuous observational phrase like, *You changed your hair,* or *That's a new style for you.* Once you acknowledge this observation, they then tell you it looks nice in a tone that's safely neutral. Not *It looks great,* or *I love it,* but a blandly neutral *It looks nice.* If someone truly likes a change you've made, they say so right at the start and do it with enthusiasm. *Wow! I love that new hair color on you!* Or *Oh my God! Those hip hugger pants make your ass look fantastic!* For further affirmation, if the person then goes out and copies whatever you've done, you know whatever you did is a rock solid improvement.

So it isn't with great glee that I receive the comments bestowed upon me by Dom and Izzy when I finally get home. I enter Izzy's house through the garage, punching in the code for the door, and then giving a token knock. Dom and Izzy are in the living room watching TV and Matthew is asleep in a portable crib that's set up near the end of the couch they're sitting on. Izzy's house has as much, maybe more baby stuff than mine does. Dom even did over one of the bedrooms as a nursery, complete with a crib, changing table, dressers, a mobile, decorative wall hangings, a toy box, and enough stuffed animals to fill a hundred fake zoos. At the time I thought he did all that because he was so excited about babysitting for Matthew, but after my discussion with him this morning, I'm beginning to think he had some ulterior motives in mind.

"Hey, you two," I say as I enter the room. I walk over to the crib and bend down to get a good look at my son. He is on his back, sound asleep, his little lips sucking every few seconds. His face is the most precious thing I think I've ever seen, and as I look at it now, I am filled with an overwhelming urge to pick him up and hug him tight. I missed him, yes, but I also realize that I enjoyed getting out of the house and away from my mommy duties for the day. And that makes me feel a twinge of guilt.

"You changed your hair color," Dom says in a decidedly neutral tone.

Uh-oh. I straighten up and stare at him. "Yeah, I thought I'd try something different."

He hesitates for several seconds and then forces a smile. "It looks nice. The layers really give it definition."

"You don't like the color."

"It looks fine," Dom insists.

"It's not you," Izzy says. Izzy isn't one to sugarcoat things. It's one of the things I value most about our friendship, but at times it can annoy the hell out of me. This is one of those times. Then, just to prove he knows me better than I think he does, he says, "This color change doesn't have anything to do with Charlie by any chance, does it?"

"No, I just wanted something different. I'm a mother now. It's a new phase of my life and I thought I'd kick it off with a new look."

"Well, I think it looks fabulous," Dom says, finally recovering from his initial shock enough to remember his manners and fake some enthusiasm.

Izzy simply arches one eyebrow at me and says nothing.

"Okay, fine," I say, shooting Izzy an annoyed look. "I've noticed that women with red hair always seem to get lots of male attention, Charlie in particular."

"Charlie has other attributes besides red hair that garner that attention," Izzy says.

"Yes, I know. Thanks for pointing out all the ways I

can't measure up." With an exasperated sigh, I plop down on the arm of the couch and run a hand through my hair. "Does it look that bad?"

"It doesn't look bad," Izzy says. "But it doesn't look like you. And if you're doing this to attract or impress Hurley, it's a wasted effort. You already have the man, Mattie."

"Do I? Because some days it doesn't feel that way."

Izzy shakes his head and gives me a patient smile. "Steve Hurley loves you, Mattie. He may not say it all the time, and he may spare an appreciative glance at another beautiful woman like Charlie from time to time, but none of that takes away from the fact that he fell in love with the original, messy, screwed-up Mattie Winston that he met a year ago. If you could see the way he looks at you sometimes when you're talking, or doing something and you don't know he's watching you . . . it's obvious how that man feels about you."

"You make it sound so simple and straightforward," I say with a little harrumph.

"The *feelings* are simple and straightforward," Izzy says. "But the circumstances that have befallen you two are anything but. I mean think about this for a moment. Hurley has gone through several huge changes in his life over the past year and a half. First he had to leave his job in Chicago and come here to what must seem like a Podunk town by comparison. Then he meets you and feels an instant attraction, but you're married to someone else, someone who he is forced to investigate as the primary suspect in a murder. Not to mention that you were on that suspect list, too. He finally gets past that, and the two of you are working toward hooking up when he discovers that he's not only still married to a woman he thought he divorced fifteen years ago, but he has a daughter he never knew about. And within a matter of months he ends up as his daughter's sole parent as well as the father of a new baby with you. I don't know what sort of life plan Hurley saw for himself when he came here, but I'm betting it was a far cry from the reality he's had to deal with. Considering everything that's happened, I'm amazed that Hurley is as calm and collected as he is, because on the scale of life stressors, he racked up a bazillion points this past year."

Everything Izzy has said is true, and I realize then that I've been kind of selfish in dealing with all this stuff. Granted, I've been through some pretty major stresses and changes over the past year, too, but when compared to what Hurley's had dished out to him, I've only hit the halfway mark on the Stress-O-Meter, whereas he's well into the red zone. And then my mind takes a bizarre detour as I wonder whether or not one can order a Stress-O-Meter from Amazon.

"You're right," I say to Izzy. "I need to be more patient and understanding with Hurley. And I will, just as soon as this crap with Emily gets sorted out."

"Did she turn up?" Izzy asks.

I shake my head. "Hurley promised he'd call me if she did and I haven't heard a word."

"That's worrisome," Izzy says with a frown.

"Yes, it is," I agree.

Dom, who knows that my primary coping mechanism is to soothe my troubled soul with food, says, "Would some hot apple crisp topped with hard sauce make you feel a little better?"

"I do believe it would," I tell him with a smile. And it does.

* * *

An hour later, I have Matthew home and tucked into his crib, my boobs are drained and tucked into my sleep bra, and my dog, Hoover, and my two cats, Rubbish and Tux, are all tucked into my bed. I should be sleeping—my body is bone tired—but my mind is whirring along at a hundred miles an hour. I'm wide awake, worrying about Hurley and Emily. After tossing and turning for half an hour, I sit up, turn on the light, and call Hurley on my cell.

"Feeding time?" Hurley says when he answers.

"No, Matthew's asleep. I should be, but I can't stop worrying about Emily. No news at all?"

"Nothing. There's no sign of her anywhere here in town. Johnny said something when I talked to him earlier about how Emily has been talking about Chicago a lot lately. So that got me to wondering if she might have tried to go back. I don't remember the names of any of her friends there, other than a couple of first names, but I have some guys checking to see if she might have bought a bus ticket."

"Did she have enough money to do that?"

"Yeah, she did. The cash stash I had in my closet is gone."

"You had a cash stash?"

"Of course. Doesn't everyone? You never know when you might need to take off in a hurry, and if you want to stay off the grid, you can't use credit or bank cards."

I'm about to ask him why he thinks he might need to go into hiding when I remember that we had to do just that last fall when his ex-girlfriend turned up murdered and Hurley was framed for it. So instead I ask him how much he had in his stash.

"A little over a thousand bucks."

I whistle at that. "She could have gone a long way on a thousand bucks."

"I know. I just hope that if she did take off, she was smart enough to use the money and buy a ticket rather than hitchhike."

"This is horrible, Hurley. What are you going to do?"

"I'm going to assume she left town somehow and headed back to Chicago. I'm thinking I should head down there to see if I can figure out who she might have hooked up with."

"Maybe it's time to do an Amber Alert."

"Did it an hour ago. Much as I hate to even give play to the idea, I can't rule out the possibility that she was abducted by some pervert."

"Oh, God, I hope not," I say. The horror of such a scenario is almost too much for me to consider. Something is nagging at my mind, some other question I want to ask, but I can't quite pull it out. I struggle for a few seconds, but it's no good. My brain has reached overload.

"I'm going to try to get some sleep," I tell Hurley. "But promise me you'll call the instant you know anything, okay? I'll be up a couple of times during the night anyway to feed Matthew."

"I promise," he says, sounding a little irritated, and I remind myself that on the stress scale he's walking a tightrope over a tank full of hungry sharks. "Give my boy a kiss and a hug for me."

"I will. Good night, Hurley."

"Good night, Mattie."

After I disconnect the call, I grab my laptop and navigate my way to Amazon. I type something in the search box and hit enter. Then I shake my head and chuckle. Turns out you can buy a Stress-O-Meter from Amazon and one click later it's sitting in my shopping cart.

Chapter 18

As luck would have it, I'm not only able to turn my brain off well enough to go to sleep, but I also manage to remain in zombie mode during the one time I have to get up to feed Matthew. In the morning I feel reenergized and giddy with excitement when I realize that I only had to do one feeding over a period of eight hours. This is a new record for Matthew, and I'm psyched over the idea of getting four whole hours of sleep in a row. Surely an entire night of sleep can't be too far behind. I should have started adding cereal into his diet sooner.

I check my cell phone for messages or voice mail, hoping that maybe I slept so well I didn't hear the phone ring or ding, but there's nothing. I make a mental note to call Hurley when I get to the police station if he isn't there and I haven't heard from him by then. Then, even though I'm not a religious person, I mutter a little prayer toward the ceiling, asking any mighty powers up in the heavens to keep Emily safe. I figure it can't hurt to cover all the bases, and the thought of her being abducted scares the crap out of me.

It's a shock when I glance at myself in the mirror. I'm so used to seeing the pale blond version of me and this new redder me is one I'm not sure I like.

Dom shows up right on time, as usual, and I make it into the office by eight. I check in with Izzy to see if there are any autopsies pending and fill him in on Richmond's plans for the day.

"There's nothing pending at the moment," he tells me. "Go ahead and work with Richmond and I'll call you if anything comes in that I need help with. Any news on Emily?"

I shake my head. "I didn't hear anything from Hurley during the night so I'm assuming she's still gone. It's kind of scary. She's never been gone overnight before. Now he's thinking she might have gone back to Chicago." I don't mention the other, scarier possibility Hurley shared with me, fearing that saying it aloud will somehow give it life.

"How's Hurley holding up?"

"About like you'd expect. Angry one minute, worried the next, berating himself every hour."

"Look, if you need some personal time for this business with Emily, just let me know. We can make it work."

I thank him and head to my office, which is in the library. Since I have a little time before I have to meet Richmond at the station, I place a call to Dr. Maggie Baldwin.

"Hey, Maggie, it's Mattie Winston."

"Hello there. How's motherhood treating you?"

"I'm not going to lie. It's exhausting, but it's totally worth it. I can't believe how much I love this little guy."

"That's great."

"I'm calling you about Emily. Has Hurley spoken with you since yesterday?"

"About her disappearance?"

"Yes."

"He did. In fact I spoke to him just a little while ago. He called last night and left a message for me but I didn't get it and return the call until this morning. He told me nobody has seen her since yesterday morning, and that she hasn't run off with her new boyfriend. In fact, Hurley said the boyfriend seems as worried as anyone."

"And do you think we're right to be worried?"

"It's definitely concerning."

"Do you think this is another one of her attention-getting stunts? Can you shed any light on where she might be? Hurley thought she might have left town and gone back to Chicago to hook up with some old friends there. Did she ever say anything to you about anyone there she was close to?"

"Mattie, you know I can't provide you with any details regarding my sessions with Emily. If you were her parent or legal guardian, it might be different. But you're not."

I curse under my breath.

"Besides, Emily didn't share that much with me. We've only had a few sessions. If I think of something that might help, I'll give Hurley a call."

"Okay, thanks anyway."

"Sorry I can't be of more help. Unfortunately girls that age tend to be very secretive. Getting them to open up isn't easy."

"Tell me about it."

I disconnect the call and walk over to the police station. It's a bitter day, cloudy with a gusty wind that snakes its way up my sleeves and down my neck. The warmth of the station is a welcome respite, but I can't help but think about Emily. Is she warm wherever she is? Is she safe from the elements? Is she with some sick and twisted pervert? And the thought that scares me most—is she alive?

I find Richmond in his office clicking away on his computer.

"Good morning," I say, shucking my coat. "Any updates for me?"

"A few," he says, nodding, typing, and not taking his eyes off the screen. "We finally tracked down the surviving relative of Freda Herman, thanks to Laura. It isn't a son, it's a nephew. And his name is, or rather was Hartwig Beckenbauer, but he had it shortened and legally changed years ago to Hart Bauer. He's a wannabe actor who tried to make it in L.A. and failed. Now he's living in Milwaukee and performing in some revue show there that features female impersonators. He agreed to come here to talk to us because he has to drive to Madison today anyway. The plan is for him to get here around two."

He points toward the computer screen and goes back to typing. "I'm filling out the search warrant request for our Mr. Olsen and his archery equipment now, but I'm going to hold off on the one for the Haas household and the footwear. If we go out there and find a matching boot, all it does is tell us what we already know, that George Haas was with Lars Sanderson's body at one point. And if we happen to see anything else in the house that's incriminating while we're looking for other shoes, we can't touch it because we'll be limited to the footwear. Plus, if Haas did have something to do with it and had a partner, we have no idea if the partner is someone from that household. So I'm going to hold off until we can get a better grasp on some of these other suspects."

"Makes sense, I suppose," I say. "You might want to look into Axel Nilsson. He's George's best friend and he's the one he was talking to at the Quik-E-Mart. It's not likely he would have had the conversation he did with Axel if Axel was involved, but it's worth looking into."

"Got it. Laura also looked into the other legal cases involving Lars but nothing came up there. They've been settled."

Richmond finishes filling out his form and then faxes the request straight from the computer. When he's done he leans back in his chair, hands behind his head, and looks at me. "Whoa," he says, suddenly straightening in his chair. "You changed your hair."

"Yeah, I decided to switch it up a little to celebrate my new mommy status. What do you think?"

Richmond hesitates just long enough that he doesn't have to answer; like an X-File, the truth is out there. But he makes a valiant effort anyway. "It looks nice," he says, and he's smart enough to follow it with a quick subject change. "Jonas finished processing Lars's car but he didn't find anything of interest other than some fingerprints. Kirsten Donaldson's were in there, and so were Cynthia Parker's, but since they were both dating him, that doesn't mean anything. His office assistant's prints were in the car, too, but when I called and talked to her, she said she sometimes took his car for him to get it washed or serviced. So that's a dead end. I talked to some folks at the Nowhere Bar last night about the altercation between Lars and Reece Morton, and they said it was the same sort of argument they've witnessed between those two dozens of times before. Apparently they both frequent the place and their antagonistic history is a long one that tends to get vocal when the booze is flowing.

"I also went by Kirsten Donaldson's neighborhood last night to talk to some of her neighbors. No one saw her, but two people remembered seeing her car parked in the driveway early in the morning yesterday. One guy saw it around five-thirty when he left for work and the woman across the street remembers seeing it at seven forty-five when she left to go to the grocery store. So it seems her alibi is holding up."

"Wow, you were a busy guy last night," I say.

Richmond shrugs. "Time is of the essence with these cases. I also sent some guys back out to Cooper's Woods this morning to look for ATV tracks. They just called to say they found some, but only small tracks in the areas where there's still some snow on the ground. The rest of the ground is too frozen. There didn't seem to be any rhyme or reason to the direction of the tracks and they didn't find any close to the site where we found Lars's body, but there wasn't any snow nearby either. That's not to say there wasn't an ATV in the area; in fact, based on some disturbances they saw in leaves and such on the ground it looks like something might have been there, but we couldn't find any tracks to prove it."

"Bummer."

"Yeah. Heard from Hurley this morning?"

I shake my head. "I talked to him last night and he said the guys on duty were on the lookout for Emily, but there's been no sign of her. Hurley is thinking she might have tried to go back to Chicago. Have you heard anything this morning?"

"I know some guys checked with the bus and train stations in the area and came up empty. No one saw any female travelers fitting Emily's description. Of course, she might have hitchhiked her way out of town."

"God, I hope not." The abduction theory worms its way back to the forefront of my thoughts.

Richmond's phone rings and he answers it. "Richmond." After listening for a few seconds he says, "Okay, thanks," and disconnects the call. "Bridget Rutherford is here. Why don't you go up front to get her and I'll head into the interview room and turn on the AV equipment."

"Okay, but first let me tell you what I know about Bridget. She's a local who was a couple of years ahead of me in high school, and I went to school with her brother, Nate, who joined the Marines when he graduated and is now stationed overseas somewhere. Bridget married Pollard Gleason, also a local boy who made good with an investment firm in Chicago after he made bad with Bridget and got her pregnant. The marriage lasted for sixteen years, and their son, Tanner, is now a senior in high school and living full-time with his father in Chicago. Bridget came back home after the divorce, took back her maiden name, and has been living with her parents for the past two years. She works as a pharmacy tech at two of the local drug stores, and she's taking classes in hopes of one day becoming a full-fledged pharmacist. And as we both know, she's been dating Lars Sanderson, though I have no idea if that's an exclusive relationship for her, or if she's seeing anyone else."

"No local rumors about her being out and about with anyone else?"

"Not that I know of, but then I've been out of the loop for several months so I'm not as up on the latest gossip as I usually am."

Richmond heads into the room that does double duty as a conference and interview room for the station. It's fully wired for audio and visual, and there's also an adjacent observation room, though it's almost never used for anything anymore other than a secret trysting place. I head out front to the reception area, and since I entered the station this morning through the back door, I take a moment to greet the day dispatcher, Heidi.

"Good morning," she fires back just before she looks at me. For a few seconds her smile is frozen on her face. "You changed your hair," she says in a dull, neutral tone.

Damn.

"Yes, I did," I say with a smile.

"Looks nice," Heidi says, and then she quickly turns back to her switchboard and computer.

I step through the locked door that separates the dispatch and back areas of the station from the front public area and walk over to Bridget Rutherford. She is a short, slightly overweight, brunette, a year or two past forty. Judging from her hairdo and her clothing, however, her fashion sense never made it out of the eighties. Her hair is teased and blown to three times the size of her head. Her jacket is a puffy thing with wide, fold-down lapels. Half of it is neon green and the other half is a black and white checkerboard pattern.

I don't know if Bridget remembers me from our high school days. She was a senior when I was a freshman, so I doubt I was on her radar back then.

"Bridget?"

"Yes."

"Hi, I'm Mattie Winston with the medical examiner's office; I'm going to be sitting in with Detective Richmond when he talks to you this morning."

"The medical examiner's office," she echoes with great solemnity. "I guess that makes sense since Lars is dead." She shakes her head and her eyes look moist, though she falls short of actually shedding a tear. "No more love grotto."

"Love grotto?"

She blushes and waves my question away. "I'm sorry. That's my nickname for Lars's bedroom. I just can't believe he's gone. I heard he was killed with an arrow. Was it a hunting accident?"

So much for keeping the details under wraps. Apparently the gossip mill is back in full operation.

"We're not sure," I tell her. "But there are some circumstances that look irregular. That's why we're talking to as many people as we can who knew Lars." She opens her mouth to say something else but before she can I grab her arm and steer her back toward the interview room. "Please, right this way. Detective Richmond is waiting on us."

The gambit works. She doesn't say anything more until we are in the room.

Richmond greets Bridget as soon as we enter. "Ms. Rutherford, I'm Detective Bob Richmond and you've already met Mattie Winston. Thank you for coming in to talk to us today. Please take a seat."

He gestures toward the other side of the table and Bridget dutifully walks around and settles in the seat right across from where Richmond is standing. Richmond sits, and I settle in next to him. Then Richmond begins by announcing the date, the time, who the interviewers and the interviewee are, and what case it is related to. When he's done with that, he smiles at Bridget and says, "Can you please tell me the nature of your relationship with Lars Sanderson?"

She blushes again, and lowers her gaze to the table.

"We've been dating for the past year or so," she says. "It's not anything super serious, mostly just companionship and . . . well . . . sex." Her blush extends all the way to the roots of her hair.

"How often did you two see one another?" Richmond asks.

"A couple of times a week. Some weekends. My son comes up to stay with me one weekend a month so I never saw Lars on those weekends."

"When did you see him last?"

"Saturday night. I spent most of the evening and night at his place. I left around three in the morning. I was supposed to see him again on Sunday but he called off at the last minute."

"Did he say why?" I ask.

"Yeah, something about a friend who was sick."

"Did he say who the friend was?"

"No, he seemed to be in a big hurry, so I didn't ask a lot of questions. I was expecting him to call me yesterday sometime, and then I heard the news." She pauses and shakes her head, once again with the damp eyes.

Richmond gives her a second before asking his next question. "Ms. Rutherford, was your relationship with Mr. Sanderson an exclusive one?"

She looks puzzled for a moment. "I wasn't stepping out on him with anyone else, if that's what you're implying."

"Does your ex-husband know you were seeing him?"

"I don't know. We don't talk about that sort of stuff. In fact, we really don't talk at all. All of our communications are via e-mail. But if you're implying that he might have been jealous or something like that, I can assure you that's not the case. He's had himself a hot little number for the past six months who is barely older than our son."

"How does your son feel about you dating other men?" I ask.

"I don't discuss my private life with my kid. He knows I'm seeing someone, but I've never discussed any details with him."

Richmond says, "That's probably a wise approach. Now back to the question of exclusivity. Was Mr. Sanderson seeing other women?"

"I don't think so," she says. "If he was, I think I would have known. I would have sensed something. That's how my first marriage fell apart. My husband was having an affair and I figured it out. He started working late all the time, and then I noticed that his shirts sometimes smelled like perfume."

"Do you know of anyone who might have wanted to harm Mr. Sanderson?" Richmond asks.

Bridget lets out a little chuckle. "Well, he did have a knack for ticking people off," she says. "From what I hear, his business tactics were disagreeable to many, and he wasn't the most tactful person at times. Fortunately his personal side and his business side were two entirely different animals. I'm sure there were a lot of people who would like to have told him off, and probably a few who actually did. Maybe there were even some who wanted to hit him. But kill him? If that's what you're getting at, I don't see it."

"Then you're not aware of anyone making any threats against him recently?"

"No, but then I'm not sure he would tell me about it if anyone had. He never talked about himself or his day much when we were together. He always wanted to hear about me and my day. He was sweet and considerate that way," she says with a sad smile.

I'm not surprised that Lars didn't talk about himself much. That's how he managed to juggle three girlfriends, only one of which apparently knew fully of the others. The less talking you do, the less chance you have of slipping up and saying something incriminating, or somehow contradicting yourself. Clearly he had Bridget duped, and Cynthia Parker was clueless, too. Kirsten Donaldson knew Lars was seeing and sleeping with other women, but she didn't seem to care. Or did she? Maybe her nonchalance was all a façade.

Richmond asks Bridget where she was the morning of Lars's murder and she informs him that she was at her parents' house, which is where she lives. She got up at six and had breakfast with her parents, both of whom are early risers. Then they all watched TV for a while—*Good Morning America,* and Bridget is able to summarize the show for us—and then Bridget got ready for work at the pharmacy, where she arrived a little before ten. When asked about cats, she informs us that her parents have two cats, one all white and one black and white.

Her alibi is easy to verify, and as soon as we let Bridget go, Richmond does so immediately by phoning her parents. They provide the same sequence of events Bridget gave us and as a result, Richmond moves her name to the bottom of the suspect list, though he isn't willing to remove it all together. "We can't rule out the possibility that the killer may have been a hired gun," he says.

With that out of the way, Richmond calls Brad Donaldson, Kirsten's ex, and invites him to the station for a chat later. Judging from Richmond's end of the conversation, Donaldson is clearly confused as to why we're making this request, but he agrees to come at three o'clock.

"We have some time to kill," Richmond says, glancing at his watch. "I want to go to Swenson Hardware and talk to this Bo Jurgenson guy about people in the area he may know who are good with bows and arrows. Want to come along?"

"Sure, but let me give Hurley a call first to get an update on what's going on with Emily."

Richmond nods and I step out of his office and head for the break room, where I dial Hurley's number. Hurley sounds exasperated when he answers. "Any news?" I ask, though judging from Hurley's tone I know what the answer will be.

"No, nothing. It's as if she vanished from the face of the earth."

"I'm so sorry, Hurley."

"I'm on my way to Chicago to poke around and see what I can dig up in the way of old friends and contacts for her," he says. "Since she took that cash I had stashed away, I keep thinking she must have planned to go somewhere." I notice that he, like me, is afraid to give any more voice to the more frightening alternative. Was he doing so to protect me, or himself? Either way, I feel compelled to address it.

"Are you looking into the abduction idea at all?"

"Of course," he says, and I can hear the subtle undertone of fear in his voice. "Her picture has gone out with the Amber Alert and I've got cops in Wisconsin, Minnesota, Illinois, and Michigan all on the lookout."

With that out of the way, I switch to a less emotional topic. "Listen, I talked to Maggie Baldwin this morning. She wouldn't tell me anything because of the whole confidentiality thing, but she did say something that got me to wondering. She said girls Emily's age tend to be very secretive."

"Yeah, I talked to Baldwin, too. She wasn't much help. She said Emily hasn't opened up much yet."

"When I was Emily's age, my primary confidants were my sister and my girlfriends at school. There had to have been someone Emily talked to besides Johnny."

"I don't know who. I already talked to several of the kids at school and they all said the same thing, that she didn't have any really close friends other than him."

"What about cyber friends? Maybe she had someone online she was close to. Have you taken another run at her laptop?"

"I tried all the logical possibilities—her mother's name, her uncle's name, our names, Johnny's name, her middle and last name, pertinent birthdates—none of them worked."

"Would you mind if I came and got the laptop and let someone else take a crack at it?"

"Like who?"

"Remember Joey Dewhurst?"

"That giant man-child who thinks he's a superhero and runs around in a costume? He's kind of hard to forget."

I smile at the memory. "Yeah, he is. But in addition to his little idiosyncrasies, he also has that savantlike ability with computer hacking, remember?"

Hurley sighs. "I suppose we have nothing to lose by trying."

"Good. I'll come by later today and get the laptop while you're in Chicago. When are you going to get there?"

"Within the hour."

"Good luck and keep me posted on how it's going. I'll let you know if Joey comes up with anything."

Chapter 19

Richmond offers to drive and since nothing urgent seems to be coming up with Emily at the moment, I agree to ride with him. Besides, any place in town we go is only a few minutes' drive away from my office and my car.

I give Richmond an update on the Emily situation as we go, concluding with "I'm going to go over to Hurley's place when we're done here and grab Emily's laptop so I can let Joey Dewhurst take a look at it. If anyone can break into it, he can."

"Who is Joey Dewhurst?"

I give Richmond a startled look. "You've never met Joey? Boy, are you in for a treat."

"The name rings a bell, but I can't quite pull it up."

"He's a huge hulk of a guy, sweet as can be, but kind of scary looking until you get to know him. He has some sort of brain damage that he suffered at birth. It left him mentally challenged and he has the emotional maturity of a twelve-year-old boy. But he also has this savant ability when it comes to computers."

"Interesting."

"Actually, that's not the most interesting thing about

him. He also fancies himself something of a superhero. He has a costume he wears all the time, complete with a red cape and tights, and a big, yellow letter H on his chest that stands for Hacker Man."

"Wait, now I remember. Wasn't he in that picture of you that was in the paper last year, the one where you were naked from the waist up?"

"That's the one," I say with a roll of my eyes. "Nice to know you remember that part."

"Hey, for a while there you were appearing in the papers in all kinds of states of undress."

"Don't remind me. Between those pictures and Matthew's birth with all of you guys standing around gawking, I feel like everyone in town who sees me now thinks of me naked. Though at the time of my delivery, I couldn't have cared less if my hoo-ha was being shown on national television if it would have made the pain go away."

Richmond looks at me and smiles. "Yeah, I saw parts of you I probably shouldn't have, but I have to tell you, seeing your son born was the most miraculous, memorable thing that has ever happened to me, Mattie. I'd never seen a birth before. And I imagine I won't ever see one again. So while you may not be comfortable knowing I was there, know that I appreciate the fact that I was."

"Fair enough," I say.

The Swenson hardware store is an old family-run business that has been in Sorenson for as long as I have and then some. It's a dusty, cramped place, filled with every imaginable tool, nut, bolt, screw, nail, and gadget you can think of. If you try to find them yourself, you're likely to get lost among the shelves and never be seen again. But the staffers, all of whom are family, know where every single item is located. It's kind of uncanny the way they do it. You can go in and ask for something and they'll lead you so far back into the dark recesses of the place that you start to wonder if you're about to become the star victim in one of those true crime shows, and then they'll reach over, under, around, and sometimes through other stuff and grab the item on the first try. How they do it is beyond me.

Bo Jurgenson is part of the Swenson family by marriage. He's been working at the store for the past four years, ever since a bad knee injury ended his hopes of playing professional football. He looks like a football player: broad shouldered, six-four, muscular with a bit of extra meat on his bones.

"Hi there," he greets as we come through the door. "What do you folks need today?"

Richmond flashes his badge and says, "Information."

Bo frowns and takes an involuntary step back. "Is there a problem of some sort?"

"Not here," Richmond says. "I understand you're something of an archery expert."

Bo relaxes and smiles, clearly charmed by the flattery. "I'm pretty good, if I do say so myself." His smile vanishes all of a sudden and he tenses up. "Oh, wait, is this about Lars Sanderson?"

"What about Lars Sanderson?" Richmond says.

"Well, I heard he was killed yesterday with an arrow."

"Yes, he was," Richmond says with a sigh. "We're interested in knowing who might have the skill to do something like that."

Bo's brow draws down in confusion. "Skill? I'd say more of a lack of it, wouldn't you?" Richmond doesn't answer and it takes Bo a second or two to catch on. "Wait, are you saying this wasn't an accident?"

"It doesn't appear so," Richmond says. "Did you know Mr. Sanderson?"

Bo shrugs. "Hard not to know the guy given how much he's been in the local paper. He came into the store a few times, and I know some contractors who have worked with him, but I didn't know him personally if that's what you mean."

"Anybody you know have a beef with him?" Richmond asks.

"Lord, yes. I can give you half a dozen names right off the top of my head. Apparently the guy wasn't particularly tactful and his standards weren't up to par with those of a lot of folks, but I can't say I know of anyone who disliked the man enough to kill him."

"So back to the archery question," Richmond says. "Where does someone learn how to do that around here?"

Bo shrugs. "I teach at the sportsmen's club over by Marshfield."

"Do other folks from Sorenson go there?"

"Sure. Lots of them."

"How many who are good at archery?"

Bo pulls at his chin. "There are several folks in town who are good. Reece Morton used to be the leader of the pack, but he doesn't shoot much anymore. Dan Hooper is quite good. He typically places high in the tournaments the club sponsors."

"How many folks that go to the club are bow hunters?" Richmond asks.

"There are a lot of them," Bo says. "You're going to have to be more specific."

I know Richmond isn't going to want to name names, and sure enough, he switches to a different line of questioning. "Let's talk equipment. Do archers typically have identifying marks of any type on their arrows so that you can tell who an arrow belongs to?"

"Sure, especially if they're hunters. There are differences in the shafts, and in the types of points, too. And there are markings on the shaft that designate the weight and diameter. The right size and weight is necessary to get the best air time and that's determined by the bow. Probably the biggest difference is in the fletching."

"Fletching?" Richmond asks.

"Those are the feathers on the arrow," Bo explains, "though these days they're typically made of plastic."

"So if we were to show you an arrow," Richmond poses, "would you be able to tell us whose it is?"

"Possibly, if it belongs to someone I know."

"Will a picture suffice?" I ask.

"It might."

I look at Richmond. "Let me call Arnie and have him forward a clean picture of the arrow to my cell."

"Will that be big enough?" Richmond says. He looks over to Bo for the answer.

Bo flashes a cheesy grin and says, "Hey, bigger is always better."

"I can have Arnie send it to my e-mail account. If the picture I pull up on my phone isn't big enough, would you let me borrow a computer so I can log in to my e-mail?"

"Sure," Bo says. "You can use the one behind the counter."

Other customers have entered the store, so I step outside for some privacy and call Arnie.

"Hey, Mattie, how's it going?" he says. "Are you glad to be back to work?"

Am I? It's a good question, one I'm not sure I know

the answer to. On the one hand I miss my son a ton, and I'm bone-aching tired. But on the other hand, I think that if I hadn't gone back to work, I might have lost my mind over time. My sister, Desi, is a natural at this mothering stuff. She's always been a stay-at-home mom and she seems to delight in the day-to-day tedium the job entails. I, on the other hand, need something more. And that makes me question my maternal instincts.

"Yes, and no," I answer Arnie truthfully.

"Good answer," he says with a chuckle. "Sorry to hear about the troubles with Emily."

"Yeah, she's been a challenge. And that's one of the reasons I'm calling you. I need a favor."

"Fire away."

"Ironic choice of words, as you'll realize in a second. Before I get to the favor, can you take a close-up picture of that arrow from Lars Sanderson and send it to my e-mail?"

"Sure can. Give me about thirty seconds and you should have it. What's the favor?"

"I need you to get in touch with Joey Dewhurst for me. I have a laptop I need him to break into."

"Let me guess. Is it Emily's by chance?"

"It is."

"Not a problem. Where and when do you want him to meet with you?"

"How about in your office at . . ." I look at my watch. "Let's try for around noon. Shoot me a text to let me know once you get ahold of him."

"Will do."

I disconnect the call and half a minute later I hear a ding from my phone to let me know that a new e-mail has arrived. As soon as I have the picture up on my screen, I head back into the store.

"It's pretty small," I tell Richmond, showing it to him.

Bo is ringing up a sale so we stand by patiently waiting for the transaction to finish. The customer is a local plumber named Zane Michaels and as Bo is ringing up his purchases, Michaels says, "Hey, did you hear what happened to Lars Sanderson?"

Bo shoots us a look. Richmond gives him a subtle nod. "Yeah, I heard he got killed," Bo says.

"Sure did," Zane says. "Someone said he got shot with an arrow. Ain't that a kick in the butt?"

Bo says nothing, but Zane isn't about to let the topic go. "Have you heard any rumors about who might have done it? Knowing Lars, I can't help but wonder if it was an accident or if someone took him out on purpose. That guy knew how to rile people up."

"Haven't heard a thing," Bo says.

"What do you think it was: accident or murder?" Zane's voice takes on a suspenseful quality as he utters the word *murder*.

"Wouldn't know and wouldn't want to speculate," Bo says, though I'm pretty sure he would want to speculate if we weren't standing here listening. He counts out Zane's change, bags his purchases, and hands them over.

"Let me know if you hear anything, okay?" Zane says as he heads out the door.

"Will do," Bo says, giving a tip of his hat. As soon as Zane is gone, Bo looks at us and says, "Sorry about that."

"No need to be," I tell him. "The gossip mill in this town waits for no man." I walk up to the counter and hand him my phone. "Here's a picture. Can you tell anything from it?"

Bo takes the phone, studies the picture for a moment,

and then says, "Yeah, I can. That fletching is pretty distinctive and I only know of one person who uses that green and purple neon color. I know because it's a custom-made arrow. And I'm the one who made it."

My heart quickens.

"That arrow belongs to Reece Morton."

Chapter 20

After learning that Bo can provide documentation to prove he custom-made the arrow in question for Reece Morton, Richmond and I thank him and head back out to the car.

"Well that's both good news and bad news," I say. "Now we know who the arrow belongs to but it doesn't do us much good because we're pretty sure Reece couldn't have shot it, and his archery equipment is missing."

"Too bad they didn't find any prints on the arrow," Richmond grumbles as we settle into his car.

"They did find one, but it belonged to Lars."

Richmond scoffs his frustration.

"We need to think back to Reece's storage unit," I say, grabbing my cell phone as it dings with an incoming text message. "Don't those places typically have security cameras?"

Richmond looks over at me with his happy face. "They do," he says, as I read the text message. "Shall we go retrieve it?"

"I'd love to, but that was Arnie texting me to let me

know that Joey will be at our office at noon. So while you do that, I'm going to go over to Hurley's place to have a look around Emily's room and get her laptop so I can take it to Joey. Would you mind dropping me off back at my office so I can get my car?"

"Sure thing."

"I'll touch base with you before Hart Bauer's interview at two."

As soon as Richmond drops me off, I head inside to check in with Izzy. I find him in his office, busy working on the mounds of paperwork that go with the job.

"Anything going on?" I ask.

He shakes his head. "Just the usual paper chase. Anything new on the Sanderson case?"

"Some." I fill him in on our chat with Ms. Rutherford, Bo's identification of the arrow, and our upcoming chats with Hart Bauer and Brad Donaldson. "Richmond is headed to Reece Morton's storage facility now to see if he can get any security tape of the unit that might show someone accessing it recently."

"Any news on Emily?"

"Yes, and no." I tell him about Hurley heading for Chicago, and my plans to use Joey so we can hopefully get a look at Emily's laptop.

"Be careful, Mattie," Izzy says with a frown. "I get why you're going to use Joey, and I'm not disagreeing with the idea. But know that whatever he does has to be off the books."

"Of course," I say, unsure why he's cautioning me on the matter. "This isn't an official investigation."

"Maybe it should be."

"Why? It's not like this is something new and unusual. Emily has disappeared before a number of times."

"Well, not to be a pessimist," he says in a way that tells me he's going to do just that, "but what if this time is different? What if this thing goes bad? If, God forbid, we have to open an official investigation, anything Joey does with Emily's laptop could taint any evidence it might contain."

There it is: the elephant in the room. Though even Izzy is skirting around it a bit. "I understand, Izzy, but if this time *is* different, and Emily *is* in any real danger, then the faster we find her the better. What are our other options with regard to her laptop? Arnie and Jonas don't do that sort of stuff. Laura is a wiz at sleuthing out information on the Internet, and she might be able to find something on the computer if we can get it unlocked, but there isn't anyone here locally other than Joey who can hack into the thing. If we send it off to the Madison lab, who knows how long it will take them to even get to it, much less find anything?"

"Like I said, I understand why you're doing what you're doing. And I'm not saying it's the wrong choice. I just want to make sure you understand the possible ramifications it might have down the road. And I'm not talking strictly evidentiary or legal implications. If Emily does return, what is she going to think when she finds out you snooped through her stuff? If you think she resents you now, just wait."

"I get it, but I think we have to do this. Hurley is going crazy trying to locate her, and since this is different from her usual disappearing act, I feel like we need to do everything we can to find her and bring her back home. If our snooping makes her resent me even more, I'll deal with it when it happens. I'd rather have that on my conscience than the knowledge that I didn't do everything I could, especially if this does turn out bad."

"Okay," he says with a wan smile. "Good luck. I hope it works."

I leave before he has a chance to change his mind or say anything else. I make a quick stop in the locker room to pump, and then head for Hurley's house.

I have a key; Hurley gave it to me months ago when I was being stalked by a crazy man who wanted to kill me. I let myself in and take a few moments to walk through the main floor and look around. I'm not sure what it is I'm looking for, but I feel the need to scope out the entire house, and figure I might as well start on the ground floor.

I walk around the living room, checking out the magazines, looking under the chair and couch cushions, scanning the titles in the bookcase. I open up the coat closet and scan its contents. There are two jackets that are too small to be Hurley's, one made from a canvas material suitable for fall, the other a puffy, lightweight jacket that would be good for cold weather at the start of the winter or in the spring, but hardly warm enough for the current temperatures. I check the pockets in both of them and find some change, a stick of gum, and a pen.

Next I head for the kitchen. I haven't been here since right before Matthew was born, but nothing looks unusual or out of place. There is a cordless house phone and I take it out of its base and scroll through the caller ID history. Nothing leaps out at me. Off the kitchen are a small bathroom and a mudroom, neither of which offers anything of interest, so I head upstairs.

The main bathroom is to the right at the top of the stairs, so I check it out first. It's obvious that Emily has been the one using it. The countertop is covered with the detritus of a teenage girl's daily needs: skin products, makeup, scrunchies, hair bands, hair spray, mousse, deodorant, toothbrush and toothpaste. The sight of it all gives me a chill and ratchets up my anxiety a notch. If Emily had left with the intention of staying away for any length of time, wouldn't she have taken these items with her?

I open up the medicine cabinet and find two prescriptions with Emily's name on them. One is an antidepressant prescribed by Maggie, the other an antibiotic often used to treat acne. That Emily didn't take these with her doesn't alarm me as much as the makeup and toothbrush. Teenagers tend to balk at taking pills for legitimate medicinal reasons even though they'll pop a handful of unknown meds in order to get high at a party.

I poke my head in the shower and see it's stocked with shampoo, conditioner, body soap, a razor, and a net scrubber. Again I have to wonder why she didn't take these toiletries with her. Granted, she had Hurley's money with her and she could buy the stuff easily enough, but why not just take them? She could have stashed them in her backpack without Hurley knowing.

I leave the bathroom and its ominous findings, and head for the end of the hall to Hurley's room. He has his own bathroom off the bedroom, and I see that his toiletries are all missing. The bed is unmade and several items of clothing have been tossed on it, no doubt stuff that didn't make the packing effort.

Finally I head for Emily's room.

It's a mess, and I wonder how much this bothers Hurley. He's hardly a neatnik, but he's not nearly as messy as this room is. Clothes are strewn everywhere, and there is no way for me to know if Emily has taken any clothing with her. I head for her desk area. The laptop is sitting there, open but asleep. I wake it up, see the prompt for a password, and for grins I try variations of Johnny Chester's name. I know Hurley said he tried birthdates, but don't know if he knew or thought to try Johnny's. So I place a call to Laura and ask for help.

"I need a birthdate," I tell her. "It's for Jonathan Chester." I give her a few other details, such as his father's name, and as I'm holding she starts clicking away at a computer.

"Is this about Emily?" she asks. "It's a darn shame that the poor girl is having so much trouble and I feel really bad for Detective Hurley because this can't be very easy for him, suddenly inheriting a teenaged girl for a daughter who he knew nothing about and who doesn't know anything about him because her mother—"

"Laura, take a breath," I say, interrupting her run-on blab.

"Sorry," she says. I hear her actually take a breath, a deep one, and then she says, "Here you go. Date of birth is March 23, 1999."

"Thanks," I say, and then before she can start another bout of verbal diarrhea I say, "Bye," and disconnect the call. I try various iterations of the birthdate, but nothing works. I abandon the laptop and start looking at other items. On top of the desk is a picture of Emily's mother, Kate, one that appears to be a few years old. There are some art books lined up against the wall at the back of the desk and I flip through the pages looking for notes. There aren't any, so I move on to a pile of school papers with grades ranging from a C in math to an A on an English paper. Underneath everything is one of those large calendar blotters but a quick scan of the few items that are written on it reveals school-related stuff—test dates, homework assignment deadlines, a pep rally. On the far right is a stack of school books—algebra, history, and biology. Accompanying each one is a black and white composition notebook. I flip through the pages of the textbooks first and then tackle the composition books. The first one contains notes for a biology class and Emily has drawn doodles on nearly every page, some of which are excellent renditions of animals and faces, including one that I recognize as Mr. Clarkston, the biology teacher. I move on to the next one, which contains notes on U.S. history and, like the first notebook, it also contains a number of drawings and doodles in the margins of the pages. One I recognize immediately as Johnny Chester. Another one looks familiar but it takes me a second to figure out who it is. I flash back to Hurley's and my trip to the school and my visit to the girls' bathroom, and it comes to me then that the face is that of Carly Randall, the cheerleader I spoke to in the bathroom. I don't recognize any of the other faces, but assume they are classmates or friends of Emily's. The third and final notebook is similar to the first two, though the topic for this one is algebra, and it contains far fewer doodles. I suspect that's because the algebra class requires more of Emily's focused attention than the other classes do.

There are three drawers in the desk, a wide, shallow center one, and two deeper ones on either side. I open the center one first and find the expected assortment of pencils, erasers, staples, paper clips, sticky notes, a compass, a pencil sharpener, a ruler, and a collection of pens in a variety of colors. Mixed in with these items are some hair ties, several pairs of earrings, nail clippers, an emery board, and a couple of bottles of nail polish. The side drawer on the right is filled with socks of all colors and designs. Recalling my own attempts to hide things from my sister when we were younger, I examine every pair, unrolling the ones that are matched up and squeezing each and every sock to make sure nothing is hidden inside them. I come up empty and move to the drawer on the left. It's a hodgepodge of stuff. There are several comic books with titles such as *Unlovable, Runaways,* and *This One Summer.* A quick scan of the content shows they all run along the same themes: acceptance, peer pressure, trying to fit in, establishing your identity, and the problems inherent in developing and maintaining friendships in adolescence.

My heart aches for Emily, remembering the pains I experienced as the weird kid in school—the one who was freakishly tall, the one who didn't have a father, the one with feet the size of a Sasquatch—and that was among kids I'd known all my life. Poor Emily has the additional burden of being the new kid on the block, and that can't be easy on top of all the other upsets she's had in her life lately.

Beneath the comic books is another one of those composition notebooks, but the pages of this one are empty, leading me to think it's an extra. At the bottom of the drawer are some drawings of animals and people, including one of Emily's mother, Kate. The level of detail in the pictures is amazing and once again I find myself in awe of the kid's talent. Finally, at the bottom of the drawer is a collection of cards from Kate to Emily, marking birthdays, holidays, and a few just because. I read a few of the messages but then stop. They feel exquisitely personal and I feel like an unwelcome interloper reading them.

I leave the desk and move on to the dresser, where I go through every drawer, and handle every item of clothing looking for any hidden items. I strike gold in the underwear drawer where I find a half full pack of cigarettes and a lighter tucked inside an otherwise empty tampon box.

A search of the closet with a close examination inside each shoe, bag, and box reveals no more secrets. I toss the bed, looking under the mattress and the bed itself. Having exhausted the potential hiding spots, and with the noon hour rapidly approaching, I grab the laptop and head out, making sure to lock the door when I leave.

Chapter 21

It's been almost a year since the last time I saw Joey Dewhurst and he looks a little different. His hair is a smidge longer and combed back with some sort of product, and his clothes are a little more fashionable than the baggy jeans and shirts he used to wear, but his lumbering gait, immense size, and sweet face are all the same.

"Joey, you are looking really good," I say as I enter Arnie's lab area.

Joey gawks at me, as does Arnie.

"You changed your hair color," Arnie says in a neutral tone.

Uh-oh.

Joey, who often doesn't grasp the concept of political correctness or polite conversation, is less deferent. "Hi, Mattie," he says with a big smile. Then he frowns and adds, "I don't like you with red hair."

I look over at Arnie and he shrugs. "You don't like it either, do you?" I say. He gives me an equivocal look, and a little head dodge. "Oh, for Pete's sake," I say before he can hand me whatever line of bull he's thinking up.

"Don't worry about hurting my feelings. I need the truth."

"Okay," Arnie says with a shrug. "It doesn't work on you. And it smacks of desperation."

"Desperation? How?"

"Are you going to tell me that Charlie's presence has nothing to do with your decision to change?"

"Who's Charlie?" Joey asks.

"Only the most beautiful woman I've ever seen," Arnie gushes.

"Charlie is a girl?" Joey says, looking confused.

"She's all woman," Arnie says. "She has a beautiful face, gorgeous red hair, freckles that lead to all kinds of interesting places, and legs that never quit."

"You mean she walks a lot?" Joey says, forcing me to bite back a laugh.

Arnie smiles and says, "I'll explain it to you later. Let's get down to business."

Joey's attention is easily diverted. Arnie directs him to the only desk in the lab, and one of the only spots that isn't covered with some type of machinery or equipment. I hand over the laptop and explain to Joey what I want him to do.

"This belongs to Detective Hurley's daughter and she's missing. We're hoping to find some clues about where she might be if we can get into the computer and check out her e-mails and her social networking, but the computer is password protected. Do you think you can get into it and snoop around?"

"Do you think she was kidnapped?" Joey asks, his eyes wide.

"It's possible," I admit, and I see Arnie's expression change to one of dark worry. "But we're thinking that she's probably run away. She's got a lot of problems and she's disappeared before, just never for this long."

"I'll see what I can do," Joey says. As he settles into the chair at the desk, the back of his shirt rides up and I can see a flash of silky red material. Joey is wearing his Hacker Man outfit and the knowledge makes me smile.

"I'm going to run home and see Matthew and then I have some interviews to do with Richmond," I tell the guys. "But I'll keep my phone with me. Call or text me if you find anything, okay?"

"Who is Matthew?" Joey asks. "Is that your boyfriend? You should have a boyfriend, Mattie, because you're very pretty, even with red hair."

"Okay, okay, I give on the red hair," I say, holding my hand up like a traffic cop. "I'll change it back. And no, Matthew isn't my boyfriend, Joey, he's my son. I had a baby a couple of months ago."

Joey's eyes grow wide and his mouth drops open. "You had a baby? How did you do that?"

Arnie and I look at one another for a few seconds. "You can handle this one," I tell him, and then I leave before any more awkward moments can crop up.

I head home hoping for a quick lunch—giving it rather than getting it—and I'm lucky enough to catch Matthew just as he's waking from a nap. I manage to sneak twenty minutes of blissful mother-son bonding in the bedroom rocking chair nursing Matthew while Dom fixes sandwiches for us in his kitchen since my cupboards are looking a little bare. I need to get back online.

Just as we are about to sit down and eat our lunch, my phone rings. I'm hoping it will be Hurley, but it's Richmond instead. "Good news, bad news," he says. "The storage facility does have security cameras, but the footage gets recorded over every month. So we know that no one approached Morton's storage unit in the past month, but anything that happened before that is lost."

"Bummer," I say, taking a bite of my sandwich. It's liverwurst with mayonnaise and a thin slice of onion on a hard roll, a treat that Dom and I love and share once in a while since everyone else we know thinks it looks, smells, and tastes like dog food. And yes, I discovered I can order liverwurst from Amazon, but it doesn't qualify for Prime shipping and because of the refrigeration needed, the shipping costs are prohibitive. So I let Dom handle the liverwurst.

"There is some good news," Richmond continues. "Junior has been looking through Sanderson's financials and all those files we got from his home office. And he turned up some unusual transactions in Sanderson's bank accounts, including an account he established using a false name and identity."

"A false identity . . . why would he need that?"

"I'm not sure yet."

"Is there a lot of money in it?"

"Actually there's no money in it, despite the fact that Sanderson deposited several large sums of money over the past year or so, two of them over twenty thousand bucks."

"Where did it all go?"

"That's what we're trying to figure out. It looks like Sanderson wired money out of his business account into this other account, which is based out of a bank in Illinois. He then took the sums out of this account as cash a number of times, typically small amounts of one or two thousand, always less than ten thousand to avoid the IRS paperwork. He had a file in his home office filled with receipts he paid for in cash, but it turns out that some of the company names are phony, and others that he supposedly paid cash to said no such transaction ever occurred."

"Interesting," I say pondering the meaning behind it all.

"Yes, it is," Richmond agrees. "I think we need to go back to Sanderson's house and have another look around. Want to come along?"

"Absolutely," I say, swallowing and giving Dom an apologetic look. "I'll meet you at the station in ten minutes."

I disconnect the call and after grabbing the rest of my sandwich, I put on my coat. "Sorry," I tell Dom. "I'll have to share the rest of this sandwich with you in spirit only."

"That's okay," he says. "I know how it is. Duty calls."

"Thanks for lunch. I owe you." I turn to leave but Dom calls me back.

"Mattie?"

"Yeah?"

"Have you given any more thought to what we discussed the other day? You know . . . the baby thing?"

"I have, but I haven't made a decision yet," I lie. "You need to discuss it with Izzy first."

"I'm afraid to broach the subject."

"Yeah, about that . . . I think it may have been broached for you," I tell him with a guilty smile. His eyes grow huge and before he can ask me anything else, I give him an apologetic shrug and head out the door at a fast clip.

A little over ten minutes later I am in my car following Richmond back to Lars Sanderson's house. Junior

Feller and Karl Young, aka KY, are both going to meet us there. Just as we arrive, my cell phone rings.

"Mattie Winston."

"Hey, Mattie, it's Arnie. Joey got into Emily's computer."

"Fantastic!" I say. "Give him a hug for me."

"I would, but I think he'd rather it came from you."

"Take a look at her e-mails, and any social networking sites she's been on to see what you can find."

"Will do. We're looking at her e-mails already, but there isn't much there."

"Pay attention to anything that looks like it might be from people down around the Chicago area. I'm on the way to Lars Sanderson's house with Richmond and some others to search for some more evidence. And Richmond and I have meetings at two and three with some other possible suspects. If you find a smoking gun, call me, otherwise I'll check in with you when I'm done."

I hang up and call Hurley, but it flips over to voice mail. I leave him a message letting him know that Joey has gotten into Emily's computer and that he and Arnie are looking through the contents now. I ask him to call me with any updates on his end and say I'll do the same.

Richmond and Junior are already at Sanderson's front door and KY has pulled up and is headed that way, so I scramble out of my car and hurry up the walk to catch up. As I step onto the porch, I realize Junior is staring at me.

"You did something different to your hair," he says in that cursed neutral tone.

"It's temporary, okay?" I snap. Both he and Richmond stare at me as if they just saw my head spin around three hundred and sixty degrees. KY comes up on the porch and looks at all of us, sensing that something has just happened. His eyes linger on me and when I see his gaze shift to my hair, I beat him to the punch. "Yes, I did something different to my hair, and yes, I know it doesn't look great. I'm changing it back. Okay? Can we please move on now?"

Richmond turns away, slices through the evidence tape, unlocks the door, and lets us in. No one says another word about my hair, which is probably a good thing because along about now it feels like I'm wearing Medusa snakes on my head.

"Let's split up," Richmond says as we all don gloves. Then, to prove how brave he is, he says, "Junior, you and Karl take the living room, kitchen, downstairs bathroom, and laundry room. Mattie and I will take the upstairs. We've gone through the home office pretty thoroughly already, so if we don't find anything in the other rooms we'll take another look in there at the end. Use your cameras as needed."

Junior and Karl nod, and with Junior manning the camera, they head for the kitchen. Richmond hands me his camera and I follow him upstairs.

"I'm thinking if he had a cash stash somewhere, he'd want it in a private place," Richmond says, "so let's start with the master bedroom."

We head there and I have to suppress a shudder at the tacky décor, even though it's lessened slightly now that the bed linens are missing. We start with the obvious places: the dressers, the bedside stands—which contain some interesting sex toys—and the closet. We empty everything out of the closet that's on a shelf or on the floor and then Richmond looks up at the ceiling area. "No panels or ceiling covers," he says as I film. Next he starts knocking on the hardwood floor to check for loosened floorboards, but nothing turns up. With no success there, we probe the mattress for any unusual lumps. Even with gloves on, I have an overwhelming urge to wash my hands when we're done. The last place we look is in a clothes hamper that's full. We pick it up and dump out all the dirty clothes, but that's all we find in there. We move on to the spare bedroom, which is thankfully plain, sparse, and rather dusty. Once again we go through the same routine and once again we come up empty.

Back out in the hallway, I ask, "How much money are we looking for?"

"More than a hundred grand," he says. "That kind of cash would have some bulk to it so wherever he stashed it has to be big enough to hold it."

"I don't suppose he had a safe deposit box somewhere."

Richmond shakes his head. "If he does, we haven't found any trace of it—no paperwork and no key."

"All we have left up here are the bathrooms. I vote we look in the master bath first. It's more private."

Richmond nods his agreement and we start to head that way when something in the hallway catches my eye. "Richmond, look at this." I point to a small door, less than a foot square, built into the wall.

"That's just a laundry chute," he says.

I pull it open and peer inside. It's dark other than a dim rectangle of light I can see at the bottom where it exits into the laundry room. "Do you have a flashlight?" I ask.

Richmond gives me an impatient look as I hand him the camera and he hands me his key ring, which has a small flashlight on it. "If you can see down it, there's no cash stashed in there," he says. "A bundle with that much cash in it would hardly fit down that chute."

"I just want to make sure. If he has a laundry chute here, why did he have a hamper full of clothes in his bedroom? Why have a hamper at all?"

Richmond shrugs. "I don't know. Maybe he doesn't like the chute for some reason. Or maybe he dumps all his stuff down it at once."

I stick my head through the opening and can barely manage to get my hand in with the light to shine it down the chute. I finally manage to get the light in far enough to see that the chute is empty. When I go to pull my head back out, it hits the top of the chute and I feel something give.

"Ow," I say, pulling my head the rest of the way out. I palpate my scalp to make sure it's still intact. It is, so I get down on my knees and shine the light up the inside of the chute opening. A few inches above the opening is what appears to be a solid wooden ceiling. I reach in with my hand and push up on it. It gives a little so I push harder. A faint click sounds and when I pull my hand back, the ceiling drops down, swinging on an inside hinge. There is a sudden *whoosh* and something hits my fingers before plummeting down the chute.

"What the hell was that?" Richmond says.

I look down the chute and see a sack lying on the floor down in the laundry room. "It's a bag of something," I tell him. "I don't think it's big enough to be a bag of cash the size of what we're looking for, but maybe it's part of it." I pull out of the chute and Richmond sticks his head in for a look. As soon as he pulls out, he takes the camera and aims it down the chute at the sack, then up the chute at the opening with the hinged door.

"There's a magnetic catch on that door," he says when he's done. He reaches in and closes the panel, which snugs back into place with a tiny click. Then he pushes up on it until it clicks again and the door drops open. "Let's go see what we found," he says.

We head downstairs to the laundry room, hollering along the way for Junior and KY, who are still in the kitchen going through its many storage spots. In the laundry room lying on the floor beneath the chute opening is a sack about the size of a ten-pound bag of flour. Richmond hands me the camera and I start filming.

"It's heavy," Richmond says, picking up the sack. It has a drawstring tie at the top that is knotted to keep the sack closed. He squeezes the bag in several places and gives us a perplexed look. "It isn't cash," he announces. It takes him a moment or two to undo the knot and open the drawstring. Then he reaches in and pulls out a block of something. As I zoom in with the camera I see that it's a stack of what looks like credit cards rubber banded together. He removes the band and sets the cards down on top of the nearby washing machine, spreading them out. I see dozens of VISA and MasterCard logos, though none of the cards have names on them.

"These are prepaid gift cards," Junior says, looking through them. "I send them to my nieces and nephews every year for Christmas. It looks like each one of these can hold up to five hundred dollars and there are forty or fifty of them here."

"And that's just the beginning," Richmond says. He takes another stack out of the bag and hands it to Junior. He repeats this five more times until the bag is empty.

"This is brilliant," Junior says, eyeing the cards. "If he went to a bunch of different stores in different towns to buy these over a period of time, no one would be the wiser. You can get them at tons of places these days, even the grocery store. And you have to pay cash to get them, so it's a completely anonymous purchase if you buy them somewhere where no one knows you."

"Don't you have to pay a fee to activate them?" Richmond says.

"You do," Junior answers. "But if you're trying to hide a boatload of cash, those activation fees are a lot less than the taxes you'd pay on the money. Not to mention the other penalties you might have to pay if the money was obtained illegally."

Richmond nods. "So we know Lars was up to something illegal that got him a bunch of cash. I'm betting that whoever killed him knew about it and hoped to get their hands on some, if not all of that money. Now all we have to do is figure out who that is."

"And how do we do that?" I ask.

"Follow the money trail," Richmond says. "We're going to have to backtrack on every one of those phony invoices and bank deposits, and figure out when they were generated, what jobs Lars was doing at the time, and where the money might have come from."

He makes it sound easy, but I know it won't be. It will be like looking for the proverbial needle in a haystack.

Chapter 22

Richmond and I arrive back at the station fifteen minutes before we are scheduled to meet with Hart Bauer, formally known as Hartwig Beckenbauer. I make use of the time by calling Hurley again, but all I get is his voice mail. Rather than leave another message, I just hang up. Richmond disappears long enough to go downstairs to the basement evidence area to log in the bank cards we found at Lars's place. When he returns, he shares some information that Laura has dug up on Hart Bauer and we discuss how to bring it up. Once we have our plan down, Richmond asks me to go out and fetch our interviewee while he heads to the interview room and readies the equipment.

I head up front, poke my head out into the reception area, and call out Bauer's name. He hops up from his seat and flashes me a big, very white smile, closing the distance between us with three long strides.

"Follow me, please," I say without any further introduction, and then I turn and head for the interview room, assuming he will follow. He does, and when we enter the room, Richmond is standing just inside the door waiting on us. I let him do the introductions, and once he's done, he directs Bauer to the far side of the table while he and I take our usual seats.

It's hard for me to peg Mr. Bauer's age. He has nice skin for a man—smooth, unblemished, pale but not sickly so. His hair is thick and brown with blond highlights, cut short on the sides and combed back from his face. His eyes are a vibrant shade of green that doesn't look natural, and upon closer inspection I see the faint outline of contact lenses. Heightwise he has me by an inch or so, and his build is slender.

Richmond opens by stating the date and time, the case the interview involves, who is being interviewed, and who is doing the interview. With that out of the way, he informs Bauer that our session is being recorded and then gets right to the point. "Mr. Bauer, I understand that you had some issues with Lars Sanderson regarding a purchase he made from a Mrs. Freda Herman."

"I do have an issue with the man," Bauer says. "He's a con artist."

"Care to explain what you mean by that?" Richmond says.

"Sure. He stole my aunt's property. She had a farm and a nice parcel of land several miles just outside of town. I was supposed to inherit it when she died since I'm her only living relative. But when she did finally pass, I discovered that the land had been hijacked by this Mr. Sanderson."

Bauer has a fabulous voice—a deep baritone that's hypnotically soft in volume—and he enunciates with great care.

"Hijacked?" Richmond says.

"Basically, yes. Aunt Freda and Uncle Joe lived and worked on that farm for more than thirty years. When Joe died eight years ago, Aunt Freda tried to handle the farm by herself and keep it going, but it got to be too much for her. She fell behind on her bills. Then this Sanderson character comes along two years ago and offers to help her out with the bills by advancing her some money and having her sign some papers. Turns out those papers gave Sanderson ownership of the land. He sold off bits and pieces of it while letting Aunt Freda stay in her home, and then when she died, he got that, and sold it off, too. I was counting on that land to help finance my career, and what he did to Aunt Freda was incorrigible."

He makes this statement with much drama, befitting his occupation.

"You called an elder abuse hotline to complain, didn't you?" I ask, using the information Laura dug up.

"I did," Bauer says, tight-lipped. "But they didn't do anything about it."

"Actually, they did," I tell him. "According to the report, your aunt was terminally ill when Sanderson approached her, and she was looking for a way to die in her home and not have to go to a nursing home. Yes, Sanderson did sell off parcels of her land, but he used some of the money he got from those sales to fund her home care. She had nurses around the clock during the last three months of her life."

Bauer's face has darkened with anger. "He might have paid for some nurses, but it hardly makes up for the money he made off her land. He stole it out from under her."

Richmond says, "That must have made you angry."

"Of course it made me angry. That money was supposed to be mine. It was supposed to help me stay in L.A. so I could give my acting career a chance." He lets out a sigh of exasperation and folds his arms over his chest. "Look, why did you make me come here? You said this was regarding Sanderson, so I thought the bastard finally got what was coming to him and you were filing charges against him."

"We are not filing any charges against Mr. Sanderson," Richmond says.

"Why the hell not?" Bauer booms in his best stage voice.

"Mr. Bauer, where were you yesterday morning between the hours of five and eight?"

"I was in my apartment in Milwaukee, sleeping. The shows I'm in run late and I don't usually get home until three in the morning or later."

"Can anyone verify that you were there?"

Bauer frowns and narrows his eyes at Richmond. "What is this about?"

"Can you please answer my question?" Richmond says.

Bauer is pissed and it shows. "No, no one can verify that. I live alone."

"Do you own a cat?"

"God, no. I'm allergic to the beasts. Swell up like a puffer fish if I so much as look at one."

"And when is the last time you saw Mr. Sanderson?" Richmond asks, the picture of cool, calm collection, which just seems to incense Bauer even more.

"I don't know . . . a few weeks ago, I guess. I went to his office to try to reason with the guy and see if he would at least give me part of the proceeds from the sale of Aunt Freda's house, but he wouldn't hear of it. He told me to leave and not come back." Bauer pauses and looks from Richmond to me and then back to Richmond again. "Wait a minute," he says, his eyes growing wide. Then he points at me, though he's still focused on Richmond. "You said she's with the medical examiner's office?"

Richmond nods.

"Does that mean someone is dead?"

"It does," Richmond answers.

"Is Sanderson dead?"

Richmond hesitates for a second or two before he nods. "Yes, I'm afraid he is."

Bauer lets out an ironic laugh and shakes his head. "If you guys are talking to people like me, I'm guessing somebody killed him?"

"It would appear so, yes," Richmond says.

"Good," Bauer says with a defiant expression on his face. "The bastard finally got what was coming to him."

Richmond arches his brows at Bauer and leans toward him, arms on the table, his eyes holding Bauer in a piercing glare.

"What?" Bauer says with a huff. "I'm not going to lie and say I'm sad he's dead, because I'm not. I didn't kill him, but I'd buy a drink for whoever did."

A half a minute of silence ensues as Richmond and Bauer stare one another down. Richmond's glare is scary looking, but Bauer doesn't appear at all intimidated.

"Am I done here?" Bauer says finally, pushing back his chair in preparation for standing.

"One more question," Richmond says. "Do you own a bow and arrow of any sort?"

"No. Why?"

"Have you ever shot a bow and arrow?"

"You said one question, so I don't have to answer that, but I will. No, I haven't. And I'm leaving." He stands and heads around the end of the table toward the door. "If you have any more questions for me, you can direct them to my lawyer."

"Well, that was certainly interesting," I say after we escort Hart Bauer out. "Our Mr. Bauer has motive and no alibi, but I don't think he had anything to do with it, do you?"

Richmond sighs and shakes his head. "No, I don't. He seemed genuinely surprised—and pleased—to learn that Lars was dead."

"Lars definitely didn't have many fans," I say with a sigh. "Though I have to confess, what he did for Freda Herman was actually quite kind. He didn't have to let her stay in that house or pay for the private duty nurses. And yet he did. It suggests he had some kind of a conscience."

"I suppose," Richmond says, sounding unconvinced.

"Any word on the search warrant for Harry Olsen's archery equipment?"

"Yeah, I got it but I've put it on the back burner for now. We know the arrow that killed Lars belonged to Reece Morton, so I don't know what good it will do to look at Olsen's equipment," Richmond grumbles.

"We know the arrow was Morton's, but that doesn't necessarily mean it was fired from Morton's bow, does it? Will a bow leave markings on the arrow the way a gun barrel does with bullets?"

"It's possible, but there are no guarantees. And if the arrow was used with Morton's bow and then another bow, any evidence gleaned from markings on the arrow would be worthless. Plus, I've done some research on the topic based on what Bo Jurgenson told us, and learned that arrows are specifically weighted and built to fit the bow they will be shot from. Using another bow might have a deleterious effect on accuracy."

I glance at my watch and see that we have over half an hour before Brad Donaldson is due to arrive. "Listen," I say, "while you contemplate our next steps,

I'm going to head back to my office to see if Arnie and Joey have made any progress with Emily's computer. I'll be back in time for the interview with Brad Donaldson."

"Okay. Good luck."

"Thanks. I think we need it." I grab my coat and head over to my office. Once there I head upstairs to Arnie's lab area. He and Joey are right where I left them.

"Perfect timing," Arnie says. "We were just about to call you."

"Did you find something?"

Arnie looks grim and shakes his head. "We've scoured through her e-mails, and all the recent ones are about school stuff, and while she does have accounts established on Myspace and Facebook, she hasn't posted anything on them in weeks. We went through all of her Word files to see if there might be any letters, or a diary, but all we found were papers she wrote for school. We just finished looking through her browser history to see if anything there looked promising, but all we found were some fan sites she'd been to, some research stuff she did for school, and some music downloads. No searches for bus tickets, train schedules, maps, or directions."

"No communications with anyone in Chicago?"

"Nothing current. There were some e-mail exchanges months ago with one girl she went to school with in Chicago, but there hasn't been any recent contact."

"Dang it!"

"I'm sorry, Mattie," Joey says.

I pat him on his shoulder. "You don't have anything to be sorry about," I tell him. "You did exactly what I needed you to do. Thank you." I bend down and kiss him on his cheek, which makes him flush bright red. "Give me the name of the girl in Chicago and I'll pass it on to Hurley just in case."

Arnie writes it down for me and hands me the paper. "You might as well take the computer back," he says. "We've given it a thorough going-over."

I nod as Arnie closes the laptop, unplugs it, and hands it to me.

"Thanks, guys. I really appreciate it."

Joey gets up from his chair and walks toward me, arms spread wide. Smiling, I let him wrap me in a giant bear hug. "I'm glad I got to see you again, Mattie," he says.

"I'm glad I got to see you, too, Joey. Thank you for helping me."

Joey releases me and, as I turn to leave, the door opens and Laura walks in. "Hello everyone," she says. "How are things . . . ?"

It's an amazingly succinct greeting for her and the reason behind it becomes readily apparent. She is gaping at me, her mouth hanging open, her greeting frozen in time. "You did something different to your hair," she says after a few seconds of stunned silence. The fact that my hair has stunned her even though Joey is in the room speaks volumes.

"It's a temporary thing," I say with a self-conscious stroke of my hair. "An experiment gone wrong. I'm changing it back as soon as I can." Then to divert attention away from me, I add, "Have you been over at the PD all day?"

She nods. "Jonas and I have been processing through all those files on the Sanderson case. Any good suspects yet?"

I see Arnie frown. No doubt he doesn't like it when

Laura has to spend time with Jonas, given that both men are vying for her attention.

"Lots of them," I tell Laura. "But no one in particular yet."

Laura finally looks at Joey and after a moment of study, she walks over to him and extends a hand. "Hi, I'm Laura."

Joey's mouth is hanging open and he's standing all rigid and stiff, like he's been Tasered.

"Laura, this is Joey, a friend of mine," Arnie says.

"You're really pretty," Joey says, finally finding his voice.

"Thank you," Laura says with a coquettish tilt of her head and a big smile.

Arnie rolls his eyes. Now that there are two other men who are gaga for Laura, things could get very tense.

I figure it's a good time to escape and head downstairs to check in with Izzy. After I update him on the hunt for Emily and our progress on the Sanderson case, he says, "I just brought in a new body from the ER. It looks like a heart attack, but the circumstances were a little unusual and the guy had no history of heart trouble, so I plan to post him in the morning."

"What time?"

"Figure on coming in at eight as usual. We'll do it first thing. Why don't you head home after your next interview? You had a long day yesterday. Go home and spend some time with that boy of yours."

"Are you sure?"

He waves me away. "Get while the getting is good. Tell Dom I should be home around seven. I'm going to stay a little later tonight and try to get caught up on some paperwork."

"Anything I can help with?"

"No, but thanks for the offer." I turn to leave but he stops me. "Mattie?"

"Yeah?"

"Thanks for the honest talk yesterday about this thing with Dom. You raised some valid points and I appreciate your candor."

"No problem."

"I'm curious about something. Would you actually consider serving as a surrogate for me and Dom?"

"No, but I didn't tell Dom that yet. I think it's a valid option for the two of you, just not with me as the surrogate. Frankly, pregnancy wasn't the glowing, tons-of-fun experience people led me to believe it would be. So if I ever go through that torture again, it's going to be for my own kid. Besides, I think it would be a situation ripe with potential, and I don't mean that in a good way. I don't want to do anything to jeopardize our friendship. I hope that's okay."

Izzy smiles at me. "It's more than okay. It's a relief. I was afraid I was going to have to fight both you and Dom on the matter. I'm not against the idea in general, just involving you in it. You're absolutely right that it has the potential to jeopardize both our friendship and our working relationship. And since I'm technically your boss, asking you to have my child seems like the worst kind of sexual harassment and abuse of power."

"I hadn't thought of that," I say, giving him a grudging look of admiration. "But I'm glad you did. It's a perfect excuse to give Dom, and one that doesn't make me look selfish."

"You're welcome."

"Let him down easy for me, okay?" I say with a wink and a smile.

"I'll do my best."

"You know, Dom is right about one thing. You'd make a great father, Izzy. You're kind, smart, loving, generous, and even fun at times."

"Good try, but I told you, I can't give you a raise until you've been on the job for a full year of continuous work, and that started over when you quit and came back."

I shrug and wink again. "It was worth a try." I turn to leave, but after taking a couple of steps I stop and look back at him. "All joking aside, I meant every word of that, Izzy."

He smiles warmly and says, "Thanks. See you in the morning."

Chapter 23

Brad Donaldson arrives promptly at three, driving up in a Hummer. Kirsten wasn't kidding when she said she hadn't married him for his looks. He appears to be in his mid-fifties and he's a short, portly fellow with a ruddy face that hints of a close relationship with the bottle. Tiny blue veins crisscross his cheeks, and his nose is red and bulbous. His eyes are a weird color that looks like a cross between light brown and spinach green, and there are bags beneath them big enough to pack for a week. His hair is salt and pepper along the sides, but the top of his head is very nearly bald with just a few iron-gray strands tying the two sides together. His face is jowly and he's sporting a five o'clock shadow on both of his chins.

I'm convinced Kirsten had to have been a trophy wife until I greet Brad Donaldson and introduce myself. He smiles and his face is transformed. The skin tightens a little, the eyes reveal a sparkling glint of light, and his cheeks look rosy and healthy. Then he speaks and for a moment I'm mesmerized. His voice is deep, soothing, and mellow. The combination of that smile and the mellifluous voice leaves me feeling oddly drawn to the man.

Brad Donaldson manages to muddle my senses even more once we get him settled in the interview room and start talking with him.

"Mr. Donaldson, we're looking into the death of Lars Sanderson," Richmond starts. "Do you know the man?"

"You're kidding, right?" Brad says. "You can't live in this town for any length of time and not know Sanderson. He's a noisemaker."

"What do you mean by that?" Richmond asks.

"I mean the guy knows how to rattle people's cages and he doesn't seem to care who he pisses off. You got to respect a guy like that. He knows what he wants and he goes after it without letting social mores or peer pressures get in his way."

"Tell me about your marriage to Kirsten," Richmond says, switching gears.

I don't know if he's hoping to rattle Donaldson, but if he is, it isn't working. "Kirsten and I had a great time of it for a number of years," he says, smiling fondly. "But in the end I lost her because I tried to hang on too tight. She was a hard one for me to lose. I really loved her. Still do, in fact. But I let my insecurities get in the way of my happiness and I drove her away."

"She took a lot of your money with her when you split up," I say.

Donaldson shrugs. "It was our money. She took half and that was fair. We both worked hard for it. Besides, I have more than enough to meet my needs and you can't take it with you, so why not spread it around and let those you care about enjoy it?"

"What is it you do for a living?" Richmond asks. He

already knows the answer, but getting people to talk about themselves is a way of relaxing them and getting them to feel confident. When people are relaxed and feeling confident they tend to slip up and say things they shouldn't.

"I own a chain of home improvement stores," he says. "And I do some contracting on the side. It's a family business that's been handed down for three generations. My son will hopefully be the fourth."

"Your son?" I say with a questioning look. "I thought you and Kirsten had two daughters."

"Kirsten and I do have two daughters," he says. "My son is the product of a dalliance I had when I was younger, before I met Kirsten. I didn't know about him until two years ago. His mother died and left him information about me in case he wanted to look me up. Turned out he did and we've been trying to make up for lost time ever since."

"Were you aware that Mr. Sanderson and your ex-wife were seeing one another?" Richmond asks.

Donaldson's smile shifts ever so slightly, and his brows draw together. The smile is still there, but it doesn't look as warm or as genuine all of a sudden. "I know she used him as an escort for social functions on occasion," he says, rubbing one temple with his fingers.

"Apparently it was much more than that," I say.

Donaldson's demeanor changes so fast it leaves me stunned. The magnetic smile is gone, his entire face is a red, raging mass of flesh, and his eyes turn cold and mean-looking. He opens his mouth to say something but stops before a single word comes out. His face goes slack for a few seconds and then the charming, captivating Brad Donaldson returns. "Kirsten is free to do what she wants and see whomever she wants," he says in that wondrous, calming voice.

It's like someone flipped a switch. And before the Hulk-esque side of Donaldson could fully emerge, it was flipped back again. It's creepy, curious, and intriguing. I want to flip that switch again.

Apparently, so does Richmond because he says, "Mr. Sanderson and your ex-wife were lovers, Mr. Donaldson. Kirsten told us she slept with Lars on a regular basis."

I watch Donaldson closely, waiting for him to turn green and bust out of his clothes. There is a faint hint of a thundercloud on his face for a few seconds, but his placid, friendly smile remains in place. "Like I said, she's free to do what she wants. I no longer have a say in that."

"So it doesn't bother you that the woman you love is sleeping around?" Richmond prods.

"I won't say it makes me happy," Donaldson says, "but I've moved on. I have a new woman in my life now and Kirsten's life is her own." His tone and his facial expression read sincere, but the muscles in his jaw are popping like water drops on a hot skillet.

Richmond makes a couple of other statements intended to rile the man, but Donaldson's self-control is firmly in place and he refuses to be goaded. Tiring of the game, Richmond eventually moves on. "Can you tell me where you were yesterday morning between the hours of five and eight?"

Donaldson thinks a moment before he answers. "I was in bed until around six-thirty, and then I got up, showered, and headed for my store on the west side of Madison. I think I got there around seven forty-five or so, and I didn't leave there until nearly eleven."

Richmond asks, "Can anyone verify that you were home between five and seven?"

Donaldson shakes his head and his smile broadens.

"Nope," he says, "because I wasn't at home. I was at Liz's house."

"Liz?" Richmond says.

"Liz Markham, my girlfriend," Donaldson says. He takes a business card and a pen from his coat pocket and writes something down on the back of the card. Then he pushes it across the table toward Richmond. "Here's her number. Call her. She'll vouch for me. And just to clarify, I was there until about seven-thirty. Her house is located on the west side of Madison, only a few miles from my store."

Richmond places the card on the table in front of him. "Mr. Donaldson, do you own a bow and arrow of any type?"

"Yes, I do," he says. "Why?"

"May we take a look at them?"

Donaldson contemplates this request for half a minute or so, and the silence in the room is so great, I can hear the second hand on the wall clock ticking its way around. "I suppose so," he says finally. "They're at my house. Do you want to go look at them now?"

"That would be great," Richmond says. "Why don't you drive there and we'll follow along behind."

I'm surprised Donaldson has agreed to Richmond's request and I half expect him to change his mind. But he doesn't. We send him out front to his Hummer while Richmond and I head out the back door to his car. Richmond throws me the keys—a first. "I'm going to call the girlfriend," he says. "You can drive."

As soon as we are in the car I say, "Wow, did you see how Donaldson changed from smooth operator to insanely jealous ex-husband in the blink of an eye?"

"Sure did. He's a charming guy but I have to say it's not hard to imagine that green-eyed version of him killing someone."

"And yet he got it under control really fast. I don't know who his therapist is but I'd bet money he's been seeing one and he or she is really good. Either that or Donaldson is on some kickass meds. Maybe it's both."

I find Donaldson waiting for us at the parking lot entrance in front of the building and I wave him on. He pulls out and I fall in behind him as Richmond dials the girlfriend's number. He puts the call on speaker and lets me listen in as he identifies himself and then asks his questions. Liz basically supports Donaldson's time line, though her times are estimates that fall within five or ten minutes of his. Liars and people who know they have to cover something up tend to get their stories very straight, so I suspect she's telling the truth.

Donaldson lives in a lakefront home located ten miles outside of town. A few decades ago, many of the homes in the area were small summer cottages that served as second homes to those who could afford a lake house. But during the housing boom of the nineties the cottages gave way to tightly packed palatial homes, and now the wealthy and the upper middle class rub elbows along the lakefront year-round.

The outside of Donaldson's house is a stunning stone and wood mansion that hogs up most of the lot space. On either side his neighbors' houses are only about ten feet away. I pull into Donaldson's driveway behind his Hummer and alongside a garage. Once we're out of our cars, Donaldson says, "I typically keep my archery equipment in a basement storeroom, but at the moment it's in my pickup."

"Why is that?" Richmond asks.

"It's deer hunting season," Donaldson says in a Captain Obvious tone.

Donaldson walks over to the garage door and punches in a number code on the lock. The door rises, revealing a shiny, metallic-blue Ford F-150 king cab. Donaldson opens the door to the truck and sticks his head inside. A moment later he comes out with a puzzled look on his face. "They're gone," he says, looking at us.

Richmond and I exchange looks, and then Richmond asks, "Who would have access to your garage?"

"No one but me," he says. "Wait, my son might. He's been here several times and I told him what the passcode was so he could use the truck. Maybe he came by to borrow the stuff. Turns out he likes archery and took some lessons when he was a kid. In fact, he still has the bow and arrows he used when he was little. I'm getting him some new equipment for Christmas."

"Can you give me your son's name and contact information?" Richmond asks, taking out his notebook. He sounds irritated and I can't say I blame him. It seems like every step forward in this case requires two steps back.

Donaldson hesitates, frowning, but finally complies. "His name is Jeff Hunt, but he can't have anything to do with this. He doesn't even know Lars Sanderson."

"Address?" Richmond says.

Donaldson's frown deepens. "He lives in Portage in his mother's home. He inherited the place when she died." He then provides us with the street address.

"Are you sure your equipment isn't in the house?" I ask. "Maybe you took it inside and don't remember doing it."

"If I took it anywhere, it would have been to the basement storage room," he says.

"Mind if we take a look there?" Richmond asks.

Donaldson thinks about it for a moment, sighs, and then nods. We leave the garage and head between Donaldson's home and the neighboring one on the left until we reach the backside of the house. The lot slopes down toward the waterfront and on the second level, which would be the main level if entering from the street side of the house, there are floor-to-ceiling windows in what I assume is a living area. No doubt they provide a stunning view of the lake. Donaldson enters the house through a ground-floor entrance into a finished basement area furnished as a game room. There are several pinball machines along one wall, and a beautiful mahogany pool table with maroon felt and a stained glass lamp overhead in the center of the room. Deeper in I see a Foosball table, an air hockey table, and of course, the requisite large-screen TV with a variety of gaming equipment. I wonder if the basement has always been furnished this way or if Donaldson added this stuff after he found out about his son.

We follow Donaldson through the game room and out a door at the far end that takes us into an unfinished storage area. Here we find various types of outdoor play equipment: set-ups for badminton, volleyball, and croquet, plus fishing gear, kites, ski jets, and some archery targets on hay bales. But nowhere can we find any bows or arrows.

When we are done, I pull Richmond to one side. "Should we ask him if we can look through the rest of the house?"

Richmond nods, and then does just that.

"I think I've been quite accommodating thus far," Donaldson says, looking troubled. "But I am concerned that my equipment has gone missing, and I'm guessing such equipment has significant meaning in this case. So until I have some time to think about the consequences, I'd like to hold off. If you want to paw through the rest of my life, you'll have to get a warrant."

Richmond looks annoyed and tired. "Fine," he says. And without another word, he turns to leave.

I scramble along behind him and when we get back to the car he grumbles, "Give me the keys."

I do so and get in on the passenger side.

"This case is tweaking my nerves," Richmond mutters.

"Did you see those targets on the hay bales? That's what Reece Morton said he had in his storage locker. Is there any way to tell if the ones Donaldson has might be Morton's? There were pieces of hay on the floor in that storage unit. Maybe there's a way to match it to the hay in those bales."

Richmond thinks about it. "Maybe, but first we have to get access to them and Donaldson is done accommodating us for now. I'll have to try for the search warrant and hope for the best."

"What do you want to do in the meantime?"

"Are you up for a trip to Portage?"

"Sure, but I want to take my own car in case something comes up with Emily."

"That's fine. We can caravan. Besides, it will be fun to watch people's reactions as you drive that hearse through town."

Chapter 24

Forty-five minutes later Richmond and I are in Portage pulling up in front of a cute little yellow Cape Cod with a red front door. There's a newer model SUV in the driveway and a two-car detached garage that looks newer than the house and is nearly as big. The reason the SUV is parked in the driveway is apparent because the garage door is open. It's already dark outside and the garage is lit up inside. In it is a mid-sized boat on a trailer, a motorcycle, a snowmobile, and an ATV. A man who looks to be in his late twenties is kneeling beside the snowmobile working a tool in the engine compartment, and various mechanical parts are scattered around him on the floor.

As Richmond and I walk up the drive, I lean over and say, "Do you think it's fate that this guy's last name is Hunt?"

Richmond chuckles and, in response, the young man inside the garage looks up, sees us, and smiles curiously.

"Are you Jeff Hunt?" Richmond asks as we reach the garage opening.

"I am," the man says, grabbing a towel to wipe his

hands. He gets up from the floor and takes a few steps toward us. "Can I help you?"

Richmond flashes his police badge and I show my ME's badge for good measure. "I'm Detective Bob Richmond with the Sorenson Police Department," Richmond says. "This is Mattie Winston with the ME's office. We'd like to ask you a few questions."

"Regarding what?" he asks with a tentative smile.

Rather than answering this question, Richmond looks around the garage and nods approvingly. "You've got some sweet toys here," he says. "I'm a little envious."

Hunt looks around the garage and his smile broadens.

"Are they all yours?" Richmond asks.

Hunt nods. "They are. The boat is new. I just bought it this past summer. I've had the motorcycle and the ATV for a little over a year, the snowmobile for two."

Richmond looks back out at the driveway. "The car looks new, too."

"Bought it in the fall," Hunt says, his smile fading. "Look, I own all of this stuff, if that's what you're getting at. I didn't steal any of it. My father purchased the boat and the car but the titles are in my name."

"I don't think you stole anything," Richmond says. "That's not why we're here. But as long as we're on the subject, what do you do for a living?"

"I work for my father managing his stores."

"What kind of stores?" Richmond asks. We, of course, already know the answer but I've learned from watching Richmond work that he likes to chat people up on seemingly innocuous matters and then toss out the occasional zinger. It's effective. Most folks end up experiencing a seesaw of calm and anxiety that keeps them unsettled. And unsettled people often say interesting things.

"Home improvement stores," Hunt answers. "My father is Brad Donaldson and he owns a chain of twenty stores throughout central Wisconsin. I manage the ones in this region—four stores all together—as sort of an internship. Dad is grooming me to eventually take over for him and run the company."

"Wow," Richmond says. "That's a lot of responsibility for a young man. How old are you?"

"Twenty-seven. I have an MBA," he adds, sounding a bit defensive.

Richmond gives him a look of grudging admiration. "That's impressive. How come you aren't working today?"

"Tuesday and Wednesday are my days off because I work every weekend and I have to process payroll on Mondays. The weekends are our busiest days at the store. That's when all the weekend warriors come in."

Richmond chuckles. "I'm betting some of them keep you busy asking a million questions, right?"

Hunt shrugs. "Sometimes, yeah. What is it you're here for again?" he asks with a hint of impatience.

"We're looking into the death of a man in Sorenson that might have been a hunting accident. Do you hunt, Mr. Hunt?" Richmond asks in an amused tone.

"I've gone out a time or two with my father, but we're solely bow hunters."

"You don't use a gun?" Richmond asks.

Hunt shakes his head.

"Well, then," Richmond says with a dismissive wave of his hand.

"I've never hunted with a gun," Hunt says, "and, to be honest, I'm not a big fan of hunting in general. I only went because I was trying to bond with my father. And I do love archery. My dad and I both do."

"Bows and arrows?" Richmond says with a hint of excitement in his voice. "That's fascinating. I've always wanted to take lessons in archery. Are you any good?"

"Decent enough," Hunt says with a hint of boastfulness. "My mom gave me lessons when I was little, so I've had some practice."

"Do you own your own bow?"

"An old worn one," Hunt says. "The same one I used when I was younger. It's in my storage shed out back."

"Can you show it to me?" Richmond asks. Hunt looks hesitant, so Richmond adds a little incentive. "It sounds like you've got a good handle on the sport and it's something I've always wanted to do. Any chance you could give me a five minute crash course on the basics?"

Hunt frowns and scratches his head, leaving a faint grease smear on his ear. Finally he smiles, shrugs, and says, "Sure, why not? But don't expect much. My set is far from state of the art."

He turns and leads us through the garage, out a back door, and into a small yard. Some thirty feet behind the house is a small utility shed. As we start to cross the yard toward it, I hear the sound of a cell phone ring behind us in the garage.

"That's my cell," Hunt says, stopping in his tracks. "I forgot, my dad called me a bit ago and I let it go to voice mail because I had my hands in that engine. I should probably call him back."

Richmond and I exchange looks. Based on the way we left things with Brad Donaldson, I can guess why he's calling his son. Will he tell him to cooperate? Or will he tell him to blow us off? I'm thinking the latter and, apparently, so is Richmond because he comes up with a quick comeback that might yet let us achieve our goal.

"Is your shed locked?" he asks.

Hunt shakes his head.

"Mind if I take a peek at your equipment while you call your dad?" Richmond looks and sounds like a kid in a toy store. "I promise I won't break it, or try to shoot any arrows. I just want to get a feel for the equipment."

"Yeah, sure. Go ahead," Hunt says with a smile, waving us on. "Just give me a minute and I'll join you in case you have any questions."

"Thanks, bud!" Richmond says. And as Hunt heads back into the garage, we beat feet to the utility shed. There is a hasp on the door with a piece of wood stuck through it as a lock. As Richmond pulls the wood out he says, "We need to try to get a sample of the dirt in the wheels of that ATV. We can compare it to the dirt out by Cooper's Woods."

"Good thinking. George Haas did say he heard an ATV out there."

"I have some gloves in my coat pocket," Richmond says. "When we get back to the garage, find a way to distract Hunt for me and I'll get a sample."

I nod my understanding as Richmond opens the shed door. It takes a moment for my eyes to adjust to the darkness, but items slowly start taking shape: a lawnmower, a weed whacker, various gardening tools, and in the back corner, a hay bale with a big target on it. Hanging on the wall beside the hay bale is a compound bow, a simple bow, and two quivers full of arrows. Richmond takes out the flashlight he has attached to his belt and turns it on.

One quiver holds ten small wooden arrows with green, plastic fletching on them. The other quiver holds eight arrows. Seven of them have black and yellow fletching but the eighth one has neon purple and green fletching, identical to the arrow that killed Lars.

"Whoa," Richmond says. "Would you look at that. We need to film this."

"Do you have your camera?" I ask him. "I don't have mine on me."

"Mine is in the car." He hands me his keys. "I'll wait here while you go and get it." As he takes out his cell phone and starts taking some still pictures of the bows and arrows, I turn to head back to the cars. And I find myself face-to-face with a scowling Jeff Hunt.

"I just talked to my dad," he says, glaring at us. "You people lied to me. Your dead guy wasn't shot with a gun; he was killed with an arrow."

"I never said he was shot with a gun," Richmond says. "I told you it looked like a hunting accident. You assumed it involved a gun."

"I want you to leave," Hunt says. "My father said you're on a witch hunt."

"I can't do that, Mr. Hunt," Richmond says with an apologetic expression.

"Why not?"

"Because we've just discovered that you're in possession of an arrow that matches the murder weapon."

"Murder? I thought you said it was an accident." Hunt's color pales. He stares into the shed, his eyes settling on the stuff in the corner. "Where did that come from?" he says, looking genuinely puzzled.

"Where did what come from?" I ask.

"That bale of hay with the target on it. That's not mine."

Richmond and I exchange looks. "Whose is it then?" Richmond says.

"Hell if I know." Hunt takes another step closer, peering into the corner. He scratches his head, looking genuinely puzzled. "That quiver on the right is my dad's, and that's his compound bow. But that arrow with the purple and green fletching isn't his. And it isn't mine, either. My dad's arrows are all yellow and black."

"So you're trying to tell me that an archery target, a hay bale, and a stray arrow mysteriously ended up in your backyard utility shed and you don't know anything about it?" Richmond says with high skepticism.

Hunt looks at Richmond, then at me, then back at Richmond. His face darkens. "I'm going to call my father back," he says. "And then I'm going to contact a lawyer."

"You do whatever you feel you need to do," Richmond says. "But this stuff is being confiscated as evidence in a murder investigation. Please don't leave the premises."

Hunt's face is a dark mask of anger, but I can also see a hint of fear there. He spins around and strides back toward the garage.

"I need to get some backup here," Richmond says, punching a number in his phone. "Looks like we're going to do a meet and greet with the Portage police."

"Are you going to arrest Hunt?"

Richmond shakes his head. "This stuff alone isn't enough, particularly since we can't know yet if the hay bale is from Reece Morton's storage unit. And having a matching arrow doesn't prove anything either. We might be able to match up some markings on this bow and the arrow we took out of Lars, but that's going to take time." He sighs and shakes his head again. "We can't arrest him yet, but we definitely need to have a chat with him. And I need to get a search warrant for his house and garage." He pauses and shakes his head. "I'm going to put a watch on Hunt. With Brad Donaldson's money at his disposal, it would be all too easy for him to disappear."

As he makes his call, I head back across the yard and out to his car to get the camera. Jeff Hunt is in the garage on his phone—no doubt talking to his father—and he glares at me as I walk by. By the time I return to Richmond, squad cars are rolling up out front. I hand Richmond the camera and watch as he starts filming.

"What motive does Jeff Hunt have to kill Lars?" I ask, thinking aloud.

"I don't know exactly," Richmond says. "But a lot of those fake receipts Lars had were for building supplies. There must be a connection there somehow."

"What do you want me to do?"

He pauses in his filming. "This is going to take a couple of hours, maybe longer. Why don't you head home and get in some time with the kid? I'll instruct the Portage guys on what we need and stay until we have the evidence secured. We can regroup in the morning. I'll call you at your office."

"Okay."

It sounds ideal on the surface, but it's just a shift of focus from one crisis to another.

Chapter 25

During my drive home, I call Hurley.

"Hey, Sunshine," he says. Despite the cheeriness of the words, his tone is one of dismal depression.

"I take it you haven't had any luck."

"Nope. I've tracked down some of Emily's old friends from here, but none of them claim to have seen or heard anything from her since she left Chicago."

"The guys didn't find anything useful on the computer, either. The only e-mail exchange she had with anyone in Chicago was with a friend named Chloe Bannerman and that was months ago."

"I haven't talked to her yet," Hurley says. "I'll look her up this evening, and I've got a couple of other names to check out. If they don't pan out, I'll probably head home in the morning."

"Okay. I'll talk to you tomorrow then if I don't hear any news from you tonight."

There's a pause for a few seconds and then he says, "I've got a very bad feeling about this, Mattie. The longer this goes, the more convinced I am that something really bad has happened to her. I've got the guys checking up on some of the known pedophiles and sex offenders in the area to see if any of them look suspicious."

"I can barely force myself to even consider that option, Hurley. It's just too horrible."

"I know." He sighs slowly, heavily. "I'll never forgive myself if something like that has happened to her." He pauses, and I stay silent, not knowing what to say. Then he adds, "Give my boy a hug and a kiss for me." His voice cracks, and he sounds so sad and forlorn, it makes me want to cry.

When I get home, Matthew is awake and bright-eyed, sitting in Dom's lap, smiling and gurgling at the colorful, noisy toy Dom is playing with.

"How are my two favorite guys doing?" I ask. I set my purse and the laptop down on the coffee table and hold my arms out to Matthew. As soon as my son sees me, his face lights up and his legs start to kick. I pick him up and give him a hug, closing my eyes to relish the moment.

My dog, Hoover, is sitting nearby and he thumps his tail and looks at me with his big brown eyes, waiting patiently for his turn. The poor guy has gotten used to being second banana now that Matthew is here. I walk over and give him a scratch on his head.

"Rough day?" Dom says.

"Could have been worse."

"Any news on Emily?"

I shake my head. "I talked to Hurley a bit ago and he's got a few more people to talk to in Chicago. If nothing pans out, he's going to head home in the morning." I start to add that he's also looking into the sex offender thing, but I can't give it voice. The thought is there, dark and lurking in the back of my mind all the time. But it's as if it's locked behind a door, and giving it too much thought or a voice would release it and make it real somehow.

"How's Hurley holding up?"

"Not well. He's really beating himself up over this."

Dom sets the toy aside and gets up from the couch. "If you're home to stay, I'm going to head home, too."

"I am," I tell him. "Izzy wanted me to tell you he'll be home around seven."

"Then I best get dinner started," he says. "I'm making his favorite tonight: beef tenderloin with roasted baby potatoes."

"What's the occasion?"

"I decided we're going to have the talk."

"The talk?"

He nods. "The baby talk."

"Oh." While I'm glad to hear that Dom is finally going to broach the subject with Izzy, it also panics me a little. I don't how much hope Dom is putting on my willingness to be a surrogate for them. "Good luck," I tell him.

My cell phone rings, and as I shift Matthew in my arms so I can get the phone out of my purse, Dom waves at me and says, "Later."

I'm hoping the call will be Hurley with some good news, but when I glance at the caller ID I see that it's my sister, Desi, instead.

"Hey, Desi," I answer.

"I heard about Emily," she says. "Have you found her yet?"

"No. Hurley is in Chicago looking for her."

"How long has she been gone?"

"Since yesterday morning sometime."

"Oh, Mattie. How awful!"

"How did you hear about it?"

"Erika told me. One of her friends has an older

sister who's a classmate of Emily's and she told the younger sister, who then told Erika."

And so the grapevine goes.

"And then I saw the Amber Alert," Desi goes on. "You don't think that boyfriend of hers had anything to do with it, do you? I heard she's been seeing a Chester boy."

"I don't think so. Johnny Chester seems to have avoided branching off his family tree the way his father and grandfather did. He's as concerned as we are."

"That has to be frustrating for you," Desi says. "Why don't you and Matthew come over for dinner tonight? I've got a big pan of lasagna made, and it's been too long since I've seen that adorable nephew of mine. And maybe we can brainstorm about Emily."

I'm tired, and the thought of having to pack Matthew up for a trip sounds like work. But it's been a while since I've seen my sister and her family, and her mention of my niece, Erika, has given me an idea. Even though Erika is still in middle school this year, she knows a lot of the same people that Emily knows. Maybe some of her connections could shed some light on Emily's whereabouts.

"I'd love to," I tell Desi. "What time?"

We'll be eating around seven. Any time before then is fine."

"Okay. Let me feed and change Matthew and then we'll be over."

Matthew isn't particularly hungry at the moment, so after trying to nurse and having him fall asleep at my breast, I put him in his crib and go out to the kitchen to pump. While disconnecting I manage to spill on myself, so I head into the bedroom to change. One of the new shirts I ordered from Amazon is still in the package in my dresser drawer. I figure now is as good a time as any to wear it and take it out. Beneath it is a composition book, a black and white notebook just like the ones Emily had in her room. Mine was a gift—or perhaps a trick—from Dr. Maggie. She gave it to me with instructions to use it as a diary of sorts, to record my feelings and thoughts. I wasn't required to share it with her, and didn't. Seeing it now makes me wonder about the empty composition book I found in Emily's desk drawer. Had that come from Maggie, too?

It doesn't matter one way or the other, but I decide to call Maggie anyway. It's after five, so I'm not sure if she'll answer, but she does. Either she is done for the day or has no client at the moment.

"Maggie, it's Mattie."

"Did you find Emily?"

"No, not yet. I have a question for you."

"Okay, as long as it's not a question about what I discussed with Emily."

"Not directly. I went through her bedroom today and I found one of those black and white composition books in her desk drawer, like the one you gave me. She had several others that she was using for notes for school, but this one wasn't labeled, so I thought maybe it was an extra. But when I ran across mine a little bit ago, it got me to wondering. Did you give Emily one of those composition books?"

"I did. Did you read it?"

"There was nothing to read. It was empty."

"Hunh. I guess she handed me a line then, because she told me she was using it."

"I wish she had. It might have helped."

"You didn't find any other papers she wrote stuff on?"

"Nothing except schoolwork. And the only things I found there were some drawings and doodles."

"Sorry. Listen, I have a patient who just arrived. Is there anything else I can help you with?"

"No, that's all I needed. Thanks, Maggie."

I hang up and finish getting myself ready for the trip to Desi's house. Hoover is sitting next to the coffee table and, after sniffing the laptop, he rests his chin on it and lets out a little whimper.

"Did my mother teach you guilt lessons when you were over there?" I ask him.

In response he thumps his tail vigorously and beseeches me with those brown eyes.

"Okay, okay," I say, and Hoover springs into action. It's as if he can read my mind because seconds later he's standing by the front door, looking back at me expectantly, his whole butt wagging with excitement.

I glance over at Matthew, who is sound asleep, and figure now is as good a time as any for a little doggie attention. Hoover's enthusiasm is contagious as he bounds out of the house and runs toward the woods, stopping every few feet to look back and make sure I'm coming with him. I don't want to be out of sight of the house so I don't venture too far, but I let Hoover run ahead and explore to his heart's content. After a few minutes of hearing him rustling through dead leaves and sniffing like a hyped-up cocaine addict, the sounds grow dimmer. Then I don't hear them at all.

"Hoover!" I yell. "Come on, boy. Come on back."

I wait and listen, but there's no sign of him, so I call to him again. "Hoover! Come!" I whistle for good measure, sure he'll come bounding through the trees any second. But he doesn't. I look back at the cottage—it's well within sight—and venture a little deeper into the trees before calling out again.

There's no sign of him and I curse my stupidity for letting him out without a leash even though I've done it a number of other times and he's never wandered far and always returns with little or no prompting. I need to go looking for him, but I'm not going to leave Matthew unattended and I don't have my phone with me to call anyone. Reluctantly, I turn back and head inside to gather up my kid and a flashlight.

My doorbell rings just as I'm trying to stuff Matthew into his snowsuit. It's like trying to thread overcooked spaghetti through the eye of a needle, so I give up for the moment and put Matthew in his bassinet in the living room while I go to the door. Standing on my porch is my ex-husband, David, whom I haven't seen since Matthew's birth.

Hoover dashes past David's feet and mine, runs over to the bassinet, sniffs a couple of times, and then plops down on the floor beside it.

"Your dog was over at my house barking," David grumbles.

"I'm sorry. I took him out for a quick walk and he went running off on me. He's never done that before. I was just about to go looking for him."

David is staring at my head and judging from the expression on his face, I've come up lacking somehow. "You changed the color of your hair."

Yeah, yeah. I make a mental note to call Barbara as soon as possible to schedule an undoing. Then I mentally amend my note, realizing that the word *undoing* might not be the best choice in a funeral home setting.

"I wanted to try something different," I tell him, running a hand through my hair.

"Well, if different is what you were after, you got it."

His tone is snippy and it ticks me off. I'm not going to stand here and be insulted by the man, even if my hair does look like crap. "Thanks for bringing Hoover home," I say, edging the door closed. "I need to be somewhere, so if you don't mind."

David's eyes shift from me to the bassinet and before I have the door half closed he says, "I can't believe you went through with this. Is this really what you want? Being a single mother? Being the talk of the town?"

I know I should just shut the door and be done with him. I know he's goading me. And I know that if I play this game with him, it's going to leave me frustrated and angry. But the gall of his comment is more than I can ignore. "You made me the talk of the town long before I did," I shoot back. "Besides, my situation is temporary."

"Really?" David says, his tone rife with skepticism. "Is Hurley going to do the right thing finally and offer to marry you?"

"Hurley has always wanted to do the right thing. He asked me to marry him months ago. I'm the one who's been holding out."

I start to shut the door again, but David puts out a hand to stop it. "I'm sorry," he says. "I didn't come over here intending to start a fight with you. It's just that . . . you and . . . things . . . Oh hell, I don't know what I'm trying to say. Things have changed a lot in the past year."

"Yes, they have." It's an understatement of astounding proportions. "We've both moved on and made some big changes. For the better, I think."

"Is it better, having a kid?" he asks, peering past me toward the bassinet.

"Life is definitely more hectic and my energy levels are much more taxed. But Matthew is the best thing that has ever happened to me. Nothing in my life, no person in my life, has ever made me happier."

David switches his gaze back to me. "Can I see him?"

I'm taken aback by his request. "I really am supposed to be somewhere," I say, stalling and looking pointedly at my watch.

"Please, just a quick peek."

"Okay." I step back and wave him inside. "But make it quick."

David walks past me into the living room and heads for the bassinet. He's about three feet away when Hoover utters a low guttural growl.

"It's okay, Hoover," I say.

David stops where he is and looks back at me. "He isn't going to bite me, is he?"

"Not if I tell him it's okay. He's very protective of Matthew."

"Matthew," David echoes, with a curious tone. "How did you come by the name?"

"It's a masculine variation on Mattie," I tell him. "His middle name is Izthak, after Izzy."

I can tell David is still leery of Hoover so I walk up to the bassinet with him and we stand there together looking down at my sleeping son. "He has Hurley's hair," David says after a bit.

"Yes, at least so far. That could change, though."

He stares for a few more seconds and then looks over at me. "Are you really happy, Mattie?"

I smile. "Yes, I am. I'm exhausted beyond belief and would give my right arm for a full night's sleep, but I wouldn't trade him for all the sleep in the world. I wouldn't even trade him for ice cream."

David laughs. He knows my ice cream addiction well.

Matthew stirs at the sound, stretching one fisted hand and sucking with his lips. Then he opens his eyes, looks up at David, and smiles.

I glance at David's face, curious to see his reaction. He smiles back at Matthew—a genuine, spontaneous response—but after a few seconds the smile fades into a frown. "I always thought you and I would be sharing an experience like this," he says. "I guess I really mucked things up, didn't I?"

"Yeah, you kinda did."

He looks at me with warmth, sincerity, and a hint of regret. "I truly am sorry for any hurt I caused you, Mattie. And I'm glad you're happy."

"Thank you." While it's nice to hear this long overdue apology, I'm wary of the sudden change in David's demeanor. Our relationship has been so marked by rancor and nastiness up until now, it's hard to accept this newer, remorseful version of him.

Matthew kicks his arms and legs, screws his face up, and starts to cry. I feel my milk let down and curse the timing. "That cry means it's mealtime," I say to David, hinting yet again that it's time for him to go. I check Matthew's diaper, find it's wet, and go about changing him. He stops crying and starts cooing at me instead.

David either didn't get the hint or has chosen to ignore it, because he stands there watching me as I work. When I'm done, I pick Matthew up and hold him close to my chest. "Is there anything else?" I ask, bouncing Matthew in my arms and giving David an impatient look.

"No, I guess not," he says, and heads for the door.

"Thanks again for bringing Hoover home."

"You're welcome." He finally leaves and as I watch him head off into the woods, I hold Matthew close, literally embracing my new life as I say good-bye to my old one.

Chapter 26

I swear my sister, Desi's, house smells better than any place on Earth. It doesn't take much to smell better than my place right now, given that the primary aromas are wet and dirty diapers, and unwashed dog. But Desi is always baking or cooking something yummy and delicious, and tonight is no exception. The house smells like Italy, the air fragrant with the scents of oregano, basil, and tomatoes.

"Oh, my," Desi says as soon as I enter. "You've changed your hair."

"Yeah, yeah. I hate it, okay? Let's move on."

"Let me see the little guy." Desi grabs Matthew's carrier from me and the rest of the family appears and swarms around the two of them. Even my brother-in-law, Lucien, makes goo-goo eyes and baby noises, chucking Matthew under his chin. It's a softer side of Lucien that I rarely get to see.

After several minutes of oohing and aahing, my thirteen-year-old niece, Erika, takes Matthew out of his carrier seat and settles on the couch with him in her lap. My nephew, Ethan, is curious, but less so than when he's examining one of his bug specimens. He has an interesting and creepy collection of six- and eight-legged critters, most of which are dead, thank goodness. The two that are alive are scary enough: Fluffy, his tarantula, and Hissy, a three-inch-long Madagascar hissing cockroach. Fortunately they are caged up in what are hopefully escape-proof containers, though I'll never think of the term *hissy fit* in quite the same way again.

"I want one of these," Erika says, bouncing Matthew in her lap.

"Hey, don't go getting any ideas," Desi says. Then she shifts her attention to me. "Any word on Emily?"

I shake my head. "Not yet. Hurley's still in Chicago looking for her."

"She wouldn't go to Chicago," Erika says. "She hated that place."

"Why do you say that?"

"When she went with us to the water park this summer she kept talking about how the kids in Chicago always made fun of her because she didn't wear designer clothes and couldn't afford to do a lot of stuff. And from what I hear, the kids here are doing the same thing. Christine Randall said that her sister, Carly, was joking about how Emily was trying to cozy up with some of the cheerleaders who let her think they would accept her as a friend, but all they're really doing is laughing at her behind her back."

My heart aches for Emily hearing about this. I can remember how hard it was to break into some of the cliques when I was in high school. Kids can be so cruel.

"That's horrible!" Desi says to her daughter. "I hope you don't condone that sort of behavior, Erika."

"Of course not," she says.

"I know Carly Randall," I tell Erika. "I went to school

with her mother. And I talked to her yesterday when we were at the school. She never said a word about any of this."

"Of course not," Erika says, looking at me like I'm as dense as a concrete block. "You're a grown-up for one, and you're connected to Emily. That's two strikes against you."

"Why do the other girls dislike Emily so much? Is it because she's the new kid?"

"No, it's more than that," Erika says, playing with Matthew's feet. "One of the other cheerleaders, Olivia Mason, likes Johnny Chester and she's pissed off that Emily is dating him."

"Hey, watch the language," Desi chastises. "Particularly around the little guy."

"Sorry," Erika says, rolling her eyes. "Anyway, Christine says the other kids think Emily is weird because she's so quiet and shy. And then when Johnny started showing interest in her, Olivia and her friends got really mad."

"It sounds like I need to have another chat with Carly," I say, angered that the girl lied to me, and angrier yet that Emily has had to put up with that sort of mean-spirited, cliquish behavior.

Erika looks panicked. "Don't tell her I said anything. I don't want to make anyone mad at me."

"I won't tell," I promise.

Desi nods toward the kitchen and says, "Dinner is almost ready. Want to give me a hand?"

I look over at Erika, who is now holding Matthew over her shoulder. "You okay with him for now?"

"Heck, yeah. I'll keep him forever if you let me."

I follow Desi out into the kitchen and help by getting the dining room table set and filling water glasses. We chat about Matthew and how things are going now that I'm back to work.

"It's hard leaving him," I tell her, "but I have to admit it's also been kind of a relief to get away for a little while. I'm not as good a mom as you were."

"Don't be ridiculous," Desi says, taking the lasagna out of the oven and setting it on the stove. "You're a great mom."

"I try, but the lack of sleep and the never-ending schedule of feedings and changings and laundry and bottle cleaning drives me crazy."

"You're doing it alone and that makes it doubly hard. Even with help it's hard, especially for those first few months."

"You did it and loved it," I say. "Twice."

"Oh, I had my moments. Trust me," she says with a chuckle. "There were days when I fantasized about running away from home the way Emily has."

The sobering change of subject throws us into an awkward silence. After a few seconds, Desi takes the lasagna into the dining room and sets it on the table. Then she comes back and takes some buttery garlic bread from the broiler and dumps it into a bread basket.

"Let's eat," she says.

I run out to the car and get the little bouncy seat I have for Matthew and place him in it in front of the TV. I can see him from the dining room table and watch as he stares at the changing colors on the TV screen. Every few minutes he kicks his legs and thrashes his arms with excitement, and I can't help but wonder what's going through his mind.

The dinner conversation starts out with updates on what the kids are doing in school, but it inevitably comes back to Emily.

"I went over to Hurley's house and looked through her things, thinking I might find a diary, or some notes, or something that would give us a clue, but there was nothing. Don't most kids her age keep a diary of some sort?" I look over at Erika. "Do you have one?"

Erika hesitates just long enough to tell me she's lying. "Heck, no," she says. "But if I did have one, I'd hide it really well and make sure no one else could find it and read it."

By the time we're done eating, Matthew starts to fuss so I grab him from his seat and head out to the kitchen to feed him. I settle on a stool at the bar and let Matthew nurse while Desi does the cleanup.

After a few minutes, Desi walks over and leans across the bar toward me. "Erika does have a diary," she says in a low voice. "And no doubt she'd be shocked to know that I not only know where she keeps it, I read it."

"You do?"

"Oh, yes. I remember all too well what a teenaged girl is like and I want to make sure I keep tabs on her. I check all of her e-mails, the browser history on her computer, her social networking posts . . . all of it. So far she's been a pretty good kid, but she's starting to show a lot of interest in boys, so things could change in a heartbeat."

"Where does she hide the diary?" I ask, thinking it might give me a clue on where else I might look for one in Emily's room.

"There's a tear in the lining on the bottom of her box spring and she stuffs it up inside there. The diary has a lock on it and I don't know where she keeps the key, but it's easy enough to pick the lock with a bobby pin. I used to do it with yours all the time."

"You read my diary?"

"Of course I did," she says with a laugh. "You had that pretty blue book with the gold clasp and lock on it, remember? All I had to do was bend the end of a bobby pin, stick it in the lock, and turn it. Easy-peasy."

"You stinker," I say with a laugh, putting Matthew over my shoulder for a burp. "Did you read anything dicey in there?"

"Oh, yeah. I read all about how you lost your virginity to Mitch Dalrymple."

I gasp. "You didn't!"

"I did," she says, with a sly grin. "When I read the part about how he broke your heart I wanted to kill the guy."

I shake my head in awe. "I can't believe you read that."

"You had no secrets from me, Mattie."

"Did you ever tell Mom?"

"No, I wasn't that mean. Besides, if I'd squealed you would have stopped writing in the diary and then what would I have done for entertainment? I was getting bored with those Nancy Drew mysteries we used to stage."

That memory makes me laugh. "Those were fun, weren't they?"

"Yes, they were," Desi says with a chuckle. "Remember how we used to write notes in invisible ink?"

"How could I forget? We almost burned the house down."

Desi and I experimented with different ways to write notes back and forth using invisible ink. My science teacher in school had shown us how to do it using either lemon juice or milk, and writing on a piece of paper with a cotton swab or toothpick dipped in one of these. Once it dried, the reader would have to heat the paper by holding it over a candle or other flame source. Since we had a gas stove, Desi used that to heat a message I'd written in lemon juice. But she got a little too close to the flame and the paper started to burn. She dropped it on the counter where it caught a roll of paper towels on fire. Panicking, she grabbed a carton of milk that was on the counter and threw it on the flames. I squirted lemon juice from a bottle on top of that. The fire was put out, but not before it had burned the bottom of the kitchen curtains and left a burn mark on the countertop. Not to mention that there was spilt, curdled milk everywhere.

Our clean freak of a mother had a major meltdown, and Desi and I joked about the term *major meltdown* even as we quaked in fear every time Mom walked into the kitchen and started sniffing. She could detect a single molecule of sour milk from a mile away and she made me and Desi scrub that kitchen from ceiling to floor a dozen times over the next two weeks.

"Those secret notes were a lot of fun," I say, reminiscing. "I should have written my diary notes out in invisible—" I stop as a flash of an idea comes to me. "I need to go," I say, getting up with Matthew on my shoulder.

"What?" Desi says, looking worried. "Is something wrong?"

"No, but I need to go check on something."

I quickly get Matthew and myself bundled up and say my good-byes. Then I get in my car and drive to Hurley's house. As soon as I'm inside, I head upstairs to Emily's room and set Matthew down on the floor. For the sake of being thorough, I get down on my hands and knees and examine the underside of Emily's bed, looking for openings or tears in the box springs.

There aren't any, so I get up and head for the desk drawer and the empty composition book. I open the book and carefully examine the pages. I can't visualize anything written on them, but the paper has a slight wavy quality to it that makes me think something might be on it.

I head for the dresser and the underwear drawer, remove the lighter I'd found earlier inside the tampon box, and carry it back to the desk. It takes me a minute to open the notebook in a way that allows me to single out a page. I have to set it on the edge of the desk with the page hanging over the side and some books weighing down the rest of the notebook. Then, holding the page in one hand and the lighter in the other, I flick a flame into existence and wave it back and forth beneath the page. Nothing happens so I try moving the lighter closer to the page until I create a small brown spot that nearly ignites. Still nothing is visible.

Frustrated, I toss the lighter aside, and open up the middle desk drawer that holds all the pens. It doesn't take me long to spot one that looks different from the others. It's shorter, and there is a small, clear plastic nub on one end of it. I remove the cap on the other end and expose a tip made of soft white plastic. There is no obvious roller ball or other device to facilitate ink flow and when I try to write on a piece of paper, nothing appears. I try depressing the clear plastic nub on the other end, but it won't move. Then I see a small button on the side of the barrel. When I depress this, a bluish light emits from the clear button at the end. When I shine this light on the piece of paper I'd tried to write on a moment before, a bright white line appears.

I shine the light over a page in Emily's composition notebook, and my heart skips a beat as I see dozens of words spring to life.

Chapter 27

I settle into Emily's chair and, using the light at the end of the pen, I scan and turn the pages quickly until I get to one that is empty. Then I go back to the last page with writing on it and start to read. It's the tail end of a longer note, and after backtracking a couple more pages, I find the start I need.

It takes me a few minutes to read the three-page entry, and when I'm done I take out my cell phone and call Hurley. The phone rings and then flips over to voice mail. I leave a message, telling him to call me right away because I have a lead on Emily. When I'm done, I call Richmond's number. His end rings several times until I think it's going to flip over to voice mail, too, but then Richmond answers sounding breathless and irritated.

"Richmond," he snaps, breathing heavily.

"Bob, it's Mattie. Are you at the gym? Did you finish up the stuff at Jeff Hunt's place?"

He doesn't answer me and after several seconds of silence I start to think we've been disconnected. "Bob, are you there?"

"What do you want, Mattie?" he grumbles.

"I need your help." I then explain to him what I've found and what I need.

He sighs with irritation but says, "Okay, where do you want me to meet you?"

"I have Matthew with me. I need to call Dom to see if he can watch him for me and then drop him off. How about I meet you at the station in ten minutes?"

"Fine." With that he disconnects the call, clearly annoyed with my interruption.

I place a call to Dom, who answers on the first ring. "I have a lead on Emily and need to follow up on it right away," I tell him. "I've got Richmond meeting me in ten minutes to help, but I have Matthew with me. Any chance you can watch him for me for a while? I'm not sure how long I'll be."

"No problem. Just drop him off here at the house."

"Thanks, Dom. I owe you."

"And I know just how you can pay me back," he says.

Crap.

I disconnect the call and as I'm looking at the bare spot on the desktop, I flash back to Emily's laptop on my coffee table at home, and how Hoover had sniffed at it and laid his head on it. I walk over to Emily's hamper, grab a T-shirt from the top of the pile, and then grab Matthew in his carrier.

It takes me about thirteen minutes to get back to the police station and meet up with Richmond. I expect him to be past his annoyance, but judging from his expression, he's not. "I'm sorry to interrupt your gym time, but Hurley didn't answer when I called him and he's still in Chicago. I didn't know who else to call."

"It's not a problem," he says, but he isn't looking at me and his expression remains annoyed.

"I can try to call Junior or one of the uniformed guys."

"I said it's fine," Richmond snaps. A second later his expression softens. "Sorry," he says. "It really is okay. It's just that . . . I was . . . I wasn't at the gym." He shoots me a sidelong glance and his face starts to color. "I was with Rose Carpenter."

"Oh." Then I realize what he was likely doing when I called. "O-o-o-h," I say, wincing.

"Can we get going, please?"

"Right. Sorry. We need to talk to either Carly Randall or Olivia Mason, maybe both. I think Olivia is the brains behind this, but I think Carly is the one who will be more likely to talk. Plus I know her mother, Debbie. We went to school together."

"Do you want to call them first?"

I think about it for a second. "No, let's surprise them if we can. I don't want to give anyone a chance to think up a story."

"What if they aren't home?"

"Then we'll ask around until we find out where they are. Or wait for them."

Richmond doesn't look pleased with this answer but he doesn't object. Instead he says, "Ride together?"

"I'd rather take my own car. I have Hoover with me."

"Your dog? Why?"

"Because I think he might be able to help."

It only takes us a few minutes to reach the Randall house, and I park right in front and leave Hoover inside the hearse. There are lots of lights on inside as we walk onto the porch and ring the bell. And as luck would have it, Carly answers the door.

"Ms. Winston," she says, her eyes wide. She smiles,

but it looks tentative. When she glances at Richmond, the smile starts to fade.

In my best stern adult voice, one I suspect I'll need to hone over the years as my son grows up, I say, "We need to talk to you, Carly. Is your mom home?"

The smile disappears. She swallows, nods, turns back into the house, and yells, "Mom!"

Richmond and I, through some unspoken tacit understanding, both take advantage of Carly's retreat and enter the house. We stop just inside the door and wait for Debbie to put in an appearance. She enters the room carrying a dish towel, wiping her hands, and looking curiously at us with the same tentative smile her daughter had a moment ago. She gives Richmond a quick once-over but her gaze lingers on me. "Mattie Fjell, is that you?"

"It is," I say.

"You changed your hair color."

Sigh. "Debbie, we need to talk to Carly about an urgent matter."

Debbie looks over at Richmond. "You're a cop, aren't you?"

Richmond nods and Debbie looks back at me.

"And I heard you work for the ME now."

"Yes, I do. But we aren't here in any official capacity. At least not yet," I add, giving Carly a pointed look. Her eyes widen again and she takes an involuntary step back. "Emily is missing and I think your daughter knows something about it."

Debbie's smile is gone in an instant. "Who is Emily?"

"She's my stepdaughter," I say, stretching the truth a bit.

"Are you accusing Carly of something?"

"Not yet," I say in what I hope is a friendly, reassuring tone. "But I need her to answer some questions. I think Emily is hurt or lost somewhere. And I think your daughter knows where she might be." Debbie has her defense shields up. I can tell from the arms folded tightly over her chest, the grim set of her lips, the rigid posture. "Please, Debbie. Emily's life could be at stake here. I need Carly's help."

My plea works. Carly starts to cry. "I'm sorry. Olivia made me promise not to tell."

Debbie gapes at her daughter. "What did you do?"

"I didn't mean to hurt anybody," Carly sobs, giving her mother a pleading look.

"Emily wrote in her diary that you and Olivia were going to drive her to a secret place to meet Johnny. Where is the secret place?"

Carly winces and hiccups a sob. "There isn't one. We made that up. We just wanted to drop her off in the country somewhere and make her walk back to town."

Debbie gasps.

"Why?" I ask. I'm so angry with Carly I want to slap her even as some part of me realizes this is probably not the best parenting instinct I could have. "What did Emily do to you?"

"She didn't do anything to me," Carly says, sniffling. "It's Olivia who got mad at her."

"Why?"

In a long, frantic confession, Carly spills the beans. "Because Olivia likes Johnny Chester and wants him for herself. The two of them were friends back before Emily came because Olivia is friends with Johnny's older sister, and Olivia was hoping something more would develop between her and Johnny. But when Emily showed up, Johnny was totally into her and Olivia got mad. She's been pretending to be a friend to Emily to keep tabs on her and Johnny so she could find a way to drive them apart. It was supposed to be

Emily who got kicked out of school because of the weed. Olivia slipped it into her coat pocket and then wrote an anonymous note to the principal's office that someone in the school was dealing weed. She knew Johnny was a straight arrow and wouldn't like that Emily had weed on her. The principal brought in a cop with a drug-sniffing dog later in the day, and that's when Olivia discovered that the jacket was actually Johnny's and Emily had only been wearing it earlier in the day. So Johnny was the one who ended up getting kicked out of school and that made Olivia even madder."

She pauses for a second and sucks in a breath before continuing. She's talking so fast, I have to focus hard on what she's saying.

"So Olivia told Johnny that Emily had set him up with the pot on purpose because Emily was into someone else and wanted Johnny out of the picture. Olivia knew Johnny wouldn't believe her right away, so she dared Brian Morgan, who has a major crush on Olivia, to kiss Emily. He did it and Olivia snapped a pic so she could show it to Johnny as proof. She thought Johnny would get mad, but instead he just looked hurt and said he wanted to talk to Emily. Problem was, his mom took away his cell phone as part of his punishment for having the weed. Olivia offered to be a go-between, figuring she could keep the two of them apart that way. So when Johnny wrote a note to Emily saying he wanted to talk to her, Olivia tore it up and told Emily Johnny wanted nothing to do with her. She didn't tell Emily that Johnny's phone was taken away because she wanted her to believe he was ignoring her calls and texts. Then Olivia faked a note from Johnny that said he was willing to hear her out but they would have to meet somewhere out of town so his mom or her dad wouldn't see them or spot his car. Olivia told Emily that the reason Johnny wrote out a paper note was because his mom was monitoring his cell phone. Olivia offered to drive Emily out to a spot she had suggested to Johnny because it was a secret place that her and I went to all the time. The plan was to drop Emily off, leave, and force her to walk back to town when she realized Johnny wasn't there. Then Olivia was going to tell her that Johnny never intended to meet her, he only wanted to punish her for framing him. She figured the two of them would hate each other by then, paving the way for her and Johnny."

She stops then and lets out a ragged breath. Clearly she's relieved to unburden herself.

"So you drove her out in the country somewhere?" I ask. Deb mutters something under her breath and she is glaring at her daughter. Carly nods. "Where, exactly?"

Crocodile tears are coursing down Carly's face. "We told her it was out in the woods by the Haas place. Olivia told me to make up some phony landmarks so Emily would wander around for a while."

"What did you tell her?" My friendly tone is gone and Carly doesn't miss this fact.

"I don't remember," she whines, looking fearfully from Richmond to me.

I'm tired of tiptoeing around and decide to play hardball. Clearly Carly feels both guilt and fear over this and I intend to take advantage of that fact. "If something bad has happened to Emily because of this, you could go to prison, Carly." I have no idea if this is true and frankly don't care as long as it has the desired effect.

Deb gasps and Carly shakes her head in vigorous denial. "It was all Olivia's idea," Carly cries.

"But you helped. What were the landmarks you gave her?"

"I told you, I made them up."

I look over at Richmond and make a give-me gesture with my hand. "Let me have your handcuffs," I say to him.

"I told her to look for a tree with a knee," Carly blurts out. "And then I think I told her to look for one that resembled a witch."

Deb's arms are folded over her chest and her expression is a mix of disappointment and disbelief. "I told you to stay away from that Olivia Mason," she says, tight-lipped. "She's not a good influence."

"You can talk about that later," I tell them. "Right now we need to head out to the woods to look for Emily and I want Carly to go with us so she can show us where they dropped her off."

"Are you taking me to jail?" Carly sobs, her eyes wide with fear. "I'm sorry. I really am. We thought she'd just walk back to town and be mad and that would be it. I don't know why she didn't come back."

"And it didn't occur to you to tell someone about it?" I ask, getting in her face.

"Olivia said we'd get into big trouble if we did that."

"Well, you got into big trouble anyway," I tell her. "Bigger trouble than it would have been if you'd said something sooner. You just better hope that we find Emily and she's okay."

I make Richmond take Carly and her mom in his car since I'm so angry with the girl, I'm afraid of what I might do or say to her. And then there's the whole hearse thing, though to be honest the idea of using it as a scare tactic with Carly has a certain appeal to me.

Richmond is on his phone as he heads to his car with Carly and Deb, asking for volunteers to meet us in the woods and help with the search. I climb into my hearse to wait for Richmond to pull out, and take out my cell phone to call Hurley.

This time he answers. "Hurley, I've got some news," I tell him. I fill him in on what I discovered with the diary, our talk with Carly, and where we're headed. "I'm thinking Emily went out there to meet Johnny and something happened to her. We're going out there now to look for her. Richmond is calling for volunteers."

"I'm on my way home," Hurley says. I can hear a mix of relief and urgency in his voice. On the one hand, knowing that Emily wasn't kidnapped by someone is a huge load off our minds. But Hurley, like me, knows that anyone who has been outside in the elements for as long as Emily has been missing might not be doing well . . . or might not be alive. "I'll be there as soon as I can, but call me with any news, okay?"

"Will do." I start to disconnect the call but I hear him call out my name. "Yeah?" I say, putting the phone back to my ear.

"You . . . I . . . thank you for helping to find my daughter . . . *our* daughter."

I smile. I suspect he wants to say something more but words of endearment don't come easily to Hurley. The only time I heard him say he loved me was when Matthew was born and he was overcome with emotion. "You're welcome," I say. And when I disconnect the call, I come up with a silent prayer that we *will* find her, and she'll be okay.

I follow Richmond's car out of town and after driving about three miles beyond the city limits on the main road, he turns onto a side road, drives on that for a mile, and then turns onto a dirt road. The dirt road ends several hundred feet in, but there is a snowmobile trail that intersects it and runs along the edge of a thick copse of trees that lies directly in front of us. Based on where we are, I figure that straight beyond that copse, maybe a mile or so as the crow flies, is what's left of the Haas farm. In fact, the woods in front of us are likely part of the remaining Haas acreage.

We park the cars and Richmond gets out of his and directs Carly and her mother to do the same. I grab the shirt I removed from Emily's hamper, take a flashlight out of my glove box, and after leashing Hoover, I get out and join the others. Richmond is on his phone directing someone on the other end to our location.

"Is this where you and Olivia dropped Emily?" I ask Carly.

She nods, her tearstained face highlighted in the moonlight. At least we have a full moon to help us with our search. "We told her to go straight into the woods from the end of this road, to look for a tree with a knee in it, and then turn right. Then she was supposed to look for a tree that resembled a witch and turn left. We said there was a small shed back in there and that's where Johnny was waiting. She asked how Johnny got out here, and where his car was. Olivia told her he probably came at it from the other side of the woods because there was a farm there where he could hide his car, but it was a longer hike to the secret place."

Richmond disconnects his call and says, "We should have some help out here in a few minutes."

"You wait for them," I tell him. "I'm going in."

"I don't think that's wise, Mattie."

"I don't care." I kneel down in front of Hoover and put Emily's shirt up to his nose. "Remember Emily?" I say to him as he sniffs the shirt, and he wags his tail. "Let's go find her."

I stand, turn on my flashlight, and repeat the command. "Go find Emily."

Hoover dutifully takes off toward the woods, his nose to the ground. Seconds later we are scrambling through thick underbrush that snags and drags at my feet and pants legs, and for a minute or two, Hoover follows a crazy zigzag pattern that makes me wonder if he's really on the scent. After scrambling over branches, through dead bushes and leaves, and under a fallen trunk that's wedged in the fork of another, nearby tree, Hoover stops for a moment and sniffs the ground.

I shine my flashlight in front of me, scanning the trees. And miraculously, off to the right, I see a tree that has a weird split in the bottom of its trunk that creates a right angle. Darn if it doesn't look like a knee. Hoover is still sniffing at the ground, so I put the shirt in front of his nose again. "Come on, boy. Help me out here. Go find Emily."

Hoover understands the *go find* command, because I use it with him in play all the time, telling him to go find his ball, or his bone, or his toy. He has enough of an understanding of these object words that he always gets the specific item I've requested and brings it to me. But I have no idea if he understands what *Emily* means. He's spent time with her before; she stayed in my cottage one night several months back and she and Hoover bonded. So I can only hope that Hoover somehow comprehends that the smell of Emily on her shirt and the *go find* command means he should sniff out Emily.

I'm encouraged when he takes off in the direction of the knee tree and then angles off to the right. The trees begin to thin in number, making our walk a little easier. Behind me I can hear voices and motors that I assume mean our volunteer searchers have arrived. And I realize that if I can hear them, maybe Emily can, too.

"Emily!" I holler. "Are you out here? Can you hear me?" I listen for a response, but I don't hear anything. Then Hoover's head pops up, his ears perk forward, and he whines. "What is it, boy? Do you hear something?" He angles his head to one side, then the other, then with a burst of energy he lunges forward, ripping the leash from my hand. He takes off at a full run and I follow. I don't want to lose him here in the woods and I'm about to call out to him when I think better of it, not wanting to confuse him over the task at hand. Instead I take off after him as fast as I can. Seconds later I've lost sight of him, but I can hear him running through the underbrush and I follow the sound. Then I hear him bark and my heart leaps. I stumble between the trees, trying not to trip, following the sound of his barks. And suddenly I break through into a small clearing. Hoover is about thirty feet away, staring at the ground, barking like crazy.

Over the next few seconds my mind whirls through a bunch of scenarios as I try to make sense of the scene. *Clearly Emily isn't anywhere to be seen so why is Hoover barking? Is he barking at something on the ground? Clothing? An animal? Or, heaven forbid, is he barking at something* in *the ground? Did Carly tell me the whole truth? Were those girls crazy enough to have killed Emily and buried her out here?*

My feet start moving forward and I shine my flashlight at the ground in front of Hoover. I can tell that something about it is odd . . . there is a depression . . . a void. *Oh God, is it a grave?* As I draw closer I see that it's definitely a hole, and then I feel the ground beneath my feet change. I stop, sweep a foot through the dead leaves, and reveal a series of wooden boards. I'm about six feet away from Hoover now, and I can see that the hole isn't in the ground per se, but rather in the boards. The rotted, broken edges of several of them are about five feet in front of me.

I realize I'm standing over some kind of underground pit or bunker, and those freshly broken boards fill me with both hope and dread. Carefully I work my way toward the hole, testing each footstep, shifting my weight in increments. About a foot from the hole's edge I feel the ground sag beneath me so I step back and get down on my knees. Hoover has stopped barking, but he's staring into that hole and wagging his tail. He looks at me for a second, then back into the hole. I crawl up to the edge on all fours and shine my flashlight down into the abyss.

It's a bunker hollowed out of the ground with planked walls and a dirt floor. And lying on that floor in the beam of my light is a body.

Chapter 28

"Emily!" I cry out. And my prayers are answered when I see the body move. "Thank God, you're alive. Can you hear me?"

She is lying on her left side and she nods weakly. "I think . . . my leg . . . is . . . is broken," she says, her voice cracking. "I'm so cold. Mattie, please help me."

"Help is on the way, honey," I tell her. "You hang in there." I look back the way I came and yell as loud as I can, "I found her! She's over here!" I wave my flashlight at the trees and yell again. "Richmond! Can you hear me?"

"We hear you, Mattie. Keep your light pointed this way."

I do as instructed and moments later I see several bouncing balls of light through the trees coming my way. I turn back toward Emily, and I'm shocked to see that Hoover is inching himself into the hole. I'm afraid he'll fall and hurt himself, and I'm about to yell to him, but after bellying partway down the wall, he leaps the rest of the way, landing just fine. Then he goes over to

Emily, nudges her with his nose, and starts licking her face.

"Hoover," she says in that weak voice. I see the faintest hint of a smile on her face as she lifts her arm and wraps it around his neck.

Hoover lies down beside her, his head alongside her face, his body warming hers.

I look back and see Richmond and KY enter the clearing. "She's down in some kind of underground bunker," I tell them. "She's alive, but she's hurt. We're going to need an ambulance, and maybe the fire department, too, to get her out of there."

Richmond nods and gets on his phone. He and KY are still walking toward me and I hold up a hand to stop them. "Be careful. These boards covering the hole are old and rotted. I don't want you guys falling through, too."

"What the hell is this?" KY asks, edging up to the place where Hoover had been moments ago.

"These woods are part of the Haas farm, and back in the day it was rumored that they had a still out here where they produced illegal moonshine. I'm guessing this is where it was."

Emily moans, making my heart ache. "Em, talk to me. Stay with me. Tell me where you hurt."

The only response I get is another moan. I look over at KY and say, "I'm going down there. I can't wait for the ambulance."

Behind me, Richmond says, "Don't be stupid, Mattie. Wait for the fire crew to get here."

"I can't, Richmond. She's going into shock, and if I don't do something now we could lose her. Every second matters at this point. I'm not going to stand by and let her die."

I crawl on my hands and knees over to where KY is squatting. The opening there doesn't have sharp-edged planks sticking out, and some of the wall planks are accessible. I figure I can back down over the edge on my belly and when I drop, the fall will only be a few feet. When I reach the edge by KY, I lie on my stomach and stick my feet over the side. I inch my way back, feeling for toeholds in the plank wall. When I get to waist level, I look at KY. "Can you help me?"

He looks hesitant, but nods. I set my flashlight down as KY gets on his knees. He grabs me under my arms and holds tight as I continue inching my way into the hole. I manage to get my boobs to the edge, and realize they are so full they feel like they're ready to burst. "Okay, let me go," I tell KY.

He does so and I half slide, half fall down into the bunker. I land on my feet but immediately lose my balance and fall backward, landing on my butt.

"Are you okay?" KY asks, grimacing.

"I'm fine. Toss me my flashlight." He does so, and then I flip over onto my hands and knees and crawl to Emily. I grab her hand, which is frightfully cold, and I flash on all the similarly cold, rubbery hands I've had to fingerprint. The image strikes fear in my heart and I shake it off and start rubbing that hand, determined to get some warmth into it. My efforts are rewarded moments later when I feel Emily's fingers curl around my hand.

"Atta girl, Em," I tell her. I take off my coat and lay it over her. Then I give Hoover a pat on the head. "Good boy." I try to let go of Emily's hand but she grabs mine in a death grip.

"Don't leave me," she whimpers.

"I won't leave you, Em. Not now, not ever. But I do

need to take a look at that leg. Hang on to Hoover for a few minutes, okay?"

She nods, looking up at me with pleading eyes. I feel an instant, powerful wave of guilt for every bad thought I had about this kid over the past few months. And I vow to myself that somehow, some way, I'm going to make it up to her.

I crawl down to her legs and the smell of stale urine wafts up to me. The poor kid was forced to lie here so long she had to pee in her pants. And wet pants in this cold weather could be deadly. In fact, the only reason she isn't already dead from hypothermia is because the weather warmed up over the past couple of days, and there wasn't any rain or snow. Plus the bunker provided some protection from the wind. Emily is lying on her side, the broken leg—and based on the angle it has, it is definitely broken—on top of the good leg. I shine my flashlight along her pant leg and see blood—fortunately all of it dried—on the lower part of it. I gently palpate this area through the pants, soliciting a moan from Emily. Midcalf I feel a hard, angled deformity that tells me she has a compound, open fracture. I need to get her pants off her, both to warm her up and to get a better look at her leg.

"KY, got a knife of any sort?"

"A pocket knife. You want it?"

"I do. Toss it down to me. And see if we can get a blanket or two down here." He tosses me the knife and then disappears. I open up the knife blade and start cutting the seam in Emily's pants, starting at the ankle and working my way up. It's slow going because even the slightest movement makes her moan in pain. Every time she moans, Hoover licks her cheek. When I finally have the break exposed, I wince. It's a bad one, the shattered end of her tibia protruding through her skin and the broken end of her fibula visible just inside the open wound. The skin around the wound is hot and red, a sign of pending infection. I check for pulses in her foot, relieved to feel them, but frightened by how weak and thready they are.

KY returns with a blanket and tosses it down to me. I cut the remainder of the pants away and pull the wet material from Emily's body. Then I cover her up with the blanket. In one of the pants pockets I find Emily's cell phone. The screen is shattered and when I try to turn it on, nothing happens. Either the battery died completely or it's broken, which explains why Hurley had no luck tracking it. Off in the distance I hear the sound of sirens approaching and I move back up to Emily's head. "Help is on the way," I say softly. "Hear those sirens?"

She grunts a response.

I lift the edge of the blanket and lay down beneath it, extending the front of my body along the backside of hers, taking care not to touch the injured leg. I drape an arm over her torso and snug myself up against her backside. And then I tighten my hold slightly, hugging her close. It's an effort to both warm her and reassure her.

"Emily, I need you to do something for me, okay?" I say just above a whisper. "I need you to stay awake, and focused. I need you to listen to me. Do you hear me?"

She mutters a halfhearted assent.

"Johnny never knew about you coming out here," I tell her. "Some very stupid, very despicable girls played a nasty trick on you because they're immature, insecure, and mean-spirited. They were hoping to drive you and Johnny apart, but it didn't work. Johnny is crazy with worry about you. So is your dad. He'd be here right now if he could but he went to Chicago to search for you. He's on his way back and he'll be here as soon as he can."

"Chicago?" Emily whispers.

"Yep, Chicago. He's been searching for you since you went missing. He even abandoned a case we're working on so he could focus on finding you."

I feel Emily's shoulders start to tremble and hear her suck in a sob. "I'm sorry," she stutters.

"You don't have anything to be sorry about," I tell her. "We're just glad you're okay."

"Johnny isn't mad at me?"

"Nope, he's just worried about you. We've all been worried about you."

"I didn't think anyone would look for me," she sobbed. "All those times I ran off . . ."

"Of course we looked for you, silly," I say, tightening my grip on her. "Look, I know you have to feel kind of lost and adrift with all the changes you've had in your life. Your dad kind of feels that way, too. Both of you have had to make some really big adjustments in your lives. We all have. We're trying to figure out our personal definition of family, and right now it's our little group of four: you, your dad, me, and Matthew."

"Where is Matthew?"

"He's with Dom and Izzy." I hear the sound of urgent voices drawing near and know that help is close at hand. "Listen, Emily, the rescue people are going to get you out of here and to the hospital. But it isn't going to be easy for you. They're going to have to move you and that's going to hurt. They can give you pain medicine, but it won't make the pain go away. It's only going to dull it. So you're going to have to be very brave. I know you're strong, and I know you're tough. You have to be to get through everything that's happened to you in the past year. So dig down deep and find all the strength you have left, okay?"

She nods, but she also starts to weep. Above us is a lot of commotion and I look up to see several men with ropes and a litter.

"You're going to need an IV and some pain meds," I tell them. "And a splint. She has an open tib-fib fracture of the right leg."

Moments later there are three men in the bunker with us. I release my hold on Emily and get up to assist them. I call Hoover to me so the EMTs can get to Emily. He gets up, but then he walks over and lies down near Emily's head. He's out of the way enough for now, so I let him be because Emily seems to be taking comfort in his presence. She stretches a hand out and pets him.

"If you give me the supplies, I'll start an IV on her," I tell the EMTs. "You guys can splint that leg."

They don't argue; they know me from when I worked in the ER and know I can handle the task. The supplies are handed to me and I scoot around to the front side of Emily and explain to her what I'm about to do. "I need to start an IV on you. Do you know what that is?"

She nods.

"It means a needle stick but it will be quick and it will be worth it. Because once we have the IV in, they can give you some pain medicine. And by giving it through the IV it will work much faster."

She nods again.

I make quick work of the IV while the paramedic beside me holds a flashlight so I can see, and then I start some fluids running. "What have you got for pain?" I ask him.

"Morphine," he says, taking her blood pressure. "She's 98 over 60."

"We're ready with the splint," the two guys at Emily's feet say. "Let us know when we can go."

The EMT beside me rummages in a kit, pulls out a syringe of morphine, and hands it to me.

"Emily, are you allergic to anything?"

"I don't think so."

"Okay, then I'm going to give you some pain medicine through this IV. It will make you feel better but like I said before, it won't make the pain go away completely, okay?"

She nods.

I look over at the paramedic and speak in a low voice. "I'm thinking we should start with four milligrams. She's a little shocky and I don't want to drop her pressure too much more." He nods his agreement and I push the medication into the IV line. "Keep an eye on her pressure," I tell him. After giving the medication a minute to circulate, I look over at the paramedic and he gives me a thumbs-up as he finishes taking another blood pressure. I take Emily's hands in mine and lean down by her ear. "This is it," I say. "Be strong. Squeeze my hands if you need to." She looks up at me with fear in her eyes, but there is also determination. She nods, and I look over at the two guys who are ready with the splint and say, "Go."

The next few minutes are marked by rapid reassurances and muffled moans as Emily bravely bites back the screams trying to box their way out of her lungs. I know the pain has to be horrible even with the morphine on board, and she squeezes my hands so tight as they splint her leg that my fingers all go numb. In the end, I'm duly impressed by the girl's fortitude. By the time they have her splinted and wrapped in the litter, ready to hoist out of the bunker, she is calmer. The IV fluids have perked her up. Her eyes are brighter, and there's some color in her cheeks.

KY and a fireman drop a ladder and with some help we get Hoover out of the bunker by tying a special vest around him and lifting him out. Once I climb out, I help the crew hoist Emily's litter out of the bunker and then wait with her as they climb out of the hole. Once we're all ready to hike out, I grab one of the handles on the litter and help carry her through the woods to the waiting ambulance.

It's a bumpy trip for Emily and she winces in pain several times, but when I ask her if she needs more pain medicine, she insists she'll be fine. "I don't want to fall asleep," she says. "That's the only way I kept going when I was lying down there. When I got really cold I kept telling myself that I couldn't fall asleep. I was afraid that if I fell asleep, I'd die."

"That was smart of you. And very brave," I add with a smile.

"Except I did fall asleep a couple of times," she said. "I'd get mad at myself every time I woke up because I was afraid that if I did it again it would be the last time and I'd never wake up again."

"That takes a strong will and some incredible inner strength," I tell her. "You have no idea how proud I am of you."

She manages a weak smile at this. "Will you ride with me to the hospital?" she asks.

"Is it okay if I follow right behind you? I have Hoover and they won't let him ride in the ambulance. Plus I have my car here and not many people are comfortable driving it."

She smiles again, bigger this time, and my heart leaps. "That's right. I forgot you have that cool hearse."

"Yes, I do. And just imagine what people are going

to think when they see a hearse screaming down the road following an ambulance that's running with full lights and sirens." This time she chuckles and the paramedics manage a snort, too. "I need to call your dad and let him know you're okay," I tell her, taking my phone out with my free hand. "Want to talk to him?"

She nods and I dial Hurley's number on my cell. I don't waste a second of time on greetings, identification, or guessing games when he answers. "We found her, Hurley. She fell into an old abandoned bunker and broke her leg, but she's okay. We're on our way to the hospital now."

"Thank God," Hurley says. "I'm still about half an hour away."

"You should know that she didn't run away," I tell him mostly for Emily's benefit. "She was duped and lured out into some woods by some girls at her school. I'll fill you in on the details later. Hold on and I'll let you talk to her."

I hand my phone off to Emily and as soon as she hears her father's voice on the other end, she bursts into tears.

"I'm so sorry if I scared you. I didn't mean to," she sobs. She listens for a minute and squeezes her eyes closed. Then she says, "Okay, bye," and hands me my phone back.

"Hurley?"

"I'm here."

"She's going to need surgery on that leg."

"Okay, I'll be there as soon as I can. If they need to take her before I get there, have them phone me. Can you stay with her?"

"Of course I can. She even asked me to."

"She did? Maybe there's hope after all."

"Drive carefully. I'll see you soon."

We reach the ambulance and I stand by and watch as they load Emily in. "I'll be right behind you," I tell her just before they close the doors. And then I create a bit of a spectacle as I pursue a lights-and-siren, full-out ambulance down the highway and through town with my midnight blue, slightly used hearse.

Chapter 29

The ER staff has changed a lot since I worked here, but there are a few die-hard nurses and techs I recognize. Because of the hour, my closest coworker, Syph, isn't on duty, but other nurses I know well are, and I know the doc on duty, too. This helps expedite things since legally I'm not allowed to authorize care for Emily, but many of the folks who work here know my current life situation with Hurley.

By the time Emily is settled in and medicated with enough of the good stuff to send her to la-la land, Hurley arrives. He rushes into the room like a stiff breeze, and stops at the foot of Emily's stretcher. After looking at her, he looks at me and rears back. "What the hell?" he says.

"What?" I say, totally confused.

"What did you do to your hair? I almost didn't recognize you."

"Oh yeah, that," I say glumly. "It was an experiment that didn't work out the way I hoped. I'm going to change it back as soon as I can."

He nods and looks back at Emily. "How is she?" he asks in a low voice.

"She's better now that they have her medicated," I tell him. "She's badly dehydrated and a little hypothermic. That's why she has that machine and special blanket blowing on her. She has an open leg fracture that will have to be reduced surgically and will leave her at great risk of infection. But at the moment she's comfortable and she's going to be okay. The orthopedic doctor hasn't arrived yet but they expect him anytime."

Hurley walks over and gives me a kiss on the cheek. "What the hell happened?" he asks, straightening up and running a hand through his hair. "Where was she and how did she get there?"

I fill him in on the story as I know it based on Carly's confession. "If what Carly said is true, this girl Olivia was the mastermind behind it all," I conclude. "Once we got Emily here, Richmond headed to Olivia's house to speak with her and her parents. I'm not sure what the outcome will be. The good news is, Johnny had nothing to do with this. Apparently his only fault is being too darned attractive to too many girls."

Hurley walks over to the bed and leans down to kiss Emily on her forehead. Though she was snoring seconds ago, her eyes flutter open and she smiles when she sees Hurley.

"Hey, kiddo," Hurley says. "You had us pretty worried."

"I'm sorry. I didn't mean it, not this time."

"Don't worry about that. The important thing is that you're safe now and we're going to get that leg taken care of."

"It's pretty bad, isn't it?" she says, her brows furrowing.

"Mattie says it will be a long recovery, but eventually we can make you good as new."

Emily rolls her head toward me and manages a weak smile. "I thought you were an angel coming to take me away," she says. "I didn't recognize you at first because your hair is different."

I'm about to apologize for my hair yet again when there is some noise beyond the curtain and Mick Dunn, the orthopedic surgeon, comes into the room. He gives me a curious look and hesitates a second before he greets me—no doubt the hair again. Then he introduces himself to both Hurley and Emily, and examines the injured leg. Once that's done, he takes several minutes to explain what needs to be done, and the risks associated with it. When he's done, he asks if there are any questions.

"Will I have scars?" Emily asks.

Dr. Dunn nods. "I'm afraid so. It's hard to tell at this point how bad they will be. A lot depends on how you as an individual heal."

I'm concerned that Emily will be upset by this news, but instead she smiles and says, "I'm going to look totally badass."

Dr. Dunn pulls Hurley aside and has him sign the consent for surgery. While they're occupied with that, I walk over to the bed and tell Emily I need to go home to take care of Matthew but that I'll keep up on how she's doing through Hurley.

"Do you think Dad is mad at me?" she asks me, her brow furrowed with worry.

"Of course not," I tell her. "He's just very tired. He's been really worried about you and I know he's glad you're safe. He loves you, Emily."

She looks doubtful. "He's never said that," she says, looking sad.

"Yeah, it's kind of hard for him to say that kind of stuff, I think. It is for a lot of men."

"Has he ever told you he loves you?"

"Once," I admit with a roll of my eyes. "He said it

when Matthew was born. I think he was overcome with emotion and it just blurted out of him."

"I bet he loves Matthew."

"Of course he does. But I've never heard him say it."

"Really?"

"Really. Sometimes people express love through their actions instead of their words."

This statement is a moment of enlightenment for me, and judging from the look on Emily's face, for her, too.

After a few seconds of silent contemplation Emily says, "You're right. I can tell he loves you by the way he looks when he's around you, and the way he talks about you when you're not there."

"That's exactly how I know he loves you," I tell her. "He talks about you constantly, and he worries all the time about whether you're safe and happy, and if you feel like you belong. And he's always telling everyone how proud he is of you, about the grades you're getting in school, and how pretty you are, and how strong you've been through everything that's happened. He's kind of new to all this fathering and emotional stuff, so we need to give him some slack. But believe me, he's dedicated to being your dad and giving you the best life he knows how."

Emily looks over at Hurley with a contemplative expression. After a moment she looks back at me and says, "I'm sorry I gave you such a hard time."

"Thank you."

She looks surprised.

"What?" I ask.

"I expected you to say it was nothing, or not to worry about it, or some other throw-away line like that."

I shrug and smile at her. "I'm not going to lie to you, Emily. You've been quite a challenge at times. But whether you believe it or not, I understand why you did it. I come from a less than normal family myself, and my father abandoned me when I was a little girl. It messed me up at times. It still does."

While investigating the case of the man who tried to kill me while I was pregnant, I learned that my father was not only a criminal, but a cop killer. And not just any cop, but Hurley's former partner. My mother swears there's more to the story, but the information the state cops dug up seems pretty straightforward.

"I didn't know that," Emily says. "Did you ever hook up with him again?"

I shake my head, even though the answer to this question isn't a simple one. While it's true that I haven't met up with my father since he left my mother and me when I was four, I'm almost certain he has not only poked his head back into my life, but was most likely the one who saved it when my potential killer finally caught up to me. But that fact doesn't mitigate the other truths. "I've learned some things about him," I tell Emily, glancing over at Hurley to make sure he's still occupied and out of earshot. "Some not-so-good things, in fact."

"Like what?"

"It's a long story, one we can save for another time. Let's get you better and get life back to normal—or what passes for normal for us—and maybe someday I'll tell you all about it. Right now I need to get home to Matthew."

"When can you come back?"

"You're going to be out of it all night tonight with the surgery, so how about in the morning?"

She nods, looks thoughtful for a moment, and then says, "Can you bring Matthew with you?"

"Sure," I say wondering how much of this newer,

kinder Emily is the drugs talking. I want to believe she's turned a corner, but I've been hopeful before only to have those hopes shattered.

"Mattie?"

"Yeah?"

"Thank you for finding me."

I smile at her. "You're welcome."

"I thought Olivia and Carly might come looking for me but when they didn't, I knew I'd been duped. And since nobody but them knew I was out there in those woods, I thought I was going to die there."

"I'm so sorry you went through that, Em. Olivia and Carly will be punished for what they did."

This makes her frown. After a few seconds she says, "How did you do it? How did you even know where to look, or who to talk to?"

I bite my lip, hesitant to tell her that I snooped into her most private life. "We looked for clues," I tell her. "Hurley and I talked to as many people as we knew to talk to, and we looked through your stuff for any hints. Your dad tried to track your cell phone but it was dead, either from being broken in the fall, or because the battery ran out. Maybe both. We even got someone to hack into your laptop and read your e-mails and your Facebook posts."

"Someone hacked into my laptop?" she says. I expect her to be mad but she looks more intrigued than anything.

"We tried a bunch of different passwords," I tell her. "Birthdays, names of family members, things like the word *password,* and some common number sequences. Whatever you picked is a good one."

"You didn't try all the family members," she says with a hint of a smile.

I give her a puzzled look. "What do you mean?"

"I used my baby brother's name," she says, and for a split second I'm confused. Then she adds, "My password is Matthew."

I'm speechless, a rare event for me.

"But I don't think there was anything on my laptop that would have helped you. Everything Olivia and Carly said was face to face."

I brace myself, swallow hard, and fess up to the rest, hoping it isn't going to damage the delicate détente we seem to have at the moment. "I read your diary," I tell her.

She looks at me, narrowing her eyes, her brows drawn down either in confusion or anger . . . I can't tell which. "What diary?"

"The one in the composition book that Dr. Baldwin gave you. She gave me the same kind of book when I was going to her and she told me to keep a diary."

Emily contemplates this a moment. Then she asks, "How?"

"I found your special pen, which is pretty cool, by the way."

Emily turns away and looks as if she is about to burst into tears.

"What's the matter? Are you in pain?"

She shakes her head. "Some of the stuff I wrote in there was just venting and—"

I stop her before she can confess to anything I don't need or want to know. "I didn't read your whole diary," I say. "I only read the last entry, the one that talked about Olivia and Carly bringing you out to meet in secret with Johnny. I figured that anything relevant in the diary would be near the end so that's where I started. Anything you wrote before that is still secret."

She looks back at me and I see doubt in her eyes. I wonder what entries had her worried. Had she bad-mouthed me? Had she admitted to some questionable behaviors?

Hurley comes back into the room and he moves to the side of the stretcher opposite me, taking Emily's hand. "Are you doing okay?" he asks her.

Emily nods. "I was so afraid you wouldn't come looking for me, that you'd think I ran away."

"We did think that initially, when the school first called."

"What made you change your mind?" Emily asks. "There weren't any clues to tell you that it was any different from the other times."

"Sure there were," Hurley says. "Your book bag wasn't at the house, Johnny didn't know where you were, and there were no messages from you."

"It was more about what wasn't there than what was," I say. And as soon as I utter those words, a mental light bulb turns on in my head.

Hurley is staring at me. "What is it?" he asks.

"I just had a flash of an idea about the Sanderson case," I tell him. "Something I need to look into. But right now I have to go home and feed Matthew. If you need me tonight, call me. Otherwise I'll be back in the morning. Actually, we'll be back. Emily asked me to bring Matthew."

Hurley looks hesitantly pleased. He gives Emily's hand a squeeze and says, "I want to see Mattie out but I'll be right back, okay?" She nods and I'm encouraged by the fact that she doesn't look angry. Hurley and I walk out of the room into the hall and head for the waiting room. As soon as we get there, Hurley pulls me to him and gives me a nice big kiss on the lips. "I don't know how to thank you, Mattie," he says when he finally lets me go.

"You can thank me by giving that child the attention she needs. She needs to know you care about her, Hurley."

"She knows."

"I don't think she does. Have you told her?"

"I show her in all kinds of ways," he says with a frown.

I shake my head. "We girls need to hear it from time to time, Hurley. All of us." I give him a kiss on the cheek. "Think about that, okay? In the meantime, I have to run before my chest turns into Niagara Falls."

We share one more delicious kiss before I reluctantly leave and head out to my car. Hoover is waiting for me and he greets me with his usual tail wag and happy face. I give him a big kiss on his furry head and tell him, "You're a good boy, Hoover. And you definitely earned your keep tonight."

I start the car and give Richmond a call. It flips over to voice mail and I figure he's probably embroiled in whatever is going on at the Mason house. So I leave a message, a long one, telling him what's on my mind. Then I start the car and head home to my boy—with a quick stop at the McDonald's drive-through to get Hoover a hamburger—feeling more hope for the future than I have in a very long time.

Chapter 30

It's a late night for me after I feed Matthew and fill Dom and Izzy in on all the events of the evening. We celebrate Emily's safe return with an intoxicating concoction Dom whipped up that he calls a Kahlúa cream cake. It's a heady mix of Kahlúa, pudding, chocolate, and sour cream that melts in my mouth, tastes like heaven, and leaves me feeling very mellow. I'm afraid to ask Dom how much alcohol is in the cake and figure I'll just pump and dump for the rest of the night so I don't get Matthew drunk.

"It sounds like Emily is finally coming around," Izzy says after we have all stuffed ourselves on the yummy dessert. "Do you think it will last?"

"I don't know," I admit. "She was scared and in shock when we first found her, and heavily medicated later on, but she seemed sincere. I'm hopeful."

"Why don't you take a personal day tomorrow," he suggests. "I can get Arnie to help me with the autopsy in the morning."

"Are you sure?" I say with a frown. "I've just come back to work after being off for eight weeks."

"True, but technically you were entitled to twelve weeks, so we have some flex room. And right now, Hurley and Emily need you more than I do."

"Thanks, and I'll take you up on the autopsy part so I can be at the hospital in the morning. But after that I think I'll be working with Richmond on our current case." I then fill him in on the thoughts I had earlier.

"Makes sense," he says. "It's certainly worth looking into."

By the time I head home it's after eleven. I fall asleep easily and Matthew wakes me just before three. I get up and grab one of the bottles I have in the fridge and call the hospital while I'm feeding Matthew to see how things went with Emily. The nurse on duty tells me that Hurley is in her room and awake, so I disconnect that call and dial Hurley's cell.

"She came through the surgery fine," he tells me. "She's pretty doped up right now but she seems comfortable."

"She and I had a good talk last night. I think she may finally be coming around."

"Let's hope so," he says.

"How are you doing?"

"I'm tired and this stupid chair is about as comfortable as a bed of nails," he grumbles. "But I'll survive."

"I plan on being there first thing in the morning, around seven. If you want, I can stay a while so you can go home and get some rest."

"Thanks, but I think I'll stay."

"Just don't tire yourself out too much."

"I'll be okay. Are you feeding Matthew?"

"I am."

"Give him a kiss for me."

"I will."

"I'll see you both in the morning."

"Call me if you need me to bring anything."

"I will. And Mattie?"

"Yes?"

"I know I don't say it much, but I love you and little Matthew."

It takes me a moment before I can speak. My throat is tight with emotion. "And we both love you," I manage finally. "As does that child in the bed, though I'm not sure she knows it. Good night, Hurley."

Matthew and I arrive at the hospital bright and early the next morning. Hurley is there in Emily's room, asleep in a chair, his hair adorably disheveled, a two-day growth of beard on his face, and dark circles under his eyes. Emily is in bed, a cast encasing her lower leg. She, too, is asleep, though her rest is augmented by the hefty pain medication in the pump at her bedside. The sight of hardware protruding from either side of the cast makes me wince. Orthopedics has never been my strong suit.

A nurse comes into the room, an old-timer named Velma whom I know from my days working at the hospital. Velma is an institution at the hospital. She's been here for more than thirty years and knows all of the deep dark secrets and where the bodies are buried.

"Hey, Mattie," she says. "Long time no see."

"It has been a while. How are you doing, Velma?"

"Can't complain. Well, I can, but nobody listens, so what's the point?"

I laugh and it wakes Hurley. He looks over at me and Matthew, smiles, and stretches.

"Who's this little guy?" Velma asks, walking over and

taking a peek at Matthew in his carrier. "I'd heard you had a kid. He's a cutie."

"Thanks. I think we'll keep him. How's Emily doing?"

"She had a good night according to the night nurses. Today will probably be a rough one for her and she has a lot of therapy ahead of her before that leg gets back to normal."

Hurley gets out of his chair, walks over to us, and wraps me in a big bear hug.

"Whoa," I say, pushing him back a ways and waving a hand in front of my face. "You should probably go home and take a shower."

"I'm happy to see you, too," he grumbles. Then he breathes in deeply through his nose and adds, "You smell fabulous."

Velma smirks at our repartee and heads over to the bed to check Emily's vital signs. The movement awakens Emily and when she sees all of us standing by her bedside, she smiles. "My whole family is here," she slurs.

Even though I know she's still under the influence, it's nice to see that her new, more positive attitude has remained intact. I take Matthew out of his carrier and walk over to the bedside with him. "Say good morning to your big sister," I tell him. And Matthew, bless his little heart, looks down at Emily, pumps his tiny fists spastically, and gives her a huge smile. She smiles in return, though hers has a stoned, dreamy quality to it.

"Can I hold him?" Hurley says. "I've missed the little guy."

His request is as natural and normal as any could be and yet it fills me with a sense of dread. How will Emily react to seeing her father cooing over his other child? Not that Hurley actually coos, but any attention he gives

Matthew right now might be perceived as rejection by Emily. Then Emily solves the problem for me.

"I've had Dad's attention all night long. It's Matthew's turn."

Relieved, I turn and hand Matthew off to Hurley. He holds his son cradled in the crook of one arm and Matthew immediately starts to cry. Hurley bounces him a little and tries to talk to him, but Matthew is having none of it. His face screws up into a tiny mask of discontent and he continues to bellow.

"Is he hungry?" Hurley asks, looking worried.

I shake my head. "I fed him right before we came here."

Hurley then lifts Matthew up toward his face and takes a big sniff of his butt. And that's when I figure out what's making my son irritable. "His diaper is clean," Hurley says.

"Yeah, but you're not. Seriously, Hurley, you need to go home and take a shower."

He hands Matthew back to me and just like that the little guy stops crying. Emily seems amused by it all, but Hurley simply looks annoyed. "Fine, I'll go home and get cleaned up. Will you stay here with Emily until I get back?"

"Of course I will," I say. "Now go before the staff starts breaking out the HazMat suits to come in here."

Hurley grabs his coat from the back of the chair, walks over to the bed, and gives Emily a kiss on the forehead. "I'll be back in about an hour, okay?"

"Take your time," Emily says in her happy state. "I'm not going anywhere." Then she giggles at her own joke.

I get a kiss on the forehead, too.

With Hurley gone, Emily and I spend the next hour and a half getting to know one another a little better.

We share openly and honestly about a lot of things: her relationship with Johnny, my relationship with Hurley, the sadness she feels over her mother's death, and the fact that she's also angry with her mother for lying to her all those years about Hurley. The topic of fathers and their influence in our lives takes up a good portion of our talk. I share with her how I felt like an outsider growing up because my father wasn't a part of my life, and how I, too, harbor some anger toward my mother for her role in it all, even though I'm not sure yet just what that role was. When she asks me if she can hold Matthew in her lap, I agree without hesitation and watch how my son smiles and gurgles at her. Clearly he likes her and feels comfortable with her, and I'm heartened by the genuine warmth Emily displays toward him.

At one point I went back to a niggling fact about her disappearance that was bothering me, one that made me think perhaps she really did intend to run away. "Why did you take your father's stash of money with you?"

Emily blushes and looks embarrassed. "I was going to try to pay it back," she says. "Johnny's father is in jail and his mom doesn't have a lot of money, and I wanted him to have some cash so he could hire a decent lawyer and fight that school suspension thing. I knew how he felt about drugs and while I didn't know where that pot came from, I knew it wasn't his. I figured someone had slipped it into his pocket as a joke or something. I had no idea they did it to try to frame him."

"Actually it was you they were trying to frame. Olivia thought the jacket was yours because you were wearing it. She slipped it in the pocket while you had it on."

* * *

Hurley comes back a little after ten, looking—and smelling—refreshed. Around eleven I leave him and Emily alone for a while to nurse Matthew. The staff lets me use the break room for privacy.

While I'm burping Matthew, Richmond calls me to follow up on the message I left him the night before. "You were right," he tells me. "I had Jonas scan through the log of the files from Lars's offices and that file wasn't there. I also had another look at the financials and the phone records, and you were right about those, too. Plus the dirt we found in the wheels of Jeff Hunt's ATV was definitely not a match. That ground where we found Lars's body is covered with pine needles and there wasn't a single one in that dirt sample. You were right about it all and given what we found, I managed to convince a judge to give me the search warrants. I'm assuming you want to be along when we execute them."

"I do," I tell him. "But there's something I think we should do first." And then I tell him my plan. He agrees, and we arrange to meet around noon.

I head back to Emily's room and find her occupied with physical therapists that have gotten her out of bed and are teaching her how to use crutches. Emily's face is pale and covered with sweat, and I can tell she's in a lot of pain. But she soldiers through it like a trooper. Once Emily is back in bed looking exhausted and worn out, I fill Hurley in on where we are with the case. Then we start discussing plans for Thanksgiving, which is only a week away.

"Desi is cooking this year," I tell them. "We're all invited and she wants me to bring some desserts."

"I can make a green bean casserole," Emily says. "My mom taught me and it's really good."

"You're on," I tell her, and I'm rewarded with a big smile.

I give both Hurley and Emily a kiss good-bye—Hurley on the lips, Emily on her cheek—and promise to return later in the day. Then I head off to hopefully catch a killer.

Chapter 31

I take Matthew home and drop him off at Dom's, then head to the police station to hook up with Richmond. I find him at his desk, typing away.

"Are you ready?" I ask him.

"I am, but there's still one piece of this that bothers me, one we haven't answered yet."

"What's that?"

"Well, we know that Lars was killed for his money, but we still don't know where it came from. We know how he tried to hide it with the phony invoices, but how did he get it in the first place?"

"I think I know the answer to that one, too," I tell him. "It came to me when I was watching Emily struggle with her pain during her physical therapy this morning. I need to make a call to Izzy first, though, to check on something."

"Go for it," Richmond says

I take out my cell phone and dial Izzy's number. He answers on the first ring.

"Hey, Izzy, it's Mattie. I have a question for you about

Lars's autopsy. Do you have any results on his tox screen yet?"

"Not for the poisons and heavy metals, but I have results from the basic screening for the common drugs: narcotics, THC, cocaine, benzos, and acetaminophen. They all came back negative."

"That's exactly what I needed," I tell him. "Thanks."

I disconnect the call and tell Richmond what Izzy told me. "Once again it's about what isn't there rather than what is," I conclude. "Do you remember the drugs we found in Lars's bedroom? There was coke, pot, and an assortment of narcotic prescriptions from different providers. Their presence would imply that Lars had an abuse problem, but his blood came back negative for all of them."

I see the light bulb turn on in Richmond's eyes. "You think he was selling the stuff," he says.

"I do. And I think he's been doing it for a while . . . with a little help from one of his girlfriends."

"Bridget Rutherford," Richmond says, hitting his desk with a fist. "Of course! She works as a pharmacy technician."

I nod. "I'm betting she's been covering for him at the pharmacies she works for. Otherwise all those prescriptions would be raising some eyebrows. The pharmacies keep counts on their narcs so I'm not one hundred percent sure how she's doing it, but I'd wager she's altered some legit prescriptions and created a few phony ones that she then faxed or called to other pharmacies in neighboring towns so Lars could pick them up. If they take their time and don't do too many at once, you can get away with something like that. I bet he accumulated a bunch of prescriptions and then sold them all at once. That would explain those large deposits he made. He probably did it when he had a project he was working on so he could fake the receipts in case anyone got suspicious and happened on to the fact that he had a lot of cash."

"It makes sense," Richmond says. "Should we go chat with her first?"

"Up to you," I say with a shrug. "But I'm inclined to go for the big guns first."

"Big guns it is then," Richmond says getting out of his chair and grabbing his coat. "I'll get Charlie and make the call. Do you want to ride with us or take that heap of yours?"

"I think I'll take the heap," I say. "I like its intimidation value."

We find Charlie and spend a few minutes discussing our strategy before we leave. Fifteen minutes later, we are pulling up in front of Reece Morton's house.

As we head for the front door, I remember Morton's annoyance with Hurley and me when we were here before because we both knocked and rang the doorbell. I'm tempted to do it again, just for kicks, but I manage to suppress the urge. Richmond rings the bell and we wait. After a minute or so with no answer, he rings it again and knocks for good measure, thus giving me the satisfaction without the guilt. But it appears it will be for naught because no one is answering.

Richmond steps off the porch, heads for the garage door, and peers in through the windows. "His car is gone," he says. "I guess we'll have to go with Plan B."

I'm a little disappointed, but there are bigger fish to fry so my mood doesn't sink much. The three of us head around to the back of the house and Reece's storage shed. Richmond has to cut off the lock on the door, but he does so with the bolt cutter he's carrying.

Once inside, he gets what we need and leaves a copy of his search warrant while Charlie films it all.

With that done, we head back to our cars and drive on to our next stop, a house Richmond has seen before but I haven't. It's an Arts and Crafts home with a detached garage in one of the older neighborhoods in town. We park out front and as we get out of our cars, I look over at the garage.

"Hold on, Richmond," I say. "I want to check on something." I walk over to the garage door, which, like Morton's, has windows in it. I peer inside and see a car parked there. Richmond and Charlie have followed me, and Richmond misconstrues my reason for peeking.

"Is she home?" he asks.

"She is if she drives a Mercedes," I say.

"She does."

I give Richmond a questioning look. "If she has this garage, which clearly has plenty of room for her car, why was her car parked in her driveway the morning of Lars's murder? With this cold weather, I would think she'd want to put the car in the garage overnight."

Richmond thinks for a moment and then rolls his eyes. "She wanted people to see the car," he says, shaking his head. "I should have caught that when I was here talking to the neighbors."

"None of them saw her, right? They only saw the car?"

Richmond nods. "I should have put that together sooner."

We turn and head for the front door, where once again Richmond rings the bell. This time we not only get an answer, we get a bonus, two of them in fact.

Kirsten Donaldson opens the door and looks at me with a curious, tentative smile. A black cat comes up and starts rubbing around her feet. "Hello," Kirsten says. She looks heavenward for a few seconds as if in thought and then adds, "I wasn't expecting you, was I?"

"Hardly," I say. "May we come in?"

I watch her debate the options and it almost makes me smile. Finally she opts for seemingly innocent politeness and waves us inside, where we find someone else sitting in the living room.

"I believe you know Reece Morton," Kirsten says to me. "But I'm afraid I'm at a disadvantage with regard to your entourage."

Richmond takes out his badge and shows it to them. "I'm Bob Richmond, a detective with the Sorenson Police Department." He then gestures toward Charlie, who already has her camera rolling. "And this is our department videographer, Charlotte Finnegan."

"Videographer?" Kirsten says with a nervous laugh. "Are you shooting some sort of documentary or something?"

"It's for evidentiary purposes," Richmond says.

To get their focus off the camera, which I know from personal experience can be intimidating and stifling, I say, "We were just at your place, Reece, hoping to have a chat with you. How ironic to find you here."

"Ironic?" Kirsten questions. "How so? Reece and I meet all the time. Our professional paths cross constantly."

"Yes, I can see where the two of you share some common interests," I say, my voice rife with innuendo.

Kirsten gives me a bemused look, but Morton is sitting in his chair, just staring at us. He doesn't look at all happy to see us.

Richmond takes over at this point, directing his comment to Reece. "Mr. Morton, the reason we went to your house is that we need to have a chat. It seems that your missing archery equipment has turned up, or at least some of it has."

"It has?" Morton says, doing a decidedly poor job of concealing his surprise.

"Yes, it has. In fact, it turns out that the murder weapon used on Lars Sanderson was one of your arrows. We know that because it has the right markings on the shaft and your distinctive neon purple and green fletching."

Kirsten shoots a nervous glance at Morton and lets out a tittering little laugh. "Surely you aren't suggesting that Reece killed Lars?" she says.

"It was his arrow," Richmond says with a shrug. "He has them specially made and the person who made it identified it, so as far as evidence goes, it's pretty darned good."

Morton shifts his gaze and glares at Kirsten.

"But Reece told me his equipment was stolen," Kirsten says quickly. "So the fact that it's his arrow doesn't mean anything."

I shake my head and say, "Not true. We have no proof that Reece's equipment was stolen, just his say-so. And if he's a killer, he's clearly going to want to eliminate the equipment that would implicate him. Nobody's going to believe some story about it being stolen."

"Nope, afraid not," Richmond says. He takes his handcuffs out and approaches Reece.

Morton's eyes grow wide with fear. "No wait," he says. But before he can say another word, Kirsten jumps in.

"Reece, it's always best in these situations to say nothing."

"Shut the hell up!" he snaps, glaring at her again.

"How the hell did my arrow end up in Lars, huh? Tell me that. It was supposed to be Jeff's arrow."

Kirsten looks at us and makes an air circle with her finger alongside her head. "I don't know what he's talking about," she says in a tone of disbelief.

Morton points a finger at her. "She's the one who did this," he seethes. "I didn't kill Lars. She did."

Kirsten scoffs. "Don't be ridiculous. What possible reason would I have for wanting Lars dead?"

"His cash stash, perhaps?" I say.

Kirsten is momentarily caught off guard by this but she recovers quickly. "What cash stash?" she says in a mocking tone.

"The one you learned about when you went snooping through his office files," I say. "That's the real reason you were in his house the day he was murdered, isn't it? You still hadn't found where he'd hidden the cash, and you didn't think anyone had found his body yet. So you went back to his place to search."

"I don't know what you're talking about," she says.

"I think you do," I say. "You told us you were there that day to look for a proposal that you and Lars had discussed the night before. But you didn't leave with anything and when we went through Lars's office files, we found no such proposal. You also told us that you had called Lars before coming over that morning and left a message, but because he didn't call you back you decided to drop by. Except we checked his phone records and you never called him. Why would you? You already knew he was dead."

"Don't be ridiculous," she says. "I don't know what money you're talking about but I have no need for it. I married a rich man, remember?"

"Yes, you did. And you also divorced him. And

while you did get a nice settlement in that divorce, you've managed to blow through that money already. We checked your financials, Kirsten. The housing market has been slow to recover, your daughters are both attending expensive colleges, and it seems you have some pricey tastes when it comes to cars."

"I have a reputation to maintain," she says, looking indignant and folding her arms over her chest.

"Yes, you do," I say. "And no money to do it with. That's unfortunate for you, but at least your daughters should be well cared for by their father, right? Except that's no longer a guarantee either, is it? Because Brad Donaldson always wanted a son who would carry on with the business he built up. And when he discovered he had one, he didn't waste any time buying him all kinds of expensive toys, and grooming him to take over the company. Suddenly your girls weren't the sole recipients of his attention and money, were they?"

"You're very good at making up stories," Kirsten says with a nervous laugh. "If you think I killed Lars, you're crazy. I told you, I was home that morning. Surely you checked with my neighbors to verify that?"

"We did," Richmond says. "A couple of them verified that your car was in the driveway until about seven forty-five."

"Well, then, there you go," she says smugly.

"Not so fast," I tell her. "We didn't say they saw *you* that morning, just your car, which for some mysterious reason was parked in your driveway rather than your garage."

"If my car was here, how could I have been in the woods where Lars was killed?"

"Lars drove you out there," I say. "You lied when you told us that you left his place the night before. You never did leave. He picked you up the evening before for one of your dates and you spent the night at his place. Then the two of you drove out to Cooper's Woods together the next morning."

"And I suppose I walked back to my house from there?" she says with a snort of derision.

I shake my head. "No need. Reece here picked you up with his ATV, took you back to a place where his car was parked, and then drove you back to your place, where you sneaked in through the back door so your neighbors would be none the wiser."

Reece, who had relaxed some when he realized the focus was on Kirsten, starts fidgeting again now that his name has been reintroduced. His tremor has become quite pronounced.

"You couldn't very well drive yourself out there," I continue, "because you needed your car to be your alibi. Plus I'm guessing that fancy Mercedes you have in the garage probably has GPS in it and that might allow the police to prove you'd been out there. And if you went with Lars, you had to have a way to get back so it would look like an accident. You needed an accomplice. And you realized that you and Reece had some needs in common. It didn't take much to figure out how Lars's death could benefit you both. Not only the money, which Reece could use for his surgery and you could use to augment your income, but all the business Lars was stealing from Reece. The idea of trying to frame Jeff for it was just an added bonus, wasn't it? You were worried because Brad was shifting so much of his attention and money away from you. First Jeff pops into his life, and then he finds a new girlfriend. He may have continued supporting your girls but you were getting cut off, weren't you?"

"That's just ridiculous," Kirsten sneers.

"We checked your bank records," Richmond says. "Up until a year ago, Brad was infusing your budget with a lot of cash. Then it stopped."

"You can't prove any of this," Kirsten says.

"Oh, but we can," Richmond counters. "Because while you didn't let the GPS in your car show you were out there, you had to have a way to contact Reece once the deed was done. So you called him. Your phone records show you made that call at six fifty-four that morning."

"So I called Reece," Kirsten says. "Big deal. Like I said before, we have common business interests. I call Reece all the time."

"But you're forgetting one thing," I point out. "Your phone also has GPS on it and it shows that you went out to Cooper's Woods that morning. Plus that ground out there by Cooper's Woods is pretty unique between all the pine needles on the ground in the woods and the nature of the soil in that glacial field. I'm betting the soil sample we took from the wheels on Reece's ATV just a little bit ago will be a match."

Finally Kirsten starts to realize that her crime might not have been as perfect as she originally thought. Her eyes look wild and panicked for a moment; then a level of calm seems to return and that tells me she has one last gambit.

"Lars was killed with an arrow, and I don't own a bow and arrow. Nor do I know how to shoot one."

"You probably didn't until Reece taught you how," I say. "That's why his equipment was missing. He took it out so he could teach you how to use it. He might not be able to shoot very well anymore because of his Parkinson's but he can still teach it. That's the one part

I haven't figured out yet. . . . Where did you hide the equipment while you were practicing?"

Kirsten just smiles. It's obvious she isn't going to spill the beans yet, so I try one more prod. "Did you use Reece's arrow to frame him, or was it insurance in case he decided to talk?"

It doesn't get Kirsten talking, but Reece bites. "I'm not going down for killing Lars," he says. "She did it. She killed him. She came up with the whole idea. But she was supposed to use Jeff's equipment, not mine." He glares at Kirsten. "You stabbed me in the back, bitch, and I'm telling them everything I know."

"Shut up, Reece!" Kirsten snaps.

"Too late for that," he says. "You're a traitor."

"You're not making any sense, Reece."

"You set me up!"

"You're being ridiculous. I—"

"How could you? You purposely tried to pin this on me. I trusted you and you stabbed me in the back!"

"I—"

"Why else would you have used one of my arrows?"

"It was an accident!" she snaps. Too late she realizes what she's just said. She clamps a hand over her mouth, almost as if she's trying to take back the words. Her eyes squeeze closed for several seconds, and then she opens them, drops her hand, and looks at me. "He was dealing drugs, you know," she says in a dull voice. "He was ruining our town, ruining people's lives, and all so he could make a buck. He deserved to die."

Richmond, who is still holding his handcuffs, walks over to Kirsten. "Kirsten Donaldson, you are under arrest for the murder of Lars Sanderson." He continues reciting her Miranda rights while cuffing her hands behind her back. I walk over to the front door and signal to the squad car parked out front. KY gets out of the car and comes in at a trot to assist by handcuffing and arresting Reece.

As they are being escorted out of the house, Charlie gives me a high five and says, "Nice work, Mattie."

"Thanks."

"By the way," she adds. "I love what you've done with your hair."

That does it. I call Barbara and book an appointment as soon as I get to my car.

Chapter 32

My sister, Desi's, house smells even better than usual. It's Thanksgiving Day, a day Hurley and I missed out on last year because we were in hiding. My mother and her live-in boyfriend, William, are here, as are Izzy and Dom. Hurley, Emily, Matthew, and I all arrive together and we are greeted with open arms by everyone except my mother, who doesn't like to touch people because of the germ risk.

Emily has been home for a week now, and she's doing great both physically, mentally, and emotionally. Apparently her near-death experience out in the woods has shaken some sense into her. She has apologized to both me and Hurley numerous times, and her attitude is light-years away from the sullen, angry teenager I knew a short time ago. The realization that she chose Matthew as her password for her computer gave me hope, and so far those hopes have been realized. It's been a week without theatrics, tantrums, or sulking.

Both Olivia and Carly are being dealt with, though in an amazing act of maturity and forgiveness, Emily pleaded with her father that he not press any charges.

Hurley confided in me that he's agreeing to Emily's request, mainly because he doesn't have any crime he can pin on them other than possession of marijuana, and that one would only stick if Olivia confesses to it. The girls lied, and they played cruel tricks on both Johnny and Emily, but they didn't break any laws worth pursuing. Word about what they did got out and both girls are now suspended from school and pariahs among those who used to call them friends. To Emily, this seems like punishment enough.

From the moment we arrive at my sister's house there is a lot of oohing and aahing over Matthew again, but this time there is as much, if not more, coddling of Emily. She is eating up every bit of the attention she's getting, and the huge smile on her face puts one on mine.

Hurley has been home all week playing nursemaid with Emily, showering her with his undivided attention. I realize that this is Hurley's way of saying he cares. The words don't come easy for him, but his actions speak loud and clear. Most of our talk during the week has been by phone, and it's been centered around Emily, her recovery, and what was going to happen with the girls who set her up. So when Hurley and I find ourselves alone in a corner of the living room at one point, I bring him up to speed on the Sanderson case.

"I heard they found some pieces of hay in Kirsten's trunk," he says. "I'm guessing those are from the bales that were missing from Morton's storage unit?"

I nod. "Kirsten has been hauling them around for the past six months, setting them up whenever she and Reece got together for a lesson. As a broker she had access to several rural properties and she and Reece used them to set up the targets for practice so no one would see them."

"Six months?" Hurley says, shaking his head. "They were planning this for a long time."

I nod. "Kirsten is one smart cookie. And a very good liar. You know that key you asked her to give you when we found her at Lars's house?"

Hurley nods.

"She gave you a key to something else and kept the key to Lars's town house. And Lars never gave her that key. She had it from when she sold all those town house units for Lars. She had keys to every one of them back then and she kept copies of them all. And she used the one for Lars's unit to go in and snoop around. That's how she found out about his cash stash. She saw the same bank statements we did and realized that he had to have cash lying around somewhere. She told Richmond that Lars used to talk about his security blanket all the time and she knew that meant his cash stash."

Hurley shakes his head. "It was quite the elaborate plan. How on earth did you figure it out?"

"It was something I said when we were talking to Emily at the hospital. In figuring out where she might be, it was more about what wasn't there than what was. She had that diary notebook, the same kind that Maggie Baldwin gave me, and Maggie told me that Emily claimed she was using it. Yet it appeared empty. Then I remembered the invisible ink thing Desi and I used to do.

"Same thing with the Sanderson case; it was about what wasn't there. Kirsten said she was in Lars's place looking for a proposal she had given him the night before. Yet we never found one. She also said she tried to call him before she came over, but there was no record of any call. Plus, it's bothered me from the start that Reece Morton's equipment mysteriously went missing. I might have bought into someone stealing his bow and arrows, but why were the hay bales he used as targets also missing? That didn't make much sense to me. But once we got a look at Reece's and Kirsten's phone records, it did. Reece called Kirsten from his car that day when we followed him to his storage unit, and they cooked up the story about the equipment being stolen. It turned out that he lied to us when he told us that the combination to the lock on that unit was his birthdate. Kirsten told him to say that to make it more plausible that someone could have broken into the unit."

Hurley shakes his head, but he's wearing an expression of grudging admiration. "She's a clever gal," he says. "And ruthless."

"No kidding," I agree. "The other thing that bothered me was why there were no fingerprints on the arrow that killed Lars. I know that archers sometimes use gloves, but there still should have been prints on that arrow from when it was loaded into the quiver, or when it was made. Bo custom-made that arrow, so wouldn't his prints be on it somewhere? The fact that they weren't suggested to me that someone had wiped those arrows down and the only reason to do that would be to cover up evidence. Then, of course, we found one of Reece Morton's arrows at Jeff Hunt's place, mixed in with Hunt's arrows. And interestingly enough, all of those arrows had prints on them except for one—Reece's."

"I assume Kirsten planted the arrow there?" Hurley says.

I nod. "She did. She never meant to use Reece's arrow

on Lars. That was a mistake. But she was so nervous when she was getting her equipment ready that she accidentally mixed one of Reece's arrows in with the other ones. So when she went to put them back, she threw another one of Reece's arrows in there to make sure Hunt looked guilty. She was the one who took the archery equipment from Brad Donaldson's car and planted it in Jeff's shed. She knew the code for the garage door because she used to live there. And she knew that Jeff's own archery equipment was too rinky-dink to do the job. So she used Brad's equipment and then put it in Jeff's shed to frame him."

"How did she get Lars out to the woods in the first place?"

"She told him that old man Cooper wanted to meet with him because he was thinking about selling the land. The only caveat was that Cooper wanted to keep the woods as is for the next five years because he'd already sold land permits to hunters who came there every year. Since Cooper is an avid hunter himself, Kirsten convinced Lars that if they pretended to be hunters when they went out to the property to meet with him, it would help sway the old man's decision and assure him that the land would be used the way he wanted. She knew Lars didn't like guns or hunting, so that's how she explained the bow and arrow she took with her. It was her intention once they got out there to simply shoot Lars with the arrow. But the sun was just coming up at the time, and she was nervous, so her first arrow—which *was* one of Brad's—missed. Lars had his back to her at the time and he thought she'd fired the arrow carelessly. He got angry and started yelling, and when he went to get the arrow out of the tree it ended up in, Kirsten grabbed the rock and hit him on the head with it. It knocked Lars down but it didn't kill him. While he was lying there, Kirsten fired the second arrow, the one that killed him. She did it fast before he could recover and didn't realize until after the fact that the arrow wasn't one of Hunt's. After that she was in a hurry to get out of there because she didn't know if any nearby hunters might have heard them. In her haste, she remembered to grab the first arrow she fired, but she forgot about the rock. She headed deeper into the woods and came out by a field a mile or so away, and then called Reece to come and get her with the ATV, something they had arranged ahead of time."

"Wow, that woman is one conniving, evil witch," Hurley says.

"I know," I agree. "It almost makes me mad that they offered her a plea bargain in exchange for a confession. They should lock her up and throw away the key."

By the time dinner is ready, we all gather around the two tables my sister has put together. I have a large envelope I bring to the table with me and my sister sees it and gives me a questioning look.

"You'll see soon enough," I tell her.

Once we're all settled, instead of saying grace, Desi asks that each of us mention one thing we are grateful for. "I'm grateful for this big extended family," she says, starting us off.

Lucien says, "I'm grateful that the women in my life are so understanding." This generates some giggles from both me and Desi.

William is next, and with a loving look at my mother, he says, "I'm glad that after our date sank like the *Titanic,* Mattie had the good sense to fix me up with her mother."

More giggles.

My mother is next and her response is typical of her

hypochondriacal, germophobic self. "I'm grateful that Ebola virus seems to be going back into hiding."

Next up is Hurley. With a surprising amount of sincerity and a little hitch in his voice, he says, "I've always wanted to be a father, so I'm grateful for getting two kids in less than a year." This garners smiles all around, but none bigger than Emily's.

It's my turn, and I look over at Emily with genuine affection. The kid has wormed her way into my heart, though I didn't realize just how much until this latest debacle. "I'm grateful that Emily made it home safe and sound."

Izzy is next, and he looks over at Dom, smiles, and says, "I'm grateful for this incredible man who has enriched my life in so many ways."

Dom makes a face like he's about to cry and leans over to kiss Izzy on the cheek. Izzy, never one for public displays of affection, tolerates it but blushes. When he's done with his kiss, Dom says, "I'm grateful that Izzy has seen the light and agreed to look into us adopting a child!" He claps his hands with glee and smiles, and everyone around the table whoops. There is a chorus of "Congratulations" and other kudos.

When the commotion dies down, Desi says, "Emily, you're up next."

Emily smiles, looks at her dad, and then at me. "I'm grateful that Mattie didn't give up on me," she says. And then she starts to cry.

Erika, who is sitting next to Emily, reaches over and gives her a hug. Then, in a not so subtle stage voice, Erika says, "Way to go, E-one. Between you and Dom, I've got one tough act to follow."

Erika's comment has the desired effect. Emily starts to laugh and everyone else chuckles, too.

"E-one?" I ask once Erika releases Emily.

Erika shrugs. "We decided that since there are three of us whose names start with the letter E, that we would call ourselves E-one, E-two, and E-three." She points to Emily, herself, and then Ethan as she lists the nicknames.

Ethan says, "I think it's stupid."

Erika rolls her eyes at her brother, tosses an arm over Emily's shoulders, and says, "And that's why I'm grateful to have a new sister."

Despite the tears coursing down her cheeks, Emily has a huge smile on her face.

"Okay, E-three," Desi says, moving the attention away from the girls. "You're the last one and the food is getting cold."

Ethan ponders for a few seconds and then says, "I'm grateful there are bugs in the world."

There is a moment of silence as we all exchange looks. Then Erika says, "You are such a dweeb."

"Shut up," Ethan counters.

In an effort to lighten the mood even more and divert attention away from the kids, I grab the large envelope I've been holding in my lap. "I have a little gift for all of you," I say. Then I remove the contents. "It occurred to me that I don't have any pictures of Matthew to pass around or show to anyone, so I had some made and just got them yesterday. Unfortunately, it seems my son hates having his picture taken as much as I do, and he's equally as photogenic. There was only one shot out of about fifty where he wasn't crying, and this is it."

I pass pictures around the table and get mixed reactions. My mother gasps, Hurley groans, Izzy laughs, Dom says, "Oh, my," and everyone else sniggers. Matthew's only picture with a smile also has a huge snot bubble coming out of his nose.

"That's impressive," Lucien says, nodding slowly. "He's good with the bubbles. I wonder if I could do one that big."

There is a chorus of groans and a collection of disgusted expressions around the table.

And then my sister, in her cheerful, optimistic way, says, "Happy Thanksgiving, everyone. Let's eat."

If you like the Mattie Winston series,
you might also enjoy the Mack's Bar Mysteries
by Allyson K. Abbott.
Keep reading for a peek at *In the Drink*, available now!

Chapter 1

Dear Ms. Dalton,

It is my understanding from all the hype I've heard and read recently in the local media that you are some kind of crime-solving savant who can literally sniff out clues. I find this claim both intriguing and highly suspect, and frankly I don't believe your ability—whatever it is—can beat out a brilliant mind. Therefore, I would like to put you to a series of tests. If you pass the first test you will move on to the next phase, and so on.

Fail it and I will leave a body for you somewhere here in the city. It won't be a random death. It will be someone you know, someone who is close to you, someone who is a significant part of your life. Should this occur, perhaps you will be able to interpret the clues I will provide and figure out who I am. I rather doubt you can do these things, but I do value a good challenge and I'm eager to see what you can accomplish.

I do have a few rules. You must figure things out using your wits and your "special ability" without any help from the police. That means your friend—or is he a boyfriend?—Detective Albright cannot be involved in any way. If I get wind of his involvement, there will be dire consequences. I do hope you understand how strict I will be if you opt to cheat because the lives of many people will depend on your willingness to play by my rules.

Each phase of this test will be timed. If you do not achieve the goals I lay out for you within the time parameters I have set, I will kill someone else and the game will go on. I do hope that the added stress of knowing your failure will cost someone their life won't interfere with your supposed abilities. But if it does, so be it. Let us begin.

The letter you now hold in your hand is your first clue. There is something very unique about this letter and if you can figure out what that is, it will lead you to the second clue. You must achieve this by nine p.m. on December twelfth or experience the consequences.

I doubt you will succeed. In fact, I'm counting on your failure. And lest you think this is a prank, I have left something for you to prove there are no "happy days" ahead if you fail to take me seriously. I will be watching you.

Good luck.

An intrigued fan

I read the letter three times in a row, slower each time, unwilling to believe what I was seeing. Then I picked up the envelope, convinced there had been a mix-up and I wasn't the intended recipient. But there was no mix-up. It was addressed to Mackenzie Dalton and the address of my bar appeared below the name. There was no return address—hardly surprising given the contents and nature of the letter—but there was a Milwaukee postage meter stamp.

With shaking hands I set both the letter and the envelope down on my desk, realizing too late that I had contaminated both by touching them. I studied the letter some more, this time focusing on the structure and design as opposed to the words. The handwritten letters were done in a simple calligraphic style with varying widths in the strokes, suggesting the use of a fountain pen. The paper was basic and white, the kind sold in hundreds of stores for use in copiers, printers, and the like. The envelope was equally as generic. In fact, I had identical ones in my own desk: business-sized, plain white, with an adhesive strip on the flap covered by a removable piece of paper. This eliminated the need to lick an envelope, and based on what I had learned watching the occasional crime show, it also eliminated a potential source for DNA.

I read the letter again, stopping when I reached the imposed deadline. I glanced at my watch, saw that it was just past four in the afternoon, and cursed under my breath. Since it was Friday the eleventh of December, I had less than thirty hours to figure things out. Another look at the meter stamp told me that the letter had been posted three days ago, meaning it had likely been sitting on my desk for two. I might have had more time if I hadn't procrastinated on opening my mail, but I'd received way more than the usual amount of late. That's because I was getting a lot of personal letters and cards mixed in among the bills and sale flyers that made up my usual deliveries.

The sudden spate of personal mail was from people who had heard about me in the news over the past few weeks when my involvement with the local police during a recent high-profile kidnapping and murder case had become known. While many of the letters were supportive, some had been skeptical, and a few had been downright mean. As a result, I'd stopped opening them after the first couple of weeks and began tossing them into a pile instead. Today was the day I'd decided to tackle them, though for one brief moment I considered simply throwing all of them away unopened. Fortunately, or unfortunately—I wasn't sure yet—I hadn't done that.

I ran my hands through my hair and then immediately regretted doing so as one long fiery-red strand fell onto the offending letter.

Way to go, Mack. Like you haven't contaminated this thing enough already.

I leaned back in my chair, distancing myself—at least physically—from the letter, and indulging in a moment of self-pity. Why this? Why now? Wasn't my life stressful enough already? I wished I could climb into a time machine and go back a year, knowing what I knew now. Maybe then I could fix things, prevent things, change the future. Maybe my father would still be alive, and his girlfriend, Ginny, would still be alive, and the man I considered both a blessing and a curse wouldn't have entered my life yet. Then again, maybe he wouldn't have entered it at all. Would that have been a good thing?

The man is Duncan Albright, a homicide detective here in Milwaukee. He entered my life around two months ago when I found Ginny's body in the alley behind the bar I own, the bar my father bought back before I was born. My father named it after himself—Mack's Bar—and then gave me the name Mackenzie so I could carry on the legacy. Some might have been annoyed by such presumptuousness, but I was always content with the assumption that I would carry on both the name and the business. This was made easier by the fact that I literally grew up in the bar; my father and I lived in an apartment above it. But the legacy became a little harder to bear when the bar became mine alone last January after my father was murdered in that same back alley where I found Ginny.

Duncan wasn't involved with the investigation into my father's murder because he didn't live or work in Milwaukee then. When I met him he was relatively new in town, having arrived only months before Ginny's murder, a fact that came into play while he was investigating the crime. Because he was not well-known in town, he decided to do a little undercover work by pretending to be an employee in my bar. I wasn't very keen on the idea at first, but Duncan's threats to shut me down if I didn't cooperate helped me decide to go along. Still, I didn't like it for several reasons. For one, he was convinced the killer was one of my employees or customers, and to me that idea was unfathomable. My employees and some of my long-term customers were like family to me. The idea that one of them might be a cold-blooded killer was an idea I could hardly bear to consider.

Another reason I wasn't too keen on having a homicide detective watching my every move was because of my disorder. I'm a synesthete, which sounds worse than it is . . . at least most of the time. Synesthesia is a neurological disorder in which the senses are cross-wired. I don't experience the world around me the way most people do. Every sense I experience is multifaceted and complex. For instance, I may taste or see things that I hear, or I may experience a smell or tactile sensation when I look at certain things or people. Both smells and tastes are typically accompanied by sounds or some sort of physical sensation. In addition to this cross-wiring, my senses are also highly acute and I'm able to smell things others can't, or hear things others can't, presumably because of my synesthesia.

I'm not alone in having this condition. There are a number of people in the general population who have it, though there are varying degrees of the disorder. People with artistic inclinations seem to have a higher incidence of synesthesia than other groups of people, and there are theories that the synesthesia plays a role in artistic ability. For instance, there are musicians who not only hear music but see it in their minds as colors, shapes, or some combination of these. The "rightness" of the colors and shapes helps the musician sense when the music is right. I have a similar experience with numbers and letters. They all appear to me with colors attached, and the rightness of those colors makes me very good at both math and spelling. Defining the "rightness," however, is something I'm not good at. It's an intuitive thing, something I know but can't seem to explain to other people.

I've spent most of my life trying to hide my synesthesia. There was a time when members of the medical profession thought my sensory experiences were manifestations of a severe psychological disorder, and I started getting slapped with labels like schizophrenia. When I was a child, my classmates and friends would often tease me, calling me weird or crazy whenever I said things like *this music appears too green*, or *this apple tastes like a blaring trumpet.* It didn't take me long to realize I was different, and when you're a kid, different is the kiss of death. So I learned to keep my experiences to myself.

For many years I was perfectly content to maintain my secret, sharing it only with my father. Over time I told a few close friends about it, but for the most part no one knew. Then Duncan Albright came into my life and everything changed. I was forced to tell him about my synesthesia and try to explain how it worked because my experiences were a key element in solving Ginny's murder. And since I was a suspect, solving Ginny's murder became my main focus. In some ways my synesthesia made things more difficult, but for the most part it not only aided the investigation, it helped to solve it.

I was impressed by the fact that Duncan didn't have the same skeptical attitude many people have when they first hear me describe my synesthesia. Not that he bought into it right away, but he didn't dismiss it immediately either. Nor did he declare me crazy. And by the time we solved the case, he was beginning to think my synesthesia might be of some use to him in his job. He spent several weeks testing me, setting up scenarios and asking me to identify a certain smell from something he would briefly bring into a room and then remove, or having me enter a room and tell him if something had recently been moved or changed. I'd been playing such parlor tricks with my father most of my life, so I passed this part of Duncan's test with flying colors. And I mean this literally. The happiness I felt whenever Duncan praised my efforts made me see swirling, floating bands of color.

Parlor tricks don't solve crimes, however, so some of the customers in my bar decided to help me develop my deductive reasoning. They did this by forming a crime-solving group dubbed the Capone Club that discussed and analyzed both real and made-up riddles and crimes. The group has proven to be quite popular and it, combined with some of the publicity surrounding Ginny's murder, attracted a lot of new clientele to my bar. I thought the increased business might be transitory—the latest gimmick for people's entertainment until something more interesting came along—but so far both my business and the Capone Club have grown.

Following Ginny's murder, the secret of my synesthesia became known by more and more people, and for a while I was okay with that. For the first time in my life, it didn't feel like something I had to hide or be embarrassed about. Many people found it fascinating, and Duncan's interest in using it to help him solve real crimes made me feel like it was a valuable trait, something that could be used for good. After several weeks of Duncan's test scenarios, I was given the chance to prove my mettle with some real crimes. Unfortunately, the last one I helped him with became a top news item. It was the headline story for days, and through some incidental events and careless slips of the tongue, my participation in helping to solve the crime became public knowledge.

This did not sit well with Duncan's bosses, particularly after the press and the newscasters claimed the local police were using voodoo, fortune-tellers, witchcraft, and hocus-pocus to help them solve their cases. In addition to the embarrassing public relations nightmare, Duncan was chastised for putting a civilian—namely me—in harm's way. He was placed on suspension for two weeks while the powers decided his fate, and then their two-week decision stretched into three. I'd begun to fear Duncan would lose his job, but this past Monday he was finally allowed to return to work. Because of his suspension, Duncan had deemed it wise for us to keep our distance until the furor died down, so I haven't seen him for several weeks, though we've spoken on the phone a handful of times. It's been hard for me because

Duncan and I were starting to explore a more intimate relationship when all this happened, and the sudden separation left me with some emotional baggage. It was also hard for me because the local reporters were determined to get a story highlighting the strange barkeep with the weird ability, and for the past two weeks they have stalked me relentlessly. Some of them have been professional enough to be up-front about the reason they were hounding me, but others have come into the bar pretending to be customers, hoping to pry a story loose from me, or from some of my employees, close friends, and patrons. Fortunately, those folks in the know are devoted and reliable, and as far as I know no one has discussed me, my synesthesia, or my involvement with the police with anyone. I thought the press would quickly lose interest, and that their inability to get anything out of anyone in the bar would deter them from writing their stories, but that wasn't the case. What they didn't know they made up, sensationalizing and speculating along the way. They turned me into a Milwaukee freak show.

So while I'm normally a very present and hands-on owner when it comes to running my bar, the recent publicity storm has forced me into hiding either in my office or my apartment much of the time. Fortunately I have a group of capable and dependable employees who can run things just fine without me, though I'm rarely more than one locked door or text message away.

Unfortunately, this need to hide coincided with the grand opening of my new expansion. After Ginny's death, I learned I was the sole beneficiary in her will. I went from counting pennies and barely scraping by, wondering from one day to the next if I was going to be able to keep the bar open, to a degree of financial independence. I bought an empty building that shared a wall with my bar, and doubled the size of my place. It was a risky move, but one I felt I needed to make to stay competitive and keep the bar alive. In an ironic twist, all the publicity helped because it kept a steady stream of curiosity seekers coming in, hoping for a glimpse of the crime-solving, psychic fortune-teller who also happened to own a bar. So while I hated all the media attention focused on me, the weeks since the mediafest began have been the busiest ever at Mack's Bar. I know some of the traffic might be transient, but I hope that once things do finally die down, there will continue to be enough business to maintain a healthy bottom line.

I was hugely relieved that Duncan didn't lose his job, but his return to work didn't help our personal relationship any. He was brought back on duty with the caveat that he wasn't to get any help with his cases from "that woman." This edict upset Duncan because he genuinely believed my synesthesia was an asset that could help him solve cases. I wanted to think it also upset him because of the strain it put on our relationship, but our last few phone conversations had been blandly polite and benignly social with little to no hint of romance or intimacy. I told myself it was because Duncan was distracted and worried about his job, but I'd harbored a fear from day one that his interest in me was more because of what I could do for him and his career than it was anything he liked about me personally. Not that there wasn't a genuine attraction between us; there was. But I wasn't convinced it was strong enough on his end to keep him interested if I was no longer of any use to him careerwise. Time would tell, I supposed, so I kept reminding myself to be patient.

But now I had this letter to deal with. If it was real—and I had no reason to think it wasn't—it was going to complicate my relationship with Duncan even more. My gut told me to tell him about the letter regardless of the writer's warning. Handling it alone was out of the question, and I had faith in Duncan's ability to help me sort it out while keeping it secret. But before I took that leap, I wanted to run it by a few other people who were among my core group of regulars, people who were the heart and soul of the Capone Club: my makeshift, substitute family.